NIAGARA

a novel

By Linda Grace

Cover design, layout
and map illustration
by Steve Rokitka
www.spinetree.org

Copyright ©2016 Big Rock Press

ISBN:
978-0-9975774-0-2

Dedication

To my parents, who gave me humor and a love of books

Author's Note

I have tried to portray an accurate description of Niagara's waterfalls and their environs, except for Cataract Lane, which is a complete figment of my imagination. I will add, however, that it is possible that it *could* exist, in another dimension of mind and memory.

My characters are fictional; any resemblance to any living person is a coincidence. I have tried to be as faithful as possible to the historical record in describing real persons and events from the past. No resemblance between my Buffalo University and existing institutions of higher learning is intended.

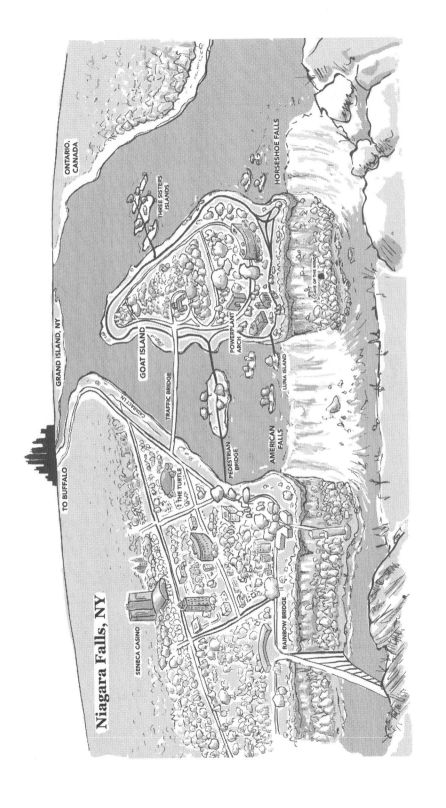

Niagara Falls, NY

TO BUFFALO

GRAND ISLAND, NY

ONTARIO, CANADA

SENECA CASINO

THE TURTLE

CATARACT LN

TRAFFIC BRIDGE

GOAT ISLAND

THREE SISTERS ISLANDS

PEDESTRIAN BRIDGE

POWERPLANT ARCH

CAVE OF THE WINDS

HORSESHOE FALLS

LUNA ISLAND

AMERICAN FALLS

RAINBOW BRIDGE

Table of Contents

PART ONE

"Betwixt the Lake Ontario and Erie, there is a vast and prodigious Cadence of Water which falls down after a surprising and astonishing manner, insomuch that the Universe does not afford its Parallel. [It is] the most Beautiful, and at the same time most Frightful Cascade in the World."

Father Louis Hennepin, 1698

CHAPTER ONE

"Don't jump! Don't jump!" Anne whispered these words as a prayer as she watched the grungy man lift one leg over the iron railing at the rim of the Niagara gorge. He hadn't seen her walk over the narrow bridge to Luna Island and, this early in the morning, no one else was on the tiny perch of land between the American and Bridal Veil waterfalls. She didn't shout or run toward him, not wanting to startle him into leaping or falling into the hundred-foot chasm.

Gripping her dog's leash tightly in one hand, keeping her eyes on the man as though she could will him into not jumping, Anne walked slowly backward over the bridge spanning the hurtling waters of the narrow falls. She took her phone out of her pocket and punched in a number she often used at the Niagara Falls police department.

Ron Gallo answered as soon as he saw her name on his caller ID. "Hi, Beautiful," he said. "Are you inviting me for breakfast?" Anne smiled. Ron was an old family friend and the age her father would have been.

"I'm standing near the bridge to Luna Island, Ron," she told him. "The Hermit is there, with one foot over the railing. I'm afraid he might fall or jump."

"All right, I'll take care of it. Don't stick around there. Get away from him."

Anne had the self-assurance of an experienced nurse, and the confidence – near arrogance – of an attractive, intelligent woman who had never yet met her match.

"Don't worry, Ben is with me," she told Ron. "I think the Hermit is more a danger to himself than anyone else."

"I'm sending a car," Ron said, and ended the call.

Anne looked down at Ben, her dog. He was panting from the heat, half-sitting by her side. She bent down to pat his big brown-and-white head. His long hair was damp from sweat, humidity, and mist from the cataracts.

Anne wasn't as confident of safety as she tried to convey to Ron. The Hermit – the man with one leg dangling over Niagara's deep, rocky gorge – unnerved her. With her experience as a triage nurse, Anne knew how to spot the dangerously simmering people, the ones whose savage pathologies were not all on the surface. It wasn't the Hermit's obvious delusional state that scared her; it was his feral ability to avoid capture by the police or mental services, and the skill with which he drew people into his world. Anne knew his actions would be unpredictable. But she didn't know if they would be dangerous, as well.

As Anne watched, waiting for the police to respond, the Hermit pulled his leg back over the top of the railing and then stood on the middle rail, facing the wide plunge basin of the cataracts. The hot rays of the sun low in the eastern sky to his left shone against his baggy white tee shirt, and gave his long gray hair the aura of a halo. The shirt and his baggy cut-off jeans were stiff with grime. His sneakers, unlaced, were full of holes.

"Roar, Niagara, roar!" the Hermit shouted into the chasm, waving his arms to the sky as he teetered on his dangerous perch. Anne couldn't hear him over the roar of the waterfalls as he ranted, "Show Man the power of Almighty God! Blast your waters into the chasm of rainbows! Flow! Flow forevermore!"

Relieved that he had pulled his leg back over the railing, Anne hurried up the forty-eight cement stairs to the plaza near the Cave of the Winds entrance, pausing a few times to let Ben catch up to her. She stood in the shade of a grove of tall maple trees, waiting, while Ben dropped on his side, breathing hard. Soon she heard sirens and saw two police cars quickly come towards her. She stood by the side of the road as the cars parked. Two officers in one car ran down the stairs to Luna Island. An officer in the other car jumped out and approached her.

"He ran off Luna Island and scooted along the path by the river, just before you got here," she told the officer, a good-looking young man with black hair.

"Ron said I should make sure you were okay," he told her.

Anne rolled her eyes. "Ron didn't need to worry about me," she said. "I've got my dog with me." The officer looked skeptically at Ben, who was now lying on his side, panting.

"That's okay," Dan said. "What's the story on this guy?"

"No one knows," Anne replied. "He just appeared a week or so ago. Looks like he's homeless, and mentally unstable. More a danger to himself than others, probably. The police have been trying to pick him up for evaluation, but he always slips away."

The officer's eyes gazed over Anne, taking in her blonde highlights and toned body; her light, loose shirt and running shorts showed her athletic figure to advantage. He flexed his muscles against his shirt. "Why did Gallo call him 'the Hermit?'" he asked her.

"One of our walkers – you know, the people who walk around Goat Island every day – first saw him splashing around in the water at the Hermit's Cascade by the bridge to the Three Sisters Islands. Don Gromosak, that's his name, got him in a conversation and the guy told him that he *is* the Hermit. The Hermit of Niagara that the little waterfall is named for. He lived on Goat Island in the early eighteen-hundreds." She shook her head to stop herself from babbling about Niagara history, a common trait among native Niagarans. "So that's what we've been calling him. It's humanizing. Better than calling him 'the latest lost soul to come hanging around the Falls because he thinks it's talking to him.'"

"That's pretty weird," the officer said. "What is he, like, reincarnated?"

Anne stared, not certain if Dan was being serious. "Not likely," she told him. "We call him that more because he *looks* like a hermit,

3

with his big dirty, baggy shirts, and raggedy jeans, and his long hair and beard. He's very unkempt."

The officer wrote in his notebook. "That's a good description. I'll keep an eye out and check to see if he shows up at St. Mary's food kitchen or anywhere around here."

"Father Joe told me he hasn't seen him at the free food pantry yet," she reported.

"So you walk around here every morning?" the officer asked.

Anne bent down and patted Ben on his head. "And evening. He needs his exercise. So do I, for that matter."

"I'll need your name and address." He caught her look. "As a witness, in case I need to reach you for more information. You must live around here."

Anne wavered. She hated guys coming on to her. But she could always complain to Ron if he started bothering her. That would end that.

"Anne Techa. I live on Cataract Lane, number 4." She gave him her home landline number.

"Do you work, Anne?"

"Yes. I began my career in emergency nursing, but now I'm on the nursing faculty at Buffalo University. And ..." she knew he was going beyond the necessary information, "I've got to get Ben home soon because I have to be on campus for a meeting by nine."

"Okay, Anne." He closed his notebook and handed her a card. "Call me if you see this guy again. Or anything else."

Anne looked at the card and saw his name. "I will. Thanks, Dan."

"I'll give you a lift home," he offered.

She smiled. "No, thanks. This guy still needs his exercise." She gave his leash a tug and the dog reluctantly rose. "Come on, Ben."

Dan got back in his car, made a u-turn, and drove back toward the mainland. For Ben's sake, Anne tried not to walk too fast along the road to the traffic bridge at First Street. She crossed to the mainland side, then turned right on a paved path that ran alongside the upper rapids. When she reached a point opposite the tip of Goat Island, she turned left off the path and crossed a treed lawn to a short lane that ran parallel to the river.

Cataract Lane was proof that things can hide in plain site, even if they are sitting next to the most famous waterfalls in the world. Among the millions of people who visit Niagara Falls every year, only a relatively few find their way upriver to the short cobble-stone street tucked between Buffalo Avenue and the upper rapids, hidden behind a woody patch of overgrown chokeberry and sumac shrubs. A remnant of nineteenth-century prosperity in the city, the street was once a private lane leading to the majestic Whitney Mansion, a columned Greek Revival building that still survives. Four houses, all facing the river, were built along the lane during the eighteen-hundreds for members of the extended Whitney family. Anne's house, built in 1888, was the youngest of the four, a sturdy Queen Anne Victorian with a turret and a deep front porch facing the river. From her windows she could see the upper rapids through trunks of century-old maple and oak trees, and hear the constant roar of the surging water.

The houses on Cataract Lane, like the city of Niagara Falls itself, had weathered good times and bad. For most of the city now, the bad times seemed to have no end. Tourists who ventured a block or so from downtown found themselves in ravaged neighborhoods. Unemployment and poverty were rampant, the newspapers full of the sad crimes they reap.

The city flourished during the nineteen-fifties when it was the famous Honeymoon Capital of the World. Its population ballooned during the next decade when New York State built the then-largest hydroelectric plant in the world along the Niagara River. Under Robert Moses, the most powerful man ever to serve in New York government, the state ripped up and paved miles of river shoreline and put hundreds of acres of Tuscarora Indian Reservation land under the waters of a reservoir. In the nineteen-seventies, the old vibrant downtown with its burlesque-era theaters and bookie joints was ripped down for urban renewal, and never regained its allure. In the twenty-first century, only the native-run Seneca Casino, whose tall glass tower dominated the city skyline with its neon waterfalls and signs, seemed to be thriving.

Cataract Lane benefited by being off the beaten path and neglected. Its houses sat rented or unoccupied for years; for a time it looked as though Robert Moses would raze them, too. But they survived his massive earthmovers, and, after hard wear, the four homes had been bought and gentrified by die-hard Niagarans like Anne. Her brother Bill had told her only a fool would buy property in Niagara Falls, especially downtown. She actually agreed, but bought the house anyway.

She saw past its neglect and the asphalt shingles someone had attached during the nineteen-thirties. Over a year, she restored it to a showcase. Since it was far too large for one person, she had an architect produce a sensitive design that created two flats – one on the first floor and one on the second – while preserving the architectural elements and historical integrity of the building. She made sure the new two-story addition at the back of the house blended perfectly, adding new kitchens and baths to each flat, and a secure back hallway. She occupied the second-floor flat, for the better views and breezes from the river. She rented the first floor to a young artist named Mari D'Angelo.

It was almost eight when Anne reached home. She just had time to feed Ben, shower, and dress, then rush to Buffalo for the special dean's meeting, which hadn't been a made-up excuse to escape Dan's interrogation. The Dean of Nursing had sent a faculty-wide email out just the day before, saying she needed to inaugurate a discussion of transformational change for the nursing college. Summers were dangerous. That's when deans launched the ideas that would drive the faculty crazy. Anne wasn't looking forward to the meeting, but she didn't dare miss it. Only a big new scheme would cause the Dean to schedule the meeting on the Friday before the long Fourth of July holiday weekend, when many of the faculty would be away. Maybe that was the whole point. Attendance would be light. Anne knew that, at the very least, a new task force would come out of it, and she intended to be agile enough to avoid being appointed to it. As one of the younger faculty members and a faculty "star," she had a constant battle to keep from being over-extended.

She could not let anything distract her from her latest project. Anne was leading a large faculty and administrative committee preparing a proposal for a million-dollar financial grant from the federal Veterans Administration that would develop ways to coordinate and streamline long-term care for war veterans and their families in the Buffalo-Niagara region. With hundreds of thousands of veterans left with long-term injuries and mental traumas from extended American wars in the Middle East, there was a national need for programs to provide comprehensive health care regimens and support services not only to the former soldiers, but to the families burdened with helping men and women with lost limbs, diminished mental capacity, and post traumatic stress outbreaks. Anne's goal was to develop a pilot program that could serve as a national model that eliminated cracks in the system.

Later, as she raced across Grand Island in her pale blue Prius, Anne asked herself again when she was going to move back closer to campus instead of making these almost daily runs between Niagara Falls and Buffalo. None of her colleagues understood what they called her obsession with the Falls. She knew, though, that she would never move during the summer. On the way home she'd be glad to leave muggy Buffalo, anxious to get back to her shady street and her elegant home by the river. No need to get distracted by campus socializing or faculty politics. Then she'd walk with Ben along the upper rapids to the island that sat between the grandest waterfalls on the continent. Their primal force reminded her, as nothing else did anymore, that while change is as unstoppable as the natural forces eroding the brinks of the great cataracts, what is solid, and strong, endures. Walking by the waterfalls, she could still feel what has drawn people to Niagara for centuries – transcendence. Only there.

CHAPTER TWO

"Niagara Falls. I must be crazy."

John Lone hesitated before getting out of his car. It wasn't too late to withdraw from the deal. He could drive away without signing the papers, return to his home in the hills south of Buffalo, and save himself a hell of a lot of aggravation. He was ready to do that, and actually started the Escalade's engine. Then he remembered how happy Jerome, his brother, had been yesterday when he told him the papers were ready to sign. Jerome would take it hard if he quit now. Jerome never asked him for anything, except this.

Taking a deep breath, John opened his car door to the heat outside. The tall old trees that lined this street in Buffalo's historic Delaware district offered shade, but couldn't relieve the heat and humidity of a July day in the city by the lake. John walked quickly from his car up the slate steps of the Beaux Arts mansion that housed his lawyer's offices.

"Good morning, Mr. Lone." The attractive receptionist greeted him with a big smile; her gaze lingered on the way his tailored linen jacket fit his wide shoulders. His thick black hair was tinged with silver and flawlessly styled. He knew she was seeing his money. "Mr. Seward is waiting for you. Come right in."

John noticed the extra swing the young woman gave her hips, snug in a fitted black skirt, as she rounded her desk. She gave two quick raps, then opened a door. "He's here, Mr. Seward," she announced.

A distinguished-looking man with abundant white hair emerged from the office, his hand extended in greeting. "John, hello, good to see you again." He clasped John's hand with both of his. "How was the drive up?"

"I made it in record time," John said as the two men entered a cherry wood-paneled office and sat down in low leather armchairs. They faced each other over a polished oak table decorated with a green marble obelisk and a large bronze buffalo; a thick manila file folder lay on it.

"That new Cadillac must be a lot of fun to drive," the attorney said. "I'm sure you're anxious to finish this business and get on with the holiday weekend. I've got the paperwork all ready for you to review and sign."

"Excellent," John replied. "We can finally get this project moving."

Seward pushed the file folder in front of John. "It wasn't easy getting to this point, as you know," he commented. "The Tuscarora council put up a big stink, especially Wallace Mountview, and threatened to tie us up with the governor's office. We finally got one of their members to sign on. But the city and developer were easy to deal with. Tough to keep your name out of it, but they were all so eager to get this contract for the building that they didn't push the point of knowing who all the investors are. Especially Nick Valli, the tourism director. He was on our side all the way."

"I knew it would all fall together eventually. I appreciate your hard work and discretion, Harold."

The older man gave a thin smile. "John, if you don't mind my bringing this up again . . ." He cleared his throat. "You can get a hell of a lot of positive PR by going public with this, and it would make our future negotiations easier. You've pulled off a real coup, getting your people from every part of the state involved. It's a great, positive enterprise. Why don't you let me hook you up with a good marketing agency? The one we use, they're real professionals."

John held up his hand. "I know you have a good argument, Harold, but I have my reasons for doing it this way."

"Well, I won't argue with you," the lawyer replied. "Take your time going through these." He indicated the papers in the folder on the table. "I'll be in the library. Call for me if you have any questions, or when you're ready to sign."

John nodded. "Thanks, Harold."

He was relieved when the lawyer left him alone. He stared at the folder. Was this project going to be worth the effort, and the money? How had his brother Jerome ever talked him into it?

John rose, walked to the window, and gazed at a garden courtyard through a wrought-iron grill that had guarded this entry from intruders for more than a century. John felt the past. So many steps had gotten him to where he was now, from deepest poverty on a Seneca Indian reservation to successful enough to be able to hire one of Buffalo's best lawyers, and to sink money into an enterprise that had no hope of ever making a profit.

Life was about moving forward, not staying in the past: this was the creed that had always guided him. Taking off his sport coat, he stretched out comfortably in an armchair and quickly skimmed through the legal papers. He wasn't worried. Seward wasn't the type to screw his own client. He was a straight arrow, attentive to the details, a member of the class of lawyers who guarded old money. After he read through the main clauses and double-checked the numbers, John rose, stretched, and put his jacket back on. A short while later, a secretary notarized his signature on the contract. Lawyer and client shook hands.

When John emerged from the cool building, the Buffalo humidity smacked him in the face. He stood just outside the door for a moment, taking his time to put on his sunglasses so he could enjoy the view of his new black Cadillac Escalade. The car looked like it belonged on this street of mansions built before the twentieth century with the new money of the port city's first entrepreneurs. Lined with tall trees, the neighborhood was an upscale business district now.

John had some time to kill. He was going to drive to Niagara Falls to meet with his developer in a couple of hours to check out his new property, then see friends in Buffalo for dinner, before heading home. But now an old memory came back, and he decided to follow it.

He hurried down the steps, navigating a broken sidewalk whose cement panels were knocked awry by large, ancient oak roots. He unlocked his car, removed and carefully folded his sport coat, and placed it on the passenger seat. The digital thermometer on the dashboard indicated the outside temperature was already over one hundred degrees. Maybe he shouldn't have been so dismissive at dinner last night when Jerome was talking – again – about the state of the planet. But John couldn't convince himself to worry too much about it, not when there were so many more imminent things to think about.

John turned on his engine and waited for cool air to waft over him before he drove to Delaware Avenue and turned left. He was pleased with his morning's work. It made him feel generous, expansive; he knew he was doing something for others, not himself, and it was a rare, surprisingly pleasurable, feeling.

For years, John Lone had encouraged the popular impression of himself as a ruthless business investor. Non-Indians, of course, would always be suspicious and wary of dealings with a Seneca man who got his start selling gas and smokes on the Cattaraugus reservation. They thought he was tied in with the powerful Seneca business establishment and its casinos. But though he had connections and investments there, John prided himself on being independent of any close ties, either business or personal. His investments were international, and diverse. He didn't need to account for himself to anyone. He even made a point of not living on the reservation, but just south of it, on land he purchased, bit by bit, until now he owned hundreds of acres of sprawling, wooded territory in the hills of southern New York.

John knew that his independence as well as his awesome net worth had prompted the lead partner of Buffalo's most distinguished law firm to take on a complicated contract involving Indians from across the state. It felt good to have his new project, White Pine Enterprises, met with enthusiasm instead of suspicion. In approaching Harold Seward, he and his brother Jerome had appealed to the Buffalonian's sense of history when they said they wanted to purchase the abandoned Turtle building near the American Falls to create a living center for native arts that would involve all six of the Iroquois nations of New York State. Jerome, who had a doctorate in Native American Studies from Buffalo University and was on the adjunct faculty there, would be the artistic director. Given the sensitivities and political implications of such an endeavor, he wanted to keep the project under wraps as long as possible. He wanted full control.

John didn't want to deal with any local preservation disputes about the Turtle building or – especially – with any city, state or Indian politics. He'd had to fight as hard against the chiefs and clan mothers as against the white authorities when he started setting up his business-es on his home reservation more than thirty years ago. He was out of those early businesses now, thankfully. After he'd gotten his business degree from BU, he'd sold the franchises and invested his money as a partner in some of the first successful Indian casinos in the country. But he still wasn't getting any respect from his own people. Early on, he'd tried a few times to get on the Seneca council, but there were too many factions. He'd turned his back on tribal politics long ago. But that didn't stop certain people from trying to bring him and his family down. His mother, the formidable Louise Lone, often talked about grievances going back generations.

After driving a few blocks down Delaware, John drove his car through a tall black iron gate into sprawling Forest Lawn Cemetery, burial place of a former United States president and Buffalo's worthiest citizens for almost two centuries. He parked just inside the gate, next to the elegant columned office building. The humidity smacked him again as he left the cool car.

Heat waves shimmered up from the paved plaza, across which stood a tall granite pedestal topped by the bronze statue of a man – it was the graven image of John's ancestor, Red Jacket, the famed Iroquois orator. Larger than life, the leader stood proudly atop a stone column. His right hand was extended in greeting, or warning; his left hand held the long wooden handle of a stone axe. He was dressed in traditional clothing, including the two-feather *gustoweh*, or feather headress, of the Seneca people. On his chest hung the large silver "peace" medal given to him by President George Washington.

"Sa-go-ye-wat-ha. He-keeps-them-awake."

John read the translation of Red Jacket's Seneca name carved on the pedestal. "Died at Buffalo Creek January 20, 1830. Aged 78 years." Underneath that inscription, these words were carved in the stone: "When I am gone and my warnings are no longer heeded, the craft and avarice of the white man will prevail. My heart fails me when I think of my people, so soon to be scattered and forgotten."

The words of the most famous spokesman of the Iroquois nations rang across the centuries. John knew Red Jacket's life story well; his family was of the Wolf clan, and his mother said they were related by blood. When he was a child, his mother periodically brought him, Jerome and their sister Loraine up to Buffalo from the reservation some sixty miles south, just to visit this gravesite. She'd beg rides and sometimes they even hitchhiked. Once, as the small family trudged up Delaware Avenue, raggedy and seemingly lost, a policeman had stopped them, thinking they were homeless vagrants. But Louise Lone faced him down. She was going to show her children their famous ancestor, so they would know that once there had been greatness in their people, and their family.

Red Jacket was born around 1750 in the Finger Lakes region at a time when the Six Nations – the Haudenosaunee, the People of the Longhouse, the Iroquois – held sway over all of what is now New York State. The Seneca were "Keepers of the Western Door," members of a centuries-old peaceful confederacy with the Cayuga, Onondaga, Oneida, and Mohawk nations, later joined by the Tuscarora fleeing bloodthirsty English settlers in the south. He was a brilliant and fierce spokesman, who negotiated not only with the British and Americans before the Revolution, but with the first seven United States presidents, playing an important role in native efforts to slow the unstoppable wave of white settlement.

John squinted at the polished figure atop the shimmering column. Before the bronze statue was restored a few years ago, it was badly corroded, so that when John first saw his ancestor as a child, it looked as though tears were running down his face. John often wondered how Red Jacket was able to survive the ruinous transformation of his world. He was a member of the last generation of native people who, in their youth, did not live under white domination, did not claim land as personal property, did not use money. Their spirits were attuned to every nuance of the physical world. Every ceremony began with lengthy thanks to the Creator for his generous gifts. Then the invaders came, men whose voracious greed swallowed everything, even their sworn words. Unlike his contemporary, the warrior Tecumseh, whose spirit rode to earth on a comet, Red Jacket did not have the lucky fate to die young, in battle. Words were his weapons. He lived long enough to compromise, and to die in his own bed, on a reservation that was a pitiful remnant of the wondrous land he had been born into.

He stayed true to himself, John thought, as well as he could. He never lived among whites, never accepted their religion. He refused to use their language; the eloquence they celebrated was filtered through translation. John was certain that if he could hear Red Jacket speak in the ancient Seneca language, he would understand him through the pure force of his words.

Red Jacket, like most brilliant figures, was still controversial. Traditional Indians said he would never enter the land of the Creator, as punishment for selling land. John saw a man who tried to hold on to as much as possible in negotiations with cheats and liars. It wasn't as though he had much of a choice. The whites were going to get the Indians' land if they had to kill every last Indian to do it, and they almost did.

As he looked up at Sagoyewatha's face staring in the direction of the Niagara River, John knew that this monument wasn't erected to honor Red Jacket or his companions and friends, buried alongside him – Young King, Captain Pollard, Little Billy, Destroy-Town, Tall Peter. This statue was a symbol of the conquest of the Iroquois, erected on the western end of the former Buffalo Creek reservation that was Red

Jacket's final home. The whites called him "the last of the Senecas." The Gilded Age elite who erected this monument did so in a sentimental haze of regret for the loss of the noble savages and the maidens in the woods. They considered the Iroquois "a race of the human family fast fading from the earth," as one speaker at the ceremony put it. A regrettable loss, but inevitable.

Yet now, against all probability, here was a proud, full-blooded Seneca man standing before the statue of his ancestor. The orator's words burned into John's brain. His people were scattered, he conceded, but certainly not forgotten. What would Red Jacket think of the twenty-six-story Seneca casino now towering over Niagara Falls? Wouldn't he be proud to know the Six Nations were still standing up to New York State over sovereign matters?

John felt new resolve. He would make sure they weren't forgotten. He was going to build a showcase of Six Nations art, history, and culture right next to Niagara Falls, the most famous natural wonder in the world. Senecas would own two glittering attractions at the Western Door.

The Turtle building, which had been vacant for more than thirty years, was built for just this purpose. The turtle shape of the building was meant to represent creation beliefs. The State of New York had funded the project, but the museum died amidst squabbling over control and loss of funds. The building was now a crumbling shell.

John had resisted his brother's idea of resurrecting the Turtle for years, but Jerome was persistent. John dismissed arguments about "giving back" and "supporting the native community." John was self-made and didn't feel he owed anything to anyone. But he did succumb to pride, to the notion that the museum would bring him respect, however begrudged, from the native communities across the state. That was why he made the effort to have White Pine's corporate board include representatives of each of the Six Nations.

John knew there were rumors that the mysterious White Pine Enterprises was going to operate another casino, or even a smoke shop, in the building. The traditionals were warning people against getting involved with it, even though they didn't know who was behind the effort. They always expected the worst. Well, soon they'll find out there is honor and pride among native businessmen, John thought, and that I'm not the asshole they think I am. Only after the project was announced to acclaim would he reveal his role in it – subtly, of course, through carefully managed leaks. He'd let Jerome be out front as the face of the project. He himself would be humble, reluctant to take credit. Everyone would have to eat their words about him and his family! John grinned in anticipation of his vindication.

"We're still here, father," John said, looking up at his ancestor's carved face. "They haven't gotten rid of us yet."

Sa-go-ye-wat-ha, standing high above the lamentation engraved in stone beneath his feet, stared beyond John.

After a moment, John turned away, anxious to be gone before he started to rehash the past. It didn't do any good, it just clouded judgment. He hurried back across the hot pavement with hardly a glance at a statue of a comely shepherdess holding a rose. He remembered the quote carved in the pedestal under her feet: "You become responsible forever, for what you have taken. You are responsible for your rose." It was a quote from a Frenchman, Antoine de Saint-Exupéry, and he didn't like it.

In his car, he drove quickly back through the gates onto Delaware Avenue. He drove several blocks to a ramp onto the New York State Thruway, and raced along the river, then across Grand Island, north to Niagara Falls.

He pulled off the Parkway at the downtown exit. He cruised slowly around the Turtle, inspecting its crumbling facade, and resigning himself to having to spend more than his original estimate on repairs. Then he parked, and walked to Prospect Point, where he spent a long time leaning against the iron railing, watching the water flow over the American Falls in its powerful cascade. The cool mist relaxed him.

When he finally turned away from the cataract, the first thing John saw was the Turtle's head, looming over the landscape.

CHAPTER THREE

Phoebe pulled Leonard by his arm out of a crush of people listening to a blues band in front of a stage on Old Falls Street. "It's too hot," she said. "Let's find some shade." They walked a block to Prospect Park and bought ice cones from a vendor. Phoebe twisted her long blonde ponytail nervously and complained about the line the entire time they waited. After they got their cones, they dropped on the grass under a massive maple tree and slurped the ice, which was already melting. Sticky red strawberry syrup covered their hands.

"So what did you think of Mari?" Phoebe asked; her hazel eyes were fixed on Leonard. "She looks cool, doesn't she?"

Leonard shrugged his shoulders.

"I really think she might give you some work, if I ask her in the right way," Phoebe said. "Bring your notebooks tomorrow and I'll show them to her. She'll love your drawings, they're awesome. She keeps telling me how she needs help keeping up with her orders for Niagara pictures now that the tourists are back. She wants to spend time on her real art, she says."

Leonard nodded.

"I asked my Aunt Anne if I could spend the rest of summer with her, and she said maybe. She said it depends if she can get me a part-time job with the tourist bureau. I don't want to work, but it would be worth it to get away from my dad and mom. They're driving me crazy."

Leonard gave her a keen look. "Because of me." He had no illusions. He knew Phoebe's father would freak out if he showed up at their house, long-haired and scruffy, straight from the reservation.

"You're only one thing," Phoebe told him. "They wanted me to go to summer school because my grades were so bad, but I told them no way. Then Aunt Anne came up with the job idea, even though it was past the application deadline. But she has connections, she knows everybody. It'll work."

Phoebe tilted her head back to drink the last of her melted slush. Leonard saw beads of sweat on her forehead and the back of her neck. She leaned back to lie on the grass. She put her hands under her head, and sighed dramatically. "I'm so tired after rehearsal last night. But it was worth it."

She sat up again, and looked at Leonard with shining eyes. "Can you believe I have a chance to be the Maid of the Mist?"

Leonard grinned, and shook his head. "You didn't even look like yourself."

She laughed. "Not with all that makeup and dark hair extensions."

"It was amazing how you turned yourself into another person."

"I had to." She laughed. "I couldn't exactly enter with my real name and age. Nick Valli knows Aunt Anne."

"How are you going to get away from your parents to do the contest tonight?"

"I told them I was hanging out with Aunt Anne," Phoebe told him. "They won't know. I told *her* I was going to the fireworks with *them*, and I'll go to her house when the fireworks are over and spend the night there."

Leonard shook his head. Phoebe's life was very complicated. He liked to keep things simple: tell the truth, or don't say anything. He mostly didn't say anything.

Phoebe checked the time on her phone. "I've got to get going," she said. "I'm going to get ready at Anne's house. She gave me a key to use when she's out. I hid my costume and makeup in the room at the top of the turret on her house, in a box of old books. Luckily she's in Buffalo today, so I'll have it all to myself. It's a sign, I think. I'll see you later."

Phoebe jumped up and hurried off, leaving her empty cup on the grass. She wound her way through the crowded park toward Cataract Lane. Leonard watched her until she disappeared among the flocks of tourists.

Leonard stretched out on the grass, and stared at the green canopy of maple leaves overhead. Being with Phoebe always made his head spin. If her father only knew, he thought, he wouldn't worry about them being friends. That's all they were – friends. They weren't DATING. Leonard and Phoebe, both outcasts from their high school's cliques, had found each other in the social wilderness. They were opposites, at least on the surface: Leonard seemed placid, Phoebe was hyper. Each of them was self-absorbed, but they orbited around each other in mutual disdain of everyone else.

After a while, Leonard forced himself up. He picked up Phoebe's cup and threw it with his into a recycling bin. He followed Phoebe's path until he got to the pedestrian bridge to Goat Island. He crossed it and walked toward Terrapin Point, where Rose was selling her beadwork at a table with some of the other ladies from the Tuscarora Reservation. Rose was married to his great-grandfather, Wallace Mountview. Leonard liked her. She was a small woman, with dark hair in a soft style, and a kind face. She was a lot younger than Wallace, being his third wife. He had outlived his first two wives, including Leonard's own grandmother.

Leonard was currently living with Wallace and Rose. It wasn't a perfect situation, but he knew they cared about him. He'd made the choice last year to stay with them rather than move up to Six Nations in Canada with his mother and her new boyfriend, whom he didn't like. Leonard had never known his own father, Wallace's grandson, who had been killed with four other young men from the reservation in a horrific car crash on Upper Mountain Road. Leonard was still in his mother's womb; sometimes he thought he was born with her grief of that event.

When Leonard arrived at her table, Rose and the other women

were packing up. The day was winding down, and they were exhausted. Leonard helped carry their boxes to Rose's car, which was in a nearby parking lot on the island.

"Where's Grandfather?" he asked her.

"I don't know," she replied. "He was standing here a minute ago." She looked around. "See if you can find him and I'll meet you both at the car. Here, take this box."

With a cardboard carton under his arm, Leonard went off in search of his great-grandfather. It wouldn't be hard to spot him. He was wearing a light, flowered ribbon shirt, in the Indian style that he preferred. He was tall, though a little bent now, after more than eighty years in this world. With his long white hair pulled back into a ponytail, and his distinctive face, he was a dramatic figure. He was famous, actually, in some circles, at least, for his long work fighting for Indian rights. People often stopped him to talk, and tourists loved to take his picture. Leonard knew he couldn't have gotten far. He started in the direction of the nearest men's room, because he knew that's where old men were always heading.

He found Wallace sitting on a park bench near the tourist center, staring into space. Some people were staring at him as they walked by.

"Grandfather?" He sat down next to him and gently took his arm. "Grandfather?"

Wallace slowly turned his face toward Leonard. His dark eyes were far away.

"Grandfather!" Leonard was anxious now. "Were you asleep?"

Wallace shook his head. His eyes began to focus. "Asleep?" he asked. "No."

"Are you alright?"

"Yes," Wallace said. He looked around. "Where's Rose?"

"She's packing up," Leonard told him. "We have to meet her at the car."

Wallace nodded. Leonard helped him up. Wallace leaned on his arm.

In his worry, Leonard almost forgot the box of Rose's beadwork, and had to turn back for it. He thought of all the tiny beads she pains-takingly sewed onto beautiful purses, medallions, and dolls, and how upset she would be if he lost her work. He would never forgive himself.

Between carrying the bulky box in one arm, and with his elder leaning on the other, Leonard was panting by the time they got to the car, where Rose was waiting. They helped Wallace into the back seat. Leonard was thrilled when Rose asked him to drive home, because she was tired. He'd just gotten his driver's permit. Rose told him he'd have to drive slowly, because of her nerves. Leonard headed for Portage Road to drive north to the Tuscarora reservation, where they lived in the house Wallace had built decades ago for his first wife.

Every so often, when they had to stop for a light, Leonard looked into the rearview mirror to check on Wallace. He was awake, and was looking out of the window. Everything seemed to be okay.

But Wallace was far from okay. He was trying to maintain control of his thoughts, and his emotions. He'd seen someone in the crowd of tourists at Terrapin Point, someone who brought back memories of his darkest days. A slender man, wearing a black leather jacket, even in this heat. The man was staring at him as Wallace walked toward the railing to look at the Horseshoe Falls. When Wallace saw him, he stopped cold. It was the eyes, the hooded, amber eyes, that gave Wallace a shock. Wallace closed his eyes, and when he opened them the man was gone. Wallace got himself to a bench and sat down to collect himself, until Leonard found him. Now, in the car, Wallace tried not to go back to that day in his memory, but, on the slow drive home, his mind took him there.

It was in April, 1958. He was a young man, then, but already a father and a U.S. Army veteran of the Korean War. And he was fight-ing another war, this time at home. He and the Tuscarora Nation at Niagara were battling with the most powerful man in New York State: Robert Moses.

The small Tuscarora reservation where Wallace and generations of his family lived lay on land that Moses wanted to use for the reservoir for the Niagara Power Project. The Tuscaroras fought in the courts to keep their land. But Moses had been rebuilding and paving New York State in his own vision for decades, and wasn't about to let a small community of Indians stand in the way of his progress. The struggle had been going on for years by then. The most recent court decision had allowed Moses to send surveyors onto the reservation, to scope out his plans to move his bulldozers in, scour the land of its homes and farms, and then inundate it.

That was a match on dry straw. When the surveyors arrived, accompanied by armed sheriff's deputies and state troopers, two hundred Tuscarora men, women, and children blockaded Garlow Road with their own bodies. They were there to protect their homes, on land that was settled by treaties. Wallace tried to quell his bitter feelings of betrayal when he saw the armed force. He had fought in Korea with thousands of other Indians, as allies of the United States government. He thought the Indian Wars were over. He had never expected to see weapons brought to his own home by the Americans he had fought beside. He told Teresa, his wife, to go home, and to take their young son, but she wouldn't, even though she was seven months pregnant.

Wallace and the other Council leaders stood at the front of the blockade. The standoff was tense. Three young Tuscarora men, including his friend, William Rickard, one of the leaders, were roughly pulled out of the crowd and arrested for disorderly conduct and unlawful assembly. Unlawful assembly on their own land! They were dragged away to jail over the protests and tears of the elderly men and women, and the children.

It was a terrible day. Wallace helped to establish calm and get people back to their homes to prevent further violence. He knew the fight would be a long one.

A few days later, he had an early dinner with Teresa. She'd killed one of their chickens, baked it with turnips, and made him sandwiches from the leftovers. He smiled at the memory. Then she drove him to work, an overnight double shift at the Hooker chemical plant, because she needed their car for a doctor's appointment, to check on the baby's progress. He did his shifts, then stayed to talk to his supervisor about getting some more overtime. He wanted to buy a used pick-up truck Old Paterson was selling. It would be useful for driving around his few acres, where they had apple and peach trees, and planted the Three Sisters - corn, beans and squash. They picked wild strawberries scattered in the fields, and fished in Gill Creek. Their old car was almost done for, and Wallace needed a vehicle to take his family on drives to the beach at Lake Ontario, or into the city to stroll around the falls to cool off on hot summer nights, and picnic on Goat Island. As these memories came to him in his half-awake state, Wallace felt joy, but also a pain that squeezed his heart.

He remembered standing on Buffalo Avenue near the bus stop by the plant entrance, where Teresa was supposed to pick him up. She wasn't there. He knew she would have waited for him, even if he were a bit late. But it was probably her that was late. She always had one last thing to do. There was no way for him to reach her to find out where she was.

He was tired after the two long shifts. A brisk wind flew off the river, scattering the pungent white clouds that hung close to the ground all along the street, carrying the smell of chlorine. He breathed deeply, grateful to the wind for some fresh, watery air.

To this day, Wallace berated himself for not noticing the dark sedan driving toward him down Buffalo Avenue, cruising through the plumes of white smoke seeping from cracks in the brick pavement. It slowed down and pulled to the curb near him. Two heavy-set men in dark suits got out and walked slowly toward him. One quickly flashed a badge. They stood in front of him, reeking of cigarettes and sweat.

"What are you doing here?" the bigger man asked.

Wallace glanced at them. "It's a bus stop," he said.

"Let me see some ID."

Looking the man straight in the eye, Wallace pulled out his wallet. He waved his Hooker plant pass, his driver's license, his Social Security card, and American Legion membership card in front of the man's face. "Okay?" he said. He turned to walk away from them.

One of the men grabbed Wallace's arm and twisted it behind his back. The other stepped in front of him and pulled back his jacket to reveal his shoulder holster. "We're taking you in," he said.

"For what?" Wallace yelled. He tried to pull out of the detective's grip.

"For questioning, Chief," the man said. Wallace lunged away only to see the detective's fat hand, glistening with bronze, aimed at his head.

He woke up on the hard floor of a jail cell. He tried to rise, but his head throbbed with pain and his arms and legs were limp. Over-coming his nausea, he fought himself to a sitting position. When his eyes came back into focus, he saw a rectangle of light high on a wall. And the bars. He tried to remember what happened. When he finally did, rage gave him the strength to lurch to his feet and storm the bars that held him inside this cage.

"Hey!" he yelled. "Hey! I want to talk to someone! Hey!" He yelled until his throat choked up, and his words came in a raspy whisper. He stumbled to the stone slab that he had lain on, and fell on it face down.

After waves of nausea and pain subsided, he sat up again. He saw he wasn't alone. A small, dark-haired young man was sitting opposite him, staring at Wallace through eyes hooded with heavy lids.

"Where are we?" Wallace asked him.

The young man spit on the floor. "Can you not tell?" His rough voice had a French-Canadian accent.

"I know it's a jail," Wallace replied, "but which one? City or county?"

The young man stood, and reached in his pocket. His hair was long, cut in a foreign fashion, like you'd see in Toronto. His leather jacket looked expensive. He held out a pack of Canadian cigarettes to Wallace.

That simple gesture took Wallace back to the battlefield. Though he'd pretty much stopped smoking when he left the Army after the war, he took one. He needed it badly.

His new acquaintance lit it with a silver lighter, and then took one for himself. He sat down again. Exhaling smoke and gesturing with his cigarette, he said, "The answer to your question is, what does it matter? City? County?" He snorted. "Will you find justice in either?"

"Just tell me," Wallace said. His head was starting to clear.

"You are in the In-jun Suite. That is what they," he nodded at the cell door, "called it. We are in the city jail downtown, near the falls. Not so pleasant, eh?"

Wallace took a deep drag. He tried to think what they could charge him with. Resisting arrest? They didn't say he was being arrested. Loitering? At a bus stop?

"Do not task your brain, *mon ami*," his cellmate said, as though he could read his mind. "They do not need a reason."

"Yes, they do," Wallace retorted. "They'll answer for this. I'm a member of the Tuscarora Council. I just met with the governor's man last week. And I'm a veteran, too."

"Frenchy," as Wallace had started to think of him, laughed derisively. "You did not even know what you were fighting for. For this?"

Wallace threw his cigarette, half smoked, on the floor. He could hardly breathe. He lay on his back, and stared at the ceiling.

Frenchy wouldn't shut up. "When they brought you here, I will tell you what they said to me. They said, here is a friend for you. A drunken in-jun. That is what they called you. That is what they will say in their court. And you cannot prove them wrong."

Wallace sat up so quickly he almost fainted from the pain. He felt a trickle of blood run down his face.

"I *can* prove them wrong! I just got off my shift at work. Listen you, just shut up!" He leaned against the wall and closed his eyes until the pain subsided. When he opened them again, Frenchy was still staring at him. He said, "Do you really think you can stop this man — this Moses — from taking your land?"

"What do you know about it?"

"What I hear. What I see."

"And what's that?"

"I see you here, in this place. With me. I am a man who does not

25

bend to laws, or borders."

Wallace didn't like the way the guy's eyes glared at him, dark amber under hooded lids, like a snake's. He wished he would just shut up. He was an instigator. Wallace turned away.

"The Prophet said, 'The white man is a monster, and what he eats is land.'"

Wallace spun around and stared. This man was like a snake, luring him. "What Prophet?"

Frenchy's smile was sly. "You should know this. But the Longhouse has its own prophets. What do they say?"

Wallace didn't answer. He'd never concerned himself with prophecies, only with living his life. A man who goes to war doesn't want to listen to prophets. He went to Korea knowing the risks. But now. Now it seemed as though the war had come to his own home. Armed men had marched on Garlow Road as though it were a new front. And maybe it was. Maybe he'd have to fight another war, right here.

"Moses *will* take your land," Frenchy said. "You cannot stop the monster. But you can fight in other ways. In ways that will make you rich, give you power. I can give you such work."

Wallace stared at the small, confident young man. Was he serious? His expression said he was. Wallace felt as though he were stepping on rocks in the rapids, having to move carefully, lest he slip and fall into raging waters that would hurl him into an abyss. He stared into Frenchy's compelling eyes, feeling the lure of intrigue, and revenge. But he knew what was real. "I'm not interested," he said.

Frenchy shrugged. "It's your choice."

There was a loud clang. The cell door opened. A big red-haired cop stepped inside and said, "Mountview. Come with me. You're being released." He glared at Frenchy. "You, Ang-wine," he drawled out the name. "You stay put. Immigration is on its way from Buffalo to pick you up. They were real happy we nabbed you before you got over the bridge. We made a nice little haul."

The young man spat on the floor.

The cop wouldn't look at Wallace as he led him through the

station. He left him in front of a men's room, saying, "Your stuff's next door." Wallace went into the dingy chamber and did his business. Then he looked at himself in a small, hazy mirror bolted to the cement wall. His thick black hair was matted with blood still oozing from an open cut on his right temple. He swabbed his bloody face with paper towels. Then he went to the room next door and found his jacket, hat, and wallet on a big wooden table, next to a cheap plastic tray holding black coffee in a paper cup, and a sandwich. There was a fly on the thin pink slice of bologna sticking out of the white bread. He checked to be sure all his ID cards and money were there. They were. He drank the luke-warm coffee quickly, ignored the sandwich, and went out to the front desk.

"So what's next?" he asked the cop.

"Nothing. You can go." He turned his back on Wallace.

Wallace was livid. He considered walking down the street to the *Niagara Falls Gazette* office, where he knew some reporters and the chief photographer. He could make a big deal about this, let them take pictures of his beaten face, let those rogue cops have to answer for their assault and false arrest. But as he walked down the stone steps of the station, he felt his anger seep out of him. He hurt and he was tired. This was just a little skirmish in a bigger war. He wouldn't let his wife, his friends, and his soon-to-be-born child, see him humiliated in the paper. He'd be sure not to get caught off-guard again, now that he knew the true nature of his enemy.

Wallace walked over to Falls Street, and turned toward the New York Central train station to find a phone booth. The streets were busy with tourists and shoppers. A couple of young men stood looking at the guitars and mandolins in the window of Rubin's Pawn Shop. People hurried in and out of the shops in the Gluck Building. There were lines outside Fannie Farmer's candy shop, and the popcorn store. As always, he was surprised at the number of Japanese tourists, a people so recent-ly a mortal enemy, with their black box cameras hanging from their necks.

As he walked down Falls Street, Wallace saw a column of pure white mist hovering over the trees in Prospect Park. He was drawn to it, as a pilgrim is drawn to a shrine offering purification and salvation. He hurried past the train station, and kept going, past the Cataract movie theater, which was showing *Vertigo*, and the Strand, where *South Pacific* was running. He went past the small souvenir shops, the newsstand, the french fries counter, Neisner's, Beir's department store, and Sears & Roebuck. Past the Main Restaurant, the bus terminal and the bars; then he dodged the cars cruising slowly on Riverway to reach the park's green shade. The tall oaks and maples created a haven, another world. He walked among the honeymooning couples, strolling hand-in-hand past tidy gardens of brightly-colored tulips and jaunty daffodils. People posed for pictures; everyone seemed to have one of the new small Kodak cameras, and everyone wanted pictures of every view of the approach to the falls.

Wallace felt more and more calm, as always, as he walked toward the source of the mighty roar that shook the ground under his feet. The river was as yet undiminished by water diverted for American power. When he stood at the brink of the American Falls, he watched the green-tinged torrent roar over its rocky brink to generate the clouds that displayed its force. He stood there a long time. He remembered Abraham Lincoln's words, when he first beheld Niagara: "My God! Where is all this water coming from?"

Wallace felt his clothes dampen and stick to his skin; droplets of mist washed new blood down his face. As he stood there watching the most famous waterfall in the world, Wallace thought it impossible that even a man as powerful as Robert Moses would be able to diminish Niagara's cataracts. Yet even as the water's roar overwhelmed his senses, Wallace realized how fragile it all was — the falls, the river, his home. The Monster would eat the land, and drink the river, too.

Nothing was ever the same after Moses got the Tuscarora land. He didn't get as much as he wanted, but he got enough to fracture the native community's home, enough to end the days of fishing for blue pike in Gill Creek, enough to break many hearts. But not Wallace's will to fight on. He remembered the words of Hugo Black, one of the justices on the U.S. Supreme Court who disagreed with its ultimate decision to give Moses a big hunk of Indian land: "Great nations, like great men, should keep their word."

Wallace hated the memory of those days. He tried never to think of them. But today, today he had seen a face – those eyes – that brought it all back.

Rose and Leonard had to help Wallace out of the car when they got home. He went straight to bed. Rose checked on him every hour.

CHAPTER FOUR

That evening, Anne tried to recover from a long, frustrating day by sitting on her second-story porch overlooking the river with some chilled wine and her iPad. She didn't look at her text messages or email because she didn't want to see notes from her angry colleagues. The Dean's meeting had been long and stressful. There was a rehash of "accomplishments" from the previous academic year, and warnings about budget "adjustments." The Dean spent a lot of time on metrics that showed enrollment drops in several programs and more declines in funding from the state. Then she announced the formation of an ad hoc committee to develop strategies for a "tranformational reorganiza-tion" to take the school into the twenty-first century. Not another one, Anne thought. She felt agitated just thinking about it.

A forced breeze from a fan set on the floor made the hot porch just bearable. It swayed the fronds of her potted ferns, and carried the scent of the delicate wisteria blossoms climbing on the porch railing. Ben lay near her feet, his tail slowly swishing back and forth.

"Anne!" a woman's voice called. "Are you up there?"

Anne leaned forward and peered through her plants over the porch railing. Mari, who rented the flat downstairs, was standing on the front steps, looking up at the second story.

"Yes," she replied. "Come up and have some wine with me."

Mari disappeared through the front door. Though Anne was the landlord, the two women, after living under the same roof for years, had become close friends. Both flats opened into a hallway in the back of the building that went from the cellar stairs to Anne's apartment. They usually kept the inside back doors unlocked during the day.

"I am totally beat!" the young woman said, as she sat down heavily in the other rocker, having poured herself a glass of wine in Anne's kitchen. She pulled her floral skirt up over her knees, and lifted her bare feet on the porch railing. She leaned her head back so that her long dark hair hung over the back of the rocking chair. "I spent all day at my booth on Old Falls Street. Right next to the music stage. I had to listen to loud music blaring all day and my head is throbbing. It was broiling hot. You know they're having that holiday art fair all weekend and the crowds were pretty big. And I have to do it again tomorrow!"

Anne gave her a sympathetic look. Mari's face was flushed; her long dark hair was limp, and she looked absolutely wilted.

After having a few sips of wine, to which she had added ice cubes, Mari asked Anne, "Have you seen this morning's *Niagara Chronicle?*"

"No. I was just looking at the *Times* online."

Mari handed her the front section of the local newspaper that she had brought upstairs.

"There's a story about Nick Valli and the opening of his new club in Niagara Tower – that's what they're calling the old United Office Building now. They are actually having a *beauty pageant* there tonight as part of celebrations for signing a contract with some Las Vegas conglomerate. And they're calling it the Maid of the Mist Pageant! Straight from the nineteen-fifties! I just cannot believe they actually resurrected that pathetic old myth about human sacrifice at the falls. Just look at that picture of him standing in front of the contestants in their trashy little costumes! I bet he tried to grope every one of them."

"I'm sure he did," Anne said drily. "I wouldn't put anything past him." She took a sip of wine.

"He is so desperate to open a non-Indian casino, or some sort of gambling club, he's even bringing in these Las Vegas guys," Mari said. "Pay no attention to the towering Indian casino across the street. We are going so backward." Mari fanned herself with the paper, and moved

Ben away from her legs. "It's too hot, Ben," she said, "even though I love you." She patted the dog on his head. "It's sad, but if I wanted to – if I could lower myself to – I could do really well selling images of the Maid of the Mist. Lelawala, paddling her little white bark canoe over the brink. The maiden who sacrificed herself to appease the Thunder God under the Horseshoe Falls. That was the most famous image of the falls in the nineteenth century. And the story was made up by some white guy. I think it was just an excuse to paint a naked woman. Why are all the great paintings of old myths full of naked women?"

Anne chuckled. "Not just the old ones. What about those posters for the movie *Niagara*, with Marilyn Monroe and her boobs laying across the brink of the Horseshoe Falls?"

"Things will never change," Mari said. Then she sat up straight and handed the paper to Anne. "Take a look at the girl standing behind Nick, to the right," she said.

Anne squinted at the image. It stayed blurred. Sighing, she put on her reading glasses. She hated them. They were the first tangible evidence that she was past her fortieth birthday. She stared at the photo, and finally asked, "What about her?"

"Doesn't she look like Phoebe?"

Anne squinted again. "Not at all. Oh, God! Can you imagine Phoebe in an outfit like that? And that hair! If I thought it could possibly be her, I swear I would just jump over the falls." She read the photo caption. "Her name is Ani Shanando. That's an odd name, isn't it?"

"Well, I think it sort of looks like her, a little bit. I'll save my copy of the paper, and show it to her sometime, just to get on her case."

Anne sighed, and tried to calm down, but couldn't quite manage it, even though she was convinced that Phoebe, her young niece, would have no part of a travesty like that. She was still in high school, only seventeen, for God's sake.

"By the way, I saw Phoebe downtown today," Mari told Anne. "She introduced me to Leonard."

The two women exchanged a look. "Really?" Anne asked.

"Yes," Mari replied, "and I have to say he wasn't at all what I expected."

"My brother Bill is furious with Phoebe for hanging around with – as he calls him – 'a kid from the reservation.' As if it's some huge, fenced-in camp. When you can't even tell where it begins and ends, and it's only, what, about ten square acres." She sighed. She and her older brother viewed the world from two opposing poles. "So Leonard must be, what, six feet tall and dangerous-looking. And also, if Phoebe likes him, he has to be hunky."

Mari laughed. "Not at all," she replied. "He's just a normal-looking kid, like Phoebe. In fact, he's a year younger, and shorter than she is. Why are they in the same grade?"

Anne winced. "Phoebe got held back a year in middle school," she said. "Bill blamed the teachers, the teachers blamed her. No one listened to me. I still think she has ADD."

"Well, anyway," Mari continued, "he seems like a pretty nice kid. Quiet. He didn't say much. He has long black hair and he was wearing a Tree of Peace tee shirt. Phoebe says he's related to Wallace Mountview, the famous Tuscarora chief. Is that why Bill is so against Phoebe hanging out with him? Just because he's Native American?"

"Yes, to be honest, that's part of it," Anne replied. "But Bill also doesn't want Phoebe seeing anyone. Her grades were terrible last year. She just won't work at her studies. They're at each other's throats. And now that her twin brothers are home from college for the summer, the whole house is in an uproar. The boys don't give Phoebe any slack."

Mari nodded. "Phoebe always does her own thing."

Anne wanted to change the subject. "I just can't believe that here it is, the twenty-first century, and what do we have in Niagara Falls?" she moaned, scanning over the newspaper article. "A beauty contest, right out of the nineteen-fifties. The prize is a chance to compete in Las Vegas on New Year's Eve and win a contract to perform in a casino. My God! Will they never come up with anything new and positive? And not so sexist!"

Mari's voice was mild as she said, "The karma of the whole city has to be changed before we get any enlightenment. And we're a long way from that. But think about it, Anne. This could be a big chance for one of these girls from Niagara Falls. What else is there here?"

Sometimes Anne wished she could be more like Mari, always trying to find the positive angle. It wasn't easy to do, especially in Niagara Falls. Maybe it was part of Mari's training as a teacher. Mari was in her early thirties, and had a teaching degree in art from the teachers college in Buffalo. She had taught art in grade school for a few years, until budget cuts eliminated the arts programs in the whole system. She supported herself now by selling her artworks, most of which were misty pastels, with poetry overlaid on images of Niagara Falls and rainbows; she also did occasional bartending or catering jobs. Her art was popular in the downtown tourist shops and online; it was original, and inexpensive. It wasn't easy for her to keep up with the necessary production, and to have enough for booths at all the local art fairs and shows.

Anne swallowed another sigh. She tried to concentrate on the newspaper.

"Here's a long interview with Nick Valli, Mr. Big Tourism Director," she said. "He's thrilled about his deal with Las Vegas. He's still hoping to open a non-Indian casino here. I just hope he doesn't try to rezone Cataract Lane for business again."

A previous battle over rezoning a few years before had turned the city official into Anne's mortal enemy, and vice versa, when Anne led a community group successfully against the move.

Mari said, "He's so creepy. I saw him last week when I was delivering my orders to Rainbow Blossoms. He was talking to a bunch of business types in dark suits. Trying to sell the Turtle again, I bet. I heard him tell them that I'm a beautiful and colorful local *artiste*. They all stared at me. I was so embarrassed. Hey, give me that paper, Ben!"

The dog had crept up on Mari and taken one end of the paper in his mouth, eager for a game. Anne laughed as Mari tried to pry it out of her dog's mouth. Her mood lightened; she leaned back into the thick cushions of her rocker and sipped her wine. Downriver, to her right, she observed a billowing column of water vapor trying to rise above the tree line as its droplets evaporated quickly under the bright sun.

Anne closed her eyes and listened to the river. On hot days like this, the water's roar seemed muted, more hiss than thunder. She loved living so close to the river. After college, she had lived at the opposite end of the state for ten years. But not even the excitement of New York City could free her from Niagara's spell. After particularly grueling days in the intensive care unit, as she waited on the subway platform to head uptown for her graduate classes, she'd close her eyes at the first sound of an oncoming train's rumble. At its loudest, just before the train's brakes began their metallic squealing, the noise was a faint echo of Niagara's eternal roar, and for a moment Anne would feel anchored again. Later, that kind of industrial, interrupted roar reminded her of the horror of collapsing towers, putrid smoke, and death. She left the city not long after 9/11, seeking solace and purification in Niagara's mists.

The annoying whirl of a tourist helicopter overhead snapped her thoughts back to the photo of Nick Valli, a skinny, dark-haired guy in his late forties, leering in front of a line of scantily-clad, pseudo Indian maidens, re-enacting a story made up by some white man more than a hundred years ago. It was discouraging how he was taking Niagara Falls back into the past, not the future.

Anne opposed casino gambling, and was a member of a historic preservation group that had vehemently fought against the Seneca Indian casino being built downtown. They would have fought a non-Indian casino, too. But the deal between the state and the Seneca Nation that allowed the casino to open was seen as a last-ditch effort to revive the dying city's economy. Anne was lately resigned to its existence, though she knew its inevitable social costs. She lived in fear of any new developments that could lead to the destruction of the last remnants of the city's downtown architectural history. Like Cataract Lane. She knew Nick Valli would agree in a minute to tear her house down for a new hotel, or even a parking lot. You only had to look at what was happening on the Canadian side of the river, with its skyline of tall casinos and hotels.

Anne and her fellow preservationists wanted the city attractions to focus on the beauty of the falls, and its fascinating history. She was especially eager to see the resurrection of a downtown Native American cultural center in the building called the Turtle. Built thirty years ago in the shape of a giant turtle to symbolize Iroquois creation beliefs, the former museum overlooked the American Falls; the turtle's giant red-striped head pointed toward its brink. The now-decrepit building had been unused for years. Anne feared the Turtle, and much else, would be sacrificed if casinos became the end-all of the city's economic focus. It would look like the Canadian side of the river, all new towers and glitz, until you stepped away from the river and saw the economic devastation of the rest of the city.

"Anne?"

She turned and saw that Mari was frowning as she looked at the newspaper.

"What's wrong?"

"Something in the police news. You know that woman who's always getting picked up downtown, Sheryl Poloka?"

Anne sighed. "Only too well. Father Joe and I have tried several times to get her placed in treatment. Whenever she shows up at the food kitchen, he tries to find out if she's on her medication, and usually she isn't. What happened now?"

"The police arrested her for soliciting yesterday."

"Oh, no." Anne grasped the arms of her chair and started to stand up. "I'd better call Joe and go to the city jail with him. Maybe we can get her admitted to the hospital again."

"Don't bother. The article says she was arrested and then released on five hundred dollars cash bail."

Anne dropped back in her seat. "What? Where did she get that kind of money? She lives on the street, for God's sake!"

Mari looked troubled. "Maybe she stole it, Anne. She was hanging around downtown all day yesterday. She was at my booth for a long time, being a real pest, looking at my stuff, reading the poems out loud, fingering my hand-painted tee shirts and dresses. I almost called the police, I hate to say, but then I felt so sorry for her, I just couldn't.

I mean, I went to high school with her. So I gave her one of the dresses she kept looking at, just to get rid of her. It was one of my best ones, too, purple with yellow irises painted on it. She was really happy to get it. She changed clothes somewhere, and the last I saw of her, she was wearing my dress and hitting up tourists for cash."

Mari's frequent acts of kindness impressed Anne. She exclaimed, "I hope she did steal the money! I'd rather think she stole it than that she earned that much by selling herself all day."

She sat back in her chair, rocking so hard that Ben, fearing for his legs and tail, crept closer to Mari. She felt angry and helpless. All efforts to help Sheryl had been futile; no one could force her to get help. The law sanctioned neglect and self-destruction.

"Hey, Anne." Mari was still reading the newspaper. "Did you see this article on page eight?"

"No."

"Listen to this. It says there's been an offer to buy the Turtle. So that's why I saw Nick down there the other day."

"Who's the buyer? What do they want to do with it?"

"The article says it's a new corporation named White Pine Enterprises, and there are rumors that it could be considering putting a small casino in there."

Anne's jaw clenched. Would even the Turtle, symbol of ancient beliefs, be given over to the modern creed that the primary – if not only – purpose of life is to make money? She leaned forward in her chair, resting her arms on the porch rail, careful not to crush delicate wisteria buds. In the rushing river, the rapids leaped and swirled in a summer's dance, sending sprays of water into the air. Droplets sparkled in the bright sun. The waves raced toward their oblivion, where white mist hovered low above a swirling cauldron. If she leaned out far enough, she could almost see the Turtle's giant head, looming over the brink.

CHAPTER FIVE

During dinner with his business friends at a crowded restaurant on Buffalo's waterfront, John disclosed his plan to reopen the Turtle in Niagara Falls as a museum of Haudenosaunee art, history, and culture. He was pleased by their enthusiastic reactions. They fully supported him, and immediately began giving him their own ideas of what should be displayed, and how the history should be told. When they started debating what some of the history really was, John excused himself from the table and headed for the men's room.

As he left the restroom, John almost bumped into a short, very thin man who abruptly stepped in front of him.

"John Lone," the man said, as if he knew him, holding out his hand.

John looked at him closely, and felt as though he should know who the guy was, maybe from seeing him on television. He had that sort of look – a bland, botoxed face, highly styled salt-and-pepper hair, even a hint of makeup; he was older than he first seemed. His black leather jacket was tailored to fit his slender frame. He wore a silver-and-turquoise medallion on a bolo tie, and several large rings. He stared at John through large, amber eyes under hooded lids. A shady guy if he ever saw one, John thought.

"Do I know you?" John asked. He didn't take the offered hand.

"Not yet," the man replied in a smooth, deep voice with a hint of a French-Canadian accent. "But I hope we will soon know each other well. My name is Levi Moon."

"What do you want?" John was annoyed. People were always after him for money.

"Perhaps we could go to the bar and talk?"

"I don't do business in bars. Anyway, I have to return to my table. I'm with friends."

"Please, just a moment." Levi Moon seemed to be trying to keep John's interest by the intensity of his gaze. But it was easy for John to look right over his head. He started to walk away, when the man said, "I hear you are conducting business in Niagara Falls."

John turned quickly. "What makes you think that?" He didn't try to hide his annoyance. Who had leaked it? Not Harold. It must have come out of City Hall. Those politicians couldn't keep their mouths shut.

Levi Moon smiled slyly, and shrugged his shoulders. "What does it matter? I'd like to talk to you about mutual endeavors that could be extremely lucrative."

"I'm not interested," John replied curtly. He tried to walk around him, but the slender man deftly kept in front of him.

"If you will give me five minutes ...," he insisted, taking hold of John's arm.

John glared, and Levi Moon removed his hand.

"I'm not interested in doing business with you," John told him. "Not now or ever. Now get away from me or I'll make you sorry you ever saw me."

John saw a fierce look pass over Levi Moon's face, but it quickly dissipated.

"Of course," he said, stepping aside. "Sorry to have troubled you, Mr. Lone."

John returned to his table, but couldn't relax after the encounter. That guy had nerve to come up to him like that. He was sorry he hadn't had him thrown out of the place. He couldn't get over the feeling of being watched.

The dinner group broke up close to midnight, with the men embracing and promising to get together again soon. John didn't see the strange little man again. As he climbed into his Cadillac, he felt a burning sensation in the middle of his chest, as though his ribs were on a griddle. He should have passed on that second order of extra-hot Buffalo wings. He thumped his chest with his fist, and burped. He could still taste the sauce as he began the long drive south, about sixty miles as the crow flies, to his home near Seneca Nation land in Cattaraugus County.

He drove a couple of blocks and got onto the Niagara section of the New York State Thruway going east, until he reached the main Thruway and turned south. Traffic was light at this late hour, and he made good time.

At Lackawanna he got onto Route 219, the Southern Tier Expressway, which ran due south of Buffalo, until hills nudged it a bit to the east. His headlights lit up the two lanes of the divided highway as he raced past Orchard Park and the exit for Ralph Wilson Stadium, where the Buffalo Bills played. The road started to dip as it crossed folds of land left by the crushing glaciers. Though he couldn't see them in the darkness surrounding the road, John knew the rolling wooded hills began as he passed Hamburg. At times he felt as though he were driving through a tunnel, as trees and bushes crowded the road. After about an hour, John felt a long decline in the road as he approached Springville, where the highway ended after it crossed Cattaraugus Creek. He took a short jog, then turned left again as Route 219 turned into a two-lane road that wound into high wooded hills.

John drove with his own thoughts, despite having a car full of electronics and satellite radio. He had a lot to think about, in addition to his businesses and the Turtle project. He lived with his extended family on an estate in the hills just north of Allegany State Park and the Seneca Nation's Allegany Territory. His massive house was built high on a hillside overlooking the flat farmland of Great Valley. It was built in the shape of an eagle, with the head facing west and the wings outstretched to the north and south. Behind the house, his hundreds of acres of wooded hills rose and fell, cut through with gullies and glens carved by running water. John had bought up the land over the years, bit by bit, as soon as he started making money.

John and his brother Jerome occupied suites in the southern wing of the house; he liked those views from his windows, views of woodland and hills. His mother, his sister Loraine, and her husband Andrew lived in the north wing with their two young sons. Andrew worked for John, helping manage business and running the estate. Loraine was a middle-school teacher.

Behind the house was a large building that served as a garage and work area on the first floor. His estate manager, a big man named Sherwood Seneca, whom everyone called "Woody," lived on the second floor, which also held his office, and some rooms for estate workers, who were hired to plant and tend the gardens, and do year-round maintenance on the large house and well-kept grounds.

John thought again about the dinner discussion the family had had the night before. Jerome was more obsessed about the environment than ever. Jerome loved the land, especially their own home in the ancient territory of the Senecas. He said the land was lovingly crafted by the Creator, who filled it with abundance for his children to thrive. John often teased his brother that the lovely wooded hills were, according to the same scientists he cited about climate change, built by the glaciers more than ten thousand years ago, that they were just mounds of earth called drumlins. Jerome would just ignore John's skepticism, and say that however the land came into being, it must be protected.

Jerome is too involved in his writing, John thought. It had taken Jerome, who started his graduate studies in his thirties, several years to get his doctorate. Now he was reworking his thesis into a mass-market book, an analysis of how American native cultures relate to the environment, from pre-contact through the present day. He was currently studying end-time stories.

Jerome came home upset earlier in the week, after he had driven past a woodland on the western end of their property and observed a large number of trees in a maple grove were drying out at the top. He couldn't stop talking about it. He had just taken an oral history from an Onondaga Elder on the reservation near Syracuse, who talked to him about Handsome Lake, the eighteenth-century Seneca prophet. Handsome Lake had warned that in the Last Days the maples would dry out. It would be a time when the Haudenosaunee would be divided, witchcraft would be practiced, there would be epidemics, and the earth would tremble and burn. The usual stuff, John thought, though it did seem eerily prescient, considering the state of the world right now. Last night, Jerome had talked about the Hopis, whose elders said men shouldn't disturb things that lie within Mother Earth. Things like natural gas, oil, uranium. It sounded like his smart younger brother was really starting to believe that the planet was decomposing from the inside out because humans wouldn't stop drilling, mining, fracking, burning. Jerome needed a vacation, another wilderness trek with his camera to calm him down, John thought. Mother, and finally even Loraine, both told him to take a break, and stop worrying so much about things he couldn't control. Mother told both her sons – again – that they should get married.

John eased his car through a long curve. It was no use talking about the end of the world. He was tired of all that old stuff, looking backward instead of forward. He hoped the Turtle project would distract Jerome from his worries. He was waiting for the right moment to tell Jerome about an investment he had just made, on a hunch, in a new space tourism venture. He figured once people landed on Mars, or built a colony on the moon, it wouldn't be long before the first space casinos opened. Nik Valli had introduced him to the investors from Las Vegas.

As he slowed down to go through the quiet streets of Ellicottville, with its historic houses, old trees, and its speed traps, John used his car's hands-free cell phone to call Woody, to check on things at home. It was after two in the morning. John could tell he had woken him up, but Woody was on top of things, as always. The security system was operational. The family was home, everything was quiet. John was relieved, and hoped Woody's reassurances would quell the burning he still felt in his chest.

In the center of Ellicottville, John turned left at the corner of Washington and Jefferson streets for the final stretch of his ride home. He thought there might be a sudden thunderstorm brewing – the sky darkened, then an odd glow lit the horizon. But when he pulled over and looked through his sunroof, the stars and moon were shining brightly.

He drove on, past the Holiday Valley ski resort and across the wide, flat land of Great Valley. There were no sounds except the rush of wind over his sunroof and the smooth hum of his car's engine. He liked having this long, quiet time to think. He was full of ideas for the Turtle project. Should he give his agent the go-ahead to buy some carvings by that hot new Cayuga artist in Syracuse? He'd gotten a tip about this guy, and Jerome admired him; maybe he'd take a ride out there himself, and check him out. He could make it a weekend trip with his girlfriend, Tifani, spend a couple of nights at the Oneida Turning Stone casino, play golf. He always got the royal treatment there, and lately, he thought, he needed it.

As he crossed into the outskirts of the City of Salamanca, now within Seneca Nation territory, John tried to keep his thoughts focused on his plans. At a corner with an abandoned gas station, he turned left onto Route 417. He'd come so far, and yet he knew he would always feel pain at the memory of growing up on the reservation, fatherless, in a wood-heated shack with no bathroom, his mother relying on canned meat and bricks of cheese from the government to feed her children. The memory of his baby sister, Leona, who died when the fire went out one bad winter night, while the family went out to scavenge fallen branches for wood. All that kept them together was his mother's iron will; she made sure her three surviving children – he the oldest – stayed in school and away from trouble-makers. Now they all lived in his estate in the woods, on his own land. It was his will that was carrying the family now. He wished he could get custody of his own son, Caleb, from the boy's mother, so he could live there, too, instead of just visit- ing.

Near Kill Buck he turned left off 417, onto a private single-lane road that took him onto his own estate. His house was more than a mile away, up a long slope, then down, then up again. He drove as quickly as he could on the narrow lane, which wound like a black tunnel through the long, wooded slope, weaving around rock ledges and gullies. He was eager to get home. His headlights shone with high intensity on the thick foliage that pressed close to the car. Trees stretched their limbs to touch each other across the road.

Suddenly, almost by instinct, he slammed his foot on the brake pedal and came to a screeching stop. His rear wheels skidded. He thought he had seen movement and a light in the trees ahead, not too far away. Poachers again, or thieves, or curious kids. He resisted his first impulse, to jump out and chase the intruders, remembering the personal safety training from the security firm that had installed his alarm system. He was still outside the secure perimeter. He turned off his headlights. He couldn't see a thing, except wooded darkness that defeated the moon and starlight. He righted the car, resolving to expand the borders of the surveillance system. The rich were under siege more than ever, now. He wasn't going to take any chances. He had a lot to protect.

He kept a heavy foot on the accelerator, going faster than he normally would on this road, even in daylight. He needed an antacid; his chest felt as though a relentless hand was squeezing his heart. When he saw another flash in the trees, he jammed on his brakes again, and this time the car fishtailed into almost a full turn. He tried to call Woody. The call didn't go through.

"Damn!" John reached into his glove compartment and pulled out a black case. He removed his handgun, inserted the ammunition clip, and put it on the passenger seat. On full alert now, wide awake, he turned the car around in short, rapid bursts, hitting the dirt shoulder, cursing as stones and dirt hit its polished new sides. He raced on, resolving not to look into the trees. He kept his eyes straight ahead, and concentrated on keeping his car on the road. Even in this remote, dark woodland, he wasn't safe. Evil could follow a man anywhere. That wasn't a spiritual belief, just reality.

The road dipped down again, and then emerged from the trees onto a wide, flat mown field. Beyond the field, less than a quarter mile away, the ground rose again beyond a tall iron fence. Beyond the entrance gate, solar lights bordered the long drive to the main entrance of the house. A small distance to the left of the house was the two-story garage that also served as Woody's office and living quarters. John could see a light on in a room on the second floor. It was Woody, waiting until he returned home. He saw an outside light turn on by the garage entrance; Woody must have seen his headlights approaching the security gate.

A massive sycamore tree stood to the left of the closed gate, like a sentinel. Jerome had estimated it was a sapling in the days Red Jacket walked these lands. The tree's mottled bark gleamed in the rays of the Cadillac's high-intensity headlights. John thought about the trouble they'd had putting up the security fencing, because Jerome wouldn't let them cut any old trees. The perimeter of the fence was a zigzag in some places, like around this elder sycamore. Jerome still mourned the loss of the old forests, the fields of oaks and chestnuts that once covered the hills, cut down for lumber by white settlers, or to feed fires at saltworks. John sighed, worried about his younger brother, and pressed his car's control panel to open the gate.

Shadows caught his eye. John thought he saw something caught in his headlights as they reflected off the wide smooth trunk of the ancient sycamore. He sped up. As he got closer to the tree, he was certain he saw someone in those shadows. Someone small, with hooded eyes. He aimed his Cadillac at the indistinct figure, which seemed to be waiting for him in the road, like an assassin. That made him mad.

"Okay, asshole," he muttered, between clenched teeth. "Here I come."

He pressed hard on the gas pedal. The last sound he heard was the scream.

CHAPTER SIX

The only place where she felt any peace was on Iris Island. Her island. Other people walked on it, but they were just shadows. She was the only one who belonged there, the only one who could feel its vibrations, born deep in its roots, as it sang to the tune of the mighty river.

The shadows called it Goat Island – ugly name! – because some farmer kept goats here two hundred years ago. She never called it that. At first she just called it "my island." Then she found a book someone left on a bench, and it said that people used to call this land Iris Island, for the goddess of the rainbow, because of the rainbows that arch above the basin of the Horseshoe Falls when the sun shines through the mist. She loved to look at the rainbows and imagine she was somewhere over them. She called her island – and herself – Iris, now.

She wasn't happy when the summer tourists came. It brought too many people to her private place. She made more money begging, though. She could buy food. Today she got a new dress that she didn't even have to steal. Her friend was selling dresses with pretty things painted on them, and pictures with poems about the river, at a table along the street fair. Iris read all the poems, and then she saw the dress, which belonged to her because it was her color, purple, with a yellow flower, just like her. She touched it until her friend gave it to her. She had to promise to keep away from her table, but that was okay. Iris was beautiful in her new dress.

So many people, though! She couldn't keep them all in the

shadows. It made her dizzy when she thought about it. Money was easy to get with just a smile and a hand held out when there were lots of people and they were having fun. Most times, it was hard. Those were the times when *she* was the shadow, and she closed her eyes, and then it didn't matter where the hands or the fingers or anything else went, because she wasn't there.

If only she didn't have to eat she wouldn't need money. Sometimes she tried to stop eating, but after a day or two her stomach cramped, and then she couldn't keep moving from place to place, and scoot over the stone bridge in the dark onto her island. If only people would mind their own business she could get free food at the church, the one with the steeple that was as high as the falls. Father Joe was nice, but after she learned how to trust him he confused her and took her to a place where there were no shadows. They kept trying to open her eyes, but whenever she did there was bright light and fear and voices that wouldn't stop talking. They tried to get her to stay in that place; they said she would get used to the light and the voices, but she didn't want to. She wanted to hear the song of the river, and she couldn't, if those voices drowned it out.

Oh, it was nice to feel free and not hungry and to have a new dress! Her island was hers again after dark. The people were gone. The thunder was over, too, that had been so loud, and so close, a little while ago. The fireworks. She was sitting on a rock on the small Sister island nearest to the Horseshoe, inside the deep shadows, watching the moon shine on the water, and then suddenly there were booms and flashes of light. She almost fell into the rapids! She ran to the middle of her island, where the oldest trees were, and a big rock that she had dug a little hole under where she could crawl, and she covered her face and her ears and went into her deepest space, where there were no sounds or light.

She couldn't sleep tonight. The river was singing and her island was vibrating softly. There was a new sound, like a drum, that was making her want to dance. She twirled among the tall trees clustered in the middle of the island. She danced with the fireflies, whose tiny sparks are love beams.

After she circled all her favorite trees, Iris left her grove and danced to the walking path. She circumnavigated the island, twirling and skipping. Sometimes she thought someone was dancing with her, another sprite among the trees, but when she looked close he always popped away, like a leprechaun. Near the Hermit's cascade, a flute was playing.

It was hot tonight, and that drum was still pounding, louder now. She went to her pool, Iris's pool. It was under an old thick willow whose weeping branches hung over the river on the Sister island farthest out. She had to climb over the new fences. Between two tiny islets there was a space where the water flowed deep and swiftly toward the Horseshoe and its rainbow, but for a few feet out there was a shelf of rock where the water was only a couple of inches deep. Iris loved to lie on her rocky bed, with her feet upstream so the water hit their bottoms and tickled them before it flowed around her, caressing her body and catching the long tendrils of her hair so that it splayed above her head. Iris would take her right arm and extend it into the deeper channel, where the force of the water's movement would pull on it, like a friend, urging her to come. It made her giggle. No, not now, she would say. Not yet. Someday I'll come.

She was teasing her river friend when the drumbeat got even louder. She stopped giggling and tried to listen. She lifted her head out of the water. She felt the rock shudder. It's too loud, she thought, as she started to sit up. But her right hand was still in the water, and this time her friend was insistent and wouldn't let go. She tried one last time to resist, then surrendered.

And she danced to the song of the river, under the rainbow.

CHAPTER SEVEN

Well past midnight, Anne gave up hope of sleep. A distant rumble sounded like thunder. Ben, sprawled across her legs, had his head up, listening.

Anne went to her guestroom to check on Phoebe, and found her on her back, sleeping heavily, her light hair a halo around her head. Anne gently took the buds out of her ears and got the tangled cord of her iPod off her.

Hearing more deep rumbles, Anne opened the French doors that led from her bedroom to the upper porch. When she stepped outside, Ben close behind her, she was surprised to see that the night was bright and clear, showing no sign of rain. There was a purplish glow in the sky, as though the lasers that illuminated the Horseshoe Falls were still on; the air felt electric, as though a storm were coming. Heat lightning, maybe. Over the American Falls, a tall, thin column of mist reflected reddish hues as deep as blood. Small bugs nipped at her skin, clammy from the humidity. She soon retreated back into her climate-controlled nest for another futile attempt at sleep.

Anne got out of bed as the first light of dawn shone through an opening in her bedroom curtains. At least it was Saturday, she thought, and she didn't have anywhere she needed to be. She noticed her digital clocks all blinking, and groaned. She tested lights in her kitchen: the power was out. This day was not starting well.

She dressed quickly and left the house with Ben for his morning walk. She was surprised to see Mari sitting on a wooden rocker on the front porch, huddled under a fringed shawl wrapped around her shoulders. Her legs were drawn up against her body, and her bare toes were bent around the edge of the seat. She was still in her sleep tee and shorts. Mari jumped when she heard Anne come through the front door.

Anne was shocked by the pungent scent of marijuana coming from a smoke cloud around Mari's head. She stared at her friend, who nervously looked away from her. When she was able to speak, Anne could feel how shrill her voice was. "Mari, what in the world are you doing?"

"Sorry." Mari pinched the lit end off the joint and put it in her pocket.

"Mari, I can't believe this!" Anne cried. "What if Phoebe smelled it?"

"I said I'm sorry, Anne."

Anne bent closer to look at Mari. She was pale, except for deep blue circles under her eyes. "Did something happen? Are you all right?" She stepped forward and reached down with her right hand to grasp Mari's wrist. Her pulse was racing.

"Yes, I'm okay, it's just …," Mari stammered.

"What?"

"Well, I had the most awful dream last night."

"And that's making you get high at seven in the morning?"

Mari pulled her shawl tighter around her shoulders and didn't respond. She looked ready to cry. Anne was concerned, but before she could say anything more, Ben gave a whiny bark and pulled as hard as he could on his leash. He was desperate. Anne knew she had to walk him, or he'd pee on the porch.

"Ben has to go, Mari, but I'll be back in a little bit. Go inside, now. You look awful. Come on." She took Mari's hands, noticing how cold they were, and gently pulled her out of the chair. "I'm not mad, just get dressed." Anne's voice was calm and firm, as she almost pushed Mari into the house. "The power's out," she told her. "I'll see if anything's open downtown and get us some coffee, if I can. I'll be back soon. Then we'll talk."

Mari slowly walked into the house, dragging her shawl.

Ben pulled Anne down the steps, and quickly relieved himself on the white flowers of her wiegelia bush. They followed their usual morning route to the path along the upper rapids. The river was an especially deep green, almost black. Furious white-tipped waves came from behind and rushed past her and Ben, splitting like atomic fragments as they hit the jagged rocks.

Ben squatted in his usual spot by an old willow bent away from the river by the wind and the weight of its branches. Its trunk was encircled by many disfiguring knobs, or galls, that wound around it like a belt. Anne called it the Knobby Tree.

As she waited for Ben to finish, Anne worried about Mari. She had never done anything so out of character before. And over a dream? Had she gone out last night? Did she bring someone home? Anne tried not to speculate on all the lousy things that could happen to a woman when she is alone with a man.

Walking quickly, Anne and Ben followed the path as it dipped under the metal girders of the American Rapids Bridge to Goat Island. Anne left the path and cut across the lawn and roads to Heritage Park on Old Main Street. There was an unusual silence, no electric hum in the streets.

The Punjabi food truck at the corner of Old Main and Rainbow Boulevard had power from its propane tank, and was open, servicing people from an early tour bus. Anne bought two cups of strong Indian tea and some sweet cakes, then hurried back toward the river. She saw police cars with their lights flashing rush across the bridge to Goat Island. As she hurried back to her house, she wondered if it was another Hermit sighting.

Back home, Anne saw Mari sitting on the front porch, waiting for her. She looked a little better. She was wearing a loose dress now, and her dark hair was brushed.

"Would you like to come upstairs?" Anne asked her.

"I'd rather be anywhere but inside right now. Let's go sit by the river."

They walked across the park lawn and sat at a cement picnic table near the river path. Here, the wide river's dark water gave only a hint of the fury that it would display just a bit farther downriver, past the tip of Goat Island. It was deep, and moved like a heaving, living mass toward the brink.

The day was already hot. Ben stretched out on the ground next to Anne. She waited until Mari had drunk some tea before asking, "So tell me what happened last night."

"Anne, I'm sorry about the weed. Really. I know I should be careful with Phoebe around. It was just a bit of homegrown that my friend brought over a while ago for when I get cramps. It won't happen again."

"I probably over-reacted." Anne took a sip of tea. "It's just that it was so unexpected to see you outside so early in the first place." She gave a weak smile at her weak joke.

Mari ran her fingers through her long dark hair. "I had a really bad night," she said.

"Tell me what happened."

"I just couldn't get to sleep," Mari told her. "I was kind of upset, actually. You know my friend, Karen?"

"From your meditation group?"

"Yes. She came over last night. She told me she saw Sheryl Poloka yesterday evening, wandering around Goat Island, wearing my dress. Karen said she looked really bad, really out of it. Karen called to her, but she just ran off."

"I wish Karen had called the police. They could have taken her to the hospital."

"If they could catch her." Mari looked sad. "You don't think she would jump, do you?"

Anne sighed. "I don't know."

"She seemed so normal in high school," Mari said. "Then she started using drugs and they said she was schizophrenic." She looked at

Anne. "Did the drugs come first, or the mental illness? Can they tell?"

"Not really." Anne ran a hand along Ben's hot back. "I won't tell Joe about this. It'll just upset him. He's been driving around downtown looking for her." She shook her head as if to shed her thoughts. "Now tell me about this terrible dream. It'll help to talk about it."

Mari lifted the tea to her lips, then set the cup down. Her voice was barely steady. "It was like something had me and was holding me down and raping me. I tried to fight it. I saw this evil – I can't even describe it as a face, it was just eyes, black eyes, looking down at me. It seemed to go on forever. Then suddenly it stopped. Something rolled down my body and through my legs, like a giant snake slithering off me. Then I think I actually passed out. When I woke up it was just getting light outside." She swallowed some tea.

After a long moment, Anne said, "I have some Xanax. Do you want some?"

"No. Thanks." Mari let out a deep breath. "It helped just to tell you, to make it real. Maybe I'll do some sketches, while it's still fresh in my mind, those eyes, that cave full of green light. I have to try to figure out what this means."

"It doesn't mean anything." Anne used her sternest professorial voice. "Dreams are just electrical impulses in your brain. It's like your brain is setting off sparks, to release extra energy. They're just random images. Probably because you were so upset about Sheryl."

"You know, the weird thing is, when I woke up, the comforter was off my bed, and some stuff was knocked off my night stand."

Anne was troubled. She thought about how incoherent rape reports could be. "Listen, I don't want to upset you even more than you are, but we should consider something. Did you have anyone over last night? That guy you met last week? Do you think it's possible you could have been drugged and assaulted? That it wasn't a dream?"

Mari let out a deep, whistling breath.

"Does anyone have a key to your place?" Anne asked.

"No. Not a guy, anyway. Just Karen, for emergencies." She was silent, thinking. Finally she said, "I don't think it's possible it was a real man. No."

"Ben would have barked if someone broke in. I think." Anne glanced down at Ben, who was sleeping like a rock near her feet.

"It was almost like a visitation," Mari said. "So real, but not reality."

"Well, something strange was going on last night. There were police cars rushing out to Goat Island when I was getting the tea. I think I'll walk over there and see if I can find out anything." As she started to rise, Anne thought of something. "Wait a minute!" She sat back down. "Mari, let's not totally discount my theory. The Hermit is still lurking around. Let's check all the windows and doors. It's possible that someone could have broken in last night."

"The Hermit looks like he stinks, right?" Mari asked.

"Oh, yeah. Definitely."

"Then he wasn't in my room last night. My dream visitor – evil as he was – smelled clean, like fresh river water."

CHAPTER EIGHT

Leonard was carrying two boxes of canning jars up the stone steps from the basement for Rose when a loud knock at the kitchen door startled him so much he almost dropped the heavy load of glass. He heard her steps cross the kitchen, the squeal of the old spring on the screen door, and men's voices.

He hoped she didn't get distracted by company. He wanted to get out of the house and meet Phoebe downtown, and hear from her what had happened at the contest last night. But he had promised to help Rose put up her famous wild strawberry jam. He'd thought, after the worry they'd had with Grandfather yesterday, that she might postpone the canning session. But Wallace slept deeply all night, and Rose went out at dawn to pick her strawberries. Now they couldn't wait, she said. The only bright spot was that he got to taste-test the jam. He licked some sugary residue off his arm. She'd get another ribbon at the county fair, for sure.

Leonard waited on the stairs until the visitors' footsteps stopped. Climbing into the kitchen, he saw two heavy, middle-aged men sitting around the old oak table. They were members of the Tuscarora Council. His hopes sank. Those guys would be here talking for the rest of the day. And they'd put a big dent in the jam, too.

"Put those jars down next to the sink, Leonard," Rose directed him. "And go upstairs and wake your Grandfather."

Leonard shot her a surprised look. It must be important, or she'd never disturb Grandfather while he was sleeping. Leonard almost questioned her, but she'd already started to measure out coffee. "Would you men like to try some of my new jam?" she asked the visitors.

"We smelled it coming up the drive," Chester, the larger of the two, said. "Tell Wallace not to hurry, Leonard."

The adults laughed, but Leonard was annoyed. He climbed slowly up the bare wood steps to the second floor. Feeling sticky with sugar and heat, he stopped in the bathroom to rinse his head and arms in cold water. He hesitated outside the bedroom door. He was worried about his elder, after the incident yesterday, when he seemed so out of it. Wallace wouldn't let Rose even call his doctor; he said he was okay.

Steeling himself, Leonard opened the door as quietly as he could, and looked inside. Wallace was lying on his back on the bed, wearing a white tee shirt and socks, and pajama bottoms. Leonard could feel the hot July breeze wash over him as it seeped through an open window opposite the door. The white cotton curtains blew softly inward, as the breeze rustled through the pines and maples that ringed the house. A big bug, a hornet probably, bounced off the window screen and made it ring. Leonard was relieved to see Wallace's chest moving heavily up and down, and to hear a faint growl emerge when he exhaled.

"Grandfather? Grandfather?" Leonard kept his voice low. He didn't want to wake the old man. He'd been scared last night, to see Wallace look so low. He decided the Council business could wait. He went back downstairs.

"I can't wake him. He's too tired," Leonard announced when he returned to the kitchen. He glared at Chester and Harry, who were spooning warm, luscious red jam on Saltine crackers and popping them whole into their mouths.

Rose looked stressed. "I'll get him. Leonard, stir this for me, so it doesn't burn." She handed him a dripping wooden spoon. Ignoring the smiles of the Council men, he stood in front of the stove and stirred the hot mixture of strawberries and sugar, which hadn't yet thickened. White bubbles burst on the surface of the steaming, blood-red broth. Rose had a couple of pots going, in different stages; the air was filled with a thick, sweet smell.

"So, Leonard, how's it going?" Chester asked.

"Okay." He didn't turn from the stove.

"How's your mother doing up at Six Nations?"

"I don't know."

"Well, next time you hear from her, tell her I said hey."

Leonard responded with a noncommittal grunt. He concentrated on the pot. After a few moments, Rose returned to the kitchen. She poured some coffee in a cup, added a heaping teaspoon of sugar and a lot of milk, and handed it to Leonard. "Here, give me that spoon. Take this up to him."

Leonard was glad to leave the kitchen. Upstairs, Wallace was sitting on the bed, looking a bit dazed. Leonard handed him the cup, and watched him take a long gulp. "Want me to tell them you fell back asleep?"

Wallace shook his head. "Rose said it's important. I'd better go. How's the jam coming?"

"Great. Except those guys are eating it all." Leonard sat on the bed. He loved this old house that Wallace had built for his first wife right after the war. It was lucky to be on the part of the reservation that wasn't lying at the bottom of the Niagara reservoir. Shadows of leaves played against the sloping ceiling, which was wallpapered with a soft silver-and-white pattern. The shadows seemed to weave in and out of the paper's design. Leonard started to feel sleepy himself. Wallace gulped down the coffee, and handed him the empty cup. "Tell them I'll be down in a few minutes."

Leonard returned to the kitchen, where Rose assigned him to be sure the caps on her filled jelly jars were twisted on as tightly as possible. He didn't use anything to shield his hands from the hot glass and metal. He liked to test his resistance to pain. But it burned, and he turned his face to the wall as he twisted the metal rings.

Wallace soon joined them, wearing a long-sleeved plaid flannel shirt and jeans. His long gray hair was loose, not tied back in his usual ponytail. Leonard glanced at Rose, who looked concerned. She'd clued

Leonard in on the fact that when Wallace didn't bother to comb back his hair and tie it into a ponytail, that meant he was out of sorts, or not feeling well, and that they should keep on eye on him. Wallace walked slowly to the table and sat down. Rose put another cup of coffee in front of him. Leonard continued to jerk the caps tight on the small jars lined in a row on the counter.

"What is it?" Wallace asked, as he spooned some warm jam on a cracker.

"I just talked to Thomas. It's done. He's joined White Pine after all," said Harry, with a disgusted look. "And there was an article about White Pine in the newspaper yesterday."

Wallace held a cracker, dripping with jam, halfway to his mouth. He leaned back in his chair and let out a deep breath. "I'm sorry to hear this. I thought we had him convinced to stay out of it."

"There's too much money changing hands. His wife told mine they're going to Lockport tomorrow to pick out a new truck," Harry said.

"His daughter wants to go to college," Chester added. "That's next year."

"Well," Wallace said, "then it's over."

"It really screws things up for us." When Harry was angry, the lines on his face were deep. "Now we'll never get the Turtle for our education center. All that time wasted applying for grants. We don't know what this White Pine is going to do with the building, and if we complain, all the papers will do is cover a bunch of Indians yelling at each other."

Leonard wondered what the men were talking about. It didn't matter. Another scheme somebody had, that everybody will argue about, and after a lot of yelling and screaming, and people not talking to each other, things would settle down, and everything would be the same as it always was.

"This is about the Turtle?" Rose asked.

"Yeah," Chester replied. "Some hotshot lawyers from Buffalo met with our Council a few months ago, claiming they were representing a group of Indian investors from across the state who were interested in re-opening the Turtle as a museum." He snorted. "Sure, we believe that. Their story was so blatantly a cover for something else. I think these so-called investors are just looking for a foothold downtown, so they can try to open another casino."

Harry added, "Our group has already applied for state and federal grants to re-open the Turtle, with professors from the Native American program at BU involved. Now who knows what will happen to the building. They may even tear it down, say it couldn't be repaired after all these years of neglect."

Wallace's head drooped, and he sat in silence.

Leonard knew this news would upset Wallace, who had his heart set on reopening the Turtle as an education center. He was a tradition-alist, against Indians getting involved in gambling. He said it brings corruption, and too many deals made with outsiders, deals that could jeopardize the nation's sovereignty. Leonard wasn't sure the Indian casinos were so bad. Look at the one downtown – it was the only thing making money there. It would be good to have some money, enough to get him to the places he wanted to go. Grandfather was wise, but he was old. Things weren't like they used to be. Even Rose told him he had to accept some new things; she was trying to convince him to go to Buffalo for more medical tests.

Chester banged his hand on the table. "I just remembered what I heard on the news coming over here." They all stared at him. "Did you hear anything about the falls collapsing?"

Wallace's head jerked up so quickly that Leonard thought he'd had some sort of a fit. His body jolted as though a bolt of electricity had shot up through the floor and zapped him. Rose dropped a jar and it crashed on the floor, smashing into bits. "What? What was that?"

"It was on the radio news. There was a big rock fall at the Amer-ican Falls last night, changed the whole face of it. Opened up a cave, too."

Wallace jumped from his chair, his lethargy gone. "Come on, Leonard. We've got to get a look at that!"

Rose made Leonard tighten the jars she had just filled with boiling hot jam, while Wallace quickly changed his clothes and fixed his hair. Chester drove Wallace and Leonard downtown and dropped them off near Prospect Point while he looked for a parking spot. Leonard navigated through the crowd, with Wallace following, until they reached the railing overlooking the famous cataract. The jagged brink looked as though someone had taken a giant's axe and brought it down right next to Luna Island, which seemed almost to teeter over the new rocky chasm at its side. Water spewed into the gap and bounced against the shattered rock. An ominous black hole seemed to lead right under the island. Huge slabs of gray rock lay at the bottom of the rift. Luna Island had been closed off, because officials were afraid more rock would collapse.

While Wallace gazed at the wounded cataract, Leonard texted Phoebe again. He was so close to Cataract Lane; he wondered how he could detach himself from Wallace and see her. But Phoebe texted back quickly: "Have important events today. Media stuff. Lelawala."

Lelawala – the name of the original Maid of the Mist. That was the code word. Leonard let out a deep breath. She'd done it. Phoebe had actually won the contest. She was the Maid of the Mist. Leonard's mind raced.

Wallace leaned on his arm, suddenly, and said, "Let's go home." Leonard called Chester on his cell phone and asked him to come and pick them up.

Later that evening, Leonard surfed the Internet on the old computer in the living room. Wallace and Rose were sitting nearby in cozy armchairs. She was listening to music on the radio while doing her beadwork, making soft cooing sounds, like a dove. Wallace seemed lost in his own thoughts, almost asleep, with his eyes half-closed. Leonard was frustrated with the long waits as pages downloaded on the old Dell, but they gave him a lot of time to think.

"Grandfather?" he asked.

Wallace opened his eyes.

"Where do you think that new cave goes down to? The one that goes under Luna Island?"

"Who can say? There are all sorts of caves in the gorge."

Leonard hesitated before asking the next question. "Are they true, the stories about spirits living around the falls? The Thunder Gods? And like at Devil's Hole, where the massacre was? There's a cave there, too, and the old story, about the evil spirit that lives there. And there's supposedly one behind the Horseshoe Falls."

Wallace closed his eyes again, and didn't answer. That was like him. If you asked him a question, usually he would answer, but sometimes he wouldn't, or he would respond with a question of his own, meant to make you think for yourself.

Leonard sighed and punched keys, trying to get the computer to download faster. He wondered if his elder knew the old words for the falls and its caves. He wondered how Wallace would describe the rock fall and the cave in the old language, what ancient concepts might be described. The Tuscaroras were relative newcomers at Niagara, the ancient Seneca homeland. They'd arrived less than three hundred years ago, seeking protection and sanctuary among the mighty Iroquois after being driven out of their own ancestral lands in what is now North Carolina.

Finally, his page opened up. It was the website for the big native music festival in Arizona that he and Phoebe were going to go to at New Year's. They had dreamed big and made a plan. They were going to use the tickets she won at the contest to get to Las Vegas. Then she was going to blow off the beauty contest there – which she said was stupid – and they would head for the big festival near the Paiute reservation close to the city. Phoebe wanted to buy lots of turquoise jewelry. He wanted to find his native culture. He wanted to get away from feeling always hemmed in, always on guard. Out west, maybe he would feel free. It seemed like a dream. He wondered if Phoebe would really go through with it, for him. He wondered what she might really want from him.

CHAPTER NINE

After leaving Mari, Anne headed to Goat Island to see what was going on there. She saw a crowd gathering at Prospect Point; as she got closer, she learned about the rockfall the night before from other sightseers.

"Even the falls had a bad night," she thought. Things were crazy downtown, with the crowds and traffic growing; the pedestrian bridge was closed. Anne wedged her way to the railing at Prospect Point; the sight of the dark gaping hole under Luna Island shocked her. Gulls shrieked overhead as they dove to inspect the new mound of earth and rocks piled at the far side of the cataract's brink. Anne closely examined the new face of the falls, thinking about how it took ten thousand years worth of erosion for it to get to this spot from Lewiston. Some day, according to geologists, the falls would disappear entirely; their layers of rock and shale would collapse into a series of smaller waterfalls and rapids. But not for a long time, she hoped, not in her lifetime. She pulled Ben back through the crowd and walked home. Mari and a sleepy-looking Phoebe were leaving through the back door, carrying boxes of small canvases to Mari's purple PT Cruiser parked in the alley. Her rainbow logo was on magnetic signs sticking to the side doors. Phoebe was going to help Mari at the fair for a while, then meet some friends for lunch, but be back for dinner.

Anne gave a sigh of relief when she found the power back on at home, and the A/C running. She took a shower, dressed, and sat down at her desk in the front parlor, intending to work on her grant proposal; if she was successful, the university would receive new federal funding to develop protocols for long-term treatment for thousands of military veterans dealing with catastrophic injuries such as the missing limbs and massive burns suffered by soldiers who fought in the Middle East. Anne's proposed protocols would also offer better support for the veterans' families, providing psychological therapy and training. She put a particular emphasis on veterans who were mothers, offering services like day care while they received treatment, and child-focused psychological therapy. Children suffered the wounds of their parents.

Anne's desk sat in a bay window that overlooked the upper rapids. To her right, she could see a thin column of pure white mist rising over the treetops. She opened her laptop and turned it on. But it didn't start up. Not after she tried several times. And said a prayer. And begged it. She even shook it, and felt its dead weight in her hands. She was dismayed; she couldn't remember the last time she had thought about backing up files. Oh, yes she could: never.

Anne's mind raced. What could she do? All her latest work was on that laptop, all the completed sections of her proposal and its supporting documentation. She had just written her draft of the justification of need, which she felt had been exceptionally compelling. How would she ever re-create it? It would take forever. She breathed deeply. She never panicked.

She called the number for BU's information technology services, which was on a label pasted to the inside of her PC. A recording told her the help desk was closed for the holiday weekend; service hours for the repair drop-off at the Cybrary, the campus technology center, would resume on Tuesday, though the center itself was open. Still calm, she found a hard-copy faculty directory in her desk drawer and found the contact number for the vice president for technology services. He'd asked her a few times to go to lunch with him. She called him.

"David, I'm awfully sorry to bother you on a holiday weekend," she began.

"No problem at all, Anne," he replied in a deep voice; he was one of those fiftyish administrators with carefully styled hair who took it as a matter of faith that all women – especially attractive, successful career women like Anne – wanted to bask in the wonder of their brilliance and power. "What can I do for you?"

Anne quickly explained that her laptop with her latest grant proposal files had died. She kept her voice cool and detached, for she knew that the professional price for any favors could be steep. "I have a very tight deadline on this grant, and I hate to lose time working on it over the long weekend. It's for a VA grant, David, a really important one."

There was a moment's silence. Then the VP said, "I'm texting one of my supervisors. I'll see if he can locate one of our technicians who can meet you in the Cybrary this afternoon. I'll text you in a bit when I get an answer."

"Thanks, David." The relief in her voice was palpable. "I really owe you for this."

"No problem, Anne," he replied in a smooth voice. "Will you be in your office next week? I'll drop by for lunch."

"Great," she said. "Thursday or Friday." She ended the call with a sigh. She was right. Payback would be a bitch. It would at least be a memo of support for his next big idea.

Within the hour she got a text instructing her to go to the Cybrary at three o'clock. A technician would be waiting.

Anne tried to stay calm on the drive, but the closer she got to campus, the more frustrated she felt. Every time she thought about her files, she pressed her foot harder on the accelerator. It would take days to recreate that grant proposal. The radio news on WBFO didn't help. It reported that there had been many scattered power outages on the Niagara Frontier during the night, with the largest one at Niagara Falls on both sides of the border. Even the casinos that lined the river went dark for a time. As the reporters described the rockfall at Luna Island, she concluded that it explained the rumbles and weirdness of the night before.

When Anne drove into the campus parking lot, she was surprised to see so many cars on a holiday weekend.

"Doctor Techa!"

Anne turned and saw a young man waving to her from the end of a long row of cars. As she got closer, she recognized him as one of her students, though she couldn't remember the class, or his name.

"I know you were in one of my classes last semester." Anne smiled and held out her hand. "I apologize for not remembering your first name."

"Jim," he told her, flashing a wide smile. He shook her hand. "Jim Tucker. That's okay. It was a huge class – Managing Crisis Triage Networks."

Anne gave a mock groan. "That *was* a huge class." She visualized the rows of anonymous faces rising above her in tiers in the lecture amphitheater. "But you did okay?"

"Oh, yeah," Jim assured her. "I got a B-. Everyone says that's like an A from any other professor." He looked dismayed. "Oh, sorry, I didn't mean ..."

"Don't worry," Anne told him. "I take it as a compliment." What her students learned could mean the difference between life and death for patients, and she wasn't going to pass any slackers. "So are you headed for the Cybrary?"

"Yeah," he told her. "I need to use one of the workstations. Our house lost power last night, over in Black Rock. Wireless is out, too."

"That's why I'm here, too," she said. "I'll walk there with you."

They chatted as they walked to the large open facility that was full of students huddled at desks with computer monitors. Jim circled the crowd, looking for an available spot. Anne walked to the help desk; a guy dressed in a light blue tee shirt and khaki shorts was waiting there, his head resting on his arms, so that all she could see was the back of his head and a mass of long reddish-blond hair. His breathing was regular; he was asleep.

She ahemed and coughed and tapped on the desk with no result. Finally, she said, "Excuse me!" and he woke up with a jump. He straightened his glasses and stared at Anne, who was wearing a light summer dress and sandals, looking more like a student than a professor.

"Sorry, the desk is closed. I'm just waiting for someone," he said.

"Are you waiting for me? I'm Professor Techa," she told him. She was accustomed to the confusion.

"Oh, sorry," he said.

"I'm sorry to wake you up," Anne replied. She realized that sounded sarcastic. "I mean, I'm sorry that you had to come in here on a holiday weekend. It's just that I'm rather desperate because I have very important files on this laptop and I need to work on them over the long weekend." She put it on the desk.

Without looking at Anne, the young man reached for the PC and opened it. Anne noticed his Help Desk badge with the name Quin. His hair haloed his face and grew, like a delicate fungus, on his unshaven chin and cheeks; a thick hunk of it was pulled back and forced into a ponytail at the back of his neck. Curly hair covered his bare arms and legs, giving them a reddish hue. What struck Anne as most odd was the way all his hair seemed to be standing on end, as though he had run an electrified comb all over his body.

"When was the last time you used it?" he asked.

"Yesterday, and it was fine. And no, I didn't have it charging when the power went out last night. I don't think it died from a power surge."

"What part of town do you live in?"

"I'm in Niagara Falls, actually," she replied. "Downtown, near the falls."

Quin stared at her. His eyebrows went up and his face brightened – literally. His skin was so transparently fair that the blue network of his veins was clearly visible, like a river system on a map. He turned the laptop over and started to unscrew the casing.

"Now *that's* interesting," he said.

"Why?"

"I have a theory about what happened last night." He worked the small screws.

"I don't see how the power outages could have affected my laptop," Anne told him. "It was asleep. And not plugged into anything."

Quin looked up at her, his eyes magnified by the lenses in his glasses. The glare from the room's fluorescent lights didn't dim their bright blue color. "That doesn't matter."

"Why not?"

"Because the power outages didn't have anything to do with the grid."

"What? What do you mean?"

"Well, think about it." His voice was calm. He had the casing open and was looking at the circuit board. "From what I read on the blogs, the systems failures were random, all over the place, though generally they occurred within a defined area along the river."

"So?"

"So ...," Quin took off his glasses and looked at her. "I think you guys were blasted."

"Blasted! By what?"

"You've heard of a solar flare?"

"Of course." She looked at him skeptically.

"The data is still coming in," he said, "but we're in the middle of the mother of all solar storms. Huge flares have been erupting on the sun for the past eighteen hours. CMEs – coronal mass ejections – are hurling high-energy solar particles at us, beyond anything that's been measured before. People are reporting they saw lights in the sky yesterday, like the aurora borealis. That's a sign of the solar particles hitting the atmosphere. They can disrupt radio communications and electrical grids." He stared down at her circuit board. "That's what I think happened. Circuits like this, that aren't shielded, could easily be wiped out."

Anne stared at him. "How could it happen at night?"

"What time did your clocks go dead?"

She had to think. "Six-fifty," she said. After sunrise.

He continued, "The Earth's atmosphere is so thin from global warming that solar storms are having increasingly serious effects on our planet's systems. So this blast is just the start of what we're in for."

Anne looked at him skeptically. "Do you really know what you're talking about, or is this just BS?" she asked.

He laughed. "Well, it's all based on what they taught me at MIT. Could still be crap, though. I admit that my theory hasn't been confirmed yet."

"You went to MIT? Are you a grad student here?"

"I have a postdoc research assistantship in the fall at the robotics lab. This job is just a part-time gig."

"That's great." Anne saw a glimmer of hope in his qualifications. "I have really important files there, for a VA grant. Do you think there's any way you can retrieve them?"

"I won't even ask if you backed them up on a hard drive or on the Cloud."

"Well, thanks for that." She gave a short laugh. "Quin?"

"Quin McCarthy." He was staring inside her laptop. He ran his hand through his hair.

"Fucking PC," he said, lifting it to peer more closely inside.

Anne's hopes dimmed. "What do you think?" she asked.

"Well, I can't promise anything yet. If you leave it with me, and give me a number, I'll text you when I know more. I'll start working on it now."

"Oh, I'm sorry for you to have to work on the holiday weekend," Anne lied politely.

"I'm here," he said, and shrugged.

"OK, I'll go to my office and wait around for a bit till you see what you can do. Please text me as soon as you know anything."

She gave him her cell number, thanked him profusely, and left. She drove to the nursing administration building, which was almost deserted. Anne saw the door open and lights on for the dean's suite, but she tiptoed quickly past it and hurried down the hall to her office. She knew the dean wanted her to serve on the transformational committee, as it was being called, and Anne was avoiding her invitations to meet. After unlocking her office door, she found everything intact, and working. She logged on to her desk computer to see what files for the grant she could find there, and started obsessively printing them out.

She checked her iPhone for texts every few minutes. She got several from Phoebe complaining about the heat and the people at the art fair. Finally, just before six, she got the text she was waiting for: "Retrieved most files loaded in new laptop can u get here soon"

"15 minutes," she texted back. She quickly locked up her office and rushed to the Cybrary. He was waiting at the desk, fingering an iPhone.

"I can't tell you how much I appreciate this," she told him when he stood up and handed her a new laptop.

"Well, orders came down from the highest levels that we had to take care of you," he replied.

She emitted a choked laugh. "Yes, well ..." She looked at him. He was taller than she thought he was when she saw him hunched over the laptop. "I'm sure you went above and beyond. Really, I cannot thank you enough." She hesitated a brief moment. "Let me buy you lunch sometime. You can tell me how to avoid the next solar flare."

He grinned. "Okay, sure," he said. He nodded at the laptop. I loaded all the files I could retrieve on here. You shouldn't have any problems using it. But text me if you do. I loaded my contact info in your email file."

Anne gave him her brightest smile and left.

On the way home, she stopped on Military Road to pick up Viola's steak-and-cheese subs for her and Phoebe's dinner, and a veggie sub for Mari. She knew they'd be exhausted after the fair. When she got home, she found the two of them on the front porch drinking iced tea. They looked beat. Ben was lying between their wicker chairs, panting in his sleep.

"Oh, wow, Anne, you read my mind for dinner," Phoebe said, when she spotted the subs.

"Did you walk Ben?" she asked.

"I just did," Phoebe replied. "He didn't want to go far. It's too hot."

They went upstairs and sat around Anne's dining table.

"How did the sales go today?" Anne asked. "Is there any more news about the rockfall?"

"We sold a lot today, didn't we Phoebe?" Mari said. "Phoebe is a good salesperson. She practically grabs people and forces them to buy something. Though you did leave me for longer than I expected for lunch."

Phoebe grinned, her mouth full of sub.

"When did the power come back on?" Anne asked.

"Sometime this afternoon. Downtown was a madhouse. They blocked off the bridges to Goat Island. Traffic was all snarled up," Mari reported.

"Guess what, Anne," Phoebe said. "Mari gave Leonard a job."

"What?" Anne stared at Mari.

"I told you Phoebe was a good seller," Mari said, giving the girl a look. "It's just for a few hours a week. It turns out Leonard's got some artistic talent. He stopped by the booth today and showed me his notebooks. I'm going to teach him some techniques so he can help me with my watercolors of the falls and the rainbows. And I want to start silk screening more of my designs on tee shirts. They sell well."

"Mari, you are a truly good person," Anne said, and meant it.

"Yeah," Phoebe said. "Leonard loves to do art, and he could really use the money, too."

They finished eating. Anne said, "I'm going to take Ben to go look at the falls again. Then I'm going to collapse."

"I'm going to bed now," said Phoebe, and left the kitchen. They heard her go into the bathroom.

"My friend Callista is coming over to spend the night with me," Mari told Anne.

Anne looked at her closely. "The one who's supposed to be a witch?"

"A white witch," Mari said, then quickly added, "She's going to do a cleansing ceremony of my flat – light candles, burn herbs like bittersweet and cloves to drive away dark spirits, and chant. Do you want her to do yours, too?"

"I'm not sure that's necessary," Anne replied.

"Something powerful happened last night, Anne," Mari told her. "This can't be coincidences – the rockfall, the power outages, my dream."

"Don't forget my computer crashing," Anne added. "But, Mari, those are all unrelated events. I'm sure there's a rational explanation for all this."

"Maybe there's not." Mari finished her iced tea, and went down to her flat through the back door.

"Well, Ben," Anne said, looking down at her dog, who was finishing Phoebe's sub. "Let's go walk to the falls and see if we can figure out whether it's spirits or sun spots we need to be worried about."

CHAPTER TEN

Sleep was what Jerome wanted most, but he knew it was a futile wish. Even if he were lying in his bed at home, and not sitting in a vinyl-covered lounge chair in a small room full of buzzing and beeping high-tech machines, he'd never be able to sleep. Not while John was like this, lying unconscious on the hospital bed, tethered to monitors and plastic tubing. It had been almost a week since the accident in front of their home. John had immediately been transported by ambulance to Buffalo's best trauma center.

John's fingers, toes, and eyelids were in constant motion with tiny spasms, the only evidence that his life spirit was still strong somewhere inside him. The doctors had done everything they could think of to bring him back to consciousness. They told Jerome that his brother was suffering from extreme trauma to the brain. He knew their vagueness meant they didn't know what they could do, besides wait.

Jerome closed his eyes and tried to calm himself. He'd never felt this tired before, not even after long days hiking on high peaks up in the Adirondacks. Weariness of the spirit is the worst kind. The only remedy is hope. But every day it was getting harder to hope that John would awake and be the man he was. None of the doctors could say when this vigil would end, whether John had entered what they call a "persistent vegetative state." Jerome didn't know when he would ever sleep again.

Whenever he closed his eyes he relived the moment when he saw

John's new car smashed against the huge sycamore tree. Woody was already there, trying desperately to force open the twisted door. The jaws of life had to be used to get him out.

Jerome had gone to the accident scene numerous times since, trying to figure out how it could have happened. The ancient tree was a familiar landmark; it stood alongside the road, just outside the gate of the iron security fence protecting their home. It was visible as soon as the road curved around the woods and entered the mowed field; at night, the tree's silvery skin glowed like a beacon when headlights shone on it. John knew every inch of the road and his land; he would have had to swerve off the road to hit that tree.

That sycamore was a giant, hundreds of years old; it had long ago shed its outer layers of bark. Its pale skin was wattled with patches of olive and ivory, and it sagged near its base, like an old man's chest. Its high, green canopy burst from long branches stretching to the sky like bleached bones. It had seen so much life come and go, but could shed no light on the accident. The car was totaled; the ancient tree still stood, its trunk hardly marked.

The sheriff's deputies who investigated the accident said John's car's many safety features had saved his life. Jerome held his mother back while the paramedics loaded John into the ambulance. His face was black and blue from the airbag, which terrified her. Jerome didn't see any blood. The EMTs said he'd received a bad concussion, but it didn't appear that he had any life-threatening injuries. But John didn't come out of it. Days after the accident, the doctors couldn't account for his persistent coma.

Jerome's eyes popped open when he heard movement. One of the intensive care nurses came into the glass-walled room that opened onto the central monitoring station. She checked the needles piercing John's flesh, and the monitors around his bed. She punched data into an electronic pad.

Jerome couldn't stand it. He pulled himself up from the deep chair. "Is there any change?" he asked.

"No. I'm sorry." She didn't look at him.

"Mr. Lone?" A volunteer, a gray-haired woman in a flowered jacket, stood just outside the door to John's room.

Jerome turned. "Yes?"

"Your brother has a visitor," she told him. "He's not immediate family so we can't let him in here. I told him I'd tell you he's in the ICU waiting area. His name is Sal." She smiled. "He's a real character."

Suppressing a groan, Jerome shook his head. "I can't leave my brother. Tell him my mother should be back soon."

The two women exchanged a glance.

"You need a break, Mr. Lone," the volunteer said. "Go down to the cafeteria with him and get something to eat."

"Here," said the nurse, "take this beeper. I promise I'll beep you if there's any change."

"Any change at all?" Jerome asked.

"Yes. Now go." The nurse turned back to John.

Jerome felt stiff as he walked to the lounge area. He went into a rest room and did some stretches, before relieving himself. He washed his hands and face and dried them. He combed his hair and put it back into a neat ponytail. By the time he finished, he still didn't feel energetic enough to deal with Sal, but he went to meet him, anyway.

"Jerome, how's Johnny, how's he doing?" The short, white-haired man pumped Jerome's arm, clutching his hand with bony fingers. "They wouldn't let me see him, is it that bad? Is his face gone? Oh, that would be terrible, such a handsome man. How is he? Tell me the truth – the truth, Jerome."

"He's hanging in there, Sal, that's all I can say. His face is fine. The doctors tell us we have to give it time."

Sal let go of Jerome's hand and waved his arm dismissively. "The doctors, phhhhhtt, what do they know? You're lucky if they don't kill you. Look at me. I'm barely alive. I have four doctors."

Jerome managed a half-smile. "Sal, you'll outlive them all."

"That's what they tell me." He threw his head back, and laughed. "Come on. I promised that volunteer lady I'd get you dinner. But I won't let you eat the stuff they cook here. That's for sick people. They're too weak to complain. I brought you and your momma some food from the restaurant." He retrieved a large brown shopping bag from a chair. "Come on, we'll find a table."

Jerome got a whiff of red meat and Sal's famous spaghetti sauce. Suddenly, he felt famished. He followed Sal to the elevator.

Half an hour later, Jerome leaned back in a cafeteria chair and burped. He felt human again. "Sal, you're a life-saver. That's the only real meal I've had since the accident." He gulped down some black coffee.

"I figured. Now we'll talk."

"Did you bring dessert?"

Sal smiled and wagged his finger at Jerome. "You know me." He pulled a heavy, foil-wrapped object from the shopping back.

After eating a cannoli, Jerome felt a burst of energy kick in. "Feel like walking, Sal?"

"I better. If I sit too long, my leg muscles don't wanna work."

Jerome separated out the disposable and recyclable items while Sal repacked the uneaten food. A heavyset man with sad eyes leaned over from the next table. "Got any leftovers?"

Sal reached into his pocket. "This, I gotta save for his mother," he told the man, indicating his containers, "but take this coupon. It's buy-one-meal-get-one-free at Sal's Restaurant on South Lakeshore."

"Hey, thanks." The pouches on the man's face elevated slightly. "You Sal?"

"That's me." Sal's wrinkled face beamed. "My son, he made me retire, but I still keep an eye on the kitchen, to make sure they keep up the standards. Here, have another coupon. Free drinks." Sal pushed himself up from his chair. Jerome reached for the shopping bag, but Sal took it with his left hand. "I need it for balance." He held up his cane in his right hand.

Jerome forced himself to walk slowly so Sal could keep up. It felt good to walk. Back in the ICU waiting room, they sat in chairs facing each other. They were the only ones there. Harsh shafts of light from the late-day summer sun blazed through the wide window.

"My mother should be back any time now," Jerome said. "Loraine and Andrew practically carried her out of here last night to take her home for some rest."

"Poor Louise." Sal shook his head sadly. "Her oldest boy. She's so proud of him."

Jerome rubbed his eyes. "It's been rough, Sal."

"Maybe you should take him to the Cleveland Clinic. Or the Mayo."

"I don't think John or my mother could take the move." Jerome leaned forward in his chair. He needed to confide in someone outside the family circle. Despite Sal's relentless joking around, he was savvy and smart. He'd founded one of the area's most successful Italian restaurants in the lean days after World War II.

"Sal, I'm worried about my mother," Jerome told him. "She's, well, she's getting desperate. We had a big scene here yesterday." Jerome looked around the empty room before continuing. "She insisted that Woody bring one of the Healers here, T.C. Williams, from the reservation, to do a healing ceremony. I checked with the nursing supervisor, who said the hospital wouldn't allow it. So Mother went to the medical director and got him to go along with her, as long as the healer didn't give John anything, or burn anything, or touch him."

"Your momma knows what she's doing," Sal said. "The old ways work, too. Sometimes they work better. My uncle saved my business once, saved me from the Evil Eye."

"We're not dealing with the Evil Eye here, Sal." Jerome stood up and paced the room. "Anyway, I didn't think it would hurt if he prayed and chanted. It would help mother, anyway. But it was a disaster. I guess old Mr. Williams had never been in an intensive care unit before, and when he saw John lying there, attached to all the machines, he got very upset. He wouldn't go into the room, unless he could burn smoke and do some other stuff. I don't know what exactly. He and my mother argued about it in the old language. She called him an old fool, and a coward. He said she was blind. I finally had Woody just get him out of here." He sat down, and slumped forward. "Mother is furious. She wants to take John out of the hospital. She wants to take him home. I don't know what to do."

Sal looked at him sharply. "Don't you give up hope." He poked Jerome's leg with his cane. "Johnny's a strong man. He'll come out of it." Sal shifted his weight in his chair. "I'll never forget the first time I saw him."

Jerome closed his eyes. He'd heard this story many times.

"He was walking along South Lakeshore Road, hitchhiking," Sal continued, as if telling it for the first time. "This was back in the seventies, before they widened it. The first time I saw him, I thought he was an Italiano boy with a sunburn." Sal still chuckled at his old joke. "Casey, the fishmonger, had a truck full of barrels for me, and he told Johnny he'd give him two bucks if he helped unload it. Well, Johnny worked hard, but then Casey, that sonovagun, he didn't want to pay. Tried to sneak off. Johnny, he wouldn't take that. Told Casey to give him his money. Casey had muscles, but when he called Johnny a 'lyin' Injun' – oh, Johnny was gonna take him on, no matter what. That's when I stepped in. 'I won't have no names like that,' I told Casey. 'You pay the boy or don't come back.' Casey paid all right, but he didn't like it. Threw the money on the ground and drove off like a bandit. Then Johnny wouldn't pick up the money. So I did. I dusted it off and made him take it. I said, 'You gonna let a bully like that make you lose your pay? Because of stupid words?' I could see Johnny, he had a lot to learn. So I hired him and taught him everything about running a business."

"You did good, Sal."

"Your brother worked hard for you. For you and your momma and your sister, back on the reservation, hungry, no poppa. Johnny left home to work. Every week, he gave me an envelope to send to your momma. Saved for college, too. I told all the boys who worked for me, 'You wanna work in a kitchen all your life?' There weren't no fancy chefs then. When he got his diploma from BU, I was as proud as if he was my own son."

Jerome stood up and walked to the window. He had a thin memory of his father, a silent man, smelling of alcohol, whose face was as distant as the moon's. He stared through the filtered glass at the big orange sun hovering over the tops of medical buildings and large parking lots; asphalt shimmered in the heat.

"I always knew Johnny would be a big shot someday," Sal said. "Don't you worry. He'll be all right. He's strong."

Jerome whirled around. He wanted to shout at Sal to shut up. But he couldn't. The old man was upset, too. He was just talking. Jerome forced himself to stay calm.

"Sal! How nice of you to come."

Jerome was never so glad to see his sister walk into a room. "Where's Mother?" he asked.

Loraine gave Sal a hug. "She was sleeping so hard I didn't have the heart to wake her up. I left her home."

"That's the best thing you could have done." Jerome felt relief wash over him.

"Loraine, you hungry?" Sal started to reach for his bag.

Jerome stepped forward and took Sal's hand. "Sal, thank you for coming. And thanks for the great dinner. I've got to get back inside."

Sal gripped Jerome's forearm. "You don't give up hope, you hear? Johnny's gonna make it. He's a fighter."

"I know, Sal." Jerome managed a smile, then hurried away.

CHAPTER ELEVEN

Though she watched out for him every day during her walks with Ben, Anne didn't see the Hermit for weeks after the big rockfall. Then, early one morning in late July, she saw him on Goat Island, near the bridge to Luna Island, which was still closed off while geologists were testing the stability of that end of the American Falls. The Hermit was staring at her from behind a tree along the path to the Three Sisters Island; he ran off when she spotted him.

She continued on to the Three Sisters islands, which used to be Ben's favorite place in the world. They could walk on the huge boulders right up to the water's edge. There were small coves where Anne would let Ben cool off by putting his paws in the water; she always kept a tight hold on his leash. But now all the paths were fettered with railings, and people weren't allowed to walk on the rocks anymore. Anne understood the need to protect the vegetation and keep people from doing stupid things so close to the brinks of the waterfalls. But she missed the old freedom to roam the islands at will.

Near the first stone bridge she ran into Don Gromosek, one of her fellow island walkers. He was a retired science teacher. He always had binoculars hanging from his neck, and wore a khaki vest with lots of pockets for his notebooks and cameras. His paraphernalia draped his thin frame like heavy plumage. Obsessed with the river, its islands, the falls, and all their minutiae, he observed and made notations on fauna, flora, water levels, unusual tourists, debris whizzing through the rapids, rockfalls, weddings, loose dogs, weird ice formations, weather – all the myriad happenings around the cataracts, mundane or spectacular. He made his rounds of Goat Island almost every day. He parked his car on city streets, often on Cataract Lane, and walked to the island, not only to avoid paying the state parking fees, but to protest the very existence of roads and parking lots on the island. Every few years he circulated another petition to the state parks commission demanding that the island be renaturalized to the unique biosphere it had been in the early nineteenth century. Anne signed every petition.

"Don, when was the first time you saw the Hermit?" she asked him.

"I first saw him, let's see ...," Don flipped through pages in his notebook, "on June twenty-first. Almost two weeks before the big rockfall. Here's my note: 'Tall man with long grayish beard, sitting on a rock on Asenath near the Hermit's cascade, seven-fifteen a.m.'" He read from his small, precise, handwritten notes. "He'd climbed over the fence."

"Asenath is the first island?"

"Yes."

Anne rolled her eyes. "I've never gotten used to calling them by those names. No one ever did, until a few years ago, and now it just seems like some tourist gimmick."

"Asenath, Angeline, and Celinda Eliza were General Parkhurst Whitney's daughters." Don took every opportunity to show off his knowledge of falls lore. "You should know that, Anne, since you live just down the street from his house. He was decorated for his valor in the War of 1812, and then he owned the legendary Cataract House, where Lincoln stayed with his family. He was an important man here."

"I know," Anne replied, "but they're such horrid Victorian names. They remind me of an antique sofa I found in the attic when I bought my house. It had scratchy, maroon upholstery." She hated that sofa until Mari painted the frame in bright lacquer and re-upholstered it in a fashion print. Now it sat in her downstairs foyer.

"Now, Anne," Don gently chided her. "I like the names."

Since Niagarans could debate such topics for hours, Anne changed the subject. "Do you think the Hermit could be dangerous? Or suicidal?"

"Not at all. Actually, he's very interesting. He really thinks he's the Hermit of Niagara."

"Did he actually tell you that?"

"In a roundabout way. He only speaks in rhyme, and it's hard to tell what's real poetry and what's gibberish he made up. I wrote down what he said to me a few days later when I asked him where he was from." Don read from his notes again: "'In the verdant month of June/I danced to Niagara's rugged tune/And though it took so long to learn it/give a rousing cheer for the returning Hermit.' He speaks in an English accent. Very obliging. Repeated the poem slowly when I asked him to, and didn't mind that I wrote it down."

"If he's delusional he should be under supervised care, not left to roam around. Do you think he could be convinced to go to the medical center?"

"I doubt it. He seems happy enough, roaming around the falls."

"Well, keep an eye on him, will you? Maybe we can help him somehow."

"Sure thing. Hey, look!" He lifted his binoculars skyward. "A hawk."

Anne left him and took Ben home. Her landline had a message from her friend Emily Storey, wanting to know if Anne could host a meeting of their historical preservation group during the coming week. Restless, and not quite ready to hunker down and work on her grant proposal, Anne decided to drive to the city library, where Emily ran the local history department, instead of just calling her back.

She drove down Fourth Street. Most days, her mind was too pre-occupied to dwell on the persistent disintegration of the once-proud neighborhoods she passed through. On this day, she wondered how much longer she could stand to live in a dying city. Her home, surrounded by parks, seemed like a bubble in time. She didn't think it was crazy to buy her home, as her brother had said, but she was wondering more and more how crazy it was to stay in this city.

She turned right on Main Street. The historic Main Street post office building on the corner reminded her that once there was beauty and elegance in Niagara Falls. It was built of white marble in a neoclassical style, and was actually younger than her home. Another block on, though, the urban decay of once-thriving Main Street depressed her, as it always did. The only new building was a gigantic police station. Just a block from the library, a dead seagull lay in the middle of the street.

Anne parked as close as she could to the library, not only because of the heat but also to minimize her view of the exterior; she hated the nineteen-seventies design of ribbed slabs of gray concrete set at odd angles to each other. The new library, as her mother had always called it, was the antithesis of the classic Carnegie library building that still stood a couple of blocks away.

Emily was surprised to see Anne. A stylish woman in her early sixties, she had a nervous energy that kept her fashionably thin; even her iron-gray hair seemed energized, its tiny curls constantly escaping from barrettes. They'd become good friends when Anne began researching the history of her house. Emily left her desk to greet Anne as soon as she saw her enter the room.

A white-haired gentleman in a gray suit and a scruffy young woman with badly cropped multicolored hair were sitting at tables looking at old documents. They looked up briefly as Anne entered, then went back to their work.

"Emily, I've been meaning to call you for ages," Anne said in a low voice, "but the summer has been so busy. I've had a lot of work to do, and to top it off, my niece, Phoebe, my brother Bill's daughter, is spending the summer with me."

"Oh, you poor thing." Teenagers, in general, were Emily's bane. "Well, it's good to see you, even if we have serious business to call a meeting about. It's the Turtle." Her voice grew hard. "You know it's been sold?"

"Yes, to some group from Buffalo?"

"We're not sure. Everyone is close-mouthed about it and the

city isn't releasing any information. We think it's a venture firm from Buffalo. We don't know what its intentions are. We don't even know if they plan to keep the building. What if they raze it? Of course, Wallace Mountview is devastated."

Anne knew Wallace was an old friend of Emily's. "When do you want to meet?"

"Let's say Thursday evening. That will give us time to contact everyone."

"Okay. I'll send out an email to the group." She had a thought. "I'd like to look up some information about the Hermit of Niagara."

"Francis Abbott! He's one of my favorites."

Emily walked quickly to a shelf on the opposite wall, pulling out several books without hesitation. She carried them to a table near her desk and set them down. "These newer books tell Francis' story," she whispered, as she opened them to certain pages and placed them before Anne. "I also have contemporary accounts, which I can dig out from the archives."

"Thanks. This should be enough for now." Anne settled at the table, realizing she had never focused on the Hermit's story before, despite walking past the Hermit's Cascade so often. Reading quickly, she learned he was an Englishman who visited Niagara Falls as a tourist in 1829, a time when the mighty cataracts were the definitive icon of the New World. Niagara was then on the frontier of the undiscovered country beyond. It was a beacon for travelers who wanted to experience the transcendence of Nature.

At twenty-five years old, Francis Abbot was said to be handsome, well-read, and a talented musician. But once he encountered Niagara, he couldn't leave. He convinced Augustus Porter, who owned Goat Island and had a gristmill on the shore, to let him live in a small house there. Anne read that he seemed happy living alone with his cat and dog. He could often be heard playing his violin, or a flute, or guitar. In all seasons, he bathed twice a day at the gentle waterfall now called the Hermit's Cascade. He entertained tourists by doing chin-ups and dangling like a spider from a long plank suspended over the chasm of the Horseshoe Falls, and became a tourist attraction himself.

Two years after his arrival, a ferryman saw Francis enter the river below the American Falls. It was June 10, 1831. He disappeared. A fruitless search was mounted. Eleven days later, his body was recovered miles down the river near Fort Niagara. People never settled the question of whether Francis' death was a tragic accident or whether he committed suicide. All that was left of him were his few belongings and words he had chiseled on a rock on Luna Island: "All is change, eternal progress, no death."

"'A mystic chain round his soul was wove,'" Emily hissed into Anne's ear.

"What?" she exclaimed, startled. The other two readers looked up.

"'A mystic chain round his soul was wove,'" Emily repeated, in a low voice. "From a poem about the Hermit by Lydia Sigourney, a poet of the time. She was very sincere, but not a very good poet, I'm afraid."

"Any poem that uses the phrase 'mystic chain round his soul' must, by definition, be consigned to the lowest ranks of the art," commented the gentleman sitting nearby, in an English accent.

Emily sighed. "There was so much poetry written about Niagara in the nineteenth century, and most of it is very bad, I'm afraid. 'Here speaks the voice of God …' Another overwrought poet, whom I won't name."

"That is the way of nature poetry in general, Madame," the white-haired gentleman said. "While colossal natural wonders like Niagara Falls and the Grand Canyon – we have nothing of their immensity in England, fortunately, we wouldn't know what to do with them – inspire the loftiest thoughts and deepest sentiments in the souls of men, they also inspire the most wretched rhymes. And the poems always do rhyme."

"Sylvester, I think you do not appreciate the transcendence that nature's loveliness can bring to the human soul," Emily said.

"Heavens, no," he replied. "But I do enjoy watching how humans try to absorb these wonders, and try to bring them down to their size."

"Mark Twain commented on that," Emily said. "It amuses me to remember it when I watch the tourists taking pictures at the falls." She mimicked a man's drawling voice: "'There is no actual harm in making Niagara a background whereon to display one's marvelous insignificance in a good strong light, but it requires a sort of superhuman self-complacency to enable one to do it.'"

Sylvester chuckled and Anne smiled. The young woman looked angry. She slammed a book on the table.

"*You're* being self-complacent," she said, as they stared at her. She didn't flinch from their attention, but stood up, as though she were in a classroom. Her bleached and dyed hair overwhelmed a pointy little face, marred by a couple of piercings. Her tanned, skinny shoulders barely held up her gray tank top. Her brown eyes, which bulged slightly, were blazing.

"Frankly, I think it's generational," she scolded. "You've studied people and ideas and beliefs as if they were bugs under a microscope, with soulless detachment. You never try to feel what these people felt. And then you make fun of their attempts to describe the things that give them a sense of poetry and awe."

"You're bloody right it's generational," Sylvester retorted. "I expect you go to university?"

"Yes," she hissed.

"Of course you do. You've learned empathy. Save the bloody whales. Cry for the indigenous peoples. Feel sorry for this lot or that, they've been abused, that's why they become terrorists. No thought is too insignificant to go unuttered. No emotion — God help us — is unworthy of being expressed, and indulged. God save me from twitters and all that rot."

The young woman leaned forward and was ready to launch her rebuttal, when Anne spoke up. "Let's introduce ourselves," she said in a calm voice. "I'm Anne Techa." She smiled and held out her hand in an attempt to defuse the student's anger. "I'm a professor of nursing at Buffalo University."

"I'm Chani Caroli," the student replied, not taking Anne's hand.

"I'm studying anthropology at BU."

Standing up, the man announced, with a little bow, "Sylvester Lindsay, at your service. I'm a curator for … well, I don't wish to add to Ms. Caroli's outrage, but I am employed by a well-known international auction house that specializes in antiquities." He ignored Chani's glare. "And I am a countryman of your unfortunate Hermit."

"Have you been able to identify or repair the mummies, Sylvester?" Emily asked.

"Mummies?" Chani repeated. "What mummies?"

"Well." He looked at each of them, basking in their attention, "I trust this won't go any further than this room." The three women nodded eagerly and seated themselves at his table. "I've been engaged to examine the last holdings of the Niagara Museum in Canada that formerly stood near the bell tower at the Rainbow Bridge. It was an old, dusty collection, very nineteenth-century naturalist, and more of a carnival than a museum, but it kept drawing in tourists, god bless them, until the building, unbelievably a former corset factory, was finally torn down to make room for the new casino hotel."

"I went there as a child," Anne told him. "I remember the mummies. I was absolutely repelled by them, the way they were exposed for everyone to gawk at."

"Well, you should have been," Sylvester replied. "I've seen photos of the exhibit and it was appalling. The mummies were very poorly displayed, not at all respectfully. There were seven of them, collected by – yes, Ms. Caroli – colonialist explorers looting the ancient world in the name of Western civilization more than a century ago. For years the Egyptians sent experts and envoys to Canada to get them back, and finally, four were repatriated. Emily has given me this article from *The New York Times*, dated October 25, 2003. One of the mummies was identified as Rameses I, the founder of Egypt's nineteenth dynasty. Can you imagine – a *pharoah* lying in an old corset factory? With five-legged pigs and two-headed calves? The *Times* rightly calls the place 'a freak show.'"

"It's outrageous!" exclaimed Emily. Chani's face had a look of disgust, and Anne thought with some guilt of how much fun she and her brother Bill had had taking pictures of each other next to the most gruesome exhibits.

"So you have the pharoah's mummy now?" Chani asked.

"Lord, no, and I'm very grateful for that," Sylvester replied. "He's been returned to Luxor at long last. A museum in Atlanta did the right thing, Chani, you'll be glad to know. After acquiring the mummy when the Niagara Museum's collection was broken up in 1999, they realized that they had not only stolen goods but a royal figure, no less. They sent him home, to the delight of the Egyptians, who greeted him with songs." He took a breath, then continued, "Most of the rest of the collection was sold off, or disposed of, except for a number of large crates that have been sitting in storage for more than a decade. My auction house acquired them along with contents of some local estates, and I'm trying to figure out what to do with them. I was gobsmacked when we opened one of the crates and found three mummies, still in their original display cases. And not only that. One of the sarcophagi held a gold face mask that apparently had been shaken out of its mummy's wrappings when the exhibit was moved the first time."

"Why weren't those three mummies returned?" Chani asked.

"It's not clear," he replied. "I've been told that over the years Egyptian representatives tried to repatriate the Ramses mummy and others in the museum, but that they said these three were fakes. They're only part of what I'm here to examine, though. The last remains of the museum were packed up really quickly at the end, lots of things just thrown into boxes and sent to a warehouse. Native American masks, carved ivory, jade objects. Dozens of moldy stuffed birds. My employer sent me to salvage what I can that's worth putting up at auction. It's not a pleasant task, I can tell you. I can't get the dust from the stuffed animals out of my head."

"Emily said the mummies have to be repaired," Anne said. "How were they damaged?"

"That's unclear." Sylvester hesitated. "Well, I may as well just give you the story and let you make your own conclusions." He saw the women were listening intently; he lowered his voice. "The three supposedly fake mummies were still housed in their original display case when my firm took possession of them. We moved them from a storage facility near the falls to a rented space where we can sort everything out. They were in a large glass box with its own wooden platform. The painted sarcophagi were laid next to each other; the covers were removed so that you could see the mummies inside."

Anne gave an involuntary shiver. "I remember how decayed and filthy they looked," she said. "The wrappings were flimsy and brown, and the heads and bodies dessicated."

"Exactly," Sylvester said. "When the mummies were moved out of the corset factory, a crate was built around the entire display case, and the whole thing was transported to a warehouse. Must have been quite a job. We got the crate to our facility intact. At least, it seemed intact the first time I saw it, weeks ago."

"What happened?" Chani asked.

"Our facility was broken into on the night of the big rock collapse at the American Falls," he said. "The power outage disabled the alarms. When I arrived the next morning there was a lot of damage inside. Most could be explained by ground tremors caused by tons of rock falling – broken glass, that sort of thing. But the mummies, well, that was something else." He paused, and looked at each woman before proceeding. "We found them sitting up in their open sarcophagi, as though they'd been having tea. And one of them was missing his head."

Anne felt a shiver run down her spine.

"That sounds like a sick joke," Chani said. "I hope you catch those vandals and arrest them. They had no right to destroy a display, even if it is fake."

"In a way they did me a favor," Sylvester said. "With the glass broken, I was able to get inside the display case and determine that the Egyptians were wrong. These are real mummies. I can't figure out why they didn't want them."

Anne was rubbing her bare arms, feeling a chill.

"We know the vandals were thieves," Sylvester said. "They

grabbed the gold mask and some other items. I'm about to put out a news release offering a reward for any information. I'm here today looking for any articles or documents I can find that refer to those mummies. I've not had much luck on the other side of the border. I read the diary of the man who originally collected the mummies. He wrote that one was purported to be an Egyptian general, an especially bloodthirsty one, who was buried with a golden mask, and a curse."

"Can you get the mummies back in their original positions?" Chani asked.

"We hope so, but we haven't done anything yet. We're trying to assess what damage has been done. I've called in a team of archaeologists from Toronto. They'll be here next week."

"Can I see them?" Chani's voice was eager. "I'd love to see you work. I'll even help you sort out the stuffed things."

Sylvester looked uncertain.

"I won't say anything about our generational differences," she promised. "This would really help me. I need an internship."

"I'll consider it," Sylvester replied. "Here's my card. Give me a call in a few days and I'll let you know when I'm going back there again." He looked at Anne. "You're welcome to come, too, Professor, and help bandage them up again."

"No, thanks!" Anne winced at the joke. "I don't do bandages anymore."

"It's a shame how so much history on the Canadian side is buried under casinos and roadways," Emily said. "A lot of us remember the Niagara Museum fondly." She sighed. "I went there with my parents, and I won't tell you how many years ago that was."

"And on this side of the border you have the opposite – the past falling into decay, and disappearing just the same," Sylvester said.

Anne rose to go. Now her head ached. They were back to the age-old questions of Niagara Falls: what should we keep, what should we lose, and what should we watch slowly erode into the mists of time?

CHAPTER TWELVE

"Phoebe, come on!" Anne was calling her – again – from the foyer. "You're going to make me late. I have an important meeting. And you're going to be late for work."

Not satisfied with her hair, Phoebe pulled off the scrunchy and tried again. After two more attempts, her ponytail satisfied her. She checked the mirror to be sure her shorts and cotton shirt were spotless. She gave Ben one last hug. When she opened the upstairs door, she heard Mari's voice downstairs. She stopped to listen.

"Easy, Anne," Mari was saying. "Just remember, you can return her to her parents in a few more weeks."

"She's just so thoughtless."

"What, you thought she'd change just because she's living with you?" Mari laughed. "Welcome to the real world."

"Phoebe!" Anne called again. "We're both late!"

That was Phoebe's cue to slam the door shut and walk slowly down the stairs. At first, she was amused to see Anne so angry, but then she felt a little guilty. Maybe she shouldn't give her aunt such a hard time. It was cool of Anne to let her stay all summer, so she could get away from her parents. But Phoebe couldn't change and be Miss Perfect all at once. Then Anne might suspect something, and start digging around, and find out her secrets.

Mari stepped in front of Anne and asked, "Phoebe, want to have dinner in the backyard with me tonight? Leonard will be working with me today, and I'll ask him, too. Then Anne won't have to rush back from Buffalo."

"You don't have to babysit me, Mari," Phoebe told her.

"I know," Mari replied, in a mild voice.

Anne said, "You're brave," and gave her a grateful look.

Phoebe decided to make an effort. "OK," she said, as she jumped down the last few steps and landed with a thud next to Anne. "Sorry, Anne. I'm ready now."

Anne turned, wordlessly, and went out the front door. Phoebe followed her to the car, to be driven to work. Her job in the Niagara Falls geological museum was to greet visitors and give them information about Niagara Falls. Anne knew the museum director and, as she reminded Phoebe at least once a week, had infringed on their friendship – something she hated to do – to get Phoebe the job. Phoebe wasn't exactly grateful.

"Listen," Anne said, groping through her big purse as she drove, "here's ten dollars, pick up some brownies or a cake on your way home, for dessert."

"Okay."

"I have to go to dinner with someone, but I'll be back by eight, at the latest."

"Stay out as long as you want. Mari will watch me, Auntie Anne." Phoebe smiled when Anne looked at her with a sharp expression. "I'm not a little kid anymore. You haven't gone out in forever. Go and have fun. Don't worry."

"All right, Phoebe," Anne said. They were at the geological museum. "Don't forget to walk Ben as soon as you get home. Take a plastic bag, remember. Then feed him and take him in the backyard with you, but don't give him table food, okay?"

"O-kay."

"Text me if you need me," Anne reminded her. "Bye now." She

drove off.

Phoebe stood at the curb until Anne's car raced around the corner. Then, instead of walking toward her job, she went in the opposite direction, to Prospect Park, a few blocks away. Leonard was sitting on a bench near the statue of Chief Clinton Rickard, waiting for her.

"Hey, Wolf, I have ten dollars," she said, as she plunked down next to him. "We can get breakfast before you go to Mari's."

"Good," he replied. He didn't tell her that he'd left home a couple of hours earlier and ran all the way from Lewiston to the Falls. Just to keep in training. He was very hungry.

"And guess what," Phoebe told him. "Mari invited us both to dinner cuz Anne won't be home. Don't worry," she added, "it'll be loose, in the backyard. And you can walk Ben for me."

"Okay. Let's go eat."

The pair started walking, a little apart. Leonard wore his black hair in a ponytail down his back. Phoebe's blonde ponytail bounced off the top of her head. Her platform sandals made her almost four inches taller than he was. She turned heads. Leonard was able to walk along and observe the power of youth and beauty. He was fascinated by it, and liked being a sort of invisible bodyguard to her. He let her call him "Wolf" in private; he had once told her he wanted to emulate the wolf's characteristics of intelligence, cunning, and loyalty. It started as a tease, but now it was her name for him, and he accepted it.

At a snack stand, they bought wraps and drinks, then walked back to the park. It was very hot, even under the trees; the cement plaza at Prospect Point felt like a grill. For a while, they stood at the railing overlooking the American Falls, hoping a breeze would blow the thin mist over them. At the far end of the brink, they could see the gap caused by the big rockfall, and the dark hole leading down under Luna Island.

"Did your great-grandfather tell you anything about the cave yet?" Phoebe asked.

"No."

"Do you think he will?"

"I don't know."

"That's annoying."

Leonard didn't respond, but looked hard at the cave. The rushing torrent had worn new paths around the gash; a thin curtain of green-tinged water flowed over the hole.

As they headed toward Cataract Lane along the upper rapids path, Phoebe mimicked tourists behind their backs. Leonard smiled. When they came near Cataract Lane, they stooped on the ground and hid behind trees, like spies, looking at Anne's house.

"Don't you like painting the rainbows over the falls?" Phoebe asked. "It must be fun to do that all day."

Leonard thought before answering. "I like what she taught me to do. But those tourist pictures aren't her real art. They just pay the rent, she says. She has other art that's really cool."

"Well, I like them," Phoebe countered.

Leonard didn't reply, so the discussion petered out. He never bothered to argue a point; if he disagreed with Phoebe, he would just go silent. Phoebe never tried to change his mind about anything or provoke him the way she did her family; if Leonard didn't see things her way, well, the way she looked at it, he was a guy, and a Native American, as well. They each had their own worlds. Who was she to argue with him?

"What's at the top of the tower?" Leonard asked, pointing to the third story of the curved turret that bowed out of the right corner of Anne's house.

"Mari calls it the wizard's den. It's a little round room that you get to through a door in the closet in the room I'm sleeping in. It's really neat. There are windows all around it. There's nothing in it, just some shelves with old books that Anne has, and a big snuggly fake white bear rug. Sometimes I go up there and lay on it, with my head on the bear's head, and look out the windows at the clouds. I usually fall asleep, especially if Ben is with me. Mari goes up there to meditate, sometimes. She's going to teach me how to meditate, too. She says I need centering."

"What's that?"

"I'm not sure. I think it has something to do with cramps."

They stretched out on the lawn, lacking the energy to get up. They flipped onto their backs and, through their sunglasses, gazed at the sky, which was white and hazy with heat. The deep roar of the rushing river, just yards away, overcame all other sounds.

After a while, Phoebe sat up and said, "I'm hot. Let's go inside before we fall asleep. Come upstairs for a while before you go to Mari's. We'll sneak in the back door."

Leonard, who was already asleep, woke up, and rose slowly.

They retraced their steps and cut between two houses to get to the alley behind Cataract Lane. They quietly unlocked the back door and crept upstairs.

Ben greeted them by jumping on Leonard and wagging his tail so hard his hind end rocked back and forth. They watched cartoons for a while, lying on Anne's cream-colored carpet, with Ben between them. Phoebe got some cheese and crackers out of the refrigerator; Leonard shared his with Ben, and let the dog lick his face when they were finished eating. He seemed to enjoy the slurpy cleaning.

"He really likes to lick you," Phoebe observed.

"Yeah, he does even when I'm not eating."

"Man, I'm so glad I called in sick today." Phoebe turned on her side to face Leonard, and rested her head on her hand. "I just couldn't have handled it. I was up late last night, doing Maid social media after Anne went to bed."

"Did you get many new messages?"

"Yeah. It's amazing how much work it is being the Maid of the Mist. People ask all kinds of questions, and I have to remember to stay inside her head. This one girl asked me to describe exactly what make-up I'm wearing in my picture on the web site, the brands and colors and all. And another girl wanted me to tell her what act I'll do if I win the big competition in Las Vegas." Phoebe grinned. "I couldn't tell her the truth, that I only entered the stupid contest to win the round-trip tickets, so we can get out to the desert, and go to the music festival, and have adventures. I had to pretend I'm really going to be in the contest to win. So I told her I'll do a Maid of the Mist re-enactment."

Leonard winced. "How do you keep track of who you are?"

"This is only my first reinvention," she told him. "You have to reinvent yourself pretty often, or life becomes too boring to go on. Anyway, it's all fun. And it's especially fun to do it in secret, with a new name and everything. Ani Shanando – I like being her, sometimes. Being as old as her, twenty-two, and not just seventeen. And I especially liked not having my family there, in the audience at the contest, like the other girls did. I liked being an orphan. Let's face it, family is just embarrassing. My Dad would be hyper because he needed a smoke. My mother would be moping that she had to leave the house. My brothers would be acting like total idiots. Anne would look normal, but she'd be ranting about how beauty contests exploit women, and she'd probably be wanting to throw me over the falls for even thinking about being in one." She sighed. "It was better to be lonely than have to put up with my family in public."

"Why'd you make Anne drive you to work today?"

"God, if I told her I called in sick she'd give me the third degree. She'd make me stay in bed, and ask me a million questions. Then, when she found out I wasn't sick – or sick enough for her – she'd ask me a million more questions to try to analyze me. Trust me, Wolf, hard as it was to get up and get dressed, it was easier than trying to fake her out. She is a nurse, you know." Phoebe rolled on her back, and stared at the ceiling. "Plus, then she'd give me a lecture about how grateful I should be, and how she had to ask special favors to get me the job. As if I wanted to spend my time telling stupid tourists about the falls. I mean, it's right there. Just look at it, and go home."

"Better being here than at your parents' house. At least we can hang out."

"Yeah, we have to give her that," Phoebe agreed. She turned to look at Leonard again. "And I'm earning some money for our trip. And so are you. It will be so awesome. Was there any more news on the Web?"

"This guy in Omaha sent me the new list of all the musicians that are going to be there. They're going to try to stream it online."

"That will be so cool." Phoebe sighed again, loudly. "It's so hard to wait. Sometimes I just can't stand it." She reached for the TV remote. Leonard fell asleep almost as quickly as Ben did. Phoebe tried to stay awake, but it was futile. The last thing she saw before she fell asleep was Wile E. Coyote's shocked expression as he went careening off a rocky cliff.

CHAPTER THIRTEEN

The meeting of the ad hoc faculty committee formed to develop strategies for the implementation of the Dean's proposed transformational reorganization of the nursing college turned out to be even more depressing than Anne had anticipated. She hadn't been able to avoid serving on it; the Dean had targeted her especially. No one could figure out what the Dean really wanted. As the group of frustrated academics left the stuffy conference room, Anne's colleague, Stephanie, an attractive fifty-something African-American woman wearing a stylish summer suit, asked her, "So, do you feel transformed?"

"I'm so sick of that damn word!" Anne hadn't intended to lose her cool, but felt better when she saw some fellow faculty members nod in agreement as they passed. "What does it mean, anyway?"

"I have no idea," Stephanie replied. "But it's clear who she's listening to. That new advisory committee of hers is made up of insurance executives and hospital administrators. The whole emphasis of the new curriculum is on business management, not on real nursing. She wants to divide the profession into technicians who run the machines and administrators who cut costs."

"None of that is really nursing. Why can't we talk about what really matters – patient care?" Anne asked.

"This helps me make up my mind about one thing," Stephanie said. "I'm going for early retirement next year."

Anne stopped in her tracks. "You can't." Stephanie kept walking.

Anne caught up with her. "You're too important. Not just in the college. Think of all the kids in the community who've gone into nursing because of you."

"The community will have to get with the times," she replied. "Face it, Anne. The system we knew is broken, and they're not going to put it back together again. I'm not going to train people for jobs that won't exist in a few more years. And I went into nursing to care about people, not costs. No use fooling ourselves."

"I'm not ready to give up on nursing." Suddenly, Anne felt hot tears in her eyes. She blinked them back. "Somebody's got to make sure the patients get good care."

Stephanie gave her a weak smile. "You fight the good fight, Anne. But I'm getting out while I still have my health, and my sanity."

Anne walked across the steamy parking lot in a grim mood and got into her Prius. The steering wheel was too hot to touch. She opened all the doors and waited while the air conditioner poured out cold air. Was Stephanie right? Was she blocking out reality? She closed her eyes and leaned her head back in the seat. She wanted to go home and take a long walk with Ben, by the river, and cool off in the mist from the falls, and think about how it was still flowing after thousands of years. It gave her hope. But she couldn't go home yet because she had a debt to pay.

Looking in the driver's vanity mirror, she wiped her face with a tissue and fixed her makeup. She wished she could cancel, but decided she might as well get this over with; the day was already ruined. She would just have to endure her dinner with Quin McCarthy, the post-doc techie who had retrieved her files.

Two days after he'd helped her, she'd received an email from him, instructing her how to link up to the Cloud, and sync all her devices, and advising her on other backups and hardware she should get. She had some idea what he was talking about, but just some. After a lengthy text exchange, which just confused her even more, he offered to meet with her to explain the tech-talk, and even go to her house to set up a new wireless system. Whoa. But she felt she should take some of his advice, so she decided to meet him in a neutral place; she offered to take him to an early dinner so she could get a feel to see if she could trust him near her house.

She worked in her office all afternoon until she was scheduled to pick up Quin in front of the massive science and engineering complex. He was wearing a yellow short-sleeved tee shirt and khaki shorts; the halo of hair around his head seemed less electrically charged than it had been when she met him. His tee shirt had an outline of a blazing sun and red letters that spelled, "Support climate change. Get an Arctic tan."

"Hey, hi," he said as he got in the passenger seat. He dumped an overstuffed canvas backpack between his feet.

"What kind of food do you feel like?" Anne asked.

"Anything."

"Well, if you don't mind eating outside in this heat, there's a place up by the river where we can get wings and burgers and fresh corn on the cob," she suggested. Nothing could be more casual and less date-like than Old Man River.

Quin rubbed his hands together. "I'm in!"

Twenty minutes later, they were sitting at a small metal kitchen table in Tonawanda under the awning of a wooden building with a giant blue whale on its roof. Across the busy street was a narrow park that ran along the bank of the upper Niagara River, opposite the east shore of Grand Island. Quin's first course was a foot-long hot dog covered with peppers and onions, potato wedges with bacon and cheese, and corn on the cob. He went back for baked beans and a slaw dog.

Anne picked at a grilled chicken sandwich and some cole slaw, but she didn't feel much like eating. A couple of cold beers had softened the hard edge of her earlier mood, but she felt herself sinking. Luckily, Quin was far more interested in eating than talking.

"Man, that was great," he said, licking sauce off his fingers. Finishing his beer, Quin rose, stretched, and headed for the men's room. "I've got to clean up."

While he was gone, Anne walked to a trashcan and dumped their litter. Quin returned with two lemon ices. They walked across the street to the river's shore. The rays of the sun, low in the west, cast sparkles on the river's deceptively calm surface. High-powered boats raced up and down the wide expanse of water. There was nothing to hint at the river's depth, or the speed of its underwater currents, the outflow of four great lakes, racing inexorably to the brink of the falls, ten miles downriver.

Quin sat down on the grass near the trunk of a tall maple. Anne joined him, sitting a few feet away.

"I should bring my fishing gear up here." Quin was watching two men on a dock near them as they reeled in their fishing lines and packed up their gear.

"You fish?"

"Yeah, but I've only done it in the lower river and the lake. I never thought of coming up this far. I should, though."

Anne looked at him. The red glow of the setting sun made his body shimmer with a bronze radiance. "Did your dad teach you?"

"Yeah, me and my brothers and sisters. We all fished, and my mom cooked them."

"Have you been to the fishing pier down by the power plant?"

"Yeah, my friend Pete, one of the guys I live with, and I go there sometimes. We're renting a big old farmhouse near the lake, in Porter. He has a small boat, and we mostly fish in the lake."

As they savored the cold lemon ices, Anne asked him, "Why are you here in Buffalo, Quin? Why didn't you stay in Boston?"

"I had to get out of that fucking place," he replied. "After my dissertation was finally accepted – after a few rewrites – and I couldn't find a job anywhere, with all my student loans rearing their ugly heads, I planned to head out west, live in my car, and try to get a job designing robotics systems at one of the new space venture companies starting up out there."

"Space as in outer space?"

"Yeah. That was in the fall. I stopped here to spend a few days visiting Pete, who's got an adjunct lectureship at BU. He hooked me up with a research assistantship in the robotics lab. It was only supposed to be for a semester, but they've been extending it and I'm good for the fall semester, at least. So I ended up staying here longer than I expected."

"Well, that happened to me, too, actually," Anne told him. "I was living in New York City. I'd been there for about ten years. Had a great job running the emergency unit in a big hospital. I loved it. I earned my Ph.D. in nursing while I was working. I often wonder how I ever managed it all. Then, after my mom had a heart attack, I took a leave to come back and help her. A friend at BU told them about me and they recruited me for the nursing faculty. I always intended to go back to New York, but the longer I stayed here, the harder it was to leave again. And after a while, I didn't really have anything to go back for."

She remembered the look on Jason's face when she told him she was considering accepting the position at BU; it said she had utterly lost her mind. He didn't know it was a test, or if he did, he hadn't tried to stop her. He said he couldn't make any commitments until he finished his residency. About a year after she left New York, someone sent her, in a hospital stationery envelope, his engagement announcement from the *Times*. As if she wouldn't have seen it. His fiance had a bland WASP face and an Ivy League MBA. Anne wasn't surprised; she'd always known he was ambitious, and his engagement to her would never have been printed in the *Times*. By then, Anne felt over him, focused on her new life in academia.

"Besides, everything was different after 9/11," she said softly. "You could never get away from it, couldn't forget." Quin was lying on his side, propped on his elbow, watching her closely. She took a deep breath, and went on. She rarely talked about this, but tonight it felt good to let the story out.

"After my first year at BU, my mom died suddenly, from an aneurism in her heart." She picked up a small stick lying on the ground and made circles in the hard earth. She couldn't stop talking. "It was hard. I didn't know what to do, whether to stay or go back to New York, or somewhere else. So one day I decided to walk around Goat Island to think. We used to picnic there a lot when I was a kid, with my parents, grandparents, and my brother Bill. On the way back to my car I took a detour to look at the old houses on Cataract Lane, this little hidden street along the upper rapids. My mom and I used to walk there and wonder what it would be like to live in one of those houses. We had a favorite one, a shabby old Victorian. We would talk about how we would fix it up. And that day, it had a for-sale sign on the lawn. Right then I decided to buy it. Once I moved in, finally, after months of renovation, I was finally able to calm down, walking by the river every day, hearing the rush of the water at night. It soothes me, takes me outside of myself. I even found a stray puppy along the river one day, and took him in." She smiled at the memory of the scared little furball that was now her big spoiled dog. "So now I have a house and a dog and tenure." She gave Quin a sharp look. "You'd better be careful, or you'll end up staying here until you have to be transformed, like me."

"What do you mean, transformed?"

"Our dean is planning a big reorganization. She's basically told the faculty that nursing, as we know it, as I was trained for it, needs transformational change. Don't you hate that word?"

"Yeah. It's fucking meaningless." Quin sat up. "Real transformations, like Tesla's alternating current generators here at Niagara, for example, don't happen too often. And sure as hell not by tenured faculty."

Anne ignored the inadvertent dig. "Have you seen Tesla's statue on Goat Island?" she asked him. Everyone who grew up in Niagara Falls knew the story of the Serbian genius, Nikola Tesla, who invented the generators that distributed Niagara's power across long distances.

Quin grinned. "That was the first time I ever did the tourist thing and looked up a statue. Wait here." He rose, walked across the street, and returned with two cold beers.

Drinking slowly, they watched the red disk of the sun slowly sink behind the tree-bordered horizon of Grand Island. The river, which had been shimmering with reflected sunlight a short while ago, dimmed until it was an ominous black trench. The air was still hot. Moths and mosquitoes buzzed around shafts of light coming from the restaurant and park lamps.

"Everybody is worried about being transformed now," Quin said, after a while. "We're all running around doing our little tasks, and trying not to get deleted when someone changes the program. That's why I signed up for this European project that wants to send people to Mars in another ten years or so."

Anne stared at him. "Are you serious?"

"Yeah. I figure it's the only way I'll get out of paying my student loans." When she didn't laugh, he shrugged.

"You really want to leave the planet for good? Why, when you're so young and have such good academic credentials?"

He started to reply, then stopped himself. He took a swig of beer and said, "I don't want to be a slave to some fucking corporation. Or worse, to some shitheads in a tech start-up who want to monetize their codes. Most of the corporate space plans are for space tourism, and let's face it, what's the point of that? It's like what the Maid of the Mist boats were a hundred years ago, taking people into a supposedly dangerous, alien environment. But it was all orchestrated, and not as dangerous as it looked. That's what space tourism is all about."

"I never thought of it that way," Anne said.

Quin looked closely at her. "Okay – you've been down to that fishing pier in the gorge?"

Anne nodded. "A long, long time ago. With my dad, when he was alive, and my grandfather. When I was a kid."

"Right," Quin said. "You're down there at the bottom of this deep canyon, on the shore of rushing, whitewater rapids, with more than a hundred feet of rocky gorge rising straight up behind you, and in front of you. Look upriver to your left and all you can see is wildness, the river coming straight out of the Whirlpool at killer speed, and the steep cliffs on both sides. You might as well be living hundreds of years ago. But there's this throbbing sound, and you look to the right, downriver, and on both sides of the gorge there are these massive concrete abutments for the power plants, built right into the rock, looming over you on both sides of the river, putting out millions of watts of power a minute. It's almost like instant time travel."

"Yes," Anne said softly.

"Those plants are awesome. Have you ever been inside to see the generators?"

"Actually, um, no."

"I got a special tour. It's so cool. They're huge, set inside this big marble complex behind all that concrete, under tons of rock. Putting out power. Electricity that's made out of water. Two elements: H-2-0. All that power – pure energy, Anne. People used to think Tesla did magic tricks with his generators, throwing lightning bolts around. Everything that people don't understand is magic, for a while. But Tesla, he knew. He predicted everything."

"People make even a simple rockfall into magic," Anne said. "The big rock collapse at the falls three weeks ago was just erosion, the way the falls have been eroding and moving south for thousands of years. But my friend Mari thinks the rockfall has a cosmic meaning, because she had a bad dream the same night. A lot of people seem to think it was UFOs, for God's sake, or terrorism, or an old Indian curse. Even you have a weird explanation for my computer crashing – a solar storm."

"But I'm the one who's right." Quin smirked. "And anyway, that's not a weird explanation. Solar storms are a natural phenomenon."

"Could they have caused the rockfall?"

"I think we can blame our old friend erosion for that."

"So the solar flares and the rockfall happening on the same night weren't related?"

"Probably not. That was just coincidence. Randomness. Chaos."

"Chaos," Anne repeated.

They exchanged a quick glance, then each turned away, and stared at the black river. After a while, Quin said, "This river freaks me out. You can divide it into segments, and each one is different. Up here, it's just a wide stretch of deep water. Then you get the upper rapids, the falls, then the whitewater, and the whirlpool, and ultimately it peters out into the lake. But mostly, it's a power source. When Tesla was young, he saw a picture of Niagara Falls and right away he started figuring out how to use its energy. And then once he figured out alternating current, the whole country became electrified. It changed everything."

"But it wasn't good for the Falls," Anne commented. "That power brought the chemical factories here, and all the pollution. I grew up in this city, so I know how bad it was."

"Yeah, this place was Silicon Valley in the eighteen-nineties," Quin said. "Making new stuff like aluminum and carborundum. Later, even chemical warfare weapons."

"I'm not against technology," Anne told him. "I'm a nurse, and I know how many lives it saves. I'd never want to go backward. It's just that I know the downside in a very personal way. My dad was killed in an explosion in one of the chemical plants when I was seven years old."

His face was full of sympathy. "What happened?"

She tensed. The memory still hurt. She hadn't known, at first, what woke her up in the middle of the night, but it seemed that her bed was shaking. She sat up, and heard her mother's footsteps running down the stairs, and the front door opening, and voices from the street. Cars starting. Sirens. She ran outside to her mother, who was standing in a cluster of their neighbors on East Falls Street, just two blocks over from the stretch of Buffalo Avenue where the chemical plants were; everyone was looking at the glow from the chemical factories that lined the upper river. "It's Hooker, alright," said the man next door. A white plume of smoke rose slowly in the muggy air, reflecting a reddish light. The smell of chlorine wafted toward them. Frightened, Anne took her mother's hand. The acrid chemical smell became stronger. The sirens got louder, as police cars and ambulances raced toward Buffalo Avenue. People shouted and ran. The night air seemed electrified. A haze descended over the neighborhood streets, smelling of chlorine and cigarette smoke, so thick that street lamps and car lights seemed to float in it. Flashing red lights gave everything a bloody glow.

"It was a chlorine explosion," she told Quin. "My dad was the night supervisor at the plant. He tried to help his crew get out of the disaster area. They weren't wearing masks; the company had a long history of safety violations."

"Man. I'm sorry. It must have been hard."

She didn't need sympathy anymore. Life was actually easier, in some ways, after your parents' deaths tempered your soul, hardened it to life's other miseries. She felt she could face anything now. Still, she had to make an effort to keep her voice steady. "It was all pretty ironic. I mean, he went through the Vietnam war unscathed, and then he died a hero a few blocks from where he was born. In an explosion." During her years in the ER, she had trained herself not to look for hidden meanings, or try to analyze the fates of her patients. Why did the innocent bystander take the bullet? Why did the out-of-control cab hit the pregnant woman? You could make yourself crazy doing that. She ordered herself to think clinically. "Do you know what happens when you die of chlorine inhalation?"

Quin shook his head.

"Your lungs fill with fluid. You drown on dry land." Anne spit out her words. "It's because they weren't careful enough – the men who owned and ran the chemical plants. They didn't take enough precautions to protect people from the poisons they were working with. They just wanted to make money."

"Well, that's what it's still about, isn't it, only we're at the next stage."

"What do you mean?"

"People working with technology and ignoring its dangers. Only back then, the technology dealt with chemicals and physical processes. Now it's dealing with circuits and mind processes. Man, they're making nano devices that can crawl through our brains. And growing live cells on silicon structures. We don't know what the long-term consequences will be. Just like the guys who invented those chemical processes. They didn't worry about pollution or danger. They just thought, cool, man, I'm gonna be rich. Just like today."

Anne stared at his profile; the restaurant's lights behind him formed a corona around his head. "The technology rushes so far ahead of us. And we never catch up," she said.

"I guess that's really why I'm still hanging around here. I'm trying to figure it all out, find out where I fit in, before I get in too deep, before I get trapped," Quin told her.

Anne rose, feeling a bit unsteady. "Wait here," she said. She went into the ladies room, and then bought hot caramel sundaes and coffees. She carried them across the street on a tray. Most people had left. For a long while, she and Quin sat near the water's edge, watching powerboats race back and forth. A Coast Guard patrol boat cruised slowly up and down the river, shining its spotlight as a warning to boaters. Light from the beacon was sucked into the depths of the dark river like star matter flowing into a black hole.

LINDA GRACE

CHAPTER FOURTEEN

"Jerome, please keep your eyes on the road." Loraine's voice was tense. "Stop looking behind us every three minutes."

"I just want to be sure I'm not going too fast. I don't want the ambulance to lose us."

"They won't get lost. Woody is with the driver."

"I'd rather be riding in the ambulance with John." Jerome felt his sister's look as he reflexively glanced in the rearview mirror. "What did you want to talk about?"

Loraine sighed loudly, and turned her face toward the passenger-side window. Jerome had never seen her so tired. Loraine, his older sister, was an attractive woman, but today she looked middle-aged, and beat. Almost defeated.

They were driving south on Route 219. Jerome estimated they'd be home in about an hour. He glanced in the rearview mirror. The ambulance was still behind them. "Loraine?"

"What?"

"I still think taking John home is a very bad idea."

"I know. So do I."

"Then why didn't you take my side and help me convince Mother to keep John in the medical center? At least for a while longer. This seems like we're giving up."

"Her mind was made up. She wants him home."

"Do you agree with that?"

"It doesn't matter. She's bringing him home."

"I'm afraid she's getting her hopes up too much. Or giving up hope. I don't know which it is, or which is worse."

"There's something I should warn you about," Loraine said.

Jerome tightened his grip on the steering wheel. This was it. He'd been expecting something from the way she'd been avoiding looking him in the eye since they met at the hospital earlier in the day, and said she needed to talk to him. "What is it?"

"We have a visitor at home, a man you've never met. He's convinced Mother he can help John."

"And you're telling me now?"

"There was no way to stop it. Anyway, there was nothing you could do from Buffalo. I figured that once you were home, you'd be able to handle it better, take care of it."

"Where was Woody? I told him to keep strangers away from Mother and the house."

"Don't blame him." She sighed. "Remember that day about two weeks ago, when he went up to Buffalo with all that paperwork to meet you and catch up on business? He left strict orders with everyone. I don't know what happened, but this man got through the gate and showed up at the door; Mother answered it. I was in the yard with the kids. When I came in, I tried to get rid of him, but he had Mother in a deep conversation, and she shooed me away."

"I can't believe it!" Jerome exclaimed. "How could he get through the gate?"

"The more I've thought about it, the more I suspect that he had gotten in touch with her somehow, or she with him, before he arrived, and she was waiting for him, and let him in," Lorraine replied. "He saw her a few more times, I think. I saw him in the hospital cafeteria one day. Then, the day before yesterday, he moved an expensive RV onto our property, about a mile from the house, in the field past the rock ridge."

"How come no one told me?" Jerome was furious. "Why didn't you? Why didn't Andrew or Woody?" He looked into the rearview mirror. "I'm going to fire him as soon as we get home."

"Jerome, you don't understand."

"There's no excuse for this. A stranger showing up at the house! Camping on our land!"

"Don't blame Woody. He can't stand up to Mother."

"He should have called me."

"He was going to. I told him not to."

"He reports to me. To me and no one else now that John ...." Jerome couldn't continue.

Loraine leaned toward him and touched her brother's arm. "Listen to me and try to understand. It's a very delicate situation."

Glancing in the mirror, Jerome saw that his anger had made him inadvertently speed up. The ambulance was too far behind. He slowed down. "How is it so delicate that you and Woody keep secrets from me?"

"Mother believes in this man. He has her convinced he can heal John."

"All the more reason to get rid of him."

"I told her that's what you would do. She won't hear of it. She says if we send him away she'll bring him back. Or take John to him."

"She can't even drive."

"Jerome, please ...," Loraine pressed her hands against her face, and rubbed tears from her cheeks. "It's been so difficult for all of us." She tried to keep her voice steady. "I'm not complaining. Maybe I made the wrong decision not to tell you right away. But Mother believes this man can help John. The doctors give us no hope. They say John may be in a persistent vegetative state. That's the most horrible thing of all, to see him lying unconscious, twitching, as though he's in pain. I can barely look at him. It's killing Mother to see him like that. She'll do anything to help him – I will, too. Maybe this guy *is* our last hope."

"I don't know anything about him!" Jerome banged his hands against the steering wheel. Loraine jumped in her seat. He tried to control his temper.

Speaking more calmly, he said, "Look, I wouldn't mind if she brought in healers, people from our community, men we know. Even after what happened in the ICU with Mr. Williams; he just got upset seeing John like that. I believe in the healing power of our faith, and the natural medicines. But to have some stranger come into the house, some guy in an RV." He shook his head. "What is she thinking?"

His sister sighed and leaned her head back against the seat. "I honestly don't know." She sounded very tired.

"But why didn't you tell me before now, when we're practically home? At least I could have done some checking."

"You had enough on your mind, trying to keep up with everything, including your research for your important book, living in John's hospital room. There was nothing you could do. Anyway, Woody is already checking him out. And watching him."

"So what's this guy's name?"

"Levi Moon."

"I've never heard of him. Where's he from?"

"Originally, he says, from Six Nations up in Ontario."

"I'll call some people I know there as soon as we get home."

They drove in silence for a long while.

Loraine changed the subject. "Have you seen Tifani lately? Does she know John's going home?"

Jerome shrugged. "She came last week for a little while, said she's been busy. Now that John can't take her to fancy places, she doesn't have time for him."

"That'll make Mother happy." Brother and sister exchanged a quick glance. "Me, too." Lorraine laughed. "Boy, she was just after his money, it was so obvious. We haven't heard from her, either."

Jerome, relieved at the news of one less aggravation, slowed down. They were reaching the end of the 219. His spirits lifted as he felt himself getting closer to home. He hated the city. He was going to spend tonight sleeping out in the meadow, under the stars. He couldn't wait. But he was still infuriated at being kept in the dark.

"Woody is going to hear about this," he said angrily. "And so is

Mother. She has to know she can't just bring strangers into the house. Doesn't she realize the danger she could be putting John in? Or all of us? And we still have to be sure John keeps getting good medical care. The new kind, in addition to the old."

Loraine tried to reassure him. "The medical director wouldn't sign the release until Mother promised John would continue to have daily professional nursing care and physical therapy, and that the doctors could examine him at home. She signed a lot of papers."

Jerome flicked on his turn signal. He watched to be sure the ambulance followed. He told his sister, "I'm going to keep plans moving ahead for the Turtle."

"I think that's the right thing to do," Loraine said. "Either John will be there to open it himself, or ...," her voice broke, "we'll open it in his name." She started to cry softly.

Jerome reached over and gently squeezed her hand. He swallowed hard. No matter what happened, he wouldn't let their plan for the Turtle die. It was his dream, too. He wished John had done it in collaboration with the university or with the traditional leaderships of the Six Nations, but that wasn't his way. It would have taken too long, he would have had to make compromises, he would have had to share power. He had to get things done his way. Jerome had tried to persuade him otherwise, but in the end conceded to his brother's plan. The Turtle museum was too important to quibble about how it was conceived. Once it opened, there would be time to heal rifts. Jerome thought about the young people who would be inspired there. The future was in the children, and he would do everything he possibly could to help them know and honor their culture. Every decision should be made for the benefit of future generations. Jerome tried hard to quell his fears that humanity didn't have many generations left to live on a dying planet.

PART TWO

"You can descend a staircase here a hundred and fifty feet down, and stand at the edge of the water. After you have done it, you will wonder why you did it; but you will then be too late.... I never was so scared before and survived it."

Mark Twain, 1871

CHAPTER FIFTEEN

Anne ran along the upper rapids path with Ben, trying to keep up with the parade of waves rushing toward the brink. A thunderstorm had hit just after dawn, waking her. She went outside as soon as the heavy shower was over, while the grass and pavement were still wet, to take advantage of the temporary cooling before the sun burned off the much-needed moisture. She and Ben hadn't had a good run in a long time. And, despite the fact that she had gotten home close to midnight after her dinner with Quin, and the drive back to Buffalo to drop him off at his car, she felt good, energized by their discussion and the sparks they generated in each other.

She was near the traffic bridge to Goat Island when she heard, "Hey! Aren't you Anne?"

Startled, she looked up and saw a young woman with short, brightly colored hair walking toward her. "Yes, and you're ... Chani, right?" Anne stopped and leaned with her hands on her knees, panting. "From the library?"

"Right." She looked pleased to be remembered.

"So, what are you doing here so early?" Anne asked her.

"Snooping around. Hey, nice dog." Chani bent over to pet Ben.

Anne smiled. The young woman didn't look very devious in her jeans and a green tee shirt emblazoned with *The Earth Is Your Mother*. "What are you snooping for?"

"I've been trying to get permission to do a dig on Goat Island to look for Native American artifacts," Chani explained. "But the state won't let me. They say there's no evidence that Indians ever managed to get out to the island, that it was impossible for them to do it. But that's bullshit. I don't know why they won't let me do even a small, exploratory dig."

"Because then they'd have to confront the fact that everything people have done to Goat Island is wrong." Anne felt her old anger rise. "Cutting down the old-growth trees, destroying its ecosystem, expanding the roads and parking lots – everything!"

"I need to find some evidence, or a new argument," Chani told her. "I tried to sneak onto Luna Island to see if I could poke around in the area where the rock collapse was, you know, where it's roped off, but a cop spotted me and chased me out."

"Don't ever underestimate how dangerous it is around the falls, Chani," Anne cautioned. "One slip and you're gone, even if the water is shallow."

"Oh, I'll be careful. Listen, I have a petition to the state parks commission, trying to show that I have community support to do a small dig. Will you sign it?"

"Well, I'll take a look at it," Anne replied. "Can you come to a meeting tonight? I'm in a local historical preservation group, and our executive committee is meeting at my house, just over there on Cataract Lane. I think everyone would be interested in your petition. Maybe we can help you, at least with some advice."

"That would be awesome." Chani left with a big smile on her face after Anne gave her directions to her house.

Anne crossed over the traffic bridge to Goat Island. She turned right to jog along the tree-lined path. She loved to be on the island early, before the crowds came. When she reached the bridge to Luna Island, Anne stopped at the police barricade blocking access to it. Geologists were warning another big rock collapse could be imminent. Just beyond the falls, the huge face of the Turtle loomed over Prospect Point; his eyes seemed to be staring at her. From where she stood, Anne couldn't see the cave that had been opened up by the rockfall, but she'd observed it from the mainland, where the dark jagged hole that led under Luna Island was easily visible. A thin curtain of water flowed over it like a lacy curtain. Geologists hadn't explored the cave – it was far too dangerous. She wondered what would happen if there were another rockfall. Perhaps Luna Island would disappear altogether. After pondering the relentless force of erosion for a while, she turned and walked more slowly home with her tired dog.

She tapped softly on the back door of Mari's apartment to see if she was awake. Phoebe had been sleeping when Anne returned home late the previous night. After a moment, Mari opened the door, looking half awake.

"Want some coffee?" Anne asked her.

"Yeah." Mari's sleepy vocal chords made her voice deep.

"Come upstairs when you're ready. I'll be on the front porch."

Upstairs, Ben quickly slopped up his bowl of water, then fell on the floor, panting. Anne took a quick shower and was sitting on her front porch with coffee when Mari joined her shortly afterward.

"Is Phoebe up yet?" Mari asked.

"Are you kidding, it's not even eight-thirty," Anne replied. "How was your dinner?"

"It was fun," Mari told her. "Leonard got here kind of late, looking like he just woke up. He walked Ben at suppertime, and Phoebe helped me get the food ready." Mari took a sip of coffee. "What do you think about her and Leonard?"

"Why do you ask?"

"I don't know. I can't figure out what their relationship is. They're together, but each of them seems in their own world. Sometimes it seems like they're strangers on the same path."

"I don't know how much they have in common except their secrets," Anne replied. "Phoebe has a box in her room that has some of his stuff. She says she keeps it safe for him. I don't know what's in it. I pray it isn't drugs, but I can't violate their privacy by inspecting it."

Mari nodded. "Not unless you have to. Anyway, I know some of what's in the box."

"What?" Anne set down her coffee cup.

"His drawings. That's where he keeps a lot of them. Phoebe told me. Like a lot of beginning artists, he's shy about showing his work to people. I've seen some of them, and I think he has talent. I'm doing my best to encourage him."

"Mari, you are really a good person."

"Good deeds come back to you. Besides, he's a big help to me. Oh! Remember that picture from the newspaper? Of that girl in the Maid of the Mist beauty contest?"

Anne nodded.

"Well, I showed it to Phoebe last night, just to tease her."

"What was her reaction?"

"I think I insulted her. She just stared at it. So did Leonard, who looked really uncomfortable. Then Phoebe said, 'You can't really see me in that outfit, can you?' I had to admit I couldn't. I laughed, but they didn't. It was touchy."

"Hi."

Both women jumped as Phoebe walked onto the porch. Anne looked at her watch. "You're dressed! It's still early!"

"I just heard you guys and came out to talk. Want me to make some toast?"

"Sure," Anne said, shooting a surprised, approving look at Mari. "We have time before I take you to work."

That evening, Phoebe made an effort to be useful by helping Anne get ready for the meeting and answering the door. Chani was the first to arrive, followed by Emily, who brought Anne a collection of articles about Francis Abbott.

"Is the new Hermit still around?" she asked.

"I saw him yesterday," Anne replied. "From a distance. He was walking toward the woods on Goat Island."

"I've been down by the falls several times, but haven't seen him yet. I'm dying to make his acquaintance."

"Be careful, Emily. He could be dangerous."

"Oh, Anne, you think all men are dangerous," a male voice said. Anne smiled and turned to it.

"Every man except you, Joe," she said, giving her guest a hug. "I have to apologize. I've been intending all summer to come to the food kitchen and give you a hand, but I've been so busy. Phoebe has been staying here, and I've had to go to campus a lot, and ..."

Father Joseph Flynn held up his hands.

"No more excuses." A smile broke through the ruff of his gray-flecked brown beard. "I know you're busy. I'll call if I need you."

Anne motioned Joe into the kitchen, away from Chani and Emily, who were discussing the history of Goat Island or, as Emily called it, the callous depredation of one of Earth's treasures. "Mari told me she saw a flyer at the women's center when she went for her meditation session yesterday," Anne told him. "It asked for anyone with information about Sheryl Poloka to call the police. So she's still missing?"

"I'm afraid so. No one's seen her for weeks."

"I hope she turns up safely. Let me know if I can do anything to help."

"Thanks, Anne. I know I can count on you." Joe gave her arm a brief squeeze, and went into the parlor.

Joe's soft touch made Anne feel blessed. She smiled. He was, by far, the best man she knew. Even in "civilian" clothes like the cotton shirt and jeans he was wearing tonight, he had the serene air of a man who spent much time in prayer and reflection, who saw the farthest edge of the world. He was still known around town as the "hippie priest," as Anne's brother Bill always referred to him, for his antiwar activities since the sixties and his ongoing commitment to humanitarian causes. He supervised social programs in Niagara Falls for the Catholic diocese. At St. Mary of the Cataract, the historic church downtown, he filled in by saying Masses for the diocesan priests, when they had a hard time finding substitutes. Anne did not consider herself a practicing Catholic, but she tried always to go to Joe's Masses.

Steve Garrett, a young high school science teacher, and Jay Bryant, a career civil servant in the city planning department, arrived. She gave them a few minutes to get settled with their drinks and snacks in the parlor, then called the meeting to order.

"First, I thought you would be interested in hearing about Chani's project," she told the group. "There might be some way we could advise her. I think it's an effort that could help us in the long run, if she's successful. We're all in support of getting development off Goat Island and returning it as much as possible into a more natural state."

"Thanks." Chani glanced around nervously as she sat on the floor in the middle of the room. Her thin bare arms were tanned a deep brown. A knitted cap of thick yarns muted the brightness of her hair. She shuffled through papers until she found the one she was looking for. "This project is for my master's thesis in anthropology at BU. I've been studying the aboriginal peoples of this region, especially the Neuters and the Eries, who were called the Cat People. They lived along the river and lakeshore. Not much is known about them. Some sites have been excavated, like the burial mound at Artpark and some places on Grand Island, and in Fort Erie. I'm trying to find a dig site around the falls. In my research, I learned that ancient human bones actually *were* found on Goat Island. In 1895, a workman digging a sewer trench unearthed a skull and other human bones; it was reported in the newspaper. The body was buried with its feet pointed toward the rapids. There *must* be more evidence of the early native peoples there, somewhere."

"Can you learn by studying oral tradition?" Emily asked.

"I've tried," Chani replied, "but I can't find sources. My professors won't help me. They're trying to steer me toward digging up colonial pottery shards and musket balls at Fort Niagara. Right."

"Chani, you didn't mention before that your professors haven't endorsed your project," Anne interjected.

"I think it's because they just don't want to hassle with the state," Chani replied. "But if I got the necessary permits on my own, and support from groups like yours, I think they would approve my proposal."

"I'm not sure ...," Anne began.

"Mastodons," Steve said.

"What?" Chani responded.

"You'll never get anywhere trying to dig for Native American artifacts. There are just too many political ramifications," the teacher explained. "And the state doesn't want any interference in how it manages Goat Island. So you need to say you're looking for something that won't stir up a hornet's nest. Mastodons are nice and safe. Goofy-looking hairy elephants. Great tusks. Interesting, but not political."

"No offense, but why would I try to find mastodon bones on Goat Island? I mean, how would they even get there?"

Steve got excited. He was a young man with dark, trimmed facial hair, who loved to push his students into new areas. "Remember your geology," he told Chani.

She looked confused.

"Remember that mastodons were living around here around ten thousand and more years ago," Steve told her. "And where were the falls ten thousand years ago?"

There was silence as everyone waited for Chani to answer. "Omigod," she finally said. "In Lewiston. The falls were in Lewiston."

"Right," Steve said. So the mastodons were wandering around here on a nice open plain. Maybe on this exact spot." He gave a big smile, showing strong teeth in his dark beard. "And it's not too much of a stretch to look for them on Goat Island. Charles Lyell himself, the English scientist who's known as the father of geology, reported in a speech in 1843 that workers digging for a mill on Goat Island found a mastodon tooth."

"But I'm looking for remains of people," Chani told him.

Steve shrugged. "Some mastodons have been found with spear flints in them."

"Come back to the library," Emily urged her. "I'll show you some citations of mastodon bones found around Lewiston. And, if I remember correctly, there was a mastodon skeleton in the Niagara Museum collection. Maybe Sylvester still has it."

"Wait a minute!" Anne cried. Everyone looked at her. "It would be totally unethical for you to submit a false proposal, Chani. And you know that, Steve." She glared at him. "Don't get carried away!"

"Well, maybe I just might be interested in mastodons now," Chani told her.

"Please, Chani, please work closely with the faculty in your department," Anne urged. She wondered if she should give a call and talk to someone over there. "Then, maybe we can help you."

"I'm going to do this one way or another," Chani said. "I *know* there's something to find on that island."

"Keep in touch with me," Anne told her. "Would you like to stay for the rest of the meeting?"

"No, I'm through." She gathered up her papers, stuffed them into a colorful hemp sack. "Thanks for inviting me." She gave Steve a high-five as she left the room.

"The state will never give permission for a dig on Goat Island," Jay said, after they heard the door close behind Chani. "She's dreaming."

"Have you been able to learn anything more about White Pine Enterprises, Jay?" Anne asked him.

"No. I've cornered Nick Valli a couple of times, but he won't answer my questions. He's definitely avoiding me."

"We have to find out what they intend to do with the building, whether they're preparing it for a casino or if they want to tear it down," Emily said. "We can't let the Turtle be used for anything except a learning center."

"That's right," Joe said. "Jay, you've got to get hold of White Pine's proposal."

"I'll try."

Anne said, "If they redevelop the Turtle site, it will be the start of another massive new development downtown. They'll start taking all the old homes and buildings on this end of Buffalo Avenue, and maybe Cataract Lane, too. I saw Nick driving past my house again yesterday. He does it just to annoy me, I'm sure."

The committee speculated for almost an hour about what to do. They came to no conclusions. With no new business, they adjourned.

The members stayed to chat and finish Anne's refreshments.

"Joe," Anne asked, "have you seen the Hermit?"

"Yes, a few times. Why do you ask, Anne?"

"I'm wondering if he's a danger to himself."

"I don't think so. He's just a poor deluded soul, an eccentric. But very literate. He recited some poetry for me, Shakespeare and Old English poems. Sometimes he sings."

"I've got to meet him," Emily said. She spotted Leonard and Phoebe trying to sneak past the group to get out the front door. "Oh, hello, Leonard," she enthused, walking toward the youth. "How is your great-grandfather?"

"He's fine."

"Tell him I said hello. You remember me? Emily Storey from the library?"

"Yeah, I'll tell him."

"We're going out for ice cream, Aunt Anne," Phoebe said. "Bye," she added as the two teens rushed out the door.

"You know Leonard?" Anne asked.

"His great-grandfather is Wallace Mountview," Emily said. "He's brought Leonard to the archives, to look at old maps and photos. He's trying to teach him about his Tuscarora ancestry."

"That's good. I've been wondering about Leonard's family."

"It's been so hard for Wallace," Emily said. "To develop a relationship with the boy, I mean. He had a rough time with his granddaughter, Leonard's mother, she was pretty wild, I hear. Wallace was so upset when she moved away. She went to live up in Canada. Leonard didn't want to go with her. She had a boyfriend he didn't like. That's why he's living with Wallace and his wife, Rose, now."

Anne started to pick up stray dishes. "I give them credit. It's not easy living with a teenager. It's so depressing to keep hearing about dysfunctional families. Are there any stable families left? It amazes me that I still get asked if I'm sorry I'm not married and don't have any kids. I mean, look around! Families are breaking apart all over the place. I don't know what Bill would have done if Phoebe hadn't been able to come here for the summer, give them all a break from each other. But that's just temporary. She'll be back home soon. But there are too many other kids out there who have nowhere to go. People shouldn't have them if they don't love them and take care of them."

"I agree," Emily said, following Anne into the kitchen with cups and glasses. "But, as rational people, you and I are in the minority, Anne. And maybe we're already extinct, like the mastodons."

CHAPTER SIXTEEN

"So what do you think?" Jerome asked, squinting as he shaded his eyes against the high midday sun.

The tree specialist from the county cooperative extension bureau aimed his binoculars at the line of tall sugar maples standing a way up on the grassy slope. There was no way to miss the damage. Fully the top thirds of the trees looked dingy and shriveled. This wasn't just from the summer draught. The leaves were the sickly tans and grays of brownfields.

"Let's take a closer look," Terry Caldwell said, as he lowered his binoculars.

The two men strode through the tall, dry grass and ragweed, avoiding clumps of nettles. They were in a big field on the western edge of John's extensive property. Despite the heat, Terry wore a long-sleeved shirt and his jeans were tucked into hiking boots. Jerome noticed beads of sweat falling from under his red cap and disappearing behind his sunglasses and into his blond beard. He gave off a strong odor of insect repellant and sunscreen.

"Thanks for coming out here to meet me," Jerome said, feeling sorry for the young man's discomfort. He himself hadn't yet succumbed to paranoia over ultraviolet rays and insect-borne viruses like Lyme disease. "I've been meaning to call you for some time, but this is the first chance I've gotten to have the time to come out this way." He knew he didn't need to explain. The local newspapers were still reporting on

John Lone's lack of recovery from his car accident, and what it meant for his business ventures.

Terry shrugged. "It's too bad that rain they promised last night didn't come. The drought is taking its toll on everything, even established plantings and mature trees. The farmers have taken another bad hit. I hope some state aid comes through, or a lot of them are going to go under."

"The weather channel said to expect these high-nineties temperatures all week."

"Welcome to climate change." Terry was breathing hard; he shifted the weight of his backpack. "We fry, while Washington just sits on it. Someone should tell them we won't have an economy, or even a world capable of sustaining human life, if we don't start doing something now." He snorted like an angry dog.

It didn't feel any cooler in the shade under the maples' withered canopy. Squatting down, Terry pulled off his backpack and opened it, removing notebooks, a digital camera, magnifiers, pruners, cellophane envelopes, and folded paper bags. Jerome watched as the agent examined and photographed the trees and the ground surrounding them. He collected samples of dirt, bark, and fallen leaves. Then, staring at a mature tree with low branches, he said, "I'm going to climb up and get some samples from the top."

"I'll do it." Jerome stepped in front of him. "I've been wanting to get a close look."

"You won't get sued if I fall. I'm covered."

Jerome was disappointed Terry thought it was about money. "You can come, too," he told him. "But I'm going up."

The agent grinned. "Then you can help."

Jerome went first, hoisting himself onto a thick branch. He could feel the tree's strength still coursing through its limbs. But as he passed the halfway point up, the leaves started to change. They looked as though a flame had singed them. Branches were black, and cracked.

"We'd better not go much higher," Terry warned. "The limbs look brittle."

Jerome nodded, but continued going up a few more feet. They snipped off branches and collected wood samples. Jerome used his own digital camera to get close-up images of the leaves and bark. Then they climbed back down.

"Got any ideas?" Jerome asked.

"I've never seen anything like this." Terry stared closely at a small branch with dun-colored leaves, turning it. "I'm finding no evidence of borers, or any blight I've ever heard of."

"It doesn't look like trees I've seen up in the Adirondacks, where they've been burned by acid rain. It's much worse." Jerome crushed a wide leaf in his hand; it crumbled into ash. "Maybe this is a harbinger, a sign of worse to come," he said softly.

"That's likely." Terry was packing up his samples and equipment. He unfolded a large bag, and put two branches with scorched leaves into it; he sealed it with tape, and wrote notes on the outside. "I mean, how much of Greenland has to melt before we start doing anything?"

Jerome didn't answer. No matter what scientific explanation Terry might find for what was happening to these trees, they were dying, slowly, from the top down. And maybe Mother Earth was, too. Maybe they were already in the End Days that Handsome Lake had predicted, the last days that would come when the people no longer cared for Mother Earth, no longer believed in the future, and no longer gave thanks.

The two men hiked down the slope in silence. Before he got into his truck, Terry turned to Jerome. "I'll contact you if I find out anything. I'll send out a query to see if anybody else in has seen anything like this. I might want to bring some guys down from Ithaca to take a look at those trees. Would that be okay? Should I call you first?"

"Bring them anytime. You don't have to call." Jerome handed Terry his card. "But contact me fast if you do find out anything, okay? Especially if this is spreading."

"Will do. Nice meeting you, Jerome."

They climbed into their vehicles and took off in opposite directions. Driving home, Jerome tried to quell his dreadful foreboding by noting that most of the trees still looked pretty good, just droopy from the heat and lack of rain. When he neared the main house, he stopped his car to take a long look at the ancient sycamore. Its thick canopy was beginning to turn yellow, earlier than usual. Passing through the gate, he thought he'd dealt with the most troubling news of the day.

He entered the house, and went into the first-floor office to check the voicemail on his landline phone. He had a message from New York City, from James Dalway, the private investigator he'd hired to look into the background of Levi Moon. Sitting at the desk, he pulled out a notepad and pen, and quickly returned the call. "Good to hear from you, James. Tell me what you've found."

The investigator spoke in a quick, business-like manner. "We've had limited success so far, Mr. Lone. We've only been able to trace his activities to the mid-nineties, and even there, he leaves a suspiciously weak trail. Not only haven't we been able to find any reports of criminal activity, we can't locate the usual sorts of records, like car registrations, deeds, credit reports. We've even checked in Canada, after one source told us that's where he came from."

"That's not good news, I assume, from what you're saying?"

"It's not necessarily bad news, but it raises red flags. Most people leave a pretty wide electronic trail, because most people aren't trying to cover their tracks. I'm checking prison records to see if he was locked up for a while. This guy travels a lot between the U-S and Canada, lives in a big excursion home, so he doesn't have to buy plane tickets or check into motels. He makes the rounds of the reservations – Six Nations, Garden River, Walpole Island, Akwesasne. My Canadian associate found out he crosses the border dozens of times every year, mostly at Niagara Falls, or up in northern New York, at Cornwall."

"There's nothing illegal about that. Is he a member of any of the Indian communities, the reservations?"

"None that would claim him. Some folks up at Six Nations said they knew of him, that he passed himself off as a healer there, but they seemed not to take him all that seriously. Said he's mostly a salesman. Except for one guy. He wouldn't say much to my associate, but he told him that if he was checking on Levi Moon on behalf of someone who was involved with him, then we should give that person his phone number, and he'd talk to him directly. It was strange. My man said when he pressed the guy, he said he didn't want to get involved in anything regarding Moon, but that he'd feel guilty if he didn't try to help someone who might really need it."

"Do you think I should call him?"

"There's no way to tell how reliable his word is. Could just be someone with a grudge. But I don't want to keep any information from you. Take down this number, it's up in Brantford, Ontario. You don't have to give your name, just tell him I told you to call. But I wouldn't rush to do it. We're still working hard on this, and I'm sure we'll come up with more information."

After ending the call, Jerome started to punch in the number Dalway had given him. It would be good to talk to someone who had had experience with Levi Moon, someone who might be able to explain why Jerome was so uneasy in his presence, despite the fact that there was nothing on the surface to explain the doubts or unease. The man had obviously spent money to enhance his appearance with plastic surgery, but that wasn't unusual for older men, these days. His clothes were expensive, and so was the Indian jewelry he wore. Levi Moon was always pleasant. He spent a lot of time with Mother, sitting vigil over John, and had performed some of his own prayer ceremonies in John's room, under Jerome's close observation. They seemed innocuous enough, and totally ineffective. At least it kept his mother busy.

But Jerome was angry that Moon didn't want members of their own local medicine society to see John, and he had convinced Mother to go along with him. He did this by encouraging her to talk about the past, when John first started his businesses on the reservation, and there were many disputes and bad feelings about what he was doing. The leaders then opposed John's gas and smoke shops. Mother, of course, supported everything John did, and turned her back on her own relatives when they sided with the leadership. For years, they were estranged, but as time passed, attitudes changed on both sides, and in the past few years Mother had renewed her family relationships. But talking to Moon seemed to draw the old grudges to the surface, and Mother had shut out her relatives, and the traditional community, again. She wouldn't talk to anyone. She put all her trust in Moon.

Jerome put the phone down. He didn't want to talk about all this now, with another stranger. He stood, and started to pace the room. Why was he hesitating to do what he knew he had to do? Mother — and, he suspected, Loraine — believed Levi Moon was helping John with his herbs and his smoke and his prayers. And even Jerome had to admit that sometimes John's spasms subsided a bit when Moon was doing his thing around the hospital bed set up in John's suite. At Jerome's absolute insistence, John was still receiving regular nursing care and daily physical therapy. Moon promised Mother that he'd have John awake, and sitting up, soon. She believed he could do it. Would she ever forgive Jerome if he sent away her only hope?

Feeling hemmed in, Jerome left the house. He needed to be outdoors, so he could think under the open sky. He started on the hilly path that led to the clearing where Levi Moon was camped. As he walked the dirt trail through the woods, he surveyed the treetops, looking for signs of the decay that was afflicting the sugar maples. He heard a faint rustling, and turned in time to see the shifts of color that indicated a doe, followed by two youngsters, was retreating further into the woods. He stopped walking, and leaned against the wide trunk of an ancient oak.

Rubbing his eyes, Jerome felt as though he were going crazy. What was he doing, looking for signs of the End Days, as casually as if he'd heard a report of rain and stepped outside to look at the clouds? Since John's accident, he often felt as though time had stopped, that the whole world was in stasis. Now he felt as though he and his family were going backward, back to the time of magic and prophecies. John would hate this. He didn't like looking back, though he'd never said anything negative about Jerome's decision a few years ago to get his doctorate in Native American studies. He seemed amused by it, more than anything else. He didn't know how eagerly Jerome pursued those studies, looking for guides to help him find his way. The old ways called to Jerome. He knew he could lose himself in them, and hoped that by approaching them intellectually he wouldn't succumb to pure belief, and be lost in the modern world. He only wanted to know what was important to remember, to pass on to the children, without holding them, or himself, back.

Now he wondered whether his studies had any purpose anymore, if maybe the End Days really had come. Maybe he was just giving up hope, for John, and himself, and the whole planet.

Jerome made himself walk on, following the path through the woods until it reached an overlook to a wide, grassy clearing near the southern end of the Lone property, not far from a county road. A large new recreational vehicle rested on the far side of the clearing. That was Levi Moon's expensive lair, resting on the bone-dry brown field. All set for a quick getaway, Jerome noted. The scene was too tranquil, the RV too much like a roving command post.

Jerome decided to keep a closer eye on Levi Moon, to keep him unsettled, to let him know he was being watched. He thought of a project he'd been wanting to do for a long time – to build a *gä-no'-sote*, a longhouse, the old way, downing trees with fire and stone, stripping them, chiseling them to fit tightly, covering the structure with bark. Hard work in the clear, fresh air. He decided to do it. Right in the middle of that clearing. He'd recruit a team of young guys from the reservation who were interested in learning about their culture. If nothing else, their activity would annoy Moon immensely, while giving Jerome the opportunity to watch his comings and goings.

Jerome ran his hand along the ridged gray bark of an ash tree. He would make sure nothing was wasted. No tree would be cut needlessly. They were too precious. But he would sacrifice a few for this project. He needed to build something, to see something grow. He wouldn't sit around and passively wait for the end of time.

CHAPTER SEVENTEEN

"Phoebe, watch out for that van," Anne cautioned. Phoebe was driving Anne's Prius coming back from Buffalo on the Youngmann Highway. It wasn't easy for Anne to relax. She was a much better driver than she was a passenger. But Phoebe had begged to drive, and Anne had gritted her teeth and let her.

"Anne, calm down already," Phoebe said in a steady voice.

Anne wondered if Phoebe had even seen the van as it sped past their car and then cut sharply in front of them to get on the exit lane for the south Grand Island bridge.

Phoebe glanced at her and laughed. "You're worse than my father. Admit I'm a good driver. I don't panic."

"I don't panic, either," Anne said. "If I'm driving."

"That was a NewsEye van that passed us," Phoebe said. "I wonder if they're on a story."

Anne relaxed after they crossed the busy, narrow bridge and were driving straight across Grand Island. She and Phoebe were having a good time on their annual Labor Day weekend ritual of shopping for school. They'd successfully scoured two malls. She was relieved that Phoebe seemed to be eager to get back to school, though not so eager to go back home. But it was going well, so far. She was experimenting with a new look, less casual clothes and more style. Anne even bought her a suitcase for an upcoming class trip Phoebe told her about.

"Wow, there's another TV truck coming up fast." Phoebe

watched it in the rearview mirror. The van quickly caught up to them and raced past. Anne turned off the satellite music and tuned in to WBFO.

After a moment, the announcer said: "Here's an update on that bulletin from Niagara Falls. Rescue vehicles and helicopters are speeding to the Falls, where one of the Niagara Thunder tour boats is floundering in rapids below the Horseshoe Falls. The boat is carrying a sold-out load of passengers on one of its regular runs close to the thundering cataracts."

"Oh, my God!" Anne cried. Phoebe's eyes got wide.

"The Niagara Thunder boats are one of the most popular new tourist attractions at Niagara Falls," the announcer continued. "Crowds are especially heavy today because of the holiday weekend."

"Step on it, Phoebe!" Anne ordered. Both women were pushed back against their seats by the momentum of Phoebe's acceleration.

"This is incredible," Anne said. "But what do you expect? The Canadians took the contract away from the old Maid of the Mist operators last year and sold it to the company that runs Alcatraz tours. They brought in a bunch of new computer-operated boats. The old Maid of the Mist boats never had an accident in more than a hundred years. Now this happens."

"I'm glad I'm not working today," Phoebe said. "Everyone will be freaking out."

"Not only are those new boats run by computers," Anne continued, as if she hadn't heard Phoebe, "but they don't even let you experience the falls. Do you remember how in the old boats you could stand on the deck and get all wet? Remember we had so much fun doing that when you were younger?"

"I remember."

"Well, these new boats are all enclosed, so people don't wear the plastic slickers anymore to keep dry. They only see the falls through windows and on video screens inside."

"That sounds like a good idea," Phoebe commented.

"Really?" Anne was surprised. "Didn't you like to experience the falls naturally? That's a big part of the fun."

"I'd definitely go for the new boats. Who wants to get wet?"

Anne decided not to debate the question.

"Wow, everybody's rushing now," Phoebe observed, keeping up with the flow of Thruway traffic. It slowed to a crawl on the north Grand Island bridge, because most cars were getting off on the Robert Moses exit to head directly to the Falls. Anne directed Phoebe to Buffalo Avenue, which cut through the middle of the old industrial district that bordered the river. Traffic was lighter there. Phoebe raced to Cataract Lane and screeched the car to a halt at Anne's house. They grabbed their packages and rushed up the back stairs into Anne's apartment.

Anne heard a loud thump as Ben jumped off his napping spot on her bed. "Come on, Ben." She grabbed his leash. "Let's go see what's happening."

"I'll see if Leonard and Mari are downstairs," Phoebe called to Anne. "I'll meet you on the front porch."

Soon the four humans and dog were hurrying along the river path toward Goat Island. Leonard was way ahead, running, with Phoebe trying to keep up with him. A huge rescue helicopter flew above and past them, following the river, the chop of its blades almost drowned out in the roar of water, sirens, and crowds. All the paths and roads were jammed with people flocking to Goat Island to watch the disaster unfold.

Anne lost the others in the crowd when Ben, out of habit, stopped to crap at the Knobby Tree. "Oh, Ben, not now!" she begged, as her dog leisurely circled and pawed at his selected spot. "Hurry up!"

When he was finished, Anne ran to catch up with the others, but she soon gave up hope of finding them in the crowd. The police had the bridges blocked off to cars, but were still allowing people to walk across. On Goat Island, Anne abandoned the path and cut across the wide lawn and then through the sparse remnant of old woods to get to Terrapin Point, the American overlook for the Horseshoe Falls.

She was breathless and Ben was panting by the time they had crossed the island. When she reached the front of the tourist center and saw the terraced slope that led down to the edge of the gorge, she was dismayed to see a throng of people rushing to the railing to watch the crisis unfold. The tightest crush was in the area just at the edge of the brink; from there, people could view the tumultuous basin at the foot of the Horseshoe Falls, almost two hundred feet straight down, at the bottom of the rocky gorge.

Huge clouds of white mist, churned up by the falls and four rescue helicopters, swirled out of the Horseshoe's basin and fell like rain on the crowd. Two smaller helicopters buzzed like flies around the larger ones — they were news helicopters with bright logos on their sides. The roar of the water, the din of the crowd, the piercing wail of sirens, and the metallic chop of the helicopters merged into a barrier of sound that Anne could actually feel. Ben whimpered.

"There's no way we're going to get to see anything," Anne told the dog, kneeling down to caress his ears to calm him, and herself. Then she noticed, a few yards down the slope, a white television satellite van, sticking out like a covered wagon in the midst of a buffalo herd. It was parked illegally on the grassy slope, apparently swamped when its crew tried to cut through the mob. Two videographers were making the best of their situation by interviewing people for reactions to the event.

A reporter and technician were watching live camera shots, fed from the NewsEye helicopter above, on a video monitor set up on a tripod next to the truck. Anne pushed her way through the crowd to join a cluster of people gathered around it. Onscreen, they could barely see through the mist a small, electric-blue boat leaning precariously to one side, bobbing up and down in dangerously hard jumps, as it was throttled by tremendous waves at the base of the Horseshoe. It looked as though cable lifelines from the helicopters were all that kept the small vessel from tipping over completely.

"It's one of the new boats, isn't it?" Anne asked no one in particular.

"Of course it is," a man replied.

"Anyone could see this coming," another man offered. "No computer can handle the Falls."

"Did any passengers fall in the water?" Anne asked.

"Yeah," the reporter replied. "One of the windows shattered and several people were thrown out of the boat. We don't know how many yet. They're still in the water."

"It doesn't look good," an observer said. "They'll be lucky to find the bodies."

"What happened, do they know?" Anne asked.

"Not yet," said the reporter. "We interviewed a tourist who said he was shooting video of the boat from Terrapin Point, and saw the front end dip down suddenly. Then the boat shot up again and started spinning. It took almost an hour to stabilize it, with those cables from the helicopters. The Canadians are diverting more water into the power intake tunnels, to cut down on the force of water going over the falls, but other boats haven't been able to get near enough to rescue any of the passengers yet, or move the boat. It's crazy."

"They never should have gone to those new boats," a man behind Anne said. "Which one is it, did they say?"

"*Marilyn*," the reporter said. "Come on, baby," he encouraged the bobbing vessel on the screen. "Hold on."

Anne remembered then. The new boats had been christened *Marilyn* and *Diana*, in honor of the two most glamorous women who had ever visited Niagara Falls. Marilyn Monroe spent weeks at the falls in the 1950s filming the movie *Niagara*. Anne herself experienced the excitement of Princess Diana's visit in the early nineteen-nineties – the princess had even ridden on one of the old Maid of the Mist boats to see the falls close-up with her boys. She felt a sudden chill as she thought about the sad deaths of both women. She knew it wasn't rational, but felt it was tempting fate to give those names to boats that sail in dangerous waters, just for some marketing campaign.

The crowd around the TV truck pressed closer to the screen. One of the TV crew members had an earphone and announced reports to the crowd as he received them by radio. "They finished attaching a cable from the lead helicopter to *Marilyn's* bow. They're going to try to tow her ... They're having trouble with the helicopter formation.

They're getting too close to each other. They've ordered the news helicopters to move back."

The viewers could see the result of that order on the monitor, as the news crews in the helicopter and on the ground adjusted to more distant shots of the action.

"*Hiawatha* is in position to rescue the people in the water as soon as they move *Marilyn* out."

"That's one of the old boats," a crowd member contributed. "They're still running on this side of the gorge."

"The copter's starting to tow *Marilyn*. She's moving now. Come on, baby!" the reporter yelled.

The din grew as people shouted encouragement to the rescuers, and to the helicopters, and to *Marilyn*. Anne's group crushed even closer to the video monitor, in spite of the fact that it was impossible to see what was actually happening in the water, since thick clouds of mist obscured the action.

Anne stared at the screen full of white mist until she felt her eyes blur and her head ache. Her shirt was pasted to her back as the crowd's crush added its own heat to the hot and muggy temperature. Finally, someone yelled, "She's free! They're moving her away from the rapids!"

For some moments, Anne knelt and held her hands over Ben's ears as people whooped and cheered. Onscreen, the crowd could see, first, the black cables emerging from the mist, then *Marilyn's* blue bow, then all of *Marilyn*, leaning hard on her right side, as she was slowly towed back to her home dock on the Canadian side of the river.

The on-air reporter shouted, "Let's go!" to his crew. They grabbed their cameras and started questioning people in the crowd for their eager reactions to the drama on the river.

"Did they say anything about the people in the water?" Anne asked, but everyone was too busy to answer.

She bent down and caressed Ben, who was huddled as small as he could make himself near her feet. "Poor Ben, you've been a good boy. Come on, let's go."

The dog cautiously rose to his feet. They pushed their way against the crowd, along the path toward the Three Sisters islands. Anne felt cold now, thinking about the people in the frigid water of the Horseshoe's swirling cauldron. Crossing the stone bridge to Asenath, the first island, she glanced briefly to her left at the Hermit's Cascade, where a smooth flow of water tumbled over a low, rocky ledge. They continued to Angeline, the largest, middle Sister.

Anne had never been absolutely alone on the Three Sisters in the middle of the day before. Every other human being on Goat Island was squeezed into the mob scene at Terrapin Point. "It's all ours, Ben," she told her panting companion. Throwing caution to the winds, she led Ben under the one of the railings and took him to one of his old favorite places, on the far shore, where shallow water flowed swiftly through the channel between Angeline and Celinda Eliza, the island most in the raging torrent. Keeping a strong grip on Ben's extendable leash, she let him splash happily in the cold water, which he eagerly lapped.

Anne's knees felt wobbly. She sat on a huge boulder, worn smooth by flowing water, appreciating the coolness of the deep shade. Closing her eyes, she tried to calm down, but could think only of the fate of the human beings who had just been flung into the unknowable depths of one of the most powerful rivers on the planet. The waters of four inland seas pour over the Horseshoe before they push into the narrow stone chasm of the Niagara gorge. Trapped, the waters surge on in whitewater rapids, until they turn back on themselves in a dervish dance three miles downriver, in the deadly Whirlpool.

Keeping a distracted eye on Ben, Anne wondered again why the new boats were named for ill-fated women. Nothing was too crass or insensitive anymore. In the movie *Niagara*, the human Marilyn did a famous, hip-swiveling walk as she hurried to meet her lover at Table Rock. The movie's ads compared the power of Marilyn's sex appeal to that of the raging Horseshoe Falls. Her mind racing, Anne wondered whether, when Marilyn took the pills and felt her life slipping away, did she go peacefully? Or did her fading spirit take her back to Niagara Falls, to hear its roar, as she plunged into oblivion?

A fearsome noise overhead made Anne jump. Ben froze. They

instinctively ducked as one of the rescue helicopters passed right over them, skimming the treetops. As its roar faded, she thought she heard a rustling in the bushes behind her. Fearing she would see the Hermit looming over her with an expression of homicidal rage on his face, she quickly turned around. Her nerves were on edge. But she was still alone.

"Come on, Ben." She pulled the leash until the dog sadly left his pool and followed her. As they walked home, Anne couldn't stop imagining the accident scene. *Marilyn's* passengers didn't have a chance once they were in the river. Stunned to unconsciousness by the icy, battering waves, the people would be quickly sucked under water, where the currents would have their way with them, pulling them down, down, down, toward the deep, rocky bottom, then bouncing them up again, and carrying them along, dozens of feet under the waves, into the abyss of the Whirlpool. Once inside the maelstrom, there is no escape. The river keeps its inexorable grip on its victims, some of whom it never gives up.

As Anne hurried home, pulling her exhausted dog along, she felt as though all the air around her was full of furies.

CHAPTER EIGHTEEN

It was only a scroungy stray dog, but Leonard tried to see the spirit of the wolf in it as they ran side by side on the shoulder of busy Porter Road. He liked to run long distances, not for competitions, but in the spirit of the renowned Haudenosaunee runners. If he blocked out the reality around him – pavement, cars, noise, industrial smells – he could imagine himself as a runner along the ancient trails. They ate a special white corn that gave them endurance. Grandfather told him the runners could journey from the Hudson River to the Western Door at Niagara – almost three hundred miles – in three days. Their narrow trails were like highways to the People of the Longhouse, who traveled under an almost unending canopy of massive trees: oaks, maples, chestnuts, walnuts, cedars, white pines, sycamores, ash, willows. The trails followed rivers and streams but also cut across stretches of land to reach their destinations efficiently. That network was the original Indian Internet.

The downside, as his Uncle Clint liked to say, was that the Iroquois trails were so fine that it didn't take long for the invaders to find, and use, them. The trails led the white man into the heart of Haudenosaunee lands and all the way to the Great Lakes. If not for those trails, the white man would have stumbled around lost in the forests and hills of eastern New York for decades longer, Clint told Leonard. That would have given the Indians more time to find out just what sort of people they were, and to build defenses against them. Most of all, the Indians would learn how untrustworthy they were, and that they would tell any lie to get hold of land.

Unfortunately, like all predators, the white man sniffed out the easy way to his prey. He built his roads right over the trails, and his settlements near Haudenosaunee towns ravaged in 1779 under the orders of George Washington. But they kept the names, or their garbled versions of them – Niagara, Tonawanda, Scajaquada, Chautauqua, Canandaigua, Oswego, Cayuga, Susquehanna, Chemung, Schenectady, Schoharie, Skaneateles, Ticonderoga, Oriskany, Tioga, Canastota, Cheektowaga, Chittenango, Canoga, Geneseo. Leonard matched his strides to the rhythm of the names.

That morning, Leonard had started his run from his uncle's trailer in a mobile home park in the Town of Niagara. Clint Mountview, in his sixties, lived on veteran's disability and odd jobs. His history showed in his ravaged face and heavy body. Clint was a loner, but he always made Leonard feel welcome. He'd clear off his cluttered sofa for Leonard to sleep on, and never asked any questions about why he came, or how long he'd stay. Leonard used to stay with him for weeks sometimes, when he needed a break from his mother and her boyfriends. Leonard had just spent the night visiting with Clint. He liked his uncle, and knew that his visits cheered him up. He'd brought food from Rose, which was much appreciated.

The October morning was hot and muggy. Leonard was on his way to see Phoebe to talk about their plans, and then meet up with Wallace and Rose at the annual anti-Columbus Day rally in Prospect Park. His nose itched from the acrid smell of diesel and chemicals in the air, wafting on the wind from the massive OHARAS landfill, the toxic waste dump about a half-mile away from the trailer park. Leonard remembered the night Clint told him about Vietnam. Clint had been drinking hard, the way he did when he wanted to find oblivion. He kept talking, even though Leonard pretended he was asleep so Clint would stop remembering, and crying. Clint told him when he was in Vietnam, he smelled things no living being should have to smell. So he stopped smelling. That was why he didn't mind living next to the

OHARAS dump. He said life was easier now.

Stopping for a breath, Leonard tied his red tee shirt around his waist so he could run bare-chested. He hated Columbus, the slave-master and thief. To the first peoples, this was a day for tears. Leonard had spent the previous evening on Clint's computer, visiting Indian websites that told what Columbus' "discovery" of them had brought: disease, slavery, conquest. Clint told him not to dwell on that stuff too much, because it would make him hate, and then he'd be just like a white man.

Leonard tried not to hate as his rubber soles bounced off hard pavement laid on top of the ancient trails. Columbus' modern legacy was asphalt, litter, cheap ugly buildings, and, towering over all, that mountain of toxic waste, the OHARAS dump. Clint had a good view of it from his front door, where he could watch it grow, slowly, inexorably, like a gigantic anthill.

Leonard had his own network of trails. Some of them followed exactly the ancient trails Grandfather had shown him on a map in the library. He tried to match them as he ran to meet Phoebe downtown; she was having lunch with Nick Valli to get updated about the prize trip to Las Vegas and the New Year's Eve event. She had to play the role, she told him, even though she wasn't going to be in the pageant. They didn't have many chances to see each other. Phoebe said they should "lay low," and not be seen together, so people wouldn't get suspicious. She was even working to improve her grades, so no one would suspect she had a plan.

Leonard thought about the trip as he ran. He wanted desperately to head out west, to see what it was like in wide, open spaces. He would see country that wasn't all covered over with too many people, too many roads, too many mocking remnants of how it used to be, before the white man came. Maybe there he could feel the ancient roots that bound his ancestors to Mother Earth.

When Leonard left Clint's trailer, near the railroad tracks just north of the old Porter Road, he ran for almost a mile to the city park. That's where the gray dog abandoned a pile of litter and joined him. He liked running on open grass, and enjoyed the stretch along Hyde Park Lake and Gill Creek. Grandfather said he used to fish in Gill Creek on the reservation, before Robert Moses changed the landscape. When he reached the south end of the park, Leonard crossed Pine Avenue and Hyde Park Boulevard to stay on grass along the creek. The gray dog left him to run down an alley.

Leonard turned down Niagara Street. Patches of the long street were rundown, with boarded-up old family beer gardens and stores; some businesses thrived, and many of the houses were still kept up. When he reached Portage Road, he turned left on it just to run for two blocks along the most famous Iroquois trail of all, the ancient land route around the cataracts at Niagara. At East Falls Street, he turned right for the last mile of his run. The big stone church with Polish words carved above its doorways marked the end of the older city. Ahead of him now was an empty stretch of land, once a thriving immigrant neighborhood, that ended at the back entrance of the tall, glistening Seneca casino.

Leonard had another test he made up for himself, a personal game of roulette, but one which had more dangerous consequences than just losing money. Outside the back entrance to the casino, he caught his breath, and pulled on his tee shirt. He waited for people to come out of the parking lot, and then walked into the lofty, air-conditioned lobby with a small group. For a while, he pretended to look at the art on the walls, edging closer to the big podiums that guarded the entry to the casino itself. Being underage, he wasn't allowed in.

He waited until a bus group of old people was going through the entry; one was in a wheelchair. While the security guards' attention was diverted, he scooted through and ran zig-zagged through the casino floor, to get to the main entrance directly on the opposite side of the building. A curved, carpeted aisle led him toward a stained-glass vista of a sun setting over pine trees. He ducked behind slot machines as a guard ran after him. When he got to the other end, the big guard there had already been alerted to the presence of an intruder, and was watching for him. Leonard hid behind a bank of slots and waited for his moment to rush out. That came when a busload of tourists lined up at the guards' station. Leonard ducked and crept forward, against the tide of gamblers. He managed to stay out of the guard's line of site until he was almost past the sentry. The guard did spot him, but would have had to push people aside to get to him. Leonard was quick and scooted through. The guard chased him until he got outside, but gave up quickly because of the heat. Leonard kept running with a grin on his face. That was the second time he'd done this. He knew he'd have to wait a while before trying it again.

He found the outdoor café where he was supposed to meet Phoebe. He looked right past her before she laughed and called, "Wolf, it's me!" She was sitting at a small round table only two yards away. He stared at her. She really was Ani again.

"You have to get one of these energy floats, Wolf," she told him when he sat down. "My treat. I just had the most fabulous lunch with Nick. Did you run all the way here from your uncle's? Awesome." Phoebe waved the waitress over and ordered a strawberry float for him. Her transformation was unsettling. With her hair extensions pinned tight on the top of her head, lots of makeup, fancy sunglasses, and a short, tight dress, she didn't look in the least like regular Phoebe. She looked like a supermodel. Even her personality totally changed.

"Why are you staring at me?" She giggled nervously.

"It's kind of magical. The way you change yourself."

She looked pleased. "Do you want to know what Nick told me?"

"What?"

"That I'm the most popular Maid of the Mist they've ever had. He can tell just by my online hits; people are even sending me snail mail at the tourism office."

"Do you have to answer them all?"

"I just signed my name with a digital pen so they can print it on a form letter with my picture on it." She giggled. "I almost signed it Phoebe!"

He smiled. He could see her doing that.

"Then he took me to lunch at a new restaurant in his building.

He ordered wine for me. They didn't proof me. I drank some, even though I didn't really like it."

"Don't drink alcohol, Phoebe. That's poison. It fogs your brain."

"Don't worry, Wolf, I know. I poured most of it in a plant when he went to the men's room. But it was so cool. I mean, I had lobster, for lunch!"

Leonard grunted.

She opened a small black purse, took out a mirror and lipstick, and checked her makeup. "Then Nick drove me around Goat Island for a while. He says he's going to meet me at the airport when we get to Las Vegas, in a limousine. He says I'm definitely a real contender to win the pageant in Las Vegas. A fresh young talent. That's what he said."

"Are you starting to like this?"

"What?"

"Being Ani."

Her eyes darted behind her sunglasses. "Well, it's just different, you know? I'm having fun with it. Finally, someone appreciates me. But I'll know when to quit. Don't worry. I'm definitely going to go into the desert with you."

The waitress put Leonard's drink in front of him and he gulped it down. He hadn't realized how thirsty he'd been.

"You know, Wolf," Phoebe remarked, "I know we shouldn't have a Columbus Day, because he was a genocidal maniac and all, and he really didn't discover anything that wasn't already there, but I'm still glad we have the day off from school." She stretched her legs out in front of her, and yawned.

Leonard was amazed at how Phoebe's thoughts never wandered far from her head. Sometimes he wished he could rein in his thoughts, to keep them from wandering into places where he found hot anger. He could control his thoughts best when he ran. Seeing her excitement made him even more eager for their trip. Phoebe was making it possible. He could not have done what she did – turn himself into another person, not for anybody. She said it was fun to reinvent herself. He was amazed at how completely she accomplished it. But so far there seemed to be no permanent change. He was glad of that.

"I have to go now, Wolf," Phoebe said. "I have to get home before my parents do and change back into myself. My father would die if he saw me like this. He'd jump over the falls." She motioned the waitress for the bill, and left money on the table. She stood precariously in her high heels. She slipped a couple of times on the cobbled pavement, and, like a cat, pretended she didn't.

Leonard walked her to her car; Phoebe was prey when she looked like this. Men's heads turned. He was relieved when she drove off.

He walked to Prospect Park and made his way through a mass of people congealed around a stage set up near the statue of Chief Clinton Rickard. Onstage, four men sat around a wide drum, beating it, singing. A stringy circle of protest marchers made its way around the statue. Their signs read: "*We* discovered *Columbus*." "No more genocide!" "Free Leonard Peltier." "Honor the Treaties." "Stop Climate Change."

Leonard noticed police officers watching the crowd. Some onlookers were hostile. A heavy-set man in biker clothes yelled repeatedly, "Where's the cavalry?" as he waved a small American flag. A short, intense older man, yelling about "sovereign nations," inserted himself in front of the picket line, so that the demonstrators had to walk around him. Two officers moved in when one man rushed onstage, shouting, "You should pay taxes like the rest of us, dammit!" He fought the police as they pulled him off the platform. "Enough of your free ride!" he kept yelling. "Pay your goddam taxes!"

Leonard saw these angry white men with twisted faces at every rally. Things had gotten worse lately. The economy was still bad, especially in places like Niagara Falls. People wanted to tax the Indians, breaking old treaties again. There was even a new line of attack: Congress wanted to form a commission to "renegotiate" all the Indian treaties. Leonard knew that Indians never came out ahead when that happened.

He wandered around the edge of the crowd, looking for Wallace and Rose. The drums stopped, and a young woman, wearing a bright ribbon dress and leggings, started talking about the statue nearby, which depicted Wallace's old friend, Chief Clinton Rickard. The Tuscarora chief was famous for his long battles for native rights both in the United States and Canada; his statue depicted him wearing a feathered headdress, a gift from Western Indians, and holding a wampum belt. He had led the fight in the twentieth-century for the native peoples to have free access across the arbitrary border between Canada and the United States.

Leonard wondered what he would ever fight for, or against, as he walked away from the stage to Prospect Point, to check out the cave. The dark hole under Luna Island was unchanged. The mist from the American Falls rose in a thin column, defeated by the heat. After examining the scene, he sauntered back to the rally, where his Grandfather was now speaking. He pushed his way to the front of the stage.

Pointing toward the bronze statue of his friend, Grandfather was saying, "My friend Clinton Rickard is honored here, near the border of two great countries, because the Indian Defense League of America, which he founded, united the native Americans on this continent, and fought many injustices. His spirit lives on in us, and we cannot give up our struggle." He hesitated; Leonard thought he looked tired as his eyes searched the crowd. But he continued:

"Ro-wa-da-ga-hra-de. It means Loud Voice. That was the name the clan mothers gave to Clinton Rickard. I will leave you with his words: 'The Great Spirit did not create men to destroy each other. ... Our hand is open in friendship. We do not seek hostility. We do not want to be forced into it. But we are determined to protect our rights. My experience through more than eighty years has taught me that people of good will of all races can work together to bring about justice for all and the betterment of mankind. May the Great Spirit help us all.'"

Wallace walked off the stage. The drumming resumed. Leonard made his way to the back of the stage to find him, and take him home.

CHAPTER NINETEEN

Anne sat on the front steps of her house, waiting for Quin, while Ben sniffed and peed around the bushes. They'd kept in touch during the first busy weeks of the semester, and met for quick lunches on campus a couple of times; they mostly talked about her technology. She was finally ready to accept his offer to set up a new wireless network at her home and sync all her devices. There was attraction between them that she found energizing. She knew this was a big step, inviting him to her house. He was a few years younger than she was, but so what? They were going to have a Columbus Day picnic, and then he'd work on her hardware.

Quin arrived in a battered green Jeep Cherokee, a bit late from holiday bridge traffic. After parking in front of her house, he stared at the tall maples whose branches arched over the narrow street, and the two majestic oaks that stood at the end of Anne's front walk. The air rumbled. A thin column of white mist rose in the distance above the treetops.

"What a great street," he said, as he turned in a full circle while walking up the flagstones to greet Anne. He rubbed Ben's head as the dog barked and jumped on him. "The river is right over there. And that white column is the falls?"

"Yes."

"Awesome." He whistled as they entered the foyer, which was bathed in gold and lavender as sunlight streamed through the stained-glass window on the stair landing. The pedestal table in the center of the hallway held an antique porcelain bowl filled with sunflowers and autumn oak leaves. "Is this whole house yours?"

"Yes, but it has two flats. I rent out the first floor."

Quin walked to the wall and peered closely at the paneling, running his hand along the grain. "What kind of wood is this?"

"American chestnut."

"Wow. You can't get that anymore."

"I know."

He stroked the wood banister as they walked up the staircase. Anne quickly collected the lunch she had packed, and the three of them soon emerged from the house, Ben trotting happily on his leash. They found a clear space on the lawn above Prospect Point, just across the street from the Turtle, and sat down on Anne's blanket.

A steady stream of people passed by, along the river's edge, while they ate cold roast beef sandwiches on rye bread. Anne never tired of watching the crowds around the falls.

"You must come here every day," Quin remarked. "It's like watching a parade."

"I do, and it is," Anne replied. "I've been watching it all my life, it seems. The cameras get smaller, and the fashions change, but the people don't, not in any deep way. It's odd, the compulsion to travel, maybe all the way around the world, to see Niagara Falls. I mean, what is it but lots of water falling over a cliff? And yet, even though it's surrounded by pavement and casinos, it's still one of the most beautiful sights in the world. And we're only seeing half of it, at most, because of the diversion for the power plants. Imagine if they ever let it flow at full blast!"

"Tesla got inspired just by seeing a picture of it when he was a kid. He imagined the falls turning a big wheel, making power. And thirty years later, he came here and did it."

"I still say that wasn't necessarily a good thing, for the falls, at least." Anne bit into her sandwich.

Quin laughed. "They still come, Anne. They still come."

They finished eating and tossed their trash. They walked to Prospect Point and looked out over the brink. Some bulldozers had been moved to Luna Island, near the rockfall.

"I wish they'd decide what to do about that cave-in," Anne remarked, as they stood at the railing, enjoying the cool mist blown over them by a light breeze. The jagged brown gash destroyed the symmetry of the waterfall. She didn't like this ugly reminder that some day – not in her lifetime, hopefully, but some day – the majestic falls would erode, and collapse into a long series of mundane rapids.

"I wish I could get into that cave," Quin said. "It's gotta be awesome."

"No you don't." Anne laughed. "Mari says that's where the evil spirits live."

"Cool." He grinned. "Gateway to Hell. One of my favorite video games."

They turned and walked against the river's flow toward Cataract Lane. At the pedestrian bridge, Ben got assertive, and started pulling to go on the island. He whimpered when Anne tried to restrain him. "Want to keep walking?" she asked Quin.

"Sure." He took Ben's leash and followed him across the bridge.

As they walked along the hot path, Anne couldn't resist bringing up a constant topic of her preservation group. "Did you know that once this island was as famous as the waterfalls? It was a primeval garden, with unique plant species that grew only here, in the mist, between the two cataracts. It was covered with huge old trees. And look at it now." She pointed to the large parking lot, filled with RV's, at the tip of the island. "What kind of a twisted mind would put that obscenity of a parking lot there?"

Quin smirked. "An engineer's."

"Exactly my point. Robert Moses. *He* ruined everything. Even more than Tesla."

"It's progress, Anne." When she gave him a sharp look, Quin shrugged. "I'm not saying it's good, just that it's inevitable. The human species is voracious." Anne looked away from him.

149

Terrapin Point was crowded with tourists, and they had to press their way to the railing. A perfect rainbow spanned the wide gorge, brilliant against the deep blue sky. Its Canadian foot was rooted in brown scum that collected against the bank of the old power plant built into the gorge wall; its American foot nestled in the cascading waters near Luna Island. A small boat, far below, chugged its way against the waves.

"They're not using the computerized boats anymore, not since the Labor Day accident," Anne commented. "They're only letting the old Maid of the Mist boats go near the falls."

"Yeah, I heard they're reprogramming them. They never found all the bodies, did they?"

"No. Only four out of seven."

"Pete says they'll turn up eventually, out in the lake."

"Probably." Anne straightened up. "Let's go, okay?"

"Sure."

Strolling across the western end of the island, Quin suddenly cried out, "There's my man!" He strode up to Tesla's huge bronze statue, which showed him seated, with his head bowed, looking at a document. A stone arch nearby, designed by his friend Stanford White, was all that remained of the Niagara powerhouse that once sheltered his transformational generators.

"Tesla!" Quin announced. "The man who started it all!"

"My friend Mari – she's an artist – really dislikes the style of this statue," Anne told him. "She calls it Red Nikola, because she thinks it looks like Soviet art, like those awful statues of Lenin that were torn down when the Cold War ended. And it's a very passive image, considering that Tesla electrified the world." Anne paused, and walked up to the statue's pedestal. "My mother told me she brought me here as a baby when the statue was dedicated. It was a gift from the people of Yugoslavia, and there was an identical statue in the small village there where Tesla grew up. But the statue was purposely blown up during the Balkan wars in the nineties, Emily told me, and now there's no more statue there, and no more Yugoslavia, either."

150

Quin didn't take his eyes off Tesla's sharp profile. "What would be cool would be to have a statue of Tesla standing in front of one of his coils, and have it electrified, so that it would be giving off sparks, like in one of his demonstrations, when he would send about half a million volts coursing along his whole body. Yeah, that would be cool."

"You must have studied him at MIT."

"I did an undergraduate paper on him. He held landmark patents in electricity, just about all of the early ones. He believed electricity was a life force, that it had healing powers. He was a theoretical genius, a true visionary. He even invented the radio. But he got fucked. Edison, Morgan, Astor, even Westinghouse. They rolled right over him. Because he had honor. Because he wanted to keep inventing, not just take the money and run. They took his ideas and his patents and stiffed him on royalties. He made them rich, and he died broke. Fucking typical."

"Everyone knows he was a genius, but he was out of touch with reality," Anne said. "My friend Mari even has this crazy New Age book that says he was too smart to be human, that he was really an alien who was sent here to bring humans a new technology. That's absurd, of course."

Quin threw his head back and laughed. He jumped on the pedestal and put his hand on Tesla's shoulder. Tourists moved in to take pictures and video.

"Tesla was no alien!" Quin announced. A young Asian man wearing a bright red Cornell tee shirt held up his phone to take a video. "He was an Earth-born genius, and, like all true geniuses, he worshipped his art, which, in his case, was science." Quin jumped down. "You see, Anne, the thing that makes him seem so strange to people is that he didn't do it for the money. He should have been a billionaire from the Niagara generator patents alone, but he ripped up his original deal with Westinghouse just to save his friend's company and keep the research going. Imagine that! You can't, can you?"

"Yes, I can," she retorted. "I like to think that I'd do that, if it came to it, sacrifice something I really wanted, for a principle."

He grinned. "Don't let them own your mind."

They continued their walk. Anne tried not to step on any of the fuzzy brown-banded caterpillars falling from the trees onto the walkway. After a while, she started to feel prickly, as though someone were watching her. She turned suddenly and saw him, off the path behind a tree, a few yards away – the Hermit. She stopped. Their eyes met. After a moment, the Hermit slowly backed away until he was hidden behind trees.

"Who was that?" Quin asked.

"Don't ask, it's a long story," she replied; the heat was making her cranky.

Off the island, along the river path, the white-tipped rapids rushed at them in an endless frenzy. By the time they reached Anne's house, their faces were streaked with sweat. Anne was hot, and tired, and unsure of the next step. "Are you getting hungry again?" she asked, to bridge the awkward moment. "Maybe we should go out for something to eat."

"I could use something to drink. And a bathroom."

She led him into her house and pointed him in the direction of the guest bathroom. After filling Ben's bowl with fresh water, she went into her own bathroom and rinsed off her face and arms with cold water. Staring in the mirror as she dried herself, she ordered, "Don't do anything stupid. Don't get into a situation you'll regret."

Returning to the kitchen, she found Quin sitting in a chair, rubbing Ben's head. "Man, I worked up a good sweat," he said.

"I know, it's amazingly hot, even for Indian Summer. What would you like to drink?"

"Just water."

She pulled two bottles out of the refrigerator, and each of them finished one quickly. He said, "I saw a little porch when I drove up. Can I see it from inside, the view?"

"Okay." She hesitated. "Why don't we have some chilled wine out there before you start on my computers?" She grabbed a bottle from the refrigerator and two glasses before leading him and Ben quickly through her bedroom.

Quin sat on the railing and looked in the direction of the falls, whose thin column of mist still stood sentry. Anne filled the glasses, and handed one to him.

"To Tesla," she proposed, clinking Quin's glass. "To Tesla and obstinate idealism."

He grinned, and took a deep gulp.

Anne sank into her wicker rocker. The autumn sun's slanted rays cast shadows through the tree branches. She noticed that her maples had a lot of dead branches near the top. She hoped it would rain soon. They could hear the incessant song of the rapids, dancing toward the column of mist and their doom.

Quin sat in the other chair, and put his legs up on the railing. "Man, this is such a cool house. It's weird that they'd have a little porch like this on the second floor."

"Not really," Anne told him. "In Victorian times, people thought that sleeping in the night air was good for their health. They'd sleep out on these porches. The mist of the falls was supposed to have healthy properties. Hustlers even sold bottles of Niagara water to cure diseases. Can you imagine what it must have been like to sleep out here back then?"

"Damp."

Anne smiled. They sat quietly, sipping the wine, watching the shadows deepen. Ben, sleeping next to Anne's chair, suddenly started to twitch and whimper. "He's dreaming." She reached down to stroke his head. Quin reached down, too, and ran his hand along the dog's back.

"There's this story about Tesla." Quin's arm moved slowly back and forth. "When he was a kid, in the winter in Yugoslavia. They were having a deep freeze, when it was below zero for days and days. The cold sucked all the moisture out of the air, and it was really dry, and everything was giving off sparks, you know, like when you rub your feet on a wool rug?"

Anne watched the muscles ripple under the skin of Quin's forearm as he stroked the dog. She nodded.

"Tesla had this pet cat, and when he stroked it, sitting in front of the fire, sparks flew off, and he thought, 'Is nature a cat? And if it is, who strokes its back?'"

"Was he talking about God, Quin? Or science?"

He looked at her, and their eyes locked onto each other. His hand moved slowly from Ben's back to Anne's arm, still gently stroking. His hand felt hot as his fingers glided just above her skin. "Look," he whispered. "Electricity." Glancing down, Anne saw the fair hairs on her arm stand up as his hand passed over. "I don't see sparks, but I feel them," she whispered.

Their eyes locked again. The energy field between them intensified. Anne knew she was engulfed in a wave of pheromones and testosterone, but she preferred to ignore the language of science and succumb to good old desire. "Let's go inside."

As soon as the door shut behind them, almost clipping Ben's tail as he scurried in, Quin wrapped his arms around Anne and covered her mouth with his, pulling her against him until her toes were off the ground. She wrapped her legs around him. He moaned. They fell onto her bed, and began to explore each other.

She'd never made love to a man years younger than herself before; her last lover had been close to fifty. Quin made love with exuberance rather than technique. When he entered her, Anne's body arched with his strong thrust. She moaned, in a deep voice, and dimly heard Ben yap. The curly red hair on Quin's chest glistened with sweat. Anne thought of water surging onward as red sparks, generated like magic, leaped from its depths. They were making energy, like Tesla's generators. They were making magic, and it was delightful, after she'd endured such a long time without it. A charge of orgasm shot through her body, and then his. He fell off her; they both lay on their backs, motionless, out of steam.

Ben whimpered, and jolted Anne when he flung himself onto his spot on the bed. She looked at Quin; his eyes were closed and he breathed deeply. Feeling immense satisfaction, she slipped out of bed and went into the bathroom to put herself back together. When she came out, Quin shook his head and woke up.

"Sorry." He rolled over heavily and got out of bed. He walked toward the bathroom; he was limping.

"What happened to your foot?" she asked.

"Ben nipped me when you moaned. It's cool." He closed the door.

Anne hid her smile. "Ben, you bad dog." She stroked his head, lying on her side, feeling every atom of her body still in erotic motion. She realized that this was what she had needed for a long time.

CHAPTER TWENTY

A pasty fog hung everywhere, signaling the end of autumn warmth and the beginning of a cold, damp winter. Anne began to question whether the fog was real or just in her head. It engulfed her from the moment she left her house for her early-morning drive to campus. The air temperature had fallen by thirty degrees overnight. The heavy mist oozed from the river, crept up its bank, and swaddled the Robert Moses Parkway. The river itself was an ominous gray sheet under a blanket of fog, and seemed to throb rather than flow. The high arches of the north Grand Island bridges looked as though they were poised over clouds.

Anne was rather relieved the cold weather was beginning to move in, finally, in early November. The world seemed normal again, after the late heat wave. Maybe her trees would perk up. She thought about her plans for the evening. Now that her big grant proposal had been submitted, she had some breathing space. She was going to pick up Quin on campus and take him home with her. They'd spent a few nights together since Columbus Day. She was surprised, and a little uneasy, about how eagerly she was looking forward to seeing him. As she drove along the flat, murky stretch of Thruway across Grand Island, her iPhone rang. She pulled onto the wide shoulder and set her emergency lights on, before answering it.

"Anne, it's Emily. We have to schedule an emergency committee meeting tonight."

"Why?"

"Did you see the morning paper?"

"No. I'm already on my way to campus."

"Listen to this: 'City officials have reached an agreement to sell the vacant Turtle building to a newly established Native American corporation for possible use for gaming purposes, according to a source in City Hall.'"

"Whaaat?!"

Emily continued reading. "'This newspaper was unable to confirm the report with city officials. Calls to the Mayor's office were not returned. Nick Valli, director of tourism, said it was premature to make any announcement about ongoing discussions with The Pickering Corporation, the name of the new enterprise. The city is hoping these discussions will lead to new enterprises that will bring economic benefit to the city, a spokesman said.'"

Anne was stunned. "But I thought some group named White Pine bought the building," she said.

"There are all sorts of stories going around," Emily said. "Listen, I'll call everyone about the meeting. Can we do it at your place? About seven?"

She was sorely tempted to say no.

"Anne! Can you hear me?"

She almost said she couldn't do it, but this was serious. "Yes, sure, Emily. See you then."

Anne felt the day got darker after that call. She presented her morning lecture in a daze, trying to concentrate. Anne saw the students' faces wrapped in mist; she couldn't focus on any of them. Later, during office hours, a young woman came in to tell Anne she was dropping out of nursing to major in health policy fiscal management. Once upon a time, Anne would have tried to change her mind. But she couldn't now. The dean's committee on transformational change for the nursing school was bogged down in a fundamental debate over the role of the nurse in a technology-driven, profit-based health care system. As she signed the student's paperwork, Anne wished her luck in her new career, in which she'd never have to assess a human being, only data.

Anne had her car lights and heater on at four o'clock when she picked Quin up in front of the engineering complex. The earlier gray drizzle had turned to slushy rain. Quin, wearing layers of flannel under a jacket, jumped into the passenger seat, emitting drops of cold water. He flung his wet backpack on the back seat.

"Hi." She tried to smile as if nothing were bothering her.

"Man, it's wet." Quin held his gloveless red hands in front of the heater vents.

"It's like we're under the falls. That's what my mother used to say on days like this."

"Well, that seems fairly accurate today."

"We have to change plans for tonight," she told him, as she drove off. "We can still have dinner, early, but then I have to have an emergency meeting of my historic preservation committee at my house, because of an announcement in the news today."

"What announcement?"

"That a Native American corporation is buying the Turtle and plans to put a casino in it."

"What's the meeting for?"

"To try to stop it.

"How can you?"

"I don't know." Anne gripped the steering wheel hard. "That building was built for a museum, not for gambling. The Turtle represents creation beliefs. It shouldn't be reduced to a money machine for some corporation."

Quin didn't comment.

"So, do you mind?" Anne asked.

"No. I've got a new voice recognition program I can install in your computer while you have your meeting."

"Wait a minute. I'm not sure I want to have conversations with my computer."

"You will. This is cool."

Quin helped Anne get ready for the meeting by taking Ben out for his walk. She pulled a homemade banana bread loaf from the freezer to defrost. Both males were soaked and cold when they returned. Quin toweled down Ben, who gobbled up his dinner and passed out in front of the gas fireplace in the parlor. Quin changed into dry clothes. They ate hot turkey sandwiches and steamed vegetables in front of the fireplace. After that, Anne made coffee and tea and got dishes ready for the meeting.

When she returned to the parlor, Anne found Quin asleep on the floor next to Ben. She thought they were starting to look alike. She let them sleep awhile longer, then shook them both awake just before seven, and sent Quin into her small office off the parlor with coffee and a cold turkey sandwich.

Emily arrived first, with an unexpected guest. She introduced him to Anne in the downstairs foyer, as they took off their wet coats and hung them on an antique oak coat rack.

"Anne, this is Chief Wallace Mountview," Emily said. "I called him today about the newspaper story and, after we talked, I thought he should come tonight."

"Chief Mountview, it's an honor to meet you," Anne told him, holding out her hand. "I've seen so many stories about you in the newspaper."

Wallace smiled. "I'm glad to meet *you*, at last, Professor Techa." He clasped her hand with a strong grip. "I've been hoping to meet you for quite a while. You and your friend Mari have been very kind to my great-grandson, Leonard."

"Leonard is a terrific kid. He's a talented artist." Anne wanted to stare into the old man's dark eyes; they seemed as mysterious as a deep, calm pool. The wrinkles in his face exaggerated every expression, especially his smile, which widened as he said, "His grandfather, my son, was an artist."

"Please come upstairs. I've got hot coffee and tea ready."

The doorbell rang. "I'll get that, Anne," Emily offered.

Steve and Jay arrived with Father Joe. Wallace and the priest greeted each other warmly; they were old friends who had worked for social justice through the years. As they were settling down in the parlor, Emily pulled Anne aside, and whispered, "Who's that in your office?"

Quin was hacking away on the keyboard, leaning forward to stare into the monitor. His hair was gathered into a disheveled ponytail. His flannel shirt hung over baggy slacks. Ben slept next to his chair with one of Quin's work boots between his front paws.

"Quin McCarthy. He's a computer guy from campus. He's installing some new software for me," Anne told her.

Emily turned away. Anne was somewhat disappointed that her friend had not the slightest suspicion there might be more to it. But then, Quin did not look like her type. Whatever that was.

After introductions, Emily recounted the facts included in the morning's newspaper article. She asked, "Wallace, can you tell the others what you've told me about the Pickering Corporation?"

Wallace leaned forward in his chair. "This corporation was organized earlier this year under another name, White Pine Enterprises, with representatives from each of the Six Nations. These representatives were not endorsed by the traditional leaderships, who are very much opposed to gambling enterprises. They are acting individually, with – we suspect – the promise of financial reward."

"Why are people from all the Six Nations involved in this?" Jay asked. "For a casino deal in Western New York, they only need to deal with the Senecas, who have the treaty rights and the agreement with the state."

"I don't know," Wallace replied. "We've been following this project for months now. Last summer, when I questioned Thomas Johnson, the Tuscarora who joined White Pine, he assured me that there would be no gambling activities, only some sort of cultural center. Then, not long ago, we heard rumors that the plans were being changed, there was a new name, and that gambling was now an option."

"I bet Nick Valli is involved in this somehow," Anne put in. "Who, exactly, is the head of the Pickering Corporation?"

"The same man who was behind White Pine Enterprises – John

Lone."

"John Lone!" Jay exclaimed. "I used to buy his gas when I went to Chautauqua. Though I heard he sold that franchise off ages ago, and went into investments."

"Yes, that's true," Wallace confirmed. "We've been trying to set up a meeting with him. He was in a terrible car accident in July. He was in the hospital for weeks. He's back home now, but no one has seen him since the accident. I called Thomas this afternoon, and he told me that he received a letter saying that White Pine was being reorganized under the name of the Pickering Corporation, with new lawyers. He showed me the letter."

"Why are they calling it Pickering?" Anne asked.

Wallace shook his head.

"I don't know of any significance that name has around Niagara Falls," Emily remarked. "The only Pickering I can think of is Timothy Pickering, who was George Washington's envoy in negotiating the Treaty of Canandaigua with the Senecas in 1794. That's the treaty many of the current land claims are based on, because in it the United States government promised to preserve the Native Americans' lands and sovereign rights forever."

There was an uncomfortable silence.

Anne wanted to keep the meeting focused. "Is there anything we can do to stop a casino from going into the Turtle?"

"We're trying to get more information about Pickering," Wallace replied. "Our lawyers are trying to get copies of the documents."

"The first thing to do is get around all this secrecy, bring the information out into the open," Steve said.

Everyone agreed. Anne suggested that their committee also contact a lawyer. Joe said he would follow up with a friend of his. After receiving assurances that the committee, through Emily, would share information with him, Wallace started to rise.

Steve spoke up. "Chief Mountview, at the risk of sounding somewhat crazy," he said, "I'd like to ask you a question. It's about something that keeps coming up in my classroom. I teach science at the high school."

Wallace sat back down. "What is it?"

"I don't know very much about Native American beliefs, I'm sorry to say. In class, we talk a lot about current events, like the rockfall at the American Falls, and the big power outage, and the boat accident last summer, and the reports that there have been a lot of suicides, more people jumping over the falls, lately. I don't know if you've heard this, but a lot of people, especially on the blogs, are saying that so many bad things have been happening because the rock collapse unleashed some sort of evil spirit that came out of that cave that opened up. Some people say that the Indians always believed there was an evil spirit living behind the falls. You know, the old Thunder Gods stories. Other people say the evil spirit is part of an ancient Indian curse against the white man. What can I tell my students?"

Everyone looked at Wallace. He told them, "Don't take all this talk seriously."

"Would you compare these rumors to the story of the Maid of the Mist, Wallace?" Emily interjected. "Something that non-Indians make up out of their own silly notions?"

"People always seem to look for magic to explain things they don't understand," Anne said. Wallace started to rise again, but Steve persisted. "I'm trying to figure out what to say to my students. Are you saying the rumors are completely false? That there is no evil spirit, no Indian curse?"

Anne wanted to strangle Steve for badgering her distinguished, elderly guest. "The Native Americans have thousands of reasons to curse the white man, Steve," she told him. "But Chief Mountview is right. We shouldn't blame Indians when bad things happen. It's not rational. You should be teaching your students about science, not superstition."

"Now just a minute, Anne," Steve began, but Joe cut in. "I often try to imagine the falls as Father Hennepin saw them in the sixteen-hundreds," he said. "They were primal, magnificent. Who could see evil in them?"

"Mark Twain wrote a short story about Adam and Eve," Emily offered. "He put the Niagara waterfalls in Eden. He called them 'the finest thing on the estate.'"

Joe said, sadly, "The Europeans brought their old hatreds and wars here, and used religion as a weapon."

Steve responded, "With all due respect, Joe, the Indians had wars, too."

Anne and Emily glared at him.

"Yes, that's true." Wallace's deep voice was steady. "But more than five hundred years ago, the Haudenosaunee planted their weapons beneath a white pine, the Tree of Peace, and formed a confederacy that lasts today. They had found that wisdom."

"Imagine!" Joe exclaimed. "Imagine if the Europeans had never come here, what the League of Peace might have grown into, across this continent? Or if the white man had really come in peace, with true Christian principles, think what a truly new world the Indians and the Europeans could have built together."

Anne stole a glance at Wallace. His face was impassive. Not wanting the group to offend him any more than they probably already had, she stood up quickly and said, "Chief Mountview, thank you so much for coming. I hope we can work together." She turned to glare at Steve to warn him not to continue his rude questioning, and noticed that Quin was leaning back in his chair in the office, listening. "I know all of us here want the same thing, and that's to stop a casino from opening in the Turtle."

"Yes, that's the most important task before us now." Wallace rose quickly from his chair, and left the room. Emily grabbed her purse and notebooks and quickly followed.

Anne walked downstairs with them and helped with their coats. At the door, Anne said to Wallace, "I'm sorry about Steve. He likes to play devil's advocate, and he can get carried away. I hope you weren't offended."

"Unfortunately, Wallace has to endure more than his share of ignorance and insensitivity," Emily interjected. She was still angry and embarrassed.

Wallace clasped Anne's hand. "Good night." He turned away.

"I'll call you tomorrow," Emily whispered. She ran outside after Wallace.

Anne felt tired as she closed the heavy door. When she entered the parlor, Jay was telling the others about a story that would break in the morning news: the massive OHARAS landfill was leaking toxic waste into the groundwater on the western edge of its site, less than a mile from the Niagara River.

Anne exclaimed, "That's upriver from the intakes for the city water plant."

"It's been leaking for weeks, maybe months," Jay told them. "The state just confirmed it. They've been investigating what they call 'anomalous' readings at the water plant."

"The OHARAS people must have known it was going on," Joe said, angrily. "I bet they didn't report it."

"No, they didn't." Jay looked grim.

Anne felt sick. She couldn't even dredge up the old anger she felt every time she drove past OHARAS, the acronym for Omni Hazard and Radiation Abatement Services. It was a private company that had begun building its toxic mountain in the early nineteen-seventies, despite furious public opposition. Money spoke louder than the citizens, as it always did. For more than thirty years, Mount OHARAS had been growing, fed by daily loads of toxics. It was now the tallest geographical feature in the county. Millions of barrels of chemicals were buried there. And it was leaking. Anne hardly listened as the group discussed this new blow. That's what it was like to live in Niagara Falls. There seemed always to be another toxic secret ready to emerge. Abruptly, she said, "Guys, this has been a long meeting. Let's close for now, and get together again next week, okay?"

No one objected.

As he left, Joe squeezed Anne's arm. "Keep the faith, Anne. We can't give up."

"Joe, it gets harder and harder."

He smiled sadly. "I know."

Later, as Anne and Quin sat in front of the fire drinking hot chocolate, Quin asked, "Do you think the Chief answered Steve's question about the curse?"

"Yes, he told him it was nonsense, which is right."

"I think he kind of evaded the question."

"Well, it was extremely rude of Steve to bring it up. Wallace Mountview was our guest. And, anyway, things aren't really that much worse after the rockfall than they were before. People have always jumped over the falls. It's the economy more than anything." But she didn't feel like talking. She kissed Quin hard to generate a charge, and they finished in bed.

Later, snuggled in the pool of Quin's body heat, Anne slid her feet under Ben, and tried to sleep. But she grew edgy thinking about the meeting, and Wallace Mountview, and his sad weariness as he left her house. Her house, that stood on the Indians' homeland.

Then she remembered something, and an irresistible urge made her slip out of bed and tiptoe out of the room. Ben followed her; she almost shut the bedroom door on his head. She turned on the light in the hallway, and opened a polished wood door to a linen closet built into the wall. She was carrying a chair out of the kitchen when Quin emerged from the bedroom, pushing hair out of his face. "What are you doing?"

"I need to get something. Come and help me."

He followed her, tripping over Ben. Anne put the chair in front of the open closet, stepped on it, and pushed aside a box on the top shelf. She removed a large bundle from the back, and gently laid a flannel-wrapped object on the floor. As she unwound the old blanket, a soft lemon scent wafted into the air. Then he was free. She stood the Warrior on his feet.

"Awesome." Quin said as he sat on the floor next to Anne. They both stared at the carved statue. Almost three feet tall, his muscles still flexed and strong, the young native man carved in rosewood gazed straight ahead, poised as if he were ready to sprint off the carved rock he was standing on. As Anne rubbed his body with the blanket, he gleamed.

"Where did you get him?" Quin asked.

"He came with the house. He used to stand on top of the post at the bottom of the staircase, where that marble disk is now. I took him down when I moved in, because he seemed way too politically incorrect, like a tobacco store Indian. But he's beautiful, isn't he?" Anne stared at the sculpted Warrior. She couldn't pack him away again. She picked the statue up carefully. "Come on," she said, leading Quin into the guest room, where she opened the closet door. Pushing aside some of Phoebe's summer clothes to reveal the passage at the back, she went up the narrow stairs to the tower room, fumbling in the dark to find the light switch. Quin and Ben followed. She set the Warrior on top of a low bookcase, positioning him so that he gazed in the direction of the river.

"There. I don't know why, but I feel better now," she said.

A few minutes later, as she lay in bed nestled between Ben and Quin, Anne's last thoughts before falling asleep were of the alert Warrior, who was once again guarding her house, a silent sentry, watching for spirits that live in the river.

CHAPTER TWENTY-ONE

Enlarging the two images on the computer monitor in his office at home, Jerome peered closely at the screen. He had no doubt now that the maples had declined further. The first image had been taken when he met with the extension agent in August. He had just returned home with new images on his digital camera. Even the cold, wet weather hadn't slowed down the blight, or whatever it was. He fought a sense of helplessness by writing an email to Terry Caldwell and attaching his new images. "Have you brought the Cornell experts to look at the maples yet?" he asked. "Can anything more be done?"

The business landline rang. Sighing, he picked it up. "Jerome Lone here."

"Mr. Lone, my name is Patricia Sams, I'm a reporter for the *Niagara Falls Chronicle*. I'm calling to talk to you about the Pickering Corporation."

"The what? I don't know anything about it."

"I'm trying to confirm something Nick Valli, the director of tourism here in Niagara Falls, told me, Mr. Lone. He said the Pickering Corporation ..."

"Look, Ms. ... Sams, is it?"

"Yes, Patricia Sams."

"I don't know anything about what's going on in Niagara Falls right now."

"But, Mr. Lone, your brother . . ."

"That's all I have to say. Goodbye."

It felt good to hang up on the reporter, like smacking a mosquito. Jerome's usual politeness had been worn away by his having to deal with so many media calls since the accident, reporters asking about John's condition, feigning compassion while digging for a story. Jerome felt especially harrassed by this call. No doubt she was fishing for information about White Pine Enterprises and the Turtle, but Jerome was not going to say anything about the museum until John got better, or if the family decided to go on without his participation. The Turtle plans could wait. He wondered how the reporter had gotten his number at the house.

He was about to beep Woody when the office door burst open and Loraine rushed in. She stood in the middle of the room and tried to tell him something, but couldn't catch her breath. He jumped up and ran around the desk.

"What is it? John?" He grabbed her arms. "Tell me!"

She nodded. He started to rush past her, but she grabbed his shirt to keep him from running off.

"Let go, Loraine!"

She held on. "Wait. I have to, have to tell you ..." Her eyes were bugging out. She swallowed several times. "Something's happened, Jerome, but I don't know what." She wouldn't look him in the face. "I'm scared."

"Scared for John?"

She nodded.

He broke free and ran up the stairs, down the long hall to John's suite. As he opened the door to the sitting room, he smelled a strange, bitter odor. Levi Moon was burning herbs again; an acrid, purplish haze hung in the room. The bedroom door was closed. He rushed to it, and opened the door. The room was dark. Through a haze, he saw his mother and Levi Moon standing on opposite sides of the hospital bed that had been brought in for John.

Jerome spoke loudly. "What's going on? Why is it so dark in here? What's all this smoke? Is there a fire?" He turned on the overhead light, but its glare seemed dull.

His mother turned and looked at him with the first happy expression Jerome had seen on her face in months. She beckoned him. "Come. Look." Levi Moon stepped back from the bed. Without looking at Jerome, he lifted his face toward the ceiling, and stood motionless, with his eyes closed.

Warily, Jerome stepped forward into the room, watching Moon, trying to decipher the expression on his smooth face. He couldn't read it. Then he looked down at John in the bed, and felt as though he had been punched in the chest.

His brother's eyes were wide open, focused on a far horizon. His mouth was twitching, as though he were trying to speak. His rigid body shook. His mother stroked his forehead, and kept gently wiping a thin stream of drool oozing from the left side of his mouth.

As soon as Jerome's mind computed what he was seeing, he reached for the phone by the side of the bed.

"What are you doing, Jerome?" Levi Moon's voice was calm.

"Calling the doctor." He punched the direct-dial number.

With surprising force, his mother grabbed the phone out of his hand, cancelled the call, and threw it across the room. She ordered him, "You will not call anybody."

Jerome stared at her, feeling as though he was looking at a stranger. Louise Lone had always been a formidable woman – she was why their family survived. She had been a clan mother, until she stepped away from the clan during the disputes over John's early businesses. John was the only one who ever got away with crossing her. Even so, she now had a desperate fierceness in her voice that stunned Jerome. He was unnerved that her words, when they came out, sounded rough.

He had never raised his voice to his mother, and wouldn't, even now. "We should find out what's happening," he told her.

"I know what's happening," she replied.

"I can see what's happening, too, but only on the surface. We should call the doctor and see what he says. Maybe this is a good sign, but it might be a bad one. Maybe John needs new medication."

Levi Moon laughed. Jerome glared at him. Moon's hooded, amber eyes met Jerome's. They glared at each other over John's anguished body. Jerome clenched his fists, ready to lash out, when Moon blinked, and tried to calm Jerome with words. "Jerome, Jerome, can't you see what your own eyes are telling you? I've called him back. He's starting the journey home."

"I can see there's a change, but I can't tell whether it's good or bad. And neither can you."

"Oh, but I can, Jerome, I can. And so can your mother. Don't you trust your own mother?"

Jerome bit back his response. No, he didn't trust his mother, not anymore, not since she'd come under this man's influence. Her desperation made her believe in him, and he had sly words, and tricks, to keep her hopeful. Now he was using his so-called "power" on John. Staring down at his brother, Jerome could only believe he was in pain, trying to escape whatever dreadful hell his mind was trapped in. It was actually worse to see him with his eyes open, to know John had some sort of awareness, and not peaceful oblivion. He took his brother's hand, which felt warm and alive, even though it pulled against his grasp. "John? Can you hear me?"

His brother made no response. He stared far past Jerome, who held his hand firmly. After some time, Jerome, in agony, resolved to contact the doctor as soon as he was out of this room. He had to know what Moon was doing to John. He released John's hand, and turned to leave, but his mother clutched his arm.

"You will not bring any doctor here. I forbid it."

His eyes withstood her glare. "How can you, Mother? How can you stand for him to be like that? How can you not want to be sure? How can you risk John's life?"

She slapped at his face. He instinctively dodged the blow, and took it on his arm. "Don't you question my love for my oldest son!" As she turned to look at John, tears fell down her cheeks. "My handsome, brilliant son."

Jerome had always accepted the fact that his older brother was her favorite. It never mattered. "I love John, too," he wanted to tell her, in a way she'd believe. He wished he could make Moon leave the room, eliminate his influence. But the small man stood near the bed, watching them with sly eyes.

When his mother spoke again, it was in a softer voice. "I know what's best for my son. For both of my sons. Trust me, and Levi. When it's the proper time, we will call the doctors. But for now, this way is the best way."

Jerome sadly accepted defeat. "Whatever you say, Mother." As he turned, he caught a glimpse of the smirk on Moon's face. He didn't have the heart to look at John. He felt he was abandoning him. He was helpless. All he could do was watch his brother, as he watched the maples, and monitor their decline, and the end of their days on Mother Earth.

CHAPTER TWENTY-TWO

Anne timed her pickup at the Buffalo airport perfectly. She had to wait in the call-park area for less than ten minutes before Quin texted to say he had just walked off his plane from Boston. She drove quickly to the arrivals area and cut off a taxi for an open spot near the curb. A loud honk announced her arrival. Quin grinned as he opened the car door, tossed in his backpack, and got inside. They kissed a greeting. Anne quickly turned her attention to getting back on the busy road.

"How was your Thanksgiving?" she asked, as she maneuvered between lanes.

"Okay. The usual. You know. Family. How 'bout you?"

"The same. Family. We had the turkey at my brother Bill's house. Phoebe and I went shopping today. She bought a lot of clothes." Anne focused on her driving. A messy precipitation hovered between rain and snow. The roads were covered with slush that flew into her windshield every time another car passed. She couldn't go too fast for fear of hitting black ice and losing control.

"You're coming to my place, right?" she asked when she reached the exit for the south Grand Island bridge. She kept her eyes straight ahead. Driving over the Grand Island bridges at night in bad weather was always a matter of faith. There were no shoulders, and only low iron railings kept cars from hurtling over the edge into the frigid Niagara River.

"Sure. I'd really like to see Ben." His grin looked tired.

She smiled. "I'm sure Ben will be glad to see you, too."

Though Quin looked exhausted by the time they reached Anne's place, he seemed to enjoy Ben's happy greeting. After a hearty supper and some wine, they retired early.

The next morning, as she put on her makeup before they headed to campus, Anne wondered about his mood. He had seemed even more preoccupied than usual. She hoped it was just psychic meltdown after spending holiday time with family. She expected that her students would be even less alert than usual today, too.

When she emerged from her bedroom, ready to leave, she didn't see Quin. Noticing the door to the guest room closet was open, she climbed the stairs, and found Quin and Ben in the tower room. Quin was staring at the Warrior.

"Here you are," she said, surprised. "What are you doing?"

"Just looking at him. Trying to read his mind."

"Just looking at him is enough for me – he's so beautiful. I've been coming up here every week to polish him." Anne ran her finger gently along the Warrior's arm. "Look at this detail. You can see every muscle. And listen to this. Mari told me she figured out her bad dreams ended about the same time I put him up here. She thinks he's guarding the house. I told her it was just coincidence."

"Maybe it's not."

"No, Quin, not you, too! If you start believing that stuff, I won't have anybody sane left to talk to."

Quin ran his hands through his hair, electrifying it so that the top layer hovered like a halo. "Wow, the Warrior got to me. He must have got in my head."

She looked at him closely. He still seemed exhausted, though she knew he'd slept like a rock. She put her hand against his neck. His skin felt hot. "Are you feeling okay?"

"Yeah, just tired. Hey, it's getting late. We'd better go."

They drove along the Robert Moses Parkway through a gloomy mist that crept off the river, which raced past them in a field of ebony waves tipped with whitecaps. Quin stared at the heaving water. He muttered something.

Anne turned down the roaring defroster. "What did you say?"

"Patterns in chaos," he repeated. "I was just thinking about one of Carl Sagan's books, where he talks about the picture of the face on Mars. It's this geological formation that showed up in the early Martian images that were really fuzzy. It's like the man in the moon – we see a face even though we know we're only looking at craters. Sagan described how human brains evolved to find patterns, so babies could recognize their mothers' faces among the random images hitting their brains. Humans have to create some level of order. We have to believe in cause and effect, or we'll go crazy. It's like Mari's nightmares ending because you put the Warrior in the tower. Maybe her brain just deleted those images. But she's programmed to look for a reason why things happen. She makes connections that go along with her reality, just like everyone else does."

"I'm so relieved to hear you talking like this. I was afraid for a while there you'd gone over to the other side."

He gave a short laugh. "Nah. I'm comfortable with chaos. That's the only reality that makes sense to me."

Anne dropped him off at his lab building, and hurried to her class. That was the last she saw of him that busy week. She was right about her students' post-holiday moods – half of them skipped her lecture that day.

On Friday, Quin sent her an email asking to see her the next day. She told him to meet her in her campus office.

Saturday was damp and gray when she walked Ben in the morning. Though it wasn't actually raining, the dank cold permeated her jacket and his fur, so that they both were shivering and soaked by the time they returned home. Anne wanted to take a nap, but had to meet Quin. She was looking forward to seeing him, after the bleak week.

Quin appeared shortly after she arrived in her office. Taking off his ski jacket, he shook snow from it, then dropped it on the floor.

"It's snowing now?" Anne groaned. "So what's up? You look just like one of my students coming in to beg for extra time to turn in a paper."

"There's something we've gotta talk about." He sat, with a serious expression, facing her across the desk.

Anne felt her smile get tight. "What?"

"It's about a job I took this week. You're not gonna like it."

"Quin," Anne said, feeling her stomach tighten, "you don't have to apologize to me about any job. I mean, we both knew you'd be leaving Buffalo eventually. I'm not going to be angry or try to stop you."

"Hell, I wish it was as simple as that." He ran his hands through his hair; it was wet and limp. "Look, sometimes people have to do what they have to do."

"I know that. Believe me, I know that."

"Something came up when I was home last week. My dad's been sick, and he just got diagnosed with colorectal cancer."

"Oh, Quin, I'm really sorry." Anne rose and walked around the desk, sitting on another chair facing him. "Why didn't you tell me before? Is he getting treated?"

"Yeah, they're starting radiation this week at the VA in Boston. The doctor says they might have caught it in time, but it would have been better if they caught it sooner."

"That's good. The treatments are really advanced now. If the doctor says your father has a chance, then he does."

"Yeah." Quin looked down at his hands. "It's not just him I'm worried about. I never told you about my brother, Mike. He's five years older than me. He was in the Army Reserve. He got called up and blown up by an IED in fucking Iraq a few years ago."

"I'm so sorry," Anne said. She leaned forward and squeezed his hand.

"He had massive head injuries and lost his right leg," Quin said, looking at the floor. "It's been tough. I mean, he's got a prosthetic leg, but he can't work, and needs lots of rehab. He and his wife have three kids. My dad and mom were helping out a lot, with some money and babysitting so Cathy can work, but now this thing with dad kills that.

My sister and I have been sending some money, too, as much as we can, but Mike's flashbacks have been getting worse and Cathy needs more help with the kids to get him to therapy. He has PTSD and scars on his face so he won't leave the house ..." Quin stopped talking and rubbed his eyes. "He'll never just have a regular life, he'll always have to deal with this, and so will we."

"Your whole family is impacted," Anne said, thinking of her grant proposal. Quin's family was a textbook example of the range of needs she hoped to meet; she hoped more than ever that her grant would be approved.

"Yeah," he said. "So this job comes at a great time."

"So what are you going to be doing? And where?"

"It's really just a short-term project, but they're going to pay me a lot. And I get to stick around here for a while longer."

"Great. So tell me about it. Where is it?"

He met her eyes. "I'm going to set up a computer network for a new corporation. It's Pickering. The one in the Turtle."

Anne had a hard time processing this information. She stared at him. "What?" she finally blurted out.

He stood, and paced around the small office. "These guys got my name from an ad I posted online looking for freelance projects. They approached me a while ago, but I told them I wasn't interested, then, because I knew you'd be pissed, and it was just too much of a hassle. But after seeing what's happening back home ...," he shrugged, "I called and told them I was available."

Anne's mind was reeling. "Is Pickering really going to put a casino in the Turtle?"

"Not exactly."

"What does that mean?"

"Some of the plan is good, actually. You'll like it. There's going to be a state-of-the-art Indian museum and art gallery, with interactive displays. It'll be cool. That's mostly what I'll be working on, setting up the network and website. They're planning some virtual reality and hologram imaging for the displays."

"And ...?"

"And, they're also going to try something new. They're setting up a cyber casino in one section of the building."

"What, exactly, does that mean?"

"Gambling on the Internet. They're calling that part of the operation Thundering Waters CyberBucks."

"But I thought Internet gambling was illegal, or that at least you had to be on an offshore island, or something."

"Well, that's an interesting question. These guys are testing the legal limits. See, since the corporation is owned by native Americans, they could open a casino in the Turtle, theoretically. But it would be a big political hassle. So they're going online. The gamblers won't ever go near the Turtle. Only the operations center will be there."

Anne stared at him until he nervously turned away from her and walked to the window. Snow was gently falling on the peaceful, tree-filled campus. She numbly stared past him.

After some minutes passed in silence, he turned around. "This isn't like a real casino, Anne. It's just technology. You won't even know it's there."

"But it will be there." Anne felt cold and sluggish, as though the snow were burying her. "In a building that's important, that represents sacred beliefs. It's not just any other building. Why do they have to put it there?"

"Look," he said, nervously. "I'm just working on this one part of it. They're going to do it with or without me. I'm just in to get my money, then I'm gone."

"But what about morality, Quin?"

"Morality?" He stomped across the room. "What about morality for Mike, who's barely alive because of that shithead Bush? Why are he and Cheney still walking around free after their war crimes? What about the one percent – where's their morality when people are crowding food banks? What about morality for almost everyone I know who's working a crap job just to get by? Tell me where you can find morality now, Anne, and I'll go there."

"Those are all separate issues!" She felt herself getting angry. "Gambling is essentially dishonest – you know it's set up for the house always to come out ahead. It's not rich people who gamble, it's poor people. Those are the ones who end up addicted until they lose all their money and jump over the falls."

Quin's face was blazing red. "I've got news for you, Anne. The entire country is addicted to gambling. Hell, it's our national religion. Look at my father. He hasn't gone to church in thirty years, but he buys his lottery tickets every weekend. That's what he worships. He believes in magic as much as Mari does."

"Just because things are unfair doesn't give you license not to act morally yourself," Anne countered.

"Spare me the catechism class, Anne." They glared at each other for a long moment.

Anne finally spoke first, in a low voice. "What about Wallace Mountview? He had plans for the Turtle."

Quin shook his head. "I feel sorry for him, but he's living in the past, Anne. Things will never go back to the way they were. They never do. He should accept that already, and start working with guys who can make money for them. That's the only way they'll ever get ahead."

"Money isn't everything, Quin."

"Sometimes it is."

She stared at him.

He looked exasperated. "Look, I have to be straight with you. I don't see gambling as this terrible evil, like you do, and those guys on your committee. People choose to do it, or not, and if they can't handle it, well ...," he shrugged, "that's just the way it is."

"As long as there are people like Joe and me. Nurses and priests to pick up the pieces," Anne retorted. "But pretty soon there won't be many nurses left, and maybe no priests, either." She turned and walked to the window. She watched the snow bury the landscape, and ordered herself not to cry in front of him.

Quin sat down heavily on the desk. "Anne, I don't want to piss you off. It's just that I'm really stressed here, and I need to help my family."

She swallowed hard, then turned toward him. "I haven't told you where I got the money to buy my house, and fix it up, have I?"

He shook his head.

"It was the settlement for my dad's death, after the chlorine explosion. After my mother died, I found out she'd invested it. The original settlement wasn't much, but she never touched it. So it grew into enough for me to buy the house with cash when I saw it for sale." She managed a thin smile. "I must have made one of those connections in chaos, to keep from going crazy. I thought I was meant to buy it, to preserve that little piece of history."

Quin said nothing.

"Sometimes there's no compromise." She ignored the tear threatening to drop from the corner of her right eye. "Like Tesla with his inventions. And Wallace Mountview with his principles." She stopped herself from saying, "Like me, with you." She told him, "I can't be one of those people who don't believe in anything, who pretend not to see, or care. The Turtle represents ancient beliefs, Quin. How can you treat it like it's just an ordinary building?"

He looked down. He didn't say anything.

Anne got her emotions under control and spoke calmly, in her professional voice. "Well, thanks for coming by and telling me about this. I've got to get back to my work now, okay?" She sat behind the desk.

He leaned down, picked up his jacket, and put it on. "I'll talk to you later, okay?"

"Sure. Later." She fussed with her papers.

He watched her for a moment, then quickly left.

She tried to concentrate on her work. She knew it was futile, though, when a tear splashed down on her keyboard. She rubbed the back of her hand over her eyes, feeling more hot tears. She had to get out of there, before someone came by. She scooped up her laptop, donned her jacket and hat, and walked quickly through the falling snow to her car.

"Damn!" she said out loud, when she saw she'd have to brush off a heavy layer of wet snow. It was a long drive home; the snowplows were just starting to clear the streets. She had the defroster and heater on full blast. When she finally got home, she called Ben from the kitchen as she threw down her briefcase. She heard him jump off her bed. He came to her, prancing. She hugged him hard, and stroked his ears. "Come on, big boy. We're going for a walk."

Ordinarily, Anne would have enjoyed walking along the river on a day like this, with snow falling thickly but gently, covering the autumn drabness with pristine white. The river flowed darkly, the color of deep green jade, its roar muted. She didn't notice any of the details. She walked with emotions as numb as her cold nose. She didn't bother to pick up Ben's steaming dump at the Knobby Tree, where it caused a meltdown of snow. The rapids seemed to smoke and hiss as they rushed under her on the pedestrian bridge to Goat Island. She saw footprints cutting across the lawn, toward the woods, and wondered if they were the Hermit's. She walked to Terrapin Point, slowly, trying to keep her balance along the slippery path.

Icy mist filled the basin. The Horseshoe Falls was generating thick clouds of water vapor that stayed close to the river's surface, like heavy smoke swirling over a cauldron. Soon the atmosphere would reach the point where the snow and mist would merge and form a thick cloud that would settle into a dank fog. Anne stood like a statue, staring, not even noticing that the world in front of her was blurring, and disappearing.

She didn't want to see Quin anymore. It was too much. She knew she couldn't say he'd betrayed her, because she had no claim on him or his actions. But that was the way she felt. He knew she opposed that project with all her being. Well, she'd stand up for her ideals, and suffer, even if she was the last person on Earth who would bother to do so. This was another way in which she was an anachronism, obsolete. She didn't believe that every purpose in life was to make money, even for a good purpose. She believed there were other things Quin could do, even if he left town. There had to be.

A hot tear rolled down her cheek. She thought of the tragedy of Quin's brother, Mike, the victim of Bush's war game. It upset her that she couldn't feel more sympathy for Quin's tough choices. She turned toward home. It was hard to balance on the icy pavement. She was glad when she reached the top of the plaza, and didn't have to worry about slipping, and sliding right under the railing, down into the rocky chasm of the Niagara gorge. She thought about the evening ahead, and was glad she had a lot of work to do. She knew she wouldn't be checking her phone or her email. She had choices, too.

CHAPTER TWENTY-THREE

When the pilot announced they would begin their descent and land in forty minutes, Phoebe knew she couldn't wait any longer. She poked Leonard's arm. "Wolf."

He turned away from the window. With his hair pulled back in a neat ponytail, and wearing a new shirt she had bought him under his uncle's vintage leather jacket, Leonard looked cool. Phoebe beamed with confidence. They belonged where they were, in first class, on this chartered flight from Niagara Falls to Las Vegas.

"I've changed my plans, Wolf." She was blunt. "I'm not going to the music festival with you. I'm going to stay in Las Vegas and go through with the competition."

Leonard stared at her. He didn't say anything.

She hated when he did that, because then she always ended up having to explain herself. Her confidence eroded a bit. "I've been thinking about it a lot. I mean, I know our original plan was to bag the competition and go to the desert, but now I don't think it would be right for me to do that. I mean, you saw the texts and letters Ani got. I have actual fans. Nick says the whole city is counting on me."

Leonard still said nothing, so she kept talking. "I know it means a lot to you, and I don't expect you to stay in Las Vegas with me. You can still go to the desert. You have to look at it my way. I think I was meant to come here, even though I didn't know it. And now I have to do this."

Leonard looked straight at her. "I knew you were going to. You like being Ani. But it's okay. My plans have changed, too."

"What? What do you mean?" She was shocked that Leonard had a plan of his own.

"The music's just the starting point for me now. I've been online with some guys from New York who are going there, too. We're going to take off and head for the mountains, go climbing, and camping. You couldn't come."

Phoebe was even more shocked. "You were going to leave me by myself?"

He shook his head. "I knew I wouldn't have to. It all works out."

"Oh!" Phoebe wasn't sure whether she should be mad. But after thinking about it for a minute, she felt more confident than ever she was doing the right thing. They would go on separate journeys, like quests, their own ways. They would meet again in a week. But they wouldn't be the same people. She'd be a star, with a contract to perform in Las Vegas. Maybe Leonard would be a warrior, or something. They wouldn't have to stay in grungy Niagara Falls anymore, or go home at all if they didn't want to.

Phoebe checked her hair and makeup in a mirror from her big purse. She put her sunglasses on and looked across Leonard to see jagged red ridges rush by as the plane landed. Her heart pounded with excitement. In the airport, Leonard led the way, following signs to baggage claim. After they walked out of the security zone, Phoebe stood and stared. The dazzling lights of banks of slot machines and video screens disoriented her.

Leonard touched her arm and nodded toward a uniformed man holding up a cardboard sign that read, "Ani Shanando."

"I'm looking for Nick," she told him.

"Don't you remember? You're Ani here."

"Omigod! I forgot!" Startled, Phoebe doubled over laughing.

Leonard grinned, but shook his head. "Are you sure you want to do this? If you can't remember what your name is, you'll be safer in the desert."

She struggled to regain her composure. "I'm sure." By concentrating, she managed to form her lips into a haughty, painted pout. "Let's go." She walked up to the driver, a squat man with a bland face and a tight mouth. "I'm Ms. Shanando," she told him.

The driver touched his hand to the brim of his gray hat. "Let me take your bags, Ms. Shanando." He ignored Leonard. She handed him her carry-on.

"Where's Mr. Valli?" Phoebe asked.

"He's waiting in the car. I'll take you there. Is there another passenger?"

"Yes, him." Phoebe nodded toward Leonard.

The driver gave Leonard a glance, then said, "This way please."

When he turned his back on them, Phoebe looked at Leonard and gave him a quick smile. "Isn't this cool?" she whispered.

Leonard didn't reply. He just looked straight ahead.

They walked quickly through the crowded airport. Phoebe tried to look at ease in her high heels, but she tripped several times, not paying attention to where she was walking. Huge video screens displayed the stars performing on the Strip. She stopped to watch when white tiger cubs appeared on one of the screens. "See the only appearance of these famous wild animals on New Year's Day at the Desert Mirage," a voice blared. Everything was a blur of lights. Leonard's occasional steering her by the elbow kept her in the driver's wake. When she realized they were about to go outside, she said, "Wait. I have to get my suitcase."

The driver turned. "I'll take you to the car, then retrieve your luggage."

Her face turned pink. As they went outside, Phoebe was glad she had her warm, fake fur jacket on. It was a lot cooler than she expected. A line of limousines snaked along the curb. The driver led them to a white one. As he opened the door, Phoebe could see Nick Valli in the back seat, watching a video screen mounted on the interior ceiling. He turned quickly. Seeing her, he spread out his arms. "Ani, welcome to Vegas!"

Phoebe jumped into the leather interior. "Hello, Nick." She sat on the seat beside him and they air-kissed. Leonard sat opposite, facing them.

"It's great to see you, Ani. You look fabulous." He leaned forward and held out a hand to Leonard. "I'm Nick Valli. You're ...?"

"He's Leonard Running Wolf, my bodyguard," Phoebe told him.

Leonard wordlessly shook Nick's hand.

"Pleased to meet you, Len." Nick's expression never wavered from a wide smile. He leaned back against the leather seat.

The driver put his head inside the car. "Miss? I need your baggage claim check."

Phoebe rummaged through the jumble in her purse until she found the claim check near the bottom. "Here. It's a black one with wheels."

"Make it fast," Nick told the driver. "We're running late because of that snow delay."

The driver took the claim check and disappeared. Phoebe sat back and looked at Nick. His tan was deeper than usual. He was wearing a gray silk shirt, open at the neck, and black slacks. His dark hair was longer than it had been in July, and slicked back.

"Want something to drink, Ani?" Nick asked. "And you, Len?"

Phoebe saw a small refrigerator. "We'll have waters."

"Waters? Come on, we're in Vegas! Let's celebrate. How about some champagne?" Nick pulled out a dark green bottle.

"Champagne! In the car?" As soon as she blurted out the words, Phoebe flushed in embarrassment. She had to stop acting like a kid.

"Sure. Nothing's too good for our Maid of the Mist." Nick grinned.

"No," Leonard said, in a firm voice.

Phoebe glanced at him. She wouldn't have minded sipping a little champagne. But she understood where Leonard was coming from. She wanted to avoid the issue just now. "We had drinks on the plane," she told Nick. "We'll just have waters now. I'm thirsty."

"Okay, you're the boss, Ani." Nick smoothly replaced the champagne, pulled out two plastic bottles, and handed one to each of his passengers. He picked up a glass of clear liquid that he'd been drinking, and took a sip. Phoebe recognized the odor from her father's gin-and-tonics. She settled back in her seat. The driver returned with her suitcase, started the car, and pulled out into the heavy terminal traffic.

"Just wait till you see the Universe Hotel, Ani," Nick told her. "It's spectacular."

"Really?" She turned toward him. "Is it better than Castle Lake in Florida?"

Nick snorted. "Much better than Castle Lake. That's for kids. This is a playground for grown-ups."

Flushing, Phoebe decided to keep her mouth shut, like a super-model.

Leonard stared at Nick. There was an awkward silence, until Nick brought up the most comfortable topic for Western New Yorkers. "I'm glad it stopped snowing long enough for your plane to leave. I was afraid you wouldn't get here today, and that you'd miss the pageant's opening reception tonight. You know, I'm thinking of relocating out here. I love this lifestyle – fast and full of class. And, best of all, no snow. Ever." He raised his glass, and took another sip of his drink. "You missed rehearsal for tonight, but I explained what happened. You'll just have to wing it. I know you can."

"Rehearsal? For the reception?"

"Yeah, don't worry about it. You just have to stand around and look gorgeous. Piece of cake. How about some music?" Nick pushed buttons on a control pad and Beyoncé blared.

Phoebe was relieved not to have to talk. She looked out the window as the limo slowly crawled on ramps leading out of the airport. She saw a rim of jagged gray mountains in the distance, behind the perfect lines of a black pyramid. There was a row of New York skyscrapers, a tower that looked like a larger version of one at Niagara Falls, and a huge rectangular building as green as the Emerald City. She could explore the world here, she thought.

Nick shouted over the music. "You should have been here for

Christmas, Ani. It was fabulous. Santas were all over the place, handing out souvenirs and free tickets for drinks and shows. I've got a lot of ideas to try back in the Falls. *If* I go back, that is." He sipped his drink.

"Are we still going to see the baby white tigers on New Year's Day?" Phoebe asked.

"You bet, Babe. Don't ask me how much the tickets cost. They're impossible to get. But I've got a friend here from back in the Falls." Nick lifted his glass toward Phoebe. "We'll celebrate your win."

"I really want to see them," Phoebe said. "It's the only time they'll ever be shown in public. Then they're going to be released back into the wild, with their mother. That is so cool." She swallowed. She always felt like crying when she thought about baby animals.

Leonard emitted a sort of low grunt.

"Look, Ani. There's the Universe. It's brand new." As Nick leaned across her to point, Phoebe felt his taut body press against her. She followed his finger and saw, just beyond the black pyramid, a massive glass dome bordered by four metallic towers.

"Get ready to land on the Pleasure Planet." Nick sounded the way he did onstage at the Maid of the Mist contest. It was hard for Phoebe to maintain her cool, she was so impressed.

The limo made a turn and inched forward. They drove under a marquee to the main entrance of the hotel; laser lights jabbed the air in time to a banging techno rhythm. Phoebe jumped when the door was pulled open and a man with blue skin and orange hair, his chest naked, poked his head in.

Nick laughed. "Don't be afraid, Ani. All the doormen and porters look like that."

"Why?" Phoebe held out her hand to the alien stranger.

"We're on another planet, remember? The Pleasure Planet. Get into the mood." Nick grooved to the rhythm. "Someday we'll have one of these in Niagara Falls."

Phoebe laughed. As she entered the dome, she smelled the lush, humid odor of south Florida. At first glance, she saw a tropical rainforest, complete with tall waterfalls dribbling over rock formations. On her second glance, she noticed that nothing looked normal. The water had an orange tinge. None of the plant life was green. Straight ahead, dollar signs flashed above metallic slot games that looked as though they were floating in midair.

Leonard touched Phoebe's arm. "How long do you want me to stay?"

"Just come along for another few minutes," she begged him.

Nick handled the registration, turning once to ask, "Len, is that Running Wolf? One word or two?" Then Phoebe and Leonard signed in with their reinvented names.

"You have to hurry now, Ani," Nick said. "The opening reception starts in about an hour, and you have to get there early. It's in the Europa Ballroon on the fourth floor of the Jupiter Tower. You're invited, too, Len."

"We'll be there," Phoebe assured him.

"There'll be instructions in your room, Ani. You have to be in costume. When you're ready, text me and I'll meet you outside the ballroom. We'll go in together."

"I will." Phoebe started to walk away. Leonard followed her. They walked slowly until Nick disappeared into the glimmering game area.

"I should go," Leonard said.

"Don't you even want to see our suite?"

"No." He handed her his room card. "I have to hitchhike out to the Paiute reservation near the city. They have buses there to take people to the festival, where I'm meeting my friends." Feeling suddenly alone, she wouldn't look at him. "You should come with me, Phoebe," Leonard urged. "It'll be okay, I'll stay with you and we'll just go to the festival. I don't trust that guy. He's a major sleaze. Look, I won't leave you alone. Just come away from here."

"Oh, he's okay," Phoebe said. "Anyway, I can handle him. What can happen when I'm here with all these people?"

"Don't let him give you alcohol," Leonard warned. "He'll try again, but don't. And don't be alone with him."

"I won't." She flashed her Ani smile. Leonard turned to leave.

"Wait," she cried. He stopped and looked at her. "I'll meet you on the plane home, then," she said. At that moment, the thought of going home made Phoebe feel less lonely. "We'll tell each other everything that happens, and we'll celebrate."

"Okay. But be careful. And don't drink anything that guy gives you."

"I won't. Bye, Wolf. You be careful, too." She turned away quickly.

Phoebe got an unpleasant surprise when she found her room. It wasn't the luxurious suite she expected as a pageant winner, just a regular room with two queen-sized beds. The television was on, displaying the casino's many attractions, which included virtual reality adventures and "gaming from every known planet." She spotted a thick binder on the dresser. Opening it, she read, "Please read through your book of instructions as soon as you arrive. It will give you your schedule for the coming week and the pageant rules and regulations. Failure to comply with this schedule will result in your forfeiture of the opportunity to compete in the final competition. Good luck, and enjoy your stay at Universe Las Vegas, the Pleasure Planet."

Phoebe felt disappointment merge into anger. She hated all this space stuff. Why couldn't she have gotten into a contest in the casino with the dolphins and wild animals, or the New York skyline, or the Eiffel Tower? She felt as though she'd been sucked into one of her brothers' stupid computer games. There were several pages of schedule for every day of her supposedly fun-filled week, full of activities like "Mandatory Rehearsal" and "Promotional Appearance." She glanced at the clock radio. She had to hurry. She'd look at the rules later.

Phoebe was almost on time for the reception, but got confused about the elevators and was late. She was the Maid of the Mist again, though her makeup wasn't perfect because she'd had to rush. When she finally found the ballroom, she saw Nick waiting for her and looking anxious. "You're late. Come on, hurry up." He sounded mad, which made her feel terrible.

"It wasn't my fault. I kept getting lost. I couldn't remember the name of the room."

"Where's Len?"

"He'll be here later."

"If he's gambling already, he'll be broke in five minutes. He'd better let me give him some tips."

"Oh, he'll be all right. Don't worry about him. Come on, let's go in." Phoebe rushed past him into the glittering room. She tried to imagine she really was on a pleasure planet. It was hard, though, when your best friend was headed out to the desert, and you were all alone, and far from home, and wearing a skimpy outfit, pretending to be an Indian maiden.

CHAPTER TWENTY-FOUR

"Godammit, Anne, where've you been? I've left four messages for you!"

"Bill? Is this you?" Anne, just back from her morning walk with Ben, pulled off her wet cap and tossed it into the kitchen sink. The ice balls clinging to it made a rattling sound on the stainless steel. Holding the phone with her left hand, she struggled to undo Ben's leash with one hand, while straddling him with her legs to hold him as she tried to wipe a thick coating of slush off his fur with a small kitchen towel. Her brother sounded frantic.

"What's wrong? Is it Ellen's mother?" she asked.

"No, dammit, it's Phoebe. Do you know where she is?"

"Isn't she at her girlfriend's house?"

"That's where she's supposed to be but she's not there. Ellen just called. She was never supposed to be there. That little ...," Bill made a sort of gurgling sound as he groped for a word, "... *sneak* lied to us!"

Anne's mind raced. Phoebe snuck off somewhere? Where in the world would she go? And why? It wasn't possible. This must be some kind of joke she was playing. Or Bill was just jumping to conclusions again. He shouted into the phone. "Are you listening to me?"

"Sorry. I'm just shocked."

"You don't sound shocked."

"What does that mean?"

"Nothing. Just that you don't sound surprised."

"Bill, I'm a trained nurse. I don't start swearing and screaming when I'm upset."

Bill exhaled loudly. He was smoking. Anne heard the raised voices of Ellen and the twins, Josh and Jon, who were home from college for winter break, in the background.

"Do you have any idea where she is?" he asked again.

"No, I don't. I honestly don't." She racked her brain. "I haven't spoken to her since Christmas Day at your house. I asked her if she wanted to hit the sales with me this week, but she said she was going to be staying with her girlfriend – what was her name? – Jessica? – and they'd be going to the malls together." Suddenly, Anne felt very stupid. What a transparent lie. She realized that she had been so happy to hear that Phoebe was making new friends that she never questioned the story. Everything had been going so well.

"Well, she fooled all of us," Bill declared, loudly exhaling more smoke.

"Did you check her clothes? Did she take anything?"

"Ellen!" Bill yelled to his wife. Anne held the phone away from her ear. "What about her stuff? Did you check yet?"

She heard Ellen's footsteps coming toward Bill and her voice getting louder. "She took her suitcase and a bunch of clothes, I'm not sure what – she was shopping with Anne before Christmas. Her pink leather jacket and new boots, she took. The money she got for Christmas, it was in an envelope on her dresser, now it's empty." Ellen's voice rose. "Why did she do this? What am I supposed to tell Ma? Does Anne know anything?"

"No," Bill told her.

Anne could hear Ellen start to cry.

"Go lie down in the family room, I'll be right with you," Bill ordered.

As Ellen's sobs receded, Anne heard the voices of her sons trying to reassure her that their sister would be okay. They didn't sound convincing, even over the phone. "Bill, how did Phoebe leave the house with all her stuff? Did she take the car?"

"Someone picked her up the day before yesterday. No one else was home. She planned it good."

"Did any of the neighbors see anything?"

"They wouldn't know the first thing."

"Did you ask them?"

"No, and I'm not going to. I already know who to look for. That Indian kid."

Anne started to feel nauseous. "Leonard doesn't have a car."

"Maybe one of his friends has one. Or maybe he stole one. I'll find out. Do you know how to get hold of him?"

Anne couldn't imagine Phoebe running off with Leonard. She couldn't fathom what the two of them would do, or where they would go. They couldn't be that calculating. Well, maybe Phoebe could. But not Leonard. Could he? Anne knew she was resisting an obvious conclusion, but she couldn't go there, not yet. She had to investigate.

"I'll try to find Leonard right away," she told Bill. "In the meantime, have you called the police?"

"Not yet. I want to try to find her on my own first. The boys and I will check some places."

"Okay. Let me try at this end. Phoebe left some stuff here, from this summer. I'll go through that, too. And do anything else I can think of."

"Call me right away if you find out anything." Bill hung up.

Anne stood in the kitchen holding the phone to her ear for a moment, before she realized that she should end the call, too. She pulled off her jacket and slipped out of her wet jeans and socks, leaving them in a heap on the kitchen floor. Then she noticed the puddles of water leading toward her bedroom.

"Ben!" She found him curled up in a wet ball in the middle of her bed. "Ben, you bad dog!" She grabbed his collar and pulled him off. "Bad dog!" she yelled, wrenching the wet comforter and blankets off the mattress. Water had gone through the sheets, which she pulled off in a frenzy yelling, "Bad dog! Bad dog!" When she finished demolishing the bed, Anne stopped yelling, mostly to catch her breath. She got a look at herself in her dresser mirror and saw a crazy woman. Ben was cowering at her feet, whimpering.

Overwhelmed by guilt for transferring her anger to poor Ben, she hugged him, then started wiping him dry with her sheets. "I'm sorry, big guy," she repeated, trying hard not to cry from sheer frustration. The dog wagged his tail, tentatively.

As she dried Ben, Anne tried to make sense of events. What was Phoebe up to? Had she been scheming ever since last summer, when she let Anne buy a suitcase for her? She realized she wasn't concerned yet about Phoebe's safety. The girl had a plan. Anne's biggest fear was that she took off alone on some manipulative plan to wreak havoc with her parents. It was unlikely that she'd met a guy who persuaded her to run off with him. Wasn't it? She jumped up, pulled on dry socks and sweatpants, and ran down the back stairs to Mari's apartment.

"Anne, what happened?" Mari asked in surprise, as Anne burst into her kitchen.

"Phoebe's run off someplace. Bill just called. Do you have Leonard's number?"

Mari looked as though she might laugh. "You think she's run off with Leonard?"

"No, but I think he might know something." Anne quickly described Bill's call.

Mari speed-dialed Leonard's mobile number. No answer. "I have the number for his great-grandfather's house," she told Anne, as she dialed it.

"Hello, Mr. Mountview, this is Mari. Is Leonard there?" She heard a response. "Do you know where I could reach him?" She looked at Anne and shook her head as she heard the answer.

Anne took the phone. "Mr. Mountview, this is Anne Techa, Emily's friend? You attended a meeting at my house in October? The preservation group?"

"Oh, yes," Wallace responded in his deep voice. "What can I do for you, Professor?"

"We have a situation with my niece, Phoebe. I hate to bother you with this, but she seems to have gone off without telling her parents where she was going. I'm hoping to talk to Leonard, to see if she might have told him about her plans."

"Leonard's been staying with his Uncle Clint for the past few days," Wallace told her. "He didn't mention anything about any plans. But I'll try to reach him and ask him if he knows where your Phoebe might be."

"Thank you so much. Anything he can tell us would be helpful."

"Where can I reach you?"

Anne gave Wallace her number, thanked him again, and hung up the phone. She looked at Mari. "I don't know what else to do. What do you think? Did Phoebe say anything to you that gives you any idea where she would have gone?"

Mari shook her head. "Phoebe is full of secrets. She keeps her feelings and thoughts in the shadows, where they can hide."

Anne didn't have time to analyze Phoebe's psychic state. "I'm going upstairs and search some things she left in the guest room. Will you call me if you think of anything?"

"Of course." Mari's face was serious. "Phoebe's sly. She'll take care of herself."

"I hope so." Anne rushed back upstairs. A search of the guest room revealed no clues. Phoebe had left some summer clothes, but nothing else. Then Anne searched for Leonard's box. She found it under the bed, opened it, and looked inside. A couple of old tee shirts covered some art pencils and a pad of drawing paper. There were a few unfinished sketches, and a pile of practice drawings. Anne smiled when she saw drawings of Ben and her house. Then she found two computer thumb drives at the bottom of the box.

Her hope renewed, she hurried into her office. She slid one thumb drive into her computer and tried to open the files. She couldn't get past the password. She tried a dozen words; the files wouldn't open. It was the same with the other drive. Anne searched her hard drive to see if they had left any files on her home computer, which Phoebe sometimes used, but found nothing except games. She called Bill to see if he had come up with anything. Ellen answered the phone. Bill and the twins were out looking. Ellen veered between angry exhortations and tears. Anne got off the phone as quickly as she could.

The rest of the day was a nightmare of uncertainty. Anne jumped whenever the phone rang. It was usually Bill, calling to see if there was any news. She called some friends to see if by chance they'd run into Phoebe. She was tempted to call the Mountview home again, but held back. Wallace finally called her at about eight o'clock that evening to say he'd asked around, but no one had seen Leonard since the day after Christmas, not even his Uncle Clint, where he was supposed to be staying.

"Maybe they *are* together," Anne suggested. "Do you know where Leonard might have gone? Did he talk about wanting to take any trips?"

"Not that I've been able to find out. But I'll keep searching, and call you if I learn anything."

"Same here. Thanks for your help. Good night."

Anne called the Cybrary to see if she could get some advice on opening the computer files, but a recording said it was closed for winter break. In case of an emergency involving network connections, there was a number to call. She didn't dare call David again. Not yet, anyway. She quickly dismissed the idea of calling Quin. She wasn't going to go running to him begging for help. Not even for Phoebe. It would be just too pathetic, after she'd ignored all his attempts at communication with her for these past weeks. It was a mistake getting involved with him in the first place. She did feel sorry for him when she thought of his Christmas with his family, and all the stress and anxiety they were dealing with. She wouldn't give in, even though she knew he was working just down the street. She'd seen his car in the parking lot behind the Turtle during the week before Christmas. It just hardened her heart.

By midnight, she was exhausted and ready to fall into bed. But she found the bedcovers still in a heap on the floor where she'd left them, hours earlier, and the mattress was still damp. She was too tired to deal with it. Grabbing a blanket and pillow, she carried them into the living room and fell on the couch. She placed her phone on the floor where she could reach it easily. Ben stared at her as if he couldn't believe she wanted him to sleep on the floor. After she turned out the light, she heard the dog sigh and plop down beside her. After a few minutes, though, Ben rose to his feet and walked slowly to her bedroom. The last sound Anne heard before falling into a restless sleep was Ben hopping onto the bare mattress.

The next day was more of the same – uncertainty and fear juggling with anger. Anne drove to Bill's house. He told her he'd called the police, who told him that a seventeen-year-old girl who disappeared with money and a suitcase full of clothes had definite plans. With no evidence of foul play, the cops were too busy to try to find some kid who wouldn't want to be found. Bill swore a blue streak as he told Anne about it.

Ellen sat in the living room, her face a grim mask. Anne made tea and took a cup to her. She knelt in front of her. "Ellen, do you want a sedative? I can give you one so at least you can get some sleep."

Ellen stared as if she didn't understand a word.

"Ellen?" Anne observed the woman's fleshy face. Dark bags hung under her bloodshot eyes. She exuded the stale smell of a heavy smoker. Her thin, faded hair hung lifeless over her dry, cracked skin – a clear sign of estrogen depletion. Anne felt frustrated. She'd been urging Ellen to stop smoking and start taking hormones. "Ellen, come on, talk to me."

Ellen's eyes narrowed. "What if she's pregnant?" Her voice was expressionless. "What if that's why she left?"

"I'd be very surprised by that, Ellen." Anne made an effort to keep her voice calm. "I can't believe Phoebe would be that reckless."

Ellen's words came through tight lips. "There's that Indian."

"He's just her friend, Ellen. And Phoebe doesn't want a baby. You know that."

Ellen leaned forward. "I know she doesn't want a baby. She'd get rid of it. A mortal sin. She knows her father would throw her over the falls if she came home with a baby. Especially ..." She bit her lip.

"Ellen, stop it." Anne spoke sternly. "You're making yourself crazy." She stood up and went into the kitchen, pulled a brown bottle out of her backpack, and shook out two pills. After pouring a glass of cold water, she went back to the family room and gave it to Ellen, then knelt down in front of her again. "Here, take these," she said, in her firmest registered-nurse voice, as she handed her the pills. "You need some sleep."

"I don't want to take it!" Ellen replied in a loud voice.

Bill came into the room. "What's going on?"

"I'm trying to get Ellen to take a sedative so she can get some sleep."

"Good idea. Take it, Ellen."

His wife glared at him for a moment, then put the pills in her mouth, and swallowed. Anne helped her get out of the chair and walked her to the bedroom, where she fell fully clothed onto the bed. Anne pulled Ellen's shoes off and put a brightly colored crocheted afghan over her feet. "Go to sleep. You'll feel better." She didn't reply. Anne closed the door gently.

"Thanks," Bill said, when she joined him in the kitchen. "She was getting nuttier by the minute."

"She's having a hard time, Bill." Anne looked at her brother; he seemed years older than he had just four days ago, on Christmas Day. He wasn't aging well, either. He still smoked, and was about thirty pounds overweight. His dark brown hair hadn't thinned much or grayed, but it looked out of place on his face, which was fleshy and deeply lined. She felt a sharp spasm of sympathy. Bill had had a hard time. He thought the move to the suburbs would be good for the family, would make life calmer. Then he had to worry about being able to afford the house when work slowed at the construction company where he was a foreman. He was paying college bills for the twins. And now Phoebe had to do this, on top of all the other grief she'd been giving him.

Anne reached over and held his hand. "We'll find her, Bill," she told him, earnestly, looking straight into his eyes. "I know we will."

That was the nurse talking, though, trying to be reassuring. Anne had never felt so helpless before.

CHAPTER TWENTY-FIVE

Even though his friends arrived a day later than planned, Leonard knew he'd meet up with them eventually. He wandered among the festival crowds, listened to music, examined art on display, learned dance steps, and ate way too much fry bread. Late in the day, he found a display about his namesake, Leonard Peltier, and bought a paperback book of Peltier's prison writings called, "My Life Is My Sun Dance."

Leonard had absorbed the knowledge that he was named for this man without thinking too much about the actual human being behind the name. It was old, painful history. One night, when he was ten, his mom was in a good mood, for once, smoking dope with her new boyfriend. She started talking about her life, and told Leonard that it was his father who had wanted his son to be named for Leonard Peltier, a man who fought for justice for his people. Leonard wished she had said more, but she started crying when she remembered his father's laughter, and smile, and she stopped talking. She had gotten pregnant when they both were still in high school, and she was still angry at his father for dying so young, and so pointlessly. He had been in the back of a pickup truck with three other guys, partying. The stoned driver went off Upper Mountain Road at high speed. Six young men lost their lives.

Leonard spent that evening reading Peltier's book, a story of injustice and woe so powerful that when he finished it he couldn't move; he felt as though he'd been turned to stone. Since 1977, longer than Leonard had been alive, this man of the Lakota Sioux had been living in the hell of the white man's prison, convicted of killing two FBI agents who violated the sovereignty of the Oglala Sioux reservation during a time of turmoil and native activism. Even the government admitted it could not prove his guilt. But the feds had to show their strength, and their power, and make an example of someone. For many years human rights groups from around the world, and even the Pope and Dalai Lama, had been seeking his release from prison. He'd endured beatings, solitary confinement, and neglect of his medical conditions. No prisons in human history displayed more remorseless inhumanity than twenty-first-century American prisons inflicted on the human beings inside their impenetrable walls. Peltier was a living symbol, he said in his book, of how America punishes some humans for the crime of being Indian.

Now Leonard understood why Uncle Clint was always warning him never to get mixed up in anything involving the police, no matter how minor. He'd be screwed for sure. It was nothing new for Indians, Clint told him. Way back in Red Jacket's time, an Indian was sentenced to life in prison for supposedly stealing some spoons from the land speculator Joseph Ellicott. Clint told Leonard how, after the trial, Red Jacket pointed to the figure representing "Justice" on the New York State seal, and commented bitterly. His words were translated as, "Where does he live now?"

"Those spoons were worth more than a man's life," Clint told Leonard. "That's how the white man thinks. Never forget that, Leonard. Don't you ever forget it."

Leonard had to be alone after reading the book. He walked away from all the activity and found a spot where he could sit against a rock. He made himself breathe deeply; he tried to calm his mind, as Wallace had taught him. He tried to focus his thoughts away from anger and outrage, toward the peaceful center of his mind. He hadn't found that center yet. He was afraid to go too deep into himself. He was afraid of the outrage that could so easily overwhelm him, of the anger and self-hate that would let himself do what his father did, get massively high and jump into the bed of a truck driven by someone as high as he was.

Leonard tried to distance himself from any emotion, because emotions were dangerous. He fell asleep after a while, and woke up at dawn with hunger pangs, covered with dirt and sand.

Leonard finally found Jemmy, who was looking for him, too, around noon, near one of the food stands. He was wearing a purple tee shirt depicting the Hiawatha wampum belt, like he said he would. Jemmy introduced Leonard to his two friends, Darman and Terrence; they were all from the Seneca nation in Cattaraugus. Jemmy was the shortest of the three guys and had a quick smile. Darman was a bit heavy, with a big chest and skinny legs. Terrence was his opposite, lithe and quick-moving. They all wore their hair long and pulled back in ponytails.

The three of them had just ordered heaping plates of Indian tacos. "We just got here," Jemmy explained. "This is breakfast." Leonard ordered a plate, too.

After they ate, Terrence said he wanted to walk around for a while and check out the music. Leonard understood that, even though he was anxious to leave. While he waited, he checked the sleeping gear he had bought cheap as unclaimed items at the lost-and-found tent. Finally, just after sunset, they were all in a dusty old red Honda CRV, speeding northwest up Route 95 toward Miracle Lake on the huge Paiute reservation in northwest Nevada. They took turns driving, and only stopped for gas or to pee.

As they raced north, Jemmy told Leonard more about himself and the other guys. He said they were working for a rich guy and living on his estate.

"It was weird, man. This guy, Jerome Lone, came to our community center and says, I'm looking for workers to do some jobs and help me build a *gä-no'-sote*," Jemmy said.

"A what?" Leonard asked.

"That's what we said, man," Jemmy replied, laughing. "Then he explains it's a longhouse, and he wants to build it in a field on his land in the spring. He says he'll pay us, so we say, okay. Then we find out he doesn't want us to use real tools, like power saws, but we have to do it

like the ancestors did, with axes and stuff, and build fires, and strip the
bark. Some guys who said they'd do it dropped out, but we went along,
especially when he said we could live out there now, on this field near
his mansion, in a double-wide mobile home. We help out on the estate,
digging and mowing and painting. We've been mapping the trees on
the land, too. Looking for hickory trees to strip the bark off of in the
spring."

"We have to keep going to school, though," Darman put in.
"That's a drag, but he says we're fired if we drop out of school."

"We're staying at one end of the field where we're going to build
the longhouse," Jemmy said. "It's about a half-mile away from the main
house, if you walk through some woods and jump over some creeks. It's
cool. The pay is great. We're basically on call to do whatever jobs need
to get done on the estate."

"Yeah, and get ordered around by the Woodman," Darman said.
The three of them howled.

"Who's that?" Leonard asked, laughing himself.

"He's the head guy, Woody, this big dude who does the security
and stuff. He likes to give us orders."

"So why does this guy want to build a longhouse?" Leonard
asked.

"I don't know," Jemmy said. "He's a professor or something in the
American Indian program at BU. Maybe he's going to write a paper on
us, or something."

"So you guys are living all alone out in a big field?" Leonard
asked.

"Not really alone," Terrance said. "There's this weird old dude out
in the field with us, at the other end of it, near the county road. He's
got a huge RV, and some other guys living with him. He's supposed to
be a healer, but he doesn't look like a real healer to me, he looks like
he belongs on TV, telling people to call his toll-free number and send
cash. Mr. Lone tells us to keep an eye on him and let him know if
anything strange is going on, and if he gets any visitors. But we haven't
seen anything strange yet."

"Sounds interesting," Leonard commented.

"If you wanna come back with us, Mr. Lone would hire you," Jemmy said. "He said we could use a couple more guys, especially since we got so much snow this winter. It's hard to keep the roads and walks around the house clear. His estate is huge. We never get all the work done."

"It's pretty sweet," Darman added. "We've got propane for power and heat, and Mr. Lone let us put in a satellite dish. This summer, when we finish the longhouse, we'll probably move in there, at least while the weather is good."

"Only if we get windows," Terrence said.

"Oh, yeah, the windows." Jemmy laughed. "We gave Mr. Lone a hard time about it, when he asked us if we wanted to stay in the longhouse when it was finished. I said we needed windows, we had to see out, man. He said that would destroy the traditional look of the longhouse, but I said, if the ancestors had glass, don't you think they would have put in windows? So he said he'd think about it. Then he came back and said, okay, maybe we could put in some windows, but we'll put wood shutters to close over them, so they aren't too notice-able. He does want us to keep an eye on things. It's obvious he doesn't trust the old guy in the RV. So we're set up real cool out there. How about it, Leonard?"

"I ... I'll think about it," Leonard managed to say. He turned quickly to look out the window, so they couldn't see his face. He'd nev-er made friends this easily, before.

Two nights later, they were camped out in the most beautiful place Leonard had ever seen or imagined, at a high elevation where the air was so sweet he thought he could taste it. Under gigantic pines, their campsite overlooked a pure, crystal blue lake, whose waters were pierced by a shaft of jagged rock looming near its center.

On the second night, when the three others were sound asleep, Leonard moved away from their fire, because he didn't want even that small light to impede his view of the sky. Over the past few nights he realized he'd never seen the sky before, only a hazy, weak echo of it.

This trip was the first time he had ever seen a sky undimmed by human lights, the first time he ever saw stars beyond count. As he stared at the glimmering cloud of the Milky Way, he finally understood one of the things Grandfather had tried to teach him. The band of the Milky Way really did seem sturdy enough to hold the Spirits of the Ongwehónwe, the people of Turtle Island, on their last journey. Those stars were the path to the Sky World. Someday, his Spirit would take that trail.

An intense, unblinking white light rose in the west and raced across the sky. It was the International Space Station. Leonard's eyes followed its smooth path, and he wondered how many more stars beyond the earth's atmosphere he'd be able to see from there. Could he see as many as the Elders could? He envied the astronauts their heavenly perch, their weightlessness. He wished he weren't so tired, so he could stay up all night just looking at the sky.

Leonard wasn't sure he was going to return back east, even considering Jemmy's invitation, which was very tempting. There was so much to explore out here. The desert was more colorful and beautiful than he'd expected, its openness a relief from the noisy paved world of western New York. He didn't feel lonely at all under the vast multitudes of stars. Grandfather said each one was a soul. He turned on his side in the sleeping bag. In the distance, he could see the stars' reflections on the dark surface of the lake, and the giant, glimmering mass of stone that rose from it like a knife.

Then he was climbing that harsh peak. It had looked easy, at first, because it wasn't straight up like the Niagara gorge. But it turned out to be steeper, and higher, than it appeared from a distance. Halfway up, he looked down and was horror-stricken to see that the smooth, calm lake had turned into rushing green rapids. Waves reared up and licked at his feet. He climbed frantically, clawing at the sharp-edged rock, feeling as though he would fall back at any moment, and be carried by the waves into a bottomless, dark chasm. Terror made him desperate. The jagged, crystalline rock became smooth, and wet, like the rocks that sat in Niagara's rapids, and he felt himself slipping toward the abyss, even as he climbed more desperately.

"Hey, man, wake up." Rough hands were shaking him. Leonard, dazed, realized it was Darman, in the real world.

"You were thrashing around, having some wicked dream," he said. "Lucky for you I had to take a wiz." He walked off.

Leonard sat up, and rubbed his face with his hands, still feeling the terror of the dream. He looked up at the stars, and was relieved to see they were still there, shining down on him. He dropped back down, and tried to keep his eyes open, tried not to sleep. He tried to explore the star path of the Milky Way.

The starlight blurred. He saw beyond the stars, as though the sky had split open. A Warrior, proud and strong, looked down at him. Leonard had never seen so clearly, or felt so drawn in longing to any-one, in this world. He met the Warrior's gaze, and saw love there. For the first time in his life, he felt real joy. He wanted to leave this Earth, and follow the Warrior home. But the vision faded. Then he was seized with such grief that all the tears dammed up inside him from his whole life burst through. They flowed like Niagara, while he stuffed the end of the sleeping bag in his mouth so his sobs wouldn't wake the others. He saw the pointlessness of his life. He had thought he lived like a wily, lone wolf, but now he saw himself as a homeless dog, a scavenger living on the edge of human life. He turned on his side. His pain made him curl up like a baby. He hoped that when all his tears were gone, his own Spirit would follow them into the Earth. He didn't deserve to walk into the Sky.

Exhausted, he fell into a deep, dreamless sleep.

When he woke up, the guys were packing up their camping gear. His sleeping bag was twisted around his legs; his head and arms were lying on bare, rocky ground, and felt damp.

When he sat up, Jemmy came over and handed him a high-caf-feine sport drink. "Heard you had a bad night."

"Thanks." Leonard twisted off the bottle cap and took a big gulp. "I'm okay."

They spent the next days exploring and camping. It seemed way too soon to Leonard when they were back in the SUV, returning south.

He leaned back in the seat with his eyes closed for most of the drive, trying to remember the beauty of this western landscape, and to forget the desolation of his dream. They were out of food, except for candy bars, so he felt light-headed when they pulled into a rest area.

While the other guys fed all their change into vending machines, Leonard walked to an overlook that faced east. The ground below was dry and tortured, heaving in rocky folds and thrusts. Far away, the desert faded into a gray wall of mountains. He thought about his dream, and was worried that, even in the desert, Niagara Falls haunted him.

"Hey, Leonard, come on." Terrence was impatient. They all piled back into the car.

Back on the road, Leonard leaned his head back and closed his eyes. He hoped he could sleep. Then he remembered something from his vision. Behind the Warrior had stood a wooden structure, in the middle of a field surrounded by green woods. A longhouse. Was the Warrior calling him back east, to his wooded homeland? Or was he looking back in time? He thought maybe he should go back and work at the Lone estate, after all, at least until he could figure out where he belonged.

CHAPTER TWENTY-SIX

After another long day of worry about Phoebe, Anne knew what she had to do. She put Ben on his leash, at dusk, and went outside. An inch of new snow was glazed with a thin coating of ice that gleamed eerily in the last dim light of the day. She went along the river path, pulling Ben as fast as possible on the crusty snow, almost slipping a few times. The upper rapids heaved past them, a dark gray mass exuding a frozen mist. As they passed under the pedestrian bridge to Goat Island, she saw a tall, stooped figure scurry over it. Even in the gloom, she could tell it was the Hermit. He seemed to be wrapped in a blanket. She wondered where he was sleeping. She patted a hard lump in her jeans pocket. For Christmas, Mari had given her a small pocket knife with a white bone handle. She told Anne that it was a weapon against evil, that her friend Callista had cast protective spells on it. Anne had attached it to the belt loop of her jeans. It was still there. "I need all the help I can get," she thought, though she couldn't imagine ever being impelled to use it.

At Prospect Point, Anne turned toward the street, and walked straight toward the Turtle's giant head. When she reached the entryway, halfway between the Turtle's left legs, she saw lights on inside the building. She walked along the curving wall until she got to the parking lot behind the tail, and spotted what she was looking for – Quin's old Jeep. It was covered with several inches of hard snow.

Returning to the entry, she tried the doors. They were locked.

With her face against the glass, she could see down a lighted hallway, where a slender, dark-haired man was gazing at a large painting on the wall. She pounded on the iron doorframe. The man turned and saw her. He walked to the lobby and, remaining a few yards back, waved her away. She gestured him forward. Finally, he came to the door. "We're not open." His voice was muffled by the thick glass doors. "Please go away."

"Please, I just need to talk to someone," Anne yelled. "It's important. Please."

Warily, he came forward. "What do you want?"

Anne wondered if this could be her nemesis, John Lone. No, this man was wearing a denim shirt and old jeans. He was younger and much less stylish than the fashionable entrepreneur whose picture she had seen in the newspaper. He looked tired, and sad.

"I need to talk to Quin. Can you get him? Please, it's important."

"Quin?"

"Yes, he must be here, his Jeep is out back. He's the computer guy."

Jerome hesitated. "You want to talk to Quin?" he asked.

"Yes, please, it's important."

He stared at her, poised on the edge of decision.

Anne met his gaze. "I just need to give him a message."

"Is this business?"

"No." She swallowed. "It's, it's personal."

He hesitated only a moment longer. This woman looked appealing. And she had a dog, who was shivering in the cold. "Wait here," he said, and turned and walked away.

"Well, this is just great," Anne told Ben, her face burning in spite of the cold wind. "Here's the little lady trying to get into the fort because she needs a man to solve her problem. I'll never get over this humiliation, Ben."

Soon she saw Quin coming through the lobby, pulling on his quilted jacket. Her questioner unlocked the door on the inside to let him out.

"Thanks, Jerome," Quin said. "I'll only be a few minutes."

"Take your time. Just use the buzzer when you want to get back in." He pointed to a button on the side of the door.

"Thank you," Anne called to him. He closed the door, and disappeared into the belly of the Turtle.

Quin looked surprised, and wary. "What's up?" he asked, as Ben jumped ecstatically on him. "Down, boy."

"Quin, I'm sorry to disturb you." Anne could feel how stiff her voice was. Her face was still blazing from embarrassment. "But I really need your help. I couldn't just text you. It's Phoebe. She's run off somewhere, maybe with Leonard, and we can't find either of them. They left a couple of flash drives at my house, but I can't get through the passwords, and they're possibly the only clue we have. Do you think you could break into them for me?"

"Sure." Quin tried to quell Ben's enthusiasm. "Down, boy," he repeated, as he stroked the dog's ears. He gave a quick glance into the Turtle. "I need to finish up something here. It'll take maybe an hour."

"Can you come by my house then?"

He bent forward slightly to see her better in the dim light. His mouth formed a half-grin. "Sure. I'll get there as soon as I can." Turning, he pushed the buzzer. After a moment, Jerome opened the door. Before he re-entered the Turtle, Quin looked back and said, "It's cool to see you guys again." He disappeared inside.

Anne stared as the door clicked shut and the two men faded into the shadows. She was surprised at the depth of her reaction to seeing Quin again. She was happy. Pulling hard on Ben's leash, she hurried home, staying on the lighted city streets, away from the river.

Quin arrived at Anne's house almost two hours later, covered with frozen mist that coated even his mustache and beard. His face was beet red from the cold.

"Did you walk here?" Anne asked, as she let him in the front door.

He stomped his boots on the tile floor. "Yeah. It would've taken too long to chop the ice off the Jeep. Besides, I've got to go back there later."

"Thanks for coming." Anne ran halfway up the stairs before turning to wait as he pulled off his wet coat and boots, leaving them on the floor near the door. He followed her to her office, fending off Ben's new greeting, and sat at her desk. He pulled a laptop out of his backpack. She handed him the flash drives. "Can you get into these?"

"Piece of cake." He slipped one into his laptop.

"Are you hungry?" Anne's brain was on automatic pilot.

"Sure." He typed quickly.

"I'll get you something to eat." She was glad to have something to do. She brought him a cup of coffee, then put together a baked ham sandwich on rye – leftovers from Ellen's Christmas dinner. He devoured it, typing and eating with continuous, unified motion. She made him another. He was removing the first drive as she brought the second sandwich to him.

"Did you find anything?"

"Not on this one. Just games and lots of native music. Must be Leonard's."

She stepped back and leaned against the doorframe, watching Quin's fingers move quickly over the keys, slowing only when he lifted the sandwich to his mouth. After about five minutes, he announced, "Ahhh, the mother lode!"

"What did you find?"

"Email files. Look." Two grids were open on the screen, one under the address <ani@nfmail> and the other under <niagarawolf@warriornet>.

"Fabulous, Quin!" Anne threw her arms around his shoulders in a quick, impulsive hug. "I knew you could do it."

"Let's see what's in here." He clicked randomly on icons in the <ani@nfmail> grid to open the messages.

Anne's eyes scanned the screen. "These are all notes to someone named Ani. They read like they're fan mail." Anne's landline rang. She hurried to the kitchen to answer it.

"Anne, this is Mari. Anything new?"

"Where are you?"

"Downstairs. I heard Quin come in. I didn't want to come up and bother you, but I had to find out if you found Phoebe or Leonard. And did you make up with Quin?"

"No and yes, sort of. Come up. He got some email files open."

"I'll be right there."

In the office, Quin had the other file open. "Find out anything?" Anne leaned over his shoulder, resting her arm on it. He felt warm, and comforting.

"This one is definitely Leonard's. He's talking to some guy about a music festival out west at New Year's. Read this last message." He pushed his chair back.

Anne knelt in front of the desk and read: "When we meet in January, we'll head for the mountains. See you in the desert, Brother. J"

"I don't like the sound of this," she said.

"Sound of what?" Mari entered the room. "Hi, Quin."

"Hey, Mari."

"Read this message." Anne stood up.

Mari read the screen. "Hmmm. What else have you found out?"

"It looks as though Leonard was planning to go to some music festival out west," Quin reported. "But there's this other file for someone named Ani, who's in some sort of contest. We don't know who that is."

Mari's brow knit in concentration. "Ani, Ani, Ani," she repeated. "Why does that sound familiar?" She closed her eyes, and repeated, "Ani, Ani, Ani, Ani ... "

"I could do a web search but 'ani' will bring up tons of listings," Quin said. "We have to narrow it down."

"Wait a minute," Anne said. "@nfmail is the city's official email network. It's what Jay's on. Pull up the city's web site and we can search that."

Quin typed in the commands. As the laptop downloaded the site, Mari cried out, "That contest! Don't you remember, Anne? The picture!"

"What picture?"

"The girl who looked like Phoebe! The Maid of the Mist!"

"Oh, God!" Anne felt queasy. "Oh, God, you could be right."

"Here's a link to the Maid of the Mist," Quin said. Their faces moved closer to the screen as the image downloaded. Phoebe's unmistakable eyes and smile appeared, recognizable even through a mask of heavy makeup and a frame of dark hair extensions. Anne and Mari read aloud: "Ani Shanando, Niagara's Maid of the Mist."

"That's Phoebe all right," Quin said.

"She's spelled her last name wrong," Mari observed.

"What's it supposed to be?" Quin asked.

"Shenandoah, like the river. I'm sure that's what she was trying to get at. It's the name of one of my favorite Native American singers, Joanne Shanandoah. I play her music all the time when Leonard and I work."

Anne groaned. "She can't spell. How can she be the Maid of the Mist when she can't even spell her own fake name correctly?"

"Easy," Mari warned. "Don't let negative thoughts cloud your judgment."

"Here's her bio." Quin opened up another web page. "Her fake bio, that is."

Anne slumped to the floor and buried her head in her arms, resting them on her knees. "Please read it aloud. I can't get my eyes to focus on the words."

Quin glanced at Mari. She started to read: "Ani Shanando was the unanimous choice of the judges at the Maid of the Mist Pageant at the opening of the new Club Grande Niagara in July. Ani won a round trip for two and a wonderful seven nights at Universe Las Vegas. She will represent the City of Niagara Falls at Casino Resorts Internationale's Las Vegas New Year's Eve Extravaganza and Beauty Pageant, where she will have the chance to compete to win $20,000 and a performance contract with the Casino Resorts Internationale franchise."

"How could she do this?" Anne wailed.

Mari read on: "Ani was born in Niagara Falls, but left with her parents when she was just a baby. Her father, Dakota Shanando, who was part Cherokee, took Ani and her mother to live in the Southwest United States. Tragically, Ani's parents were killed when her father's small plane crashed into a mesa in the Arizona desert, leaving Ani as the only survivor." Her voice shook. "Ani lived with her grandmother in a pueblo town until she was eighteen, when she returned to New York State to attend Buffalo University. She is a senior, majoring in psychology." She doubled over with laughter.

Anne lifted her head and asked, "Is that all?"

Chuckling, Quin asked, "Isn't that enough?"

Anne jumped to her feet. "I can't believe you two think this is funny."

"Oh, Anne, it's hilarious," Mari said. "Dakota Shanando. Lived in a pueblo town. Phoebe and Leonard must have spent a lot of time thinking this up."

"I can't believe she fooled anybody with this," Anne said. "Anybody except that idiot Nick Valli, that is."

"Well, at least you know where she is," Mari offered.

"Maybe. But what if she just wanted the plane tickets so she and Leonard could go and head into the desert?"

"Call the hotel and see if she checked in," Quin suggested.

Anne googled for the phone number and called it. "Hello, can you tell me if Ani Shanando has checked in? That's S-H-A-N-A-N-D-O. She's a pageant contestant."

"Yes, she has," the clerk said after a moment. "Shall I ring her room for you?"

"Yes, please." Anne's heart was racing. After some rings, a voice-mail message clicked in. Anne hung up. "I could have left a message but I didn't know what to say. I'm sure she doesn't want to hear from me."

"Leave it for now," Quin said. Mari agreed.

"Should I call Bill and let him know we found her?" Anne asked. "He'll be so furious he'll fly out there on the first plane he can get, and that would be a disaster."

"You'd better be careful," Mari advised. "Their relationship is precarious as it is."

"She could have checked in and left without checking out," Quin suggested. "Then headed out with Leonard."

"Call and see if Leonard checked in," Mari said.

Anne redialed. The clerk informed her that no one by the name of Leonard Mountview was registered.

"Well," Quin said. "We can assume they got to Vegas, and that Phoebe for one checked into the Universe. Leonard could have a fake name, too. But they could be anywhere."

"Maybe I should fly out there," Anne said.

"And do what?" Quin asked.

"She doesn't want you to know where she is, Anne, or what she's doing," Mari argued. "She doesn't want anybody to know. Otherwise, she would have told you."

"She's on a mission," Quin said. "So's Leonard."

"But they're just kids!" Anne cried. "Anything could happen! They're either in Las Vegas, which is full of sleazeballs like Nick Valli, or else they're wandering around in the middle of a godforsaken desert, probably eating mushrooms and getting high."

"Sounds cool." Quin grinned.

Anne glared at him.

"She might win the contest and the contract," Mari offered, a suggestion that focused Anne's angry gaze on her. Mari ignored it. "Look, Anne, there's no way to force them back, even if you find them. You know they have a seven-day stay at the hotel, and then a return ticket back home. Why don't you give them the week? It's almost over. They're probably just hanging out around the hotel. They're both smart kids who know how to take care of themselves. And the pageant will keep Phoebe busy. Let them have their adventure. You and Bill can deal with it when they get home."

Anne looked dubious.

"If they're not back right after New Year's, I'll head out there with you to look for them," Quin offered.

"Me, too," Mari contributed.

"Maybe you two are right. I don't know." Anne had never felt so incapable of making a decision. "I don't know whether to call Bill or not, at least to let him know we think Phoebe is safe. I'll have to think about that some more. But I will call Chief Mountview and tell him about Leonard going into the desert. Maybe he knows people out there who can look out for him."

"Cool," Quin said. "Is there more coffee?"

"Yes, help yourself."

He rose and went into the kitchen.

"I'm glad he's here," Mari whispered to Anne.

"Oh, Mari, this is all too much." Anne pushed her uncombed hair out of her face. I feel like everything's upside down. Phoebe and Leonard must have been planning this all summer, and we never suspected a thing. I feel so stupid."

Mari nodded. "We were blinded by love."

"Don't blame yourselves." Quin returned, gulping down coffee as he came back into the office. "They lied to you. They're the ones who should feel bad, but they won't, because they got what they wanted." He drained his cup. "I've got to get back now." He left the office.

Mari nudged Anne with her elbow and whispered, "Go on!"

Anne hadn't noticed Quin had left. She was wondering how she could have spent so much time with Phoebe and not had the slightest idea what was going on inside the kid's head. "Quin, wait." Anne followed him down the foyer stairs. "Ben and I will walk back with you."

They bundled up silently and went out into the cold night. They walked a block up to Rainbow Boulevard. The wide thoroughfare was bright; few cars were out. The wind bit their faces. When they reached the street where Quin would turn toward the Turtle, Anne stopped. "I'll turn back here."

He stopped, too, and looked as though he was waiting for her to say more. She stammered, "I can't thank you enough for what you did tonight. It's such a relief to at least know where they are."

"You gonna start talking to me again?" he challenged her. "Or do

216

you still think I'm on the Dark Side?"

"I don't know what side is dark anymore. I used to think I knew a lot. Now I think I don't know anything."

"Welcome to chaos."

She looked up at his face. Illuminated by the neon waterfall lighting up the face of the towering Seneca casino a block away, his serious expression had a bluish tint. She realized that what she really wanted to do was grab him, hold onto his warm, solid body, and take him back to her bedroom where she could fling herself into an erotically charged orbit around his imperturbable reality. But she couldn't tell him that. Not yet. "Okay, truce." She managed a wry smile. "Come back after you finish tonight?"

He smiled. "Sure, cool." He bent down and rubbed Ben's ears. "See you, buddy." He turned and walked down the dim street.

Watching him recede into darkness, Anne let out a deep breath, feeling exhausted, and numb. "Come on, Ben, let's go home," she said. "Now all I've got to do is figure out who to betray – Phoebe or Bill."

CHAPTER TWENTY-SEVEN

"Ani, come along now, Honey. It's time for us to get bee-u-tee-full."

"No, not yet, Belle," Phoebe begged, as she floated on the surface of a warm pool. "Let me stay here just a little while longer. I'm soooo relaxed!"

"Sweetie-pie, if you don't come out right now, I'm gonna pour the ice from this drink right on top of your li'l head."

Phoebe surrendered, because she knew Belle actually would pour ice on her; they had to get ready for the next rehearsal. Belle was trying to help her. She was a pro. Looking up at her statuesque friend, standing on the rim of the pool, Phoebe knew she couldn't compare herself to Belle. They were in totally different leagues.

Phoebe would never forget her first site of Belle, at the contest's welcoming reception, where she was holding court in the middle of a crush of men. Standing more than six feet tall in heels, her figure was molded in a red-sequined corset; her huge breasts oozed out of its top. Her long legs were sheathed in black net stockings. Her garishly red hair was piled in big curls on the top of her head and crowned with swaying feathers. Phoebe had stared at her in awe. "Who's that?"

Nick leered when he told her, "That's Belle-Aurora Boyette, the Riverboat Queen. She represents the Paddleboat Palace Casino in Missouri. She's some competition, Ani." He added hastily, "But not in the contest. She's not the type to win." He put his mouth close to Phoebe's ear, and whispered, "As my old man would say, she's built like a brick shithouse." Phoebe had no idea what that meant, and looked at Nick in disgust.

But it turned out that she and Belle became friends. Belle seemed to look out for her, after Phoebe's disastrous beginning when she was late for the opening reception and then had no idea what to do because she hadn't read the contestant manual. The other contestants, who were professional beauties, shunned her. It was just like being back in high school. When the contestant from Texas seemed to be nice, and handed Phoebe a cold drink, Belle grabbed it right out of her hand and said, "We've got a drug test tomorrow." Later, in the ladies room, she told her, "You'd better stick close to Belle, Honey. There are a lot of rattle-snakes on this Pleasure Planet. You're gonna need my help."

Nik explained to Phoebe why the casino was called "The Plea-sure Planet" while he walked her to her room after the reception. He asked, "Did you see the big shot with the blond hair who came in for a while?" Phoebe nodded. It would have been hard to miss the sudden excitement that followed the arrival of a VIP who looked like a mov-ie-star, surrounded by a swarm of men in suits. "That's the billionaire Brit who owns this franchise," Nik told her. "It's part of his space tourism investment. He's building space planes that will take people to his casinos that will be built in space stations, or even on the moon. He's got tons of investors, and he thinks he'll be sending people up to gamble in space within the decade."

"Yeah, right," Phoebe had replied. She just didn't believe it.

Now, Phoebe knew only Belle could have gotten her out of that warm pool. She took as long as she could to dry herself, then sat down and delayed some more by wrapping her wet ponytail in the towel and twisting it to squeeze the water out. She was so tired she felt numb. She never imagined what hard work the pageant would be. Not only were there long rehearsals of the New Year's Eve show three times a day, but there were lots of promotional appearances, too. The day before, she'd shivered in her tiny Maid outfit during a parade down the Strip, won-dering all the while why it wasn't hot in the desert. She'd gazed in awe and desire at Roman columns, dancing fountains, the Eiffel Tower, the pirate ship, and all the other fabulous resorts she'd love to be staying in, rather than this space theme franchise. She wished Nick had told her what it would really be like. She hated having to interact with casino guests during her promotional appearances, and pretend to be nice. She didn't care, now, if she never met another person for the rest of her life.

At first, it seemed glamorous to be on display as one of the contestants in a big contest, and have people stare and point at her. That soon stopped being fun. In her white-fringed Maid costume, with her extensioned hair in jewelled braids, Phoebe was shocked at how many people asked her what she was supposed to be. Wasn't she obviously an Indian maid? A surprising number of people said they had no idea there were still any Indians back east. "I thought you chased them all out west ages ago," one woman told her.

During her limited free time, Phoebe escaped to her little pool, a hot tub in the back section of the sprawling complex, which had a number of pools, all named for different planets. This one was called Venus's Glade. She called it her secret waterfall, and loved to float in the warmth and watch the gentle cascade of water flow down the plastic wall. This waterfall was soothing – not like that giant horror near Anne's house. Phoebe often wondered how Anne could live with its constant roar pounding her ears. She herself slept with her ear buds on every night she stayed on Cataract Lane, to block out the sound of the falls; otherwise, she would never get any sleep. Phoebe loved staying in Anne's beautiful, peaceful house, but she didn't like being so close to the raging river – it made her edgy.

"Come on, Ani-girl, stop stalling," Belle said. "We've really got to high-tail it now."

"Okay already," Phoebe replied testily, quickly sliding her feet into her heels and standing up. She'd totally lost the self-consciousness she had, at first, when she wore her Maid outfit or bikini with heels in public. A lot of women in Las Vegas wore less than she did, and they weren't even contestants.

"What day is it, Belle?" she asked, as they waited for an elevator to take them to their rooms.

"I'm not sure, Honey. To tell you the truth, I don't know if we're comin' on ten AM or ten PM. I just know we'd better be in that hall for rehearsal in fifteen minutes." Seeing her distress, Belle put her arms around Phoebe. "You can do it, child. You just need a hug."

Phoebe tried feebly to push herself away, but when Belle's strong arms didn't give way, she surrendered. She covered her face with her towel, laid her head on top of Belle's firm breast, and sobbed.

Her friend tried to console her. "There, there, Sweetie-pie. You're just too tired for words. And I'll bet you went to float in that pool instead of sleeping, right?"

Phoebe nodded. Now she felt stupid. The trainers kept warning the contestants to get enough rest. They didn't want the girls to collapse before the pageant, or faint during the televised show. Everyone had to pass daily drug tests or be disqualified, so they couldn't use chemicals to keep going.

After breaking down in public, Phoebe was too embarrassed to lift her head off Belle's breast, so she let the older woman lead her into the crowded elevator with her arm around her, while Phoebe kept her face hidden.

"The poor child lost a bundle to a one-armed bandit," Belle lied dramatically to the people inside the elevator.

"I know just how that feels!" a woman said, in a raspy voice. Other people murmured sympathetic words. Then Phoebe felt someone tuck something into the back of her bikini panties. She was too stunned to react. When she and Belle were out of the elevator, Phoebe pulled out of her friend's arms and grabbed the item. It was a fifty-dollar bill.

"Belle, why did you say that?" Phoebe yelled. "Look what someone put in my bottom!"

Belle laughed. "Why, Honey, that's gotta be a lucky fifty. You oughta play it."

"No, thank you!" Holding the bill between two fingers, Phoebe let it drop to the floor.

"You're an uppity little thing, throwing money around like that," Belle told her. "Especially in Vegas. You might better throw it in a slot machine – you could score big."

"Maybe, but who cares?" Phoebe replied crankily. Belle raised her right eyebrow, but didn't say anything. As they walked down the hall to their rooms, three other contestants rushed past them on their way to the elevator.

"You two are going to be late again," one of them said accusingly. Belle and Phoebe made faces at her retreating back.

They reached Belle's room first. Phoebe followed her in as a short-cut to her own room, which adjoined it. They usually kept the door between their rooms unlocked.

In her room, Phoebe went to the refrigerator and pulled out a caffeine drink and high-protein snack bar. She didn't care if she was late. It wasn't like this was the real performance. She needed to pull herself together after that scene in the hallway. And think about what it meant – the way Belle had put her arms around her and held onto her. Was she a lesbian? Phoebe had to admit, once she got over the shock of being in actual physical contact with another person, Belle's body hadn't repulsed her. In fact, Phoebe had liked the way it felt to be held by her. It was comforting. Did that mean she was a lesbian, herself? Is that why she thought all the guys in high school – except Leonard, who, like her, kept strict physical boundaries around himself – were revolting? Phoebe thought so hard about this that her head started to ache.

She finished her snack and went to Belle's room, hoping Belle's manager, Val, wasn't there. He was from Europe somewhere. She liked him, but she had to hurry, and he seemed always to want to talk, in his accent that sometimes she couldn't understand. He seemed much older than Belle; his tanned complexion was thin, shriveled rather than wrinkled. His white hair was cut short and spiked straight up. He always wore tight black jeans and a black tee shirt under a leather vest; gold chains hung out of his jeans pockets.

"Belle, do you have any ibuprofen?" Phoebe yelled into the bathroom, where she could hear the shower running.

"On the bureau!" was the shouted reply.

Great, Phoebe thought, looking at the pile of cosmetics and beauty tools that covered every inch of counter space in the room. She was still searching when Belle came out of the bathroom wrapped in a short terrycloth robe. Phoebe kept her eyes off Belle as she walked over to the bureau, reached in a specific spot, and handed Phoebe a small plastic container.

"Thanks." Phoebe opened the bottle and shook two pills into the palm of her hand. She was about to return to her own room when the outer door opened, and Val walked in.

"Look what I found out in the hallway," he announced, holding up his find. "Fifty dollars!"

The two women looked at each other and started howling with laughter. Phoebe ran back to her room, doubled over, past the confused Val. She quickly shut the door behind her.

The laughter made Phoebe feel better. She was glad to be hanging out with Belle. It was fun. She liked playing a diva, and being with one. She changed quickly into her rehearsal clothes, and was ready when the door to Belle's room burst open.

"Ani girl, are you ready yet?"

"Yes, coming."

"Now remember, Ani," Belle told her as they walked to the elevator. "There's nothin' to this contest. Just *be* the personality you want them to think you are."

As she entered the rehearsal hall behind Belle, who was wearing a neon purple leotard, Phoebe realized another advantage to hanging out with her: when they walked into rehearsal late, all eyes couldn't help but be on the stately Riverboat Queen, while the slender Maid of the Mist slipped in, almost unnoticed.

CHAPTER TWENTY-EIGHT

"Y'know, Jerome, we'd get there a lot faster on ATV's." Woody's deep voice seemed to echo through the woods, which were silent except for the crunching sound of their boots on the thin ice that glazed the snow covering the trail through the woods.

Jerome stopped to turn and look at his companion. "I don't want to give them any warning that we're coming."

A grunt, accompanied by a white puff of cold breath, indicated Woody got the hint. He spoke in a lower voice. "Give me a minute." Leaning against a sturdy maple, he took deep breaths.

Jerome eyed him sharply. "You should stop smoking."

The big man's eyebrows shot up. Jerome was happy he had hit his mark. Woody tried to hide his habit, but no smoker was clever enough to eradicate all traces. Jerome was worried about Woody's health. He was overweight, even for his height. All his weight was in his huge torso; he had no butt, which amplified the impression that he was weirdly top-heavy.

"Are you sure all the guys are away?" Jerome asked.

"Yeah," Woody replied. "They left more than a week ago to drive to that big music festival in Nevada. They were really psyched, talking about camping in the desert, and smoking peyote, and picking up girls." He rolled his eyes.

Jerome smiled. He remembered when he would have loved such a journey, full of excited anticipation. It occurred to him he hadn't felt that way since long before John's accident. His research, especially, was getting him down. As he explored deeper into the past, he had less and less hope for the future. He glanced up at the treetops; the hardwoods around him had dropped most of their leaves, but many still clung to branches, like old brown rags. Even with the snow, the weather had been fairly mild so far, for December in the hills.

Woody was still talking, a sign of his nervousness. "I checked the double-wide again yesterday, just to be sure no vagrants moved in, human or animal. I wanted to be sure Moon's guests hadn't been snooping in there. The raccoons have been sniffing around, but they didn't get in. They left a lot of tracks."

"Probably looking for the junk food those kids leave around." Jerome kicked the ground with his hiking boot, turning up a hunk of moist, brown earth and leaves mixed in with the snow. It was New Year's Eve; in previous years, they usually had a lot more snow at this high elevation.

"Come on, Woody. Let's get this over with." Jerome turned and walked resolutely up the gentle slope.

It was early, just an hour past sunrise, when they crested the hill and reached the clearing on the other side. In the east, the sun glowed hazily behind a dome of silver clouds. A wide field sloped gently from the hilltop, its long brown grass bowed down in the snow. Tall dead seed heads of milkweed and thistle swayed in the chill wind. Near the path was the double-wide where the young staff members were camping. Reluctantly, Jerome turned his eyes toward the sleek RV sitting on the other end of the wide field. A row of white pines separated it from the county road just beyond. An old brown van was parked alongside it. Levi Moon had told Jerome's mother the men visiting him were his cousins, there for the holiday. Jerome felt his blood surge along his temples.

"Ok, let's go," he said. They strode across the field to the RV, and pounded on the door.

"Levi! Wake up. We're going to talk. Now!" Jerome had spent a sleepless night waiting for this moment. Woody was just behind him, stomping his big feet to announce his presence.

It was several long moments before the door opened. Archie, the largest and least attractive of Levi Moon's new companions, pushed onto the stair, forcing Jerome to step back. He closed the door firmly behind him.

"What do you want?" Archie's eyes were thin slits.

"I want to talk to Levi Moon."

"He's sleeping. Come back later."

Woody took a step forward. "As long as you guys are staying on Mr. Lone's property, you'd better be more polite. I can have a truck up here in twenty minutes to haul you out."

Archie glanced at Jerome, who met his gaze.

"Don't think he's kidding." Jerome was past any gesture of civility. "I'll drive the truck myself."

The door opened behind Archie. Levi Moon, wrapped in a heavy black coat, stepped out. "Jerome, what a pleasant surprise." Puffs of white mist spewed out with every word. "I'd invite you in for coffee, but it's a bit early."

"I wouldn't take coffee from you, Levi." Jerome glared. "It may interest you to know that I've just come back from Niagara Falls, late last night."

"How nice for you, Jerome." Moon's bland face looked puffy. "I hope you had better company than your surly friend here." He indicated Woody with a jerk of his head. "Some female company, I hope. It's so cold by the falls in winter."

"Cut the crap, Levi. You know where I've been." Jerome sucked in a deep breath of cold air. He was through playing games. "I was wondering why reporters from Niagara Falls kept calling me. I finally talked to one. Then I went to the Turtle to see the sleazy little operation you're trying to set up there. Just where do you get off setting up computerized gambling in my brother's name?"

Moon casually stepped down from the stair. "I've been waiting for the right time to explain this enterprise to you. When you hear more about it, you'll be thanking me. It'll make much more money than any of your other investments do."

Jerome stepped forward, his fists clenched. "You are not going to despoil that building, which represents sacred traditions about the beginnings of my people, by turning it into a casino. My lawyers will shut it down."

Moon was still smiling. "I welcome them to try. But I assure you, everything is in order, legally."

"It can't be. I have executive authority for my brother, and I've never signed authorization for the Pickering Corporation, as you call your phony outfit. The Turtle is controlled by White Pine Enterprises. No one else can do anything with it."

"But I do have authorization, Jerome. Ask your mother."

For the first time in his life, Jerome almost hit a man in cold anger. He forced himself not to. "Don't you dare bring my mother into this."

"But she is into this. She was the witness. She saw your brother John sign the papers giving me authority to form the Pickering Corporation, and operate in the Turtle. She signed, too."

Jerome felt the ground spin beneath his feet. Woody edged forward, breathing like a charging bull. Barely maintaining his self-control, Jerome said, between clenched teeth, "It will take me five minutes to prove that whatever signatures you have are forgeries."

"Will it now?" Moon stroked his chin. "Let's see, how could you do that?" Smirking, he turned to Archie. "Don't you think, Archie, that Jerome would have to have lawyers, and policemen, and doctors, all kinds of people, come into the Lone house and examine his brother, to see whether or not he could sign papers?"

Archie grunted.

"And don't you think Jerome's mother, poor Mrs. Lone, who has been through so much already, would have to go into court, and be questioned, and examined, and challenged?"

Woody lunged. Moon ducked behind the door while Archie thrust Woody aside. The big man landed with a thud on the ground.

"I wouldn't advise challenging the Pickering Corporation, Jerome." Moon's voice was dark, and his smarmy expression was gone. "You'll be opening up your whole life to scrutiny, and your brother's life, and even your mother's mental state. Is it really worth it?"

Jerome put his finger in Moon's face, while Woody lurched between his boss and Archie. "Yes, it is worth it, Moon. You listen to me. I will shut down your operation any way I can, and I will get you off my property and away from my family so fast you won't know where you are."

Moon lifted his head and looked down his nose at Jerome. "You'll have to fight your own mother to do that."

"Then I'll do it. For her own protection. I'll do whatever I have to. You will be out of here. And soon."

A sudden loud hissing noise came from the small man, as his face twisted in anger. Jerome and Woody instinctively jumped back. Moon leaped into the air, whirling in a circle, his black coat flying. The coat smelled rank, and as it swirled, Jerome had a vision of crows screaming in a chaotic dance.

Moon jumped back onto the top step by the door. "Now you listen to me, Jerome." His bony finger pointed like a talon. "You have no idea who you're dealing with. You can't stop me. I warn you not to stand in my way. If you try to cross me, I will bring you down. But not just you. I'll bring down your whole family. In ways you can't even imagine." The door behind him opened suddenly, and Moon seemed to be sucked inside. Archie followed quickly.

Jerome and Woody, stunned, stared at the door. After a long moment, Woody said, loudly, "Let's go get the tow truck. I'll have them out of here in an hour."

Jerome turned and walked quickly away from the RV, his every nerve and muscle screaming. As he strode quickly up the hill and into the woods, he remembered the only other time he had felt so unnerved. Two years ago, on his way to Ithaca for a conference at Cornell University, he had stopped to hike in the Enfield Glen, a deep, rocky gorge with a dramatic 115-foot cascade called Lucifer Falls. Hundreds of man-made steps carved into the shale wall of the gorge criss-crossed a trail along a thousand-foot-high elevation.

Jerome loved the Finger Lakes region in the middle of New York state, where the Onondaga kept the hearth fire for the Haudenosaunee nations. He'd camped in dozens of places there, losing himself in hills and gorges where white pines towered over silent glens. An intricate watershed of creeks and streams formed a living network of bountiful water flowing into the lakes, lifelines for spawning trout and salmon. Water streamed over layered stone in misty cascades. Wading in a brook, or lying in a glade at night listening to trees whisper and night birds chatter, he could feel the living pulse of Mother Earth.

On a cold but bright October day, he had entered the stony landscape. Jerome followed a sinuous, man-made path into a cauldron of stone formed in living rock by an ancient waterfall. The stone floor was patterned with water-carved swirls; it fell like a frozen cataract into the rushing stream below him. A raven croaked overhead. The path ahead of him looked dicey. It hugged the gorge wall on one side and had a deadly plunge into the gorge on the other. It was scarier than the Niagara gorge, which he had hiked many times. It was stark, isolated, self-contained. The skilled masonry seemed ancient, as though it had grown out of the stone, which was ever-changing through rockfalls, and alive with lichen and moss.

He kept close to the shale wall as he walked down dozens of limestone steps. Then the trail took another turn and ahead in the creek bed he saw a brink. Water gushed over a high stone ledge. Lucifer Falls formed lovely cascades as it gushed over the stone.

After taking photos, Jerome looked back along the way he had come. The stone steps he had descended blended into the shale wall, so that it looked as though his trail had disappeared and he wouldn't be able to go back. He heard another raven squawk as it flew to its nest in the gorge. He felt overwhelmed by the intensity of water and stone. He considered turning back, but saw with relief that the trail ahead turned away from the falls and began to descend along a dirt path. A wood-post fence ran alongside the path, which fell sharply down but was covered with brush and trees. Jerome longed for green. He walked forward, relieved to be walking on earth instead of stone. He heard the raven call again and looked up, not paying attention to where he stepped.

Suddenly his feet fell out from under him as he walked onto a patch of slick mud. He went down hard and felt himself sliding, as though he was being pulled, under the fence post and into the gorge. His camera flew out of his hands. For his life, he reached out and managed to grasp the sturdy trunk of a hemlock tree growing on the edge of the path. He dug his fingers into the craggy bark. He hung there for long moments, breathing heavily, forcing himself to calm down; he knew that if he let go he'd slide to the bottom of the gorge like a log in a chute.

The tree saved him. As a hawk screeched above, Jerome got a better hold and wrapped first his arms and then his body around the hemlock, digging his feet into the ground, until he could pull himself up enough to grab the fence post and hurl himself back on the trail. He never found his camera.

It was the closest Jerome had ever come to terror – until now. He knew he fell because he had let his guard down and was caught unawares. He felt like that now, only magnified, because this time the evil that was hidden had revealed itself to him.

Now halfway home, on the other side of the hill from Moon, he stopped walking and sat on a rounded boulder of silver granite, an erratic left by the last receding glacier. The tall pines swayed above his head. His hiking pants didn't warm or soften the rock's frigid surface, but he welcomed the sensation of the cold, hard rock, the feeling of still being alive.

Woody stopped. He was puffing, out of breath. He pulled out an Indian tobacco cigarette and lit it. Jerome didn't comment.

A brisk, cold wind blew in from the northwest, roaring through the trees. Breathing it in, Jerome saw the sky was darkening, with iron gray clouds building up. They'd have snow later. He rubbed his face. His nostrils still burned from the foul smell of Levi Moon. Staring at the ground, he said, "Moon's right. We can't do anything." He looked up, expecting an argument.

Woody lowered himself carefully to sit on the trunk of a fallen tree. "He's a thief, Jerome, and crazy. Crazy men will do anything. And those guys with him, they may not be as crazy as he is, but they'll do whatever he says. They're greedy, and mean, and almost as dangerous as he is."

"Did I tell you that a while back that private investigator I hired gave me the name of someone to call to ask about Moon, a guy up in Six Nations?" Jerome asked.

Woody shook his head.

Jerome stuffed his hands in his pockets, and tried to breathe in as much clean air as he could. "I called him a few days ago, before I went up to the Falls. He told me something I can't forget." He stood, and paced in a restless circle. "He told me I should get Levi Moon away from my family as soon as possible. Just before he hung up, he said, 'Don't worry about your money. Worry about your soul.'"

Woody exhaled a thick blast of white smoke.

"I'm not worried about my soul," Jerome said. "But now that I've seen what that guy was talking about, I'm worried about John's. And Mother's."

Woody stood up. "The best thing to do is get him out of here, right away. As soon as we get back, I'll call some guys and we'll haul them out. We'll go armed."

Jerome shook his head. "We can't make our move until we know exactly what to do to protect John and Mother. That's my first concern. The casino stuff can wait. I've made sure they can't get it going. I talked to the tech guy setting it up. He had no idea what was going on, but he's working for me now. Come on. Let's get home." He hurried along the trail.

Before they reached the house, the wind picked up even more, and blew icy sleet into their faces. The tall trees bent and twisted as the heavy precipitation took the last tattered leaves off their branches, and the wind rattled their limbs like bones.

CHAPTER TWENTY-NINE

"Happy New Year, America!"

The newly crowned Miss Universe Las Vegas smiled through her tears into the camera, while behind her the losing contestants gamely joined hands and sang "Auld Lang Syne" as the audience cheered and colored lasers lit up every corner of the casino's grand ballroom. They sang until the producer signaled them to stop, after the curtain came down. Their role in the pageant over, they quickly dropped each other's hands. The winner was whisked away in a bevy of casino executives. Though the audience was still singing, kissing, and drinking toasts to the New Year, the losing contestants were for the most part subdued. Except for one.

"Whooo-eeee!" a loud voice rang out. "Now we can have some fun!"

Phoebe tried to slip away. Fun? After the night's multiple humiliations?

Belle spotted her and came up behind her, a stalker in very high heels. "Ani-girl, where you goin'? Come on, let's celebrate!"

"What's there to celebrate?" She didn't want Belle to see her face, so she didn't turn around. But the Riverboat Queen grabbed her arm and pulled Phoebe to face her.

"The New Year! The end of the contest!" Belle shouted. "We have a day to ourselves in Vegas. Let's paint this town red!"

"I just want to go to my room and rest, Belle." Phoebe tried to walk around her.

Belle wouldn't let her pass. "Why, Honey, you're cryin'. Come on, let me give you a big hug." Before Phoebe could dodge her, the larger woman had her in her arms. This time Phoebe was repulsed – Belle was all sweaty. She pushed her away. "No, leave me alone."

Her friend looked surprised, and hurt.

"It's okay, Honey-chile." Belle looked closely at her. "I'm just surprised you're takin' it this hard, that's all. You didn't really expect to win, did you?"

"Well, sort of," Phoebe admitted, feeling like an idiot.

"And I thought *I* was from the sticks! Why, Ani-girl, everyone knew some witch from one of the big casinos would win. They're not going to waste their time promoting little ole us."

Phoebe stared. "You mean it was fixed? You mean I went through all this work for nothing?" She clenched her fists with righteous rage.

Belle laughed.

"Why didn't you tell me?" Phoebe shouted.

"Why, I would have, chile, if I knew you were as innocent as all that. But don't be mad at me. I don't make up the rules. I just try to get around them."

Phoebe didn't know whom to be mad at. But now she didn't feel like going to her room. She felt like getting even.

"Come on, let's not waste time here." Belle pulled on her arm. "Val's waitin' for us at the Cosmic Bar. We've got some drinkin' and dancin' and gamblin' to do!"

"Okay, Belle. Let's go!"

An hour later, Phoebe had lost count of how many glasses of champagne and cocktails she'd had – people just kept handing them to her. Then she and Val and Belle snuck behind some foliage and shared some pot. It was Phoebe's first actual inhaling of it, though she knew the smell from school. It went right to her brain cells and she suddenly felt switched on. Everything was bright, and funny – even Val looked strangely attractive. And she herself was the most beautiful of all, even if she didn't win the stupid pageant. It was fixed, not like the one back home. All she wanted to do was dance, and let people see how beautiful she was, and accept their tributes of champagne to the Maid of the Mist in her little white costume.

They went to the middle of the crowded dance floor; the DJ was playing the most danceable music she had ever heard. She let herself go with the throbbing music and lights. Belle and Val were dancing with her, and suddenly Phoebe realized how funny they were. Val's spiky hair. Belle's big pointy boobs. She started to laugh and couldn't stop. They laughed uproariously, too. The three of them had to hold each other up. Phoebe moved away from them to dance all by herself. Then she saw Nick Valli dancing with her, with a glass of champagne in each hand. His white silk shirt was unbuttoned, and open in the front; his shaved, smooth chest was glazed with sweat.

"Hey, Nick!" she shouted. "Happy New Year!" She reached for one of the glasses, but he held it back. "I want a New Year's kiss first," he told her. She giggled, put her arms around him, and kissed him on the cheek.

"That'll do for a start." Nick handed her a glass, which she emptied quickly – her mouth was so dry. "More," she demanded. Nick waved for a server. Phoebe's glass was quickly filled, and stayed filled. She lost all track of time. She waved bye-bye when Belle pranced by to tell her she and Val were going to hit the slots for a while. Later, when she and Nick were dancing to a slow song, she lifted her head from his shoulder and tried to ask him a question. It was hard to make the words come out. "Why didn't you tell me the contest was ... was ... was ... fixed?"

"Fixed? Why would you say that, baby doll?"

Phoebe was vaguely aware of Nick's hands caressing her behind. "Because I lost, that's why!" A wave of negativity swamped her brain. She pushed him away.

"Ani, Ani," Nick said soothingly, opening his arms to her. "The judges were blind, that's for sure. Come here and I'll make you feel like a winner."

Phoebe stared at him. Who was Ani? And why was Nick smirk-

234

ing at her like an idiot? She started to turn away from him. Her arm suddenly hurt, as he grabbed her with a claw-like grip. He pulled her toward him. "Let's go get something to drink," he said. He twirled her around several times in a dance step. Then she was too dizzy to say no to him. He led her off the dance floor to a private booth with soft seats and inflated plastic pillows. He motioned a waiter over and ordered two galactic-sized Cherry Eruptions. He put his arm around Phoebe's shoulder.

She became dimly aware of an annoying sensation, which confused her. She concentrated on trying to lift her arm to swat the bug that was bothering her. Then she realized Nick was licking her ear. He said, "Come on, baby, drink up." She parted her lips and tasted something like liquid cotton candy in her mouth. But when she swallowed, a burning vapor came back up through her nose, and she coughed a few times. That cleared her brain a bit. She shook her head when Nick tried to get her to drink. "No. I don't want anymore," she told him.

He set the glass down and tried to put both arms around her. She moved away from him, repulsed by his thin, sweaty face and the alcohol haze around him. His hands felt like bugs crawling all over her. She stared at him so hard she could see the short, black hairs emerging from his cheeks, like worms. Then she noticed that his lips were curled in an ugly sneer.

"Come on, Ani, cut the shit."

"What do you mean?"

"What I mean is ...," he moved even closer to her, "... start being nice to me. Remember, you owe me."

Her mouth dropped open. "Owe you! For what?"

"For what? Why, for bringing you to Vegas, and getting you on TV."

"So what?" Her outrage gave voice. "All I did was work. I had to walk around in my stupid costume and be nice to idiots all the time. I had to freeze in parades. I had to rehearse all day. And then get humiliated in the pageant. They made me stand in the very back on stage. I didn't get to say any lines. I was only on camera when they introduced me, and that was just for a second." She shoved him back. "*You* owe *me*!"

Nick grabbed Phoebe's arm and squeezed it so hard it hurt. His face got hard. He put it close to Phoebe's, and said, in a low, mean voice: "You just listen to me, you little spoiled brat. I could have blown you away a long time ago. I know exactly who you really are, Phoebe Techa, and I also know exactly how old you are. You're way too young to be drinking in this bar, and smoking pot with a couple of casino hustlers. Isn't that illegal, even here?"

Phoebe was so shocked her mind went totally blank. She tried to get her arm out of Nick's clutch. He kept talking: "You'd better stop fighting me and start being nice, or I'll call that security officer over there and have you arrested for fraud."

"Whaaaat?" Phoebe felt the word dribble out of her mouth. Her body got cold, as blood drained from her head to her feet, where it curdled. "What do you mean?"

"I mean," Nick told her, "that you came here under false pretens-es. You broke all the rules. You lied about your name, and your age, and made up a whole phony story about who you are. You took advan-tage of this corporation and its generous contest franchise, and of me, too. You could go to jail for a long time."

Phoebe started to shake. She couldn't stand to look into Nick's dark eyes, which were focused on her like a shark's, cold and heartless. She looked at his shoulder instead. "You wouldn't really tell on me, would you?" she asked in a trembling voice.

"I should," he replied coldly. "I should turn you in, and your disappearing Indian friend, and your Aunty Anne, too."

"Anne! You know Anne?"

"Unfortunately, yes. She's a real pain in the ass."

Thinking of her godmother almost sobered Phoebe up. "Honest, Anne doesn't know anything about this. She'd throw me over the falls if she knew I ever entered a beauty pageant, or came to Las Vegas." Phoebe almost wished Anne *was* there so her aunt *could* kill her. Then she wouldn't have to die of humiliation in prison.

Nick's voice softened. "But come on, Phoebe, I don't have to tell anyone the truth about you." She looked at him with hope. He took her hand and held it gently. "We can keep your little secret just between us."

"What do you want?" she whispered.

He moved his face close to hers again. "I just want us to get to know each other better, that's all. So we can team up, and leave fucking Niagara Falls. Let's talk. Why don't we go where it's more private, up to my suite?"

Phoebe shook her head. It depressed her even more to know he had a suite, and she didn't.

"Up to your room, then."

She shook her head again. "It wouldn't do you any good. I'm a lesbian."

Nick's body gave a spastic twitch and he burst into laughter. He laughed until he had to wipe tears from his eyes. "Oh, Phoebe, that's a good one. You're no lesbian. You've just been hanging around with Anne at her house of lesbos too long."

"But it's true." Phoebe's lips trembled. "And Anne didn't make me one. She's not a lesbian." Tears welled in her eyes and a big salty drop fell on Nick's hand.

"Hey." He stroked her hair. "Come on, you need someone to help you out. Someone who cares about you. A man. A man who can make you not want to be a lesbian. Come on, Phoebe, I'll take you to your room."

She let Nick pull her out of the booth. She knew she was trapped. She could feel her heart pounding against her chest bone. Her knees were shaky when she stood up. Nick put his arm around her and helped her walk to the elevator. She felt like a condemned prisoner. The trip to her room seemed to take forever.

"What a mess," Nick said, when she opened the door to her cluttered room. Phoebe wasn't embarrassed; she'd been listening to her mother say that all her life.

"I have to pee." Phoebe hurried to the bathroom as fast as her wobbly legs would carry her. Inside, she glanced at the mirror and was horrified to see how bad she looked. Her makeup was smeared, her hair hung in damp clumps, all her ribbons and feathers had disappeared, and her eyes were red and puffy. She started to cry, and cried all the while she was peeing. She was really scared. She remembered the phone next to the toilet. She'd have Belle paged. But when she carefully picked it up, she heard Nick's voice and hung up. Was he calling the police? She turned on the shower and stood under steaming hot water for a while. When she emerged, she blow-dried her hair, stalling for time, trying to keep her extensions from falling out, until Nick pounded on the door and told her to hurry up.

When she emerged, wearing a hotel bathrobe tightly sashed, Nick was standing by a room service cart that held a bucket of champagne, which he was pouring into two glasses. His silk shirt was on the floor. Phoebe's eyes darted around the room. He had pushed all her stuff off one of the beds, and fastened the inside security lock on the door. Her heart sank.

"I really am a lesbian, you know," she said, as Nick handed her a glass of champagne. "Guys don't turn me on."

"It doesn't matter," he replied. "Just drink up."

She took a couple of pretend sips. He seemed satisfied.

"I'll be right back," he said, then went into the bathroom.

Phoebe knew that if her mind was clearer, and if her brain-foot connection was working better, she'd just run. But her brain was fuzzy, and she was scared that Nick really would have her arrested. Her mind was still going around in circles when he emerged quickly from the bathroom. He had jumped in the shower and was wearing only a towel around his waist.

"Come on, drink up," he ordered.

"It tastes funny," she told him, sipping. "And there's stuff in it."

"It's just a little cork in an expensive champagne. You've never had good champagne before. Now come on." Nick sat on the bed. "Come sit by me," he ordered, patting the mattress.

Phoebe hesitated, then obeyed. As he leaned over for the TV

remote, and started to look for a music channel on the TV, she slowly became aware that her body felt heavy. She looked at her feet and tried to wiggle her toes; it was as if they had turned to stone. She turned to Nick to say something, then found she couldn't open her mouth. When he saw her struggling to talk, he smiled, and took the glass out of her hand.

"That's better," he said. With just a slight tap on her shoulder, he pushed her down, and lifted her feet onto the mattress. Then he stretched out next to her.

All at once, like a tiny spark in a fog, the realization hit Phoebe's mind – Nick had drugged her. He put something in her champagne. Just like in the anti-rape video they showed at school. She would have cried if she could make her eyes respond. She felt as if the real Phoebe had been turned into a tiny being, like Tinkerbell, who was trapped inside the skull of a big stone giant, and was banging on the inside trying to get out. Through the giant's eyes, she saw – but didn't much feel – Nick's face over hers, sucking away, and his hands groping her. He pulled on her panties and she felt his fingers go inside her.

"Get up! Get up!" cried the tiny, trapped Phoebe. "Oh, get up and run!" But the giant didn't move, even though his little prisoner screamed and cried. Nick pulled her panties off and grabbed her thighs, pulling her legs apart.

"Why, bless my soul!" a loud voice suddenly announced. "Ani, honey, what're you doin', girl?"

Phoebe tried to squirm and yell to Belle, but there was no need – her friend quickly sized up the situation. She lifted Nick right off Phoebe and hurled him onto the floor.

"You fucking bitch!" Nick yelled. He would have jumped to his feet and attacked her, but Val's heavy boot was on his chest.

"Ani-girl, do you want this louse on top of you?" Belle asked.

She couldn't respond, so she just let herself relax; tears rolled out of the edges of her closed eyes. She was so grateful Nick hadn't locked their connecting door.

Belle bent over her, felt her skin, and pulled up an eyelid. "Don't you worry, darlin'," she told Phoebe, gently stroking her cheek. "Belle and Val will take care of you." Standing, she said: "Val, honey, would you take Mr. Scumbag downstairs and show him what we do to guys who drug little girls back home?"

"I would be glad to." Val pulled Nick up, twisted his arm around his back, and pushed him out the door. Belle picked up Nick's shirt off the floor and threw it down the hallway after the two men. "And take your cheap shirt with you," she yelled. She came back into the room and went to Phoebe.

The tiny Phoebe tried to tell Belle that she was grateful, but it was impossible. Belle lifted her out of the bed, carried her to the bathroom, put her head over the toilet, and stuck a big finger down her throat. Phoebe gagged and vomited instantly. Belle wiped off her face, and carried her back to bed.

The tiny Phoebe grew back into her body, a bit. She started to cry. Belle sat down on the bed. Phoebe reached over and put her arms around her waist. "Oh, Belle. You saved me."

Belle pulled Phoebe up and put her arms around her. "There, there, darlin'."

"Belle, my life is such a mess. It's ruined."

"Nothin's that bad, Ani-girl. You just lie down here and sleep it off."

"Don't leave me, Belle," Phoebe begged her.

"I won't, Sweetie." Belle gently stroked Phoebe's back. She started to hum. Phoebe laid her head on Belle's firm bosom. She let her mind float with the melody as Belle rocked her and sang: "Hush, little Ani, don't you cry, Belle is gonna sing you a lullaby. Hush little Ani, don't say a word, Belle is gonna buy you a mocking bird..."

CHAPTER THIRTY

"See that thick layer of brown smog straight ahead?"

"Yeah," Leonard said.

"That's Vegas. We'll get there before the plane leaves, no problem."

"Thanks for going out of your way, Jemmy. I really want to drive back east with you guys, but I have to check on my friend first, and make sure she gets home okay."

"You mean see if she'll take you back," Jemmy laughed. His friends had amused themselves at Leonard's expense for days, conjuring scenes of the torrid romance going on between Leonard and his unnamed woman. Darman poked him in the back.

Leonard looked out at the high stone ridges marching along Route 95. Spruces covered the upper levels of the jagged rock formations, but the green would soon disappear as they drove further south into a landscape of scrubby Joshua trees and barren hills. Development had eaten up much of the Mojave Desert. As he gazed at the gobbled-up land, Leonard felt bad for the Paiutes who lived on the small reservation just outside the city. He knew what it was like to be surrounded by hostile territory.

He felt as though he had been riding one of the whirling dust devils that wander through the desert. His mind reeled with images: the Milky Way, striped mountains, ancient trees, far-away horizons, uncountable brilliant stars, the deep crystal blue lake with its peak rising like new earth from the void. He had known, at last, the joy of being out of the white world, with his brothers, under the open sky. He had learned that the desert was only barren from a distance, that up close it was teeming with life. He had learned that the eagle, flying high, isn't lonely at all; his sharp eyes see everything that walks upon the Earth.

Jemmy invited Leonard to return to New York with them. They were going to stop at Graceland. Terrence was convinced that Elvis was an Indian; there were web sites devoted to that discussion. Leonard wanted to, but he knew he wouldn't relax until he'd made sure Phoebe was all right. Maybe she'd even won the contest. Then he could head out with a clear mind.

As they got closer to Las Vegas, Leonard stared straight ahead as the city's skyline, nestled among high gray ridges, slowly got bigger. The casinos, like the mountains, were tricky. They were so huge that they looked closer from a distance than they really were. He'd learned that when he was running along the Strip, on his first day there.

Jemmy interrupted his thoughts. "Can't you just text her? It's easier than getting to the airport."

"I tried," Leonard said, "but I think her cell phone is dead. She always forgets to charge it. She checked out of the hotel."

"Well, we'll hang around the strip for a few hours, but we want to hit the road out of here tonight. Text us when you figure out what to do."

"Okay," Leonard said. He flushed when he heard the low chuckles of the guys in the back seat. If only they knew the real story. But he clenched his teeth, and didn't respond. No way would they understand half of it.

"Did you see the Bellagio fountains when you came in?" Darman asked.

"Yeah," Leonard replied. "I stopped to watch them when I heard some guy say they were better than Niagara Falls."

"Are they?"

"No. Not if you ever got close to the falls."

"I still want to see them," Darman said.

Jemmy leaned forward and turned the CD player on, loud. A Navajo rock group sang a song calling for justice for Leonard Peltier. The guys sang along, pounding the drumbeat on their thighs.

The Vegas skyline grew ever larger, more distinct against the gray ridge. They sped along the expressway, and soon were driving along city streets. Leonard asked, "How far to the airport?"

"Just a couple of miles," Jemmy told him.

"Let me out here."

"Gotta take a wiz?"

"No. I want to run the rest of the way. It'll be faster."

Jemmy looked at him in surprise. "You'll never make it in time."

"Yes I will."

"You won't, man."

"I will."

Jemmy shrugged and pulled over to the side of the road. Leonard grabbed his backpack, and jumped out. "Thanks for the ride. I'll text you when I'm done."

"We'll be glad to drive your woman home, too," Darman said. The guys laughed.

Leonard grinned. "Thanks. I'll see you guys later."

The tires squealed as Jemmy took off.

CHAPTER THIRTY-ONE

Phoebe couldn't remember where she was. As her brain slowly re-activated, her sensations logged on, one by one. Loud music was playing somewhere nearby. She felt some long strands of hair in her mouth as she slowly lifted her head and blinked her eyes. Gagging, she rolled over. The sunlight streaming in the window was blinding. She put an arm over her eyes. A loud voice cut through her brain like a buzz saw: "Rise and shine, darlin'!"

She froze as Belle's voice brought back memories that overloaded her brain. It all came back to her: Nick and his incredible sliminess, falling asleep in Belle's arms ... She rolled over onto her face again. She hoped she would pass out, and die, so that she'd never have to wake up again feeling so stupid and so totally physically repulsive.

"Oh, no, you don't, sweetie-pie." Belle flipped her like a pancake. She opened her eyes to see two huge mounds hovering over her face, as strong hands reached under her armpits and lifted her into a sitting position. Her brain exploded inside her skull in a fireball of sharp pain. "Leave me alone. My head hurts!"

"I just bet it does, Ani-girl," her friend replied, calmly. She yelled into the next room, "See, Val, I told you she wasn't dead yet."

Phoebe rubbed her head. "Oh, Belle, I feel so terrible all over." She sniffed and got a whiff of Nick's cologne on her body. "And I stink!" She started to cry.

"I'm startin' the shower for you." Belle strutted into Phoebe's bathroom, and came out a moment later. "Now you just hunker down in that steam for awhile, and you'll feel lots better."

"Thanks, Belle." Phoebe concentrated all her energy into making her body detach from the bed and walk into the bathroom. She didn't even stop to pee. She kept walking until she was under the hot water, so she wouldn't have to feel how raunchy she was. Only after she lathered and rinsed her whole body and her hair twice, losing most of her extensions, did she step out of the shower. She brushed her teeth and peed. Then she got back in the shower and washed again. There were bruises on her legs, arms and chest, and her back hurt. She concentrated on what she was doing. She didn't want to let herself think about the night before.

When she finished washing, Phoebe went back into the mess of her room and the din of Belle's loud music. She wished she could close the door between their rooms, but didn't have the nerve. Not after last night. She pulled on a hoody and jeans. Going to the refrigerator, she took an energy drink and breakfast bar. She felt nauseous. As she nibbled, sitting on the end of her bed, she could hear Belle and Val packing in the next room. She went to the doorway. Val was zipping up a large black suitcase. Belle, wearing a low-cut, flowing black blouse over gold pants, was standing by the bureau picking through her beauty-product pile and throwing selected items into a small suitcase on the bed. Both of them were moving in a business-like manner that Phoebe hadn't witnessed before.

"You guys getting ready to leave?" she asked.

Belle turned toward Phoebe. "You cleaned up good," she said, not stopping. "You'd better get started packin'. We've all got planes to catch."

"Belle, I need to ask you something ..."

Her friend suddenly shrieked and rushed over to hug Phoebe. "I forgot to tell you before, when you were lookin' so sickly." Belle released Phoebe from her embrace. "You're our lucky charm!"

"What do you mean?"

"Remember that fifty-dollar bill you were too prissy to keep?

Well, Val played it in the slots and hit the jackpot! So we're gonna hit Reno before goin' home. We've got a limo comin' in an hour to take us and you to the airport."

Phoebe felt a wave of relief. "You're going to take me to Reno with you!"

Belle and Val exchanged a look. Belle said, "No, honey-chile, you'd better head on home. Val and I have some serious partying to do. You couldn't keep up."

"But you said I'm your lucky charm."

"Lucky once," Val countered. "Like lightning. Doesn't hit the same spot twice."

"Please, Belle," Phoebe pleaded.

"Go get ready to leave. Then we'll talk."

"Okay." She rushed into her room and began tossing things into her suitcase. She knew she could convince them to take her. She thought about Leonard. He'd be surprised when she wasn't on the plane going home, but he'd be all right. She'd text him later. She tossed her ticket home in the trashcan, along with the contest rulebook, and went to the other room. "I'm ready, Belle," she announced.

Val was placing their suitcases by the door. Belle was on the phone for a porter. "I'll get your bag," he said, and went into her room.

Phoebe stayed close to Belle as they went down to the crowded lobby and checked out. She tried not to act nervous, but kept her eyes open for Nick. She was relieved when the three of them got into the limo. As they waited to pull into the flowing traffic, she felt a sharp pang of disappointment that she wouldn't see the baby white tigers in their only appearance ever. Tears came to her eyes but she quickly blinked them away.

After the three of them got through security at the terminal, Belle looked at Phoebe with a serious expression. "Well, honey, give me a hug. We'll say goodbye here. I'm going to look for coffee while Val takes you to your gate."

Phoebe felt a chill. "What do you mean?"

"I mean, chile, this is goodbye. You've got to be gettin' on home."

"But, I can't. I left my ticket back at the hotel. I don't remember my flight."

Val leaned forward and pulled her ticket out of his jacket pocket.

"Please, Belle." Phoebe held back tears. "I just can't go home."

"Sure you can. And I'll give hundred-to-one odds that some nice people are darn anxious for you to be gettin' there. I saw their texts and pictures on your cell phone."

"You don't understand at all. They're not nice. They'll throw me over the falls, they'll be so mad. I can't go back."

Belle laughed. "Now, you know that's a crock, Ani. Anyone, especially me, can see that you're a kid whose momma and papa spoiled her like a cream pie at a picnic on a sunny day. You ain't cut out for the fast life. You'd be crushed like a June-bug in a week's time. I don't wanna see it. I had a little sister, once."

"But, Belle, that's why I need you," Phoebe pleaded. "To teach me to be strong, and be a winner. Not just a ...," she stumbled over the painful words, "... a spoiled brat."

Belle, annoyingly, chuckled. "Bratty gets beat out of you sooner or later. And you got a good whupping out here. Just don't forget it."

Phoebe felt as though all her breath was leaving her body. "Belle, if you make me go home, I'll get arrested. Really. You don't know everything."

"Don't worry about that slimeball who was all over you. Val took care of him."

"Did you kill him?" She held her breath, hoping Val would say yes.

"He won't make trouble for you," Val told her. "I warned him."

"If he bothers you, just tell him that we'll come by and stomp him again," Belle added, laughing.

Phoebe couldn't reply. She felt sick. She folded her arms in front of her chest, and bowed her head, letting the tears fall.

"That guy's as much a fake as you are, Ani." Belle reached out to take her hand, but Phoebe angrily moved away from her.

"Now, look, Ani, we don't have much time so don't make this

hard." Belle's voice was stern. "You ain't ready to hit the road. Sure, you're bratty, but bratty ain't mean, and mean is what you have to be to survive like me. Now, don't make me get mean with you, because I like you. You make me laugh. I want us to part like friends."

"Oh, Belle." Phoebe turned toward her with an anguished expression on her face. "You're the only one who can save me. Please don't make me go home."

"I have to, kid." Belle's eyes narrowed. "You don't know how lucky you are. You got people waitin' for you to come home, wantin' you to come home. People who care about you." She paused. "Anyway, Val and I can't party if we've got to be keepin' our eyes open keepin' you out of trouble."

Phoebe recognized finality when she heard it. Wiping tears from her cheeks, she said, "I'll never forgive you, Belle."

The Riverboat Queen smiled. "Sure you will, Honey. Sooner than you think."

Phoebe hesitated until, looking from Belle to Val, she saw the hard look of closure in their eyes. She decided to go with dignity. She air-kissed Belle, and said, "Thank you for everything, except making me go home."

"You take care of yourself, little Maid of the Mist."

"I will." She swallowed hard. "I'm glad I was your lucky charm, just once." She turned quickly, and stumbled. Val turned her in the right direction. When they got to her gate, he said, "Goodbye, kid. And good luck."

"Thanks for rescuing me, Val. I hope I find a manager like you someday." She blinked hard. "Well, bye." She took a few steps toward the gate, and looked back. Val was still there, watching her, just like her father would when he told her to do something and she stalled. She considered just sitting down and doing nothing. He couldn't force her on the plane. But then what would she do? She had to think, because no way was she going home. Then she heard a familiar voice.

"Phoebe!"

As though he came out of nowhere, Leonard was standing next

to her, staring at her with wide eyes. He emitted a strong earthy aroma that smelled like some of Mari's herbs. Leonard was shocked to see Phoebe looking as she did, as though she was falling between two worlds. She wasn't Ani or Phoebe, she was a slender young woman in a baggy pink Universe Las Vegas hoodie, a bedraggled traveler. Her hair was uncombed, a mixture of dark and light, with extensions ready to fall off. And her face ... Leonard could hardly bear to look at her face. All its softness was gone, and she looked exhausted.

Val looked immensely relieved. "Get her on the plane," he told Leonard. "Take her home." He disappeared quickly into the crowd.

Leonard knew his disappointment at missing the road trip with the guys didn't matter as much as helping Phoebe now. She looked terrible, out of it. He took her arm gently. "Let's go," he said, and guided her onto the plane.

Phoebe didn't argue with him. She knew it was fate. The smell of the earth and herbs told her that magic had brought Leonard to her. He was dusty, as though he came from a different world. She stared at him as he shoved his dusty backpack and her carry-on under the seats. He looked at her, and grunted something she didn't hear. He helped her get in the window seat and slid in next to her. He pulled out his phone and started texting.

Turning toward the window, Phoebe felt as though she was living in a nightmare. The scene with Nick wasn't even the worst part. She always knew that one day she'd have to fight off a man. And she'd always believed in the big rescue, too. No, the real humiliation, she realized, came from seeing how small she was in the world. And how clueless. The other contestants were professionals. They ignored her because she was a nobody to them, a nobody who didn't have a chance of winning. Not because they were jealous of her. She was too stupid to see she couldn't possibly win. And the worst part, she forced herself to admit, was that she wouldn't ever have what it took to win a big beauty pageant, or be a supermodel. She would never work that hard for anything. She'd always be a loser. Even Belle sent her away, in the end. She was disposable.

Phoebe turned and stared at Leonard. He was changed. He was wearing a leather vest over a red tee shirt. Beaded leather straps were wrapped around his wrists. She saw he had a new tattoo on his arm, numbers and the outline of an eagle. The numbers were #89637-132, the federal prison ID of Leonard Peltier. She waited while he texted. Then, trying to make her voice sound not pathetic, she asked, "Are you going to ask me how I did in the contest?" She wanted to get that moment over with.

He glanced at her; he couldn't tell if the dark patches on her face were shadows or bruises. "I can tell," he whispered.

As Phoebe blinked back tears, Leonard let out a hard breath of exasperation. "I told you, you should have come to the desert. People wouldn't judge you by looks there. They'd take care of you. Be friends."

"I had friends." Phoebe could tell how small her voice came out. Leonard turned his face away from her.

She looked out the window, but couldn't see anything except a blur of tears. She must have dozed, because the next thing she heard was the steward's loud voice asking if she would like a drink. She shook her head and turned away. Thoughts came crowding into her mind, even though she tried to block them out. "Wolf?"

Leonard looked at her.

"Was your trip good?"

He nodded.

"I'm glad. I'm glad it all wasn't a total waste." She could tell by his expression that he was sad for her. She hated that. She was the one who had always looked out for him, before.

"Whatever happened to you back there, it doesn't matter," Leonard told her. "That was just a stupid contest, it doesn't mean anything. More important things are happening, Phoebe, things that can change the whole world. People have to decide if they want their lives to mean something." He hesitated. "You have to be careful. Money and greed are powerful forces. They could crush you."

She didn't answer.

His eyes explored her face. "You should have come with me to

250

the desert." His voice was sad. "You look crushed already."

"I'm okay." She tried to smile. "I'm just tired, that's all. I barely slept all week. I'm going to sleep now."

Turning her face, she closed her eyes, but she was far from sleep. She tried to decide where she was going to go when the plane landed. Home was out. And Anne. They would all keep yelling at her forever. She remembered some ads on TV that talked about a shelter for runaway kids in downtown Buffalo. She'd go there until she had a better plan. But she needed a disguise, in case her father already had her face on telephone pole posters. Plus, one of her fans might recognize her, and ask if she won the pageant. She couldn't face telling anyone what really happened. Turning to Leonard with sudden energy, she asked, "Wolf, do you have something sharp?"

He looked wary, but pulled his backpack up into his lap. Opening it, he fished around until he found a small sack. He shook out several stones, some of them painted, two bundles of dried herbs, a braid made of long grass, some flat gray stones, and pieces of raw turquoise. He lifted up a jagged stone as large as his palm; one end of it was chipped away. "It's a flint. Security didn't look at this too close." He touched the edge; the sharp point opened his skin. A bead of blood was on his index finger as he handed the stone to Phoebe.

"Thanks." She rubbed the stone against a lock of her hair, near her cheek, until only short, jagged ends were left. As she pulled away the extensions and cut more hair, she felt light-headed, relieved of its burden.

Leonard watched, keenly, as Phoebe's hair and extensions made a growing heap in her lap. When she had cut all the way around her head, she straightened the long strands and wrapped them round her hand the way her grandmother wound her yarn. When it was in a ball, she stuffed the tangled skein into the pocket of the seat in front of her.

"Don't leave it there," Leonard ordered. She put it into her purse. Leonard wouldn't look at her. Gathering up his stones and herbs, he replaced them in their sack, and shoved his pack under his seat. He laid his head back on his seat and closed his eyes. The muscles in his face were taut. He took Phoebe's left hand and clenched it in his, holding it tightly.

Phoebe put her hood over her head and leaned back, too; she closed her eyes. The only sensation she felt was the growing numbness in her hand, captive in Leonard's strong grip. She didn't mind. She could keep her mind focused on it, and not think about anything else. Leonard was a warrior now, she could tell. Waves of nausea passed over her every once in a while, and she remembered she hadn't eaten much for the past three days. The thought of food sickened her.

As the hours passed, the plane hurtled east. She was glad when the cabin lights dimmed, as they flew over the darkening planet below. They hit turbulence when the plane flew south of the Great Lakes, rattled by strong northwest winds. They hit a deep air pocket, and many passengers groaned at the falling sensation. Someone shouted. Phoebe hoped the plane would crash. She was exhausted, but couldn't sleep. She felt as though she was sinking into darkness. She couldn't go home. Running away would be so much work. She doubted she'd even be able to find the runaway shelter. She was so tired.

The pilot announced that a strong tailwind would get them to Buffalo twenty minutes ahead of schedule.

At that moment, Phoebe made up her mind. She had a better plan, one that would solve all her problems forever. She'd never have to tell anyone what had happened in Las Vegas. She felt good about the plan, but wondered why she couldn't stop the tears from running down her face, even though she wasn't crying. Then she understood. The tears came from a place deep inside her, her inner Niagara, which flowed relentlessly. Soon her release from her pointless life would come, in a watery dance.

She'd go over the falls like the Maid of the Mist.

PART THREE

"I stand before you now in the last hours of a death-stricken people. A few summers ago our council fires lighted up the arches of the primeval wood which shadowed the spot where your city now stands. Its glades rang with the shouts of our hunters and the gleeful laugh of our maidens. The surface of yonder bay and river was seamed only by the feathery wake of our bark canoes. The smoke of our cabins curled skyward from slope and valley. Tonight! Tonight! I address you as an alien in the land of my fathers."

Seneca Chief Honnondeuh (Nathaniel T. Strong), 1863

CHAPTER THIRTY-TWO

Mari caught Anne as she tried to sneak up the back stairs. She stuck her head out of her door before Anne reached the first landing.

"How is she?"

"The same." Anne continued walking up the stairs.

"Need some coffee? It's made."

Anne hesitated; the last thing she wanted right then was to have a conversation, even with Mari. But, god, would she love some coffee.

"Come on, Anne. You look like you really need it."

"I don't." Anne pushed her hair off her forehead. "Need it, that is. Though I concede that I probably look like I need it, but I don't."

Mari's stare confirmed to Anne that she wasn't making sense. "You do," she said.

Hesitating, Anne looked up the narrow staircase that led to her apartment. She noticed how grimy it was; each step had muddy prints and grains of rock salt on it. The place was falling apart, and so was she. Exhausted, she surrendered to the aroma of fresh coffee wafting from Mari's kitchen. "Okay, but I can only stay for a few minutes," she said. "I have to walk Ben."

Mari poured the coffee while Anne took off her heavy jacket and sat at the small bistro table in the tidy kitchen. There was a plate of cookies. She drank quickly.

"Thanks, Mari. You were right. I did need that." She reached for a cookie.

"Was it that bad?" Mari asked.

Anne nodded. No sense trying to evade the question. She knew her face betrayed her; she could feel it sag. And her eyes had to be red and puffy from crying all the way across Grand Island.

Mari sighed. She rose and retrieved the coffeepot. After refilling their cups, she sat down again. "Well, at least you know Phoebe's safe. She's in a good school, and getting counseling. She needs time now, to find her own meaning in what happened. Whatever did happen."

"Oh, Mari." Anne blinked back more tears. "I'll never forgive myself for not flying out to get her. I knew she was in over her head. But I was so angry at her, I let myself be convinced I should stay out of it. Bill's right. This is all my fault."

"It isn't, Anne." Mari's voice was firm. "You can't live Phoebe's life for her. She didn't want you involved. She lied to you. And now she has to find her own strength, and her own way forward."

Anne shook her head. She struggled for control. "I'll never forget how she looked when she got off that plane. My God, her hair! Thank God Leonard texted me so that Quin and I were there to meet her and get her right to a hospital. She was almost in shock."

"Any word about Leonard yet?"

"No." The word came out bitterly; she was still angry. "At the airport, he just handed Phoebe over to us, and took off. No one's heard from him since. Didn't tell us anything that happened."

"Has she told you anything?" Mari asked.

"No."

"I've been thinking about this so much, Anne, trying to figure Phoebe out. I think it would be a good idea not to let your imagination run away with you, about what happened out there. It may not have been all that bad, you know? Relatively speaking." Anne looked at Mari in disbelief, but Mari went on. "She lost the contest. That blow to her ego alone could have been enough to throw her totally off balance. She *can* over-dramatize things, as we know."

"You're wrong, Mari. Something serious happened. And she's dropped some hints to Stephanie." Phoebe was staying with Anne's colleague in Buffalo while she attended a private Catholic all-girls school nearby. Anne had made the arrangements, and was paying the tuition.

"What did she tell her?" Mari asked.

"Nothing much. But Stephanie says she's acting like many survivors of sexual assault. Depressed. Hardly eats. Doesn't care how she looks. Mood swings. At the hospital they found bruises on her, and traces of narcotics in her blood."

"Did they do a rape test at the hospital?"

"It was inconclusive."

Mari let out a deep breath.

Anne continued, "She sees the school psychologist, Sister Bea, three times a week. She doesn't say a word to her. They sit and stare at each other for an hour. Just like Phoebe and I did this afternoon, at lunch. She picked at a salad."

"But she's going to classes?"

"Yes. It's either that or get sent home. And that's the last thing she wants."

Mari pursed her lips and stared at her hands. The two women sat in silence. Anne picked the cookie apart, shredding it into little bits. She felt another hot wave of tears coming, and knew she had either to confess her humiliation or run out of Mari's kitchen like a madwoman.

"Oh, Mari, I just did something I shouldn't have. I've totally lost control of myself."

"Anne, you have to stop taking all the blame on yourself or you will drive yourself crazy." Mari reached across the table and gave Anne's arm a squeeze. "What happened?"

"I'm embarrassed to tell you." She shifted her eyes from Mari to the table to Mari again. "I went to Nick Valli's office."

"When?"

"Just now. Before I came home."

Mari leaned back in her chair. "What happened?"

Anne rubbed her temples. "I just wanted to find out what happened. I know he knows. When he saw me, he looked terrified. I must have looked hysterical. I think he thought I was going to attack him."

"Anne, you'd be a goddess to a lot of people in this town if you did." Mari rose and went to her cupboard. She pulled out a bottle of homemade cherry brandy, and poured two glasses. "Here, you need this more than coffee," she said, as she handed one to Anne.

"It would be worth going to jail for." Anne took a gulp of the brandy.

"Tell me what happened."

"I really shouldn't have done it. But I was so upset after seeing Phoebe. I can't help her if I don't know what happened. So after getting myself all worked up on the drive home, I went to Niagara Tower and barged into Valli's office. He was sitting on the receptionist's desk – some red-headed young thing. I'm sure he was sexually harassing her. When he saw me, he jumped off the desk and ran into his office, yelling, 'No calls, Chrissy.'"

Mari roared with laughter. Anne smiled, reluctantly. "I got into his office before he could close the door. He ran behind the desk. I'm sure he saw his life pass before his eyes. His hands were actually trembling."

"The response of a guilty creep."

"Exactly." Anne's humor drained as she relived her anger. "I leaned across the desk and demanded to know what happened to Phoebe in Las Vegas. I threatened him with legal action. I told him I was going to have him arrested for fraud, and abusing a minor, and I was going to sue him for damages for Phoebe."

"Hurray, Anne! What did he say?"

Her bluster faded; she slumped back in her chair. "He said Phoebe was the one who committed fraud. He dared me to sue him. He said any publicity that came out during a lawsuit would be a lot worse for her than for him."

"Damn his evil soul!"

"Especially since he's right." Anne tried to remember every word from the confrontation, to see if she could pick up any clues. "I know that he hurt Phoebe, somehow, or let her get hurt. I'm going to make him pay for it if I have to jump over the falls to do it."

"Callista doesn't like to do curses, but I'm going to ask her to cast a special one, just for him."

"Oh, that'll help." Anne swallowed another mouthful of brandy.

"Go ahead, be sarcastic. Do you want him to suffer, or don't you?"

"I'd like to see him rot. But not until I find out what he did to Phoebe."

"Anne, listen to me." Mari was serious. "Whatever happened, happened. Maybe the best thing to do is leave it behind, and help Phoebe deal with it, and move on. Both of you. Let me arrange a healing ceremony for her."

"I'm not sure what to do. I've lost confidence in my own judgment. And in reality, too. I checked on the city's Maid of the Mist website. It says that Ani Shanando was third runner-up in the Universe Las Vegas competition, and that she signed with an agent, and is in Los Angeles getting screen-tested. Total fiction, just like Ani's bio. Nothing seems real anymore." She stood up and reached for her jacket.

Mari stood, too. "Quin stopped by."

"What did he want?"

"To find out how Phoebe's doing. And to see you."

Anne sighed. "We've been texting, and he stayed over last week, but I feel so overwhelmed right now that I'm barely getting through my classes. I know he's been busy, too, with his research and his job." She avoided looking at Mari. "I wonder what impelled him to come by."

"It's something about Mars."

"Mars?"

"Yes. That's what he said."

Anne was curious. "I'll call him later."

"You should."

"Mars." Anne sighed. "Just what he needs." She wasn't angry at Quin, anymore, about his job with the Pickering Corporation. He told her not to worry, that the casino would never open in the Turtle. But it didn't matter to her now. She couldn't worry about peripheral issues.

Mari opened the back door and hugged Anne. "You're still mad at yourself. Please stop. And call Quin. He really cares about you, Anne."

Anne's eyes welled up again. She didn't know where to find the emotional energy to deal with anything other than Phoebe. She was also stressed about her pending VA grant. Her application had passed the first selection round, and now she was on another tight deadline to submit more demographic and financial data. All while she could barely concentrate on anything.

She tried to smile. "Thanks for the sympathy, and the brandy. I'll see you later." She walked slowly up the stairs, wanting nothing more than to crawl into bed. But Ben needed a walk.

It was cold and starting to get dark. Anne pulled the dog along wet sidewalks. It was impossible to keep warm or dry during a drizzly February in Niagara Falls. It was as though you were standing under the falls, everywhere you went.

CHAPTER THIRTY-THREE

Dear Wolf--
i hope u r reading yr email, wherever u r & i hope u r good
i'm writing this at my new school not HELL HOUSE where we used to go
its in buffalo, an all-girl school with nuns, count on anne to find it
these nuns aren't like the old kind of nun like in blues brothers, remember when we watched that?
they try to be nice i guess they are they don't push you too hard except for studies & if u look like u r trying, thyr ok
we have to wear uniforms which u will be shocked to know i don't mind because i don't ever have to think about what to wear sometimes i sleep in it it's so full of polyester it doesn't even wrinkle
I'm staying near BU with a friend of anne's, her name's Stephanie
she lives near the school so i walk there just a couple of blocks they wont let me have a car
she spies on me, but mostly she leaves me alone as long as I eat something and look like I'm studying or watching tv i can fake those things
mostly i just think
they'r worried i'm going to kill myself that's why anne doesn't want me to stay with her she's afraid i'm going to jump over the falls
i have to admit i thought about it before but now i don't want to - jump over the falls i mean
i'm still thinking about killing myself but i wouldn't want them to

find me all gross in the river

they give me these pills to take, but i don't, i save a lot of them, i have 20 now how many do i need i wonder.

i've been thinking alot about what you said, Wolf - how i should have gone to the desert with you i don't think so

we both had a quest to make, didn't we? we both had to do it. yr journey was good mine was bad but that's the way it is so at least now i know

i don't have to live 50 more pointless years in niagara falls before i figure it out

if u r reading this pls email me back, Wolf you don't have to tell me where you are or any secrets or anything.

i just want to know that u r out there, living free like a wolf or a white tiger

that will make both our quests worthwhile

your best friend still i hope, phoebe

Leonard frowned as he closed Phoebe's email. He thought about answering her, but he didn't want her to try to find him. But as he clicked on his other messages, he couldn't get Phoebe's words out of his head. Was she just being dramatic, or was she really thinking about killing herself? The image of her counting out pills in her hand scared him. He reopened her email and clicked on reply. He typed quickly:

Phoebe, you can find your strength like I found mine. One adventure isn't your whole journey it's just the start. Dump those pills you're saving!!! And don't take anymore. Listen to the voices of the trees and the wind and the animals. They can teach you. They will give you strength and courage, and help you find your sacred place, where you will be safe. Your friend still, Leonard. PS--I can't send any more messages for awhile.

Before he could change his mind, Leonard clicked send, and felt his message go.

"How're you doing?"

Leonard jumped. He hadn't heard Woody come up behind him. But then, the big man hadn't meant him to.

"I think I've got it," he reported. "I reinstalled the program. I registered you and set up your password. Now I just have to reset your preferences and run a couple of checks."

The large man scowled. Leonard was never sure how much Woody understood about the technical details when they had these little sessions. And this was just to get him back on email. But it didn't matter. Woody trusted him, and was giving him more and more stuff to do in the office.

He glanced at the date in the corner of his screen. He'd been working at the Lone estate for a few weeks now, doing a variety of jobs, from washing the household vehicles to running into town with the guys to get loads of supplies. The double-wide was a cool place to live, though the guys knew that Woody kept a close eye on them and made sure they went to school. Leonard had gone home to see Wallace and Rose, full of apologies for the distress he had caused them by disappearing for a week. He told them he needed a change of scene, and wanted to apply for work at the Lone estate. Rose quietly arranged for his school records to be transferred, after Wallace had a conversation with Jerome Lone, and they worked it out.

He had been very nervous when he showed up at the estate to apply for a job. Woody gave him a good grilling, and then said Leonard had to meet with Jerome Lone for final approval. Mr. Lone just asked him a few questions, looked hard at him for a long minute, and then signed a paper. Leonard felt sorry for him. He seemed nice, but very sad, because of his brother, who was being cared for in the mansion with everything money could buy. People whispered he was brain dead. Everyone there seemed to walk on tiptoes.

When he was telling Leonard what his duties were, Woody had said, "There's one more thing. Don't get friendly with those guys living in the RV. Stay away from them. But keep an eye on them. And let me know if you see anything strange."

Leonard wanted to ask what he meant by strange, but Woody's expression told him not to. "Okay," he said.

As the days passed, he began to understand. Levi Moon hurried in and out of the RV at all hours, often driving the long way to the main house in his black Tundra, other times trudging along the path through the woods. Anyone could see the four guys he called "cousins" weren't related to him, or to each other. Reg, Archie, Samuel, and Mal looked like they came from hard places; they looked like the meanest guys in any outlaw movie. Sometimes they tried to get the young guys to play cards, but they made up excuses. Most nights, the RV's lights were on all night. Three small satellite dishes on the roof were aimed at different points in the sky.

When Woody needed someone to set up his new computer, he seemed to like the fact that Leonard volunteered to do it, while the other guys were muttering why they couldn't. Leonard thought they were pretty harsh in the way they made fun of Woody. If he was clumsy, it was just because he was so big, and the top and bottom halves of his body didn't seem to match. The top half was large and barrel-chested; it rested on slender legs that had no butt for balance. And, face it, he was too old to learn all the new technology; he must be almost fifty.

Woody's headquarters were on the second floor of the staff building, which was behind the main house, separated by a band of evergreens. His office opened into a small apartment, where he lived. The family's vehicles were garaged and maintained on the ground floor.

Leonard was about to walk through the new email program when the door to the office opened.

"Woody, can I see you a minute?"

"Sure, Jerome." He poked Leonard.

"Just let me save this," Leonard said, half rising, while pushing on keys.

"No, don't get up, Leonard," Jerome said. "We'll step outside."

Leonard glanced at Woody. He nodded and followed Jerome out into the hall, closing the door behind them.

Letting out a deep breath, Leonard went back to work. He smiled, though, pleased that Jerome remembered his name. He glanced up at a framed photo hanging over the desk that showed Woody, Jerome, and John Lone standing together at a campsite high up on a mountain. Woody had told him it was taken up in the Adirondacks, on a hiking trip a year ago. The slopes blazed with autumn colors while beyond them continents of clouds floated in a turquoise sky. All three of them, even Woody, looked relaxed and happy.

"No, Jerome. I don't think it's a good idea."

Leonard heard Woody's voice through the closed door. He stopped keyboarding. Jerome replied, his voice muffled. Leonard inched the wheeled chair back, and listened.

"I need you to do this, Woody," Jerome said. "It'll only be one night away."

"Look, I don't want to leave while Moon and his henchmen are still hanging around. You might need me here," Woody argued.

"Andrew can handle things for one day."

"What if we get another blizzard and I can't get back right away?"

"If we get another blizzard, nothing will happen."

There was a long silence. Leonard was about to inch his chair back to the desk when he heard Jerome's voice again.

"Look, I'm asking you as a personal favor, Woody. I need that report from New York. Dan told me they finally got the goods on Moon, information that can help me get him out of here. I don't want to get it over the phone, and I don't trust email. You're the only one I can trust to meet with him. Besides, I want you to hear all the details, and ask questions, develop a strategy. Get his recommendations about what to do next."

"Jerome, my first loyalty is to John."

"Mine, too. You know that."

There was a long pause. Leonard scooted back to the desk and was furiously keyboarding when the two men came back into the office. "I'm done now," he told them. He jumped up from the chair and grabbed his jacket. As he lifted his backpack, all his stuff fell out, scattering computer manuals and sketch pads. His face reddened as he quickly dropped to pick things up, trying not to see Woody's extreme annoyance.

Jerome reached down and picked up one of his pads. He looked through the drawings. "These are quite good, Leonard," he remarked. "You've been drawing plans for the longhouse. And doing portraits of the other guys."

Leonard stood up and reached for his pad. He couldn't talk about his art with Jerome, who was an expert. He had no confidence.

"Have you had any training?" Jerome asked.

"Sort of. Not really." No way was he going to tell Jerome about Mari's rainbow pictures!

Jerome looked at him quizzically, then smiled. "Listen, next time I go up to the Turtle, I'll take you with me and we'll talk. We're setting up some scholarships. I'll tell you what you need to do to qualify. Okay?"

Leonard was too overwhelmed to answer. He could only nod, and get out of the room as fast as he could. He tore down the stairs and out of the building. Inches of new snow covered the narrow path that wound through the woods. He kicked the path open, feeling as though he were blazing a brand new trail.

CHAPTER THIRTY-FOUR

As she pulled away from American customs to drive onto the Whirlpool Rapids Bridge, Anne smiled at the memories the structure always brought her. She was eight years old again, sitting in the back seat of her father's car, squeezed between her mother and grandmother, with Bill crushed against the window. Her father and grandfather were in the front seat. They were on a Sunday drive, still digesting her grandmother's dinner that they ate after eleven o'clock Mass.

"Why do we have to take this bridge?" her grandmother always asked when they went to Canada.

"The lines are shorter, Ma," her father patiently replied. "The tourists don't come here."

"No wonder," Anne would think. One look at the ancient steel arch bridge would scare anyone away. And they were still using it. The bridge had been built downriver from the falls in the eighteen-nineties; it spanned a narrow section of the gorge, squeezing the vicious rapids below, which licked hungrily at the steel beams sunk deep into the limestone walls. Her grandmother would press her hands together and start reciting "Hail Mary's" in Polish as her father rode over the dark lower deck with its rattling wooden beams. If – the worst scare – a train was rumbling overhead, squealing its brakes and shaking the bridge even more, her grandmother would pray all the louder, taking Anne's hand in hers and holding it tightly. Anne would look at her grandmother's gold watch, a dainty little thing with a face only half an inch wide. She had two tiny little charms attached to the band, one gold and one blue enamel, each of them pressed with an image of Mary Mother of God. Anne squinted to look at the words printed on the watch face. Underneath the brand, Temple, were the words *Shock Resistant*. How comforting, Anne would think. If her grandmother's worst fears were realized, and the bridge crumpled and they were sent to their horrible deaths as the car plummeted into the worst rapids on the planet, her grandmother's watch would still be ticking.

"Citizen of what country?" The tall Canadian customs agent took her out of her reverie as he leaned over to peer through the window of Anne's car.

"U-S," Anne and Emily replied in unison, as Anne handed over her Nexus pass.

The agent bent down further to examine Anne's front-seat passenger. "Oh, hullo, Mr. Mountview." He grinned. "These lovely ladies with you?"

"Yes." Wallace was smiling. "I'm very lucky today."

Anne glanced to the back seat, where Emily was sitting. She'd been trying to think of the right word to describe Wallace's manner, and came up with "courtly." It was an old-fashioned word, but it worked. Emily said that all the Haudenosaunee chiefs she'd met were like that. It was, she said, because, in the traditional communities, the clan mothers chose the chiefs. They selected men who were wise but not arrogant, moderate but not timid. Men who would consider the impact of their decisions on the next seven generations.

They were on a mission on this sleety day in late February. Emily had asked Anne to drive her and Wallace Mountview to a meeting with Sylvester Lindsay of the auction house. He'd asked Wallace to look at the Native American artifacts among the items the auction house had in storage from the defunct Niagara Museum, and advise him what to do with them. Emily thought Anne would find the excursion interesting, but that wasn't the only reason she wanted Anne along. Wallace Mountview was almost ninety years old, and Emily was protective; too protective, Wallace would say. But Emily knew the meeting might be a strain for the elderly man, and she felt better knowing Anne was along. She also had orders from Rose.

"How long do you plan to be in Canada, ma'am?"

"Just for the afternoon. We're going sightseeing," Anne told him. It was a small lie, but you had to keep your answers simple going through customs.

The agent returned her pass. Emily and Wallace handed over their Nexus passes, which were necessary for passage over this bridge. Wallace also gave the agent his Haudenosaunee passport, with its yellow cover. The agent took the passes and passport and looked through them carefully, lingering on the passport. Wallace had warned Anne and Emily that he was going to present it at the border, on principle, and, depending on the agent, he might get hassled.

This young agent finally handed the documents back to Emily and Wallace, stood back, and waved them on.

"It was terrible when the Iroquois national lacrosse team couldn't go to the championship games in England two years ago because the U.S. and Britain wouldn't accept their Haudenosaunee passports," Emily said. "It's just unbelievable that native sovereignty is still an issue in the twenty-first century. All that nonsense about checking for terrorists. Just an excuse to deny people their rights."

"This agent was a reasonable man," Wallace said.

Emily was still indignant. "Imagine them telling YOU to show a passport."

Anne drove carefully onto the city street. There were buses to dodge, and tourists darting across the roads. She was glad Emily had asked her to join this afternoon jaunt across the river, even in the nasty weather. It felt good not to be thinking about Phoebe.

Anne avoided the tourist area by heading straight up Bridge Street, past the old railroad station, to where the street ended at the cemetery. She turned left on Stanley Avenue, then drove for a few blocks to get to Lundy's Lane. They crossed over the hydro canal on the way out of town. Anne's GPS told them when to turn on the private drive that led to an industrial park. Sylvester was waiting for them in his parked car in front of the door to a bland beige building with no signage. When he saw them he turned off the engine and got out of the car. He looked pleased to see Anne. After greetings were exchanged, Sylvester punched numbers into a keypad beside the steel door, and pushed it open.

The three visitors stood quietly while Sylvester fiddled with the light switches. Stacks of boxes filled the large space. Anne could smell dust and mold. She wished she had a face mask.

"Sylvester still has a big job ahead of him before he's finished with all this, as I saw last week," Emily said, her voice a welcome sound in the silence. "He's really grateful to you for coming, Wallace. He needs all the help he can get with the Haudenosaunee items. Very little of the collection is properly documented."

They blinked as the lights came on. Beyond the boxes near the back of the space were tables with display cases set on them.

"Let me show you this before we start," Sylvester said, handing Wallace the daily newspaper from Niagara Falls, Ontario. "I've been running this ad on a weekly basis."

Wallace glanced at the ad, then handed it to Emily. Anne peered over her shoulder to see a display ad in the classified section. Under the heading, "Reward for Information," she read, "$5,000 reward for the return of or information leading to the return of artifact shown in photo below. Gilded Egyptian mask. Warning: This artifact may contain biological contaminants dangerous to human health. Should not be handled." There was a blurry photo of a gold mask, the mouth set in a straight line, the eyes black holes. She gave an involuntary shudder, and followed Sylvester and Wallace past the piles of boxes to the tables.

The first thing Anne saw was a new sealed display case. Within it was a nineteenth-century book with faded covers.

"Ah, this is one of our treasures," Sylvester said, coming up behind her. He carefully lifted the top of the case. He took a pair of white cotton gloves from his pocket, and slowly opened the book. The binding was broken and easily opened at a particular page. Peering closely at the yellowing pages, Anne could make out the signature of "A. Lincoln,

1857" in his bold hand, prominent among the signings of lesser men.

"Three years before he was elected president," remarked Emily, peering over Anne's shoulder. "This is the guest ledger of the old Niagara Museum. Lincoln was staying with his family at the Cataract House, on the American side. Lincoln was fascinated by Niagara Falls. He visited several times, and talked about it in speeches."

"What are you going to do with this book?" Anne asked Sylvester.

"It will be placed in a specialized auction," he replied.

"It would be wonderful if it could stay in Niagara Falls and be accessible to the public," Emily said.

Sylvester smiled at her with what looked to Anne like pity. "My dear Emily," he said, "you know that would be my first choice. But you don't have the facilities to preserve this precious book, let alone the funds to purchase it."

"We barely have funds to keep the library open," Emily said. "I'm well aware of how inadequate we are."

"We should start now," Wallace said. He looked uncomfortable.

"Of course, Mr. Mountview," Sylvester replied. "My apologies. This way, please."

He turned to the left, and led them through a maze of tables piled with boxes. Anne could see by looking at the ceiling that they were in a big space. Still, the boxes hemmed them in and she felt claustrophobic. Several rows of metal tables were spread out, all of them covered with objects. On the first table was a large preserved fish more than six feet long, a sturgeon caught in the Niagara River more than a century ago. Other tables had the heads of stuffed animals, including a huge bison head with horns.

"I'm sorry this isn't better organized," Sylvester said. "We did our best to categorize things. Even in the old museum, everything was a bloody mishmash: Native American artifacts mixed in with Chinese mud figures, all displayed around the Egyptian mummies, with the stuffed buffalo being attacked by wolves right next to the giant redwood stump near the mastodon bones. My head throbs just thinking about it. We've finally gotten everything sorted out by continent, if not era. And I've had all the eastern Native American artifacts put together, Mr. Mountview, as you requested."

"Let's see them," Wallace said.

Sylvester led Wallace to a table covered with cornhusk dolls, buffalo horns, and wood carvings. Anne stayed back to look at an old exhibit she remembered from visiting the museum as a child. It was a diorama whose featured attraction was the skeleton of a mastodon. Depicted on the wall behind it were spear-toting men wearing animal furs, poised to slaughter a terrified creature. In the distance, a mother mastodon and her youngster fled the predators. "Skeleton found near St. Thomas, Ontario, 1854," a small sign read.

"I can't believe this, Emily," Anne said. "This display is exactly as I remember it from, I hate to say, thirty years ago."

Emily sniffed. "That museum was full of bad science and bad history. You know, maybe I shouldn't be sorry that it's gone." She walked over to Wallace and Sylvester, who was writing notes in a small leather notebook.

Anne walked around the space. When she saw a giant redwood stump with a tunnel carved through the middle of it, she felt seven years old again. She remembered looking through this stump at Bill, who was staring at her from the other end. Her father took a photo of them standing by the stump, dwarfed by it. She still had that photo, in an album. She moved on. The stuffed buffalo and the wolves were looking pretty decrepit in a far corner; their fur was peeling away. Scattered around them were dozens of other stuffed animals – swans, birds, foxes, squirrels, owls, beavers. She turned away. How could people have ever enjoyed looking at slaughtered animals, she wondered. And what are they going to do with the poor things? She joined Wallace and the others, who were looking at objects on a table.

"These must be returned immediately," Wallace was saying. He was pointing at a small pile of human bones, black with age, and, sadly, in an unconnected jumble.

"Can you arrange it?" Sylvester asked.

"Yes," Wallace said. He turned to another table, as Sylvester wrote in his notebook. Anne observed Wallace, noting his strained expression.

"Please tell me about this mask." Sylvester lifted a large mask carved of heavy wood, whose human-like face was creased into a grotesque smile. Long, stiff black hair framed it.

"That's a False Face, isn't it, Wallace?" Emily asked.

"What does that mean?" asked Anne.

"It's a ceremonial mask used by healers," Sylvester replied. "That is, that's what I've been told. We have about a dozen of them."

"They are passed from one healer to another," Wallace said. "They are never sold. These were stolen. They must be returned."

"That's what I thought you would say." Sylvester sighed. "My employers would rather forgo any financial return on items like this than become involved in a dispute over ownership and religious beliefs, with all the attendant negative publicity. We'll return the masks and any other items of, let's say, sensitivity. Please take a look at these other tables. Here, these corn husk dolls – what should we do with them?"

Anne asked if there was a restroom she could use. Sylvester pointed her to the back of the large space. Emily came with her. They wound their way through the maze of piled boxes again. Anne noticed a section of the space nearby was blocked off by the kind of dividers used in medical units. After leaving the restroom, Anne couldn't resist peaking behind them; Emily followed her.

When they saw what was behind the dividers, Anne was able to keep her composure but Emily shrieked. Her high-pitched yell echoed off the ceiling.

The two women were face to face with the mummies. The glass case that once surrounded them was gone. A row of examining tables had been set up, surrounded by unlit standing lights, like a surgical suite. The ancient figures were on the tables, covered with clear plastic sheets. They were sitting up. One had no head. Through the plastic, Anne could see their strips of linen, brown with age and grime. Shreds of cloth hung from their shoulders. The human forms sat stiffly, correctly, as people do when a doctor listens for a heartbeat. Anne felt her knees wobble. They looked obscene.

"Oh, my dears, I forgot to warn you." Sylvester hurried up behind them.

"What are you doing here?" Anne's voice was harsh. "Cutting them apart?"

"We've had experts down from Toronto examining them," Sylvester explained. "They're going to be prepared for shipping later this week. And not a moment too soon."

"These are human beings!" Anne cried. "You're 'shipping' them?"

"With all respect, I assure you," Sylvester said. "They're going to be repatriated to Egypt, whether they want them or not." He looked distressed. "This whole project is dreadful. It's the worst assignment I've ever had. I can't wait to return to London."

He led them quickly back to where they had left Wallace. He was gone. They found him outside standing by Anne's car, leaning against it. After quick goodbyes, Anne drove off quickly.

In the car, Emily chattered about Lincoln and Niagara Falls, trying to take their minds off the hideous experience. Anne didn't pay much attention to her as she drove back to the Whirlpool Bridge. Wallace didn't say anything. There was a backup at the American customs. Wallace showed his Haudenosaunee passport to an officious female agent, who grilled him harshly about what he was doing in Canada. Anne and Emily glared while he calmly explained he had gone to a museum with friends. Finally, she handed the passport back to Wallace, and they were allowed to return home.

Anne drove them quickly to the library.

"Thanks for the ride, Anne," Emily said, as she got out of the car. "I'll call you tomorrow."

"Okay," Anne replied. She called goodbye to Wallace, who was walking quickly to a car, where Rose was waiting for him. He gave a quick wave, but didn't turn back.

"I'm sure he's upset," Emily said. "I didn't realize about the human remains. I'm so mad Sylvester didn't tell me. I thought it was just masks and dolls."

"He must be glad he's helping to return them," Anne said. "Someone had to do it. But will you call and check on him tomorrow?"

"I'll call him tonight," Emily said. "And I'm sorry to you, too, Anne, for the fright."

"I'll get over it," Anne shrugged, and headed home. She couldn't shake the site of those mummies. She remembered the spooky thrill they had given her when she was young, seeing them with all the other exhibits. She had no feeling for them then; they were just like the other stuffed creatures, lifeless. But now, all she thought about was their humanity, and the world they had known, and how it all disappeared. They were going back home now, Anne thought, but she had a strange feeling that when the archeologists in Egypt opened the crates, all they would find would be black dust.

CHAPTER THIRTY-FIVE

Jerome kept himself moving so the bitter cold wouldn't numb his limbs. He was standing just outside the gate to the Lone estate, near the giant sycamore tree, waiting. It was pitch dark, past midnight; the wind chill put the temperature well below zero. The sky was thick with clouds; he couldn't see the stars, but every so often the clouds would shift and the full moon's light would sift through. A light scattering of snowflakes fell, lovely until a sudden gust of wind gathered them up and blasted them against his face.

A loud cracking noise broke the frozen silence and made him jump. Jerome scanned the high tree branches, dimly outlined against the snowy hillside by reflected moonlight. A lighter, popping sound drew his eyes to an old spruce that stood along the last bend of the road before the gate. The spruce shrieked as the weight of its snow-laden limbs tore off half its trunk. Sparks danced along the trunk as it split in two, sending long evergreen branches crashing to the ground. The edge of the snow cloud that erupted from the collapsing tree reached Jerome, and covered him with a dusting of snow.

The dryness must have caused those eery sparks, he thought. The temperature had been below zero for days. The frigid cold sucked every molecule of moisture from the air. Two feet of dense snow was covered with a coating of ice crystals so light they floated with any movement, like dogwood seeds in early summer.

Jerome's chapped lips stung. He ran his dry tongue over them, but that only took off another layer of skin cells. He stamped his feet. Finally, he saw what he was waiting for. A quick flash of a light coming down the road. He responded by aiming his flashlight up the road, and turning it quickly on and off. Then he waited.

A figure appeared on the road, disappearing sometimes in the blowing snow. Jerome saw him long before he heard the whisper of his cross-country skis. He wasn't out of breath when he reached Jerome. He was a tall man, dressed in sleek winter gear; a large cloth sack hung across his chest.

"Thank you for coming like this, Jake," Jerome greeted him. His low voice was punctuated by white puffs of moisture, as his breath hit the air. "Are there others?"

"Two more. On snowshoes." The man's wide face, stiff from the cold, creased into something resembling a smile. "The old guys don't like these." He held up his ski poles and motioned toward his thin skis.

Jerome nodded, his face frozen, not only from the wind, but from tension.

"Are you absolutely certain we won't be interrupted?" Jake asked.

"Yes," Jerome replied. "Only I know you're coming. You left your truck far enough away that no one could have heard it. I shut down the alarm system so nothing will go off. I sent Woody away on an overnight assignment. The family's asleep. And I don't expect Levi Moon to come out on a night like this." His throat tightened.

"We'll need time," Jake said.

"I'll do whatever I can to give it to you."

A sudden burst of wind blew clouds of biting snow around the sycamore tree. The two men covered their faces with their arms. By the time their vision was clear again, Jerome saw the others, coming toward them in slow, shuffling steps. They were bent, and wore old-fashioned snowshoes and parkas. They, too, had sacks hung across their shoulders.

"Thank you for coming to help my family," Jerome greeted the two men. He didn't know their names, and he didn't ask. Jake was an old friend from his home reservation, a member of the medicine society. For this unusual visit, Jake had called on outside help, the most experienced healers he knew, from Onondaga. Jerome was more grateful than he knew how to express. These men had come a long way, in secret, and made a grueling journey on foot, to examine John and try to help Jerome decide what to do. They were not conducting the traditional procedures, in a sacred place, because of the secrecy required. Jerome knew that Jake was troubled by that, but it couldn't be helped.

Jerome waited as the two hikers took deep breaths. They were much older than Jake, who was in his forties. Jake bent to take off his skis.

"What's the best way to get in the house?" Jake asked.

"We'll go right through the front door," Jerome told them. "It's the shortest way. If we're quiet, my mother shouldn't hear us from her wing of the house."

Moving slowly in order to keep together, the four men walked through the iron gate, which was open just wide enough for them to get through. They walked up the long drive, which was plowed but quickly being covered with the new snow. The house was dark, and silent.

Just outside the front door, the men removed their snowshoes. They entered the house, staring in the dim light at the elegant foyer with its tall palladium windows and cathedral ceiling. A carved oak staircase led in a wide curve up to an open hall that spanned the foyer from left to right. Slowly, they removed their sacks and outer coats. Forming a small circle facing each other, they began to say a prayer in low voices. The pungent odor of fresh tobacco wafted in the dry air; Jerome fought the urge to tell them to hurry. Finally, they finished.

Kneeling, the man whom Jerome thought of as Oldest Man Walking removed an object from his sack. Jerome instinctively tensed up when he heard a sound like a rattlesnake. But the man held up a large turtle rattle. My ancestors would have heard that sound, Jerome thought. He felt a thrill. Then he wondered briefly if he should tell these men to go, that he had changed his mind. But what were his alternatives? He knew he had none. It was too late to turn back. He couldn't overcome alone whatever power Levi Moon had over John and Mother. His family was under siege by powers so ancient he had thought they were extinct, like the mastodon whose bones they had found when they dug that last pond. It was easy enough to cover up the animal and move the site of the pond. But the ancient powers were strong. He couldn't not try to use them for his brother. He had to act decisively, and alone. He couldn't confide in anyone, not even Loraine or Woody. It wasn't right to make them share this responsibility. Whatever happened would be on his head. He only hoped his mother would forgive him for this, someday.

He regretted the visit by the Healers could not be done properly. He remembered how moved, and impressed, he had been when he had once observed a traditional ceremony by the False Faces, the healing society as ancient as the roots of the Haudenosaunee people. Their masks were carved from the flesh of living trees, using skills drenched with ritual. These masks could be hundreds of years old, given from Healer to Healer through generations. The memory made Jerome feel dizzy, as though his brain were lightened by the draining away of all his thoughts of this time, all the experience and learning of the modern age. He didn't need all that, he realized. All he needed were the gifts of the Creator – the Trees, and the Plants, the Birds, and the Fish, the Animals, and the Stars, and the Wind, and the Sun, and the Moon, and the ...

Oldest Man Walking brought Jerome back to the moment by putting his hand on the younger man's shoulder. Jerome looked into the man's dark eyes and felt faith, and relief. He no longer felt as though he were betraying his brother. He knew that what was happening to John was wrong. These men, hopefully, could help him.

His doubts gone, Jerome nodded and led the group across the large foyer, dimly lit by a few nightlights. Only the turtle rattle made any sound. They walked slowly up the curved oak staircase, halting at the first landing, to listen. The men took their masks out of their bags. Jerome took them to the second floor and down the long hallway to John's suite. He gave a last look back. The False Faces gleamed eerily in the hall's amber nightlights. Each one nodded. They were ready.

Holding his breath, Jerome grasped the handle, and pushed the door open. He strode through the sitting room and opened the door to the bedroom. Jake and the others were right behind him. He turned on the light. What they saw stopped them in their tracks.

John was sitting cross-legged in the center of the bed. His lank hair hung in limp strands over his wide-open eyes. His hospital gown was falling off his shoulder.

Stunned, Jerome was wary. "John? Are you awake?"

His brother didn't move. As Jerome started to walk toward the bed, he felt Jake's large hand on his shoulder, holding him back. Oldest Man Walking went forward, shaking the rattle.

"Wait," Jerome urged. "Maybe he doesn't need that now."

"He needs us more than ever," Jake said. "Go. Guard the door." The False Faces slowly walked toward the bed.

Jerome stayed where he was, uncertain, again, of what to do.

The first door burst open. Levi Moon hurried in, followed by two of his men. He hurried into the bedroom, glaring at Jerome. "Get those fools away from my patient!" His voice was rough.

"Get out of here," Jerome ordered. He looked past Moon at Archie, and Mal, standing behind him, glowering. A quiver of fear ran through him as he realized they might have weapons. He didn't let it show.

"It's you and these fakes who have to leave, Jerome," Levi Moon growled. "Or your brother will pay the consequences."

Jake moved toward Moon. Jerome held up his hand. "Wait." He pulled his cell phone from his pocket. Pressing one digit would ring the phone in his sister's room, and she could summon help. But before he could do it, the room went black. A strange, keening yell started, from Moon, Jerome thought, as he was pushed roughly to one side. He managed to stay on his feet, blinking his eyes to adjust them to the darkness. He held the cell phone close to his face so he could see its illuminated numbers to punch in the code.

A gun fired, twice. The room went silent.

Jerome felt himself pushed hard to the floor; the cell phone went flying out of his hand. He twisted his body, and tried to lift himself up. His hands slipped in liquid. He smelled blood, and wondered if it was his own. He stopped struggling for a moment, waiting for someone to turn the lights back on. He heard shouts, and heavy footsteps rushing in and out of the room.

"What's going on? Who are you? Oh, no, no, no!"

He was relieved to hear Andrew's voice. That meant help would be on the way. He thought the lights were back on, but his vision was blurred. He felt someone turn him over, on his back. Trying as hard as he could to focus his eyes in the dim light, he saw Jake, who was pushing something against his chest. It hurt. Jerome wanted him to stop pushing, so he could catch his breath, and ask him and the other Healers not to abandon John.

"Stay ... help him ...," Jerome tried to talk around the warm liquid dribbling from his mouth.

"Don't talk," Jake said. "Save your strength."

Relieved, Jerome closed his eyes. He'd done it – brought help to John. Jake and the others would find a way to convince Mother to let them stay. She believed in the old ways. Now, he needed to gather his strength. He let himself relax, and felt his mind fall softly into unconsciousness. After a while, he awakened.

When Jerome opened his eyes, Jake was gone. Another man, his handsome face full of concern, was holding him up in a sitting position. Jerome thought he looked familiar. "I think I know you," he said. "Tell me your name."

"Let's stand," the man replied.

Jerome slowly rose to his feet. He couldn't remember why he was on the floor. The man walked out of the bedroom, motioning Jerome to follow him. He complied. They went through the long hall, and down the stairs, and out the front door. He stopped walking, and stared. "Where did all this sunshine come from?"

His companion pointed ahead, to the western sky.

Jerome looked up. His gaze went past the clouds, and Mother Earth's sun, and so deep into the sky that he could see the Milky Way.

Beyond its band of brightly shining stars, he saw hills covered with multitudes of trees, marching into a distant land with peaks so beautiful that he felt like weeping. Before his feet lay a green meadow, dotted with small white flowers. The smell of strawberries was in the air. He took a step forward, then stopped, as he realized what he was seeing – the land of the Creator.

"Do I have to go now?" he asked.

The Guide held out his hand.

Jerome stared at it a long while, hesitating. There was pain in leaving his family, and the familiar, beloved landscapes of Mother Earth. But it could be that Mother Earth was dying, too, that the End Days were already underway. If he left now, he wouldn't have to watch the maples die, and all the other trees, as the beautiful, green earth withered. He wouldn't have to see the lovely creeks and waterfalls of his native land dry up, and turn to barren stone. He would hear the voices of songbirds in the Creator's land, familiar songs, and the songs of birds whose voices hadn't been heard by his people for generations.

He looked at his Guide, who was waiting patiently, and gazed again at the gorgeous high country the Creator had prepared for his children. He realized the task of healing John was for others now, the others who were left behind. He wanted nothing more than to journey among those distant mountains. Those trees!

"Remember me, John. Forgive me, Mother," he said. After a long look back, Jerome held his hand out to his Guide. "I'm ready now."

Together they began the journey to the land where there would be no End Days, only days without end.

CHAPTER THIRTY-SIX

"Leonard, we're heading to town for supplies. You coming?"

"Can't. I'm waiting for Woody to text me. His computer crashed again."

"Yeah, all by itself." Jemmy's deep laugh rang out. "Ask him how many trucks he's crashed. He could run his own salvage yard."

Darman and Terrence laughed with Jemmy.

Leonard, lying on his bunk with his laptop open, smiled.

"Maybe. But I'd better be here when he texts me to come."

"Okay, see ya later." Jemmy tossed a set of keys into the air, and jostled for them with the other guys as they left.

Leonard opened the window over his bed. A light breeze, cold but with the warm scents of pine and the awakening earth, blew into his face. He breathed the fresh air deeply.

When the sounds of the truck and its blaring radio receded, Leonard relaxed. Finally, he was alone. He needed time to think. Things had happened so quickly, and were so at odds with what he thought he knew, that he wondered what was real anymore.

Leonard closed the window and pulled its thin curtain shut. He sat up and lifted the front part of his mattress, the side against the wall. Carefully, he pulled the turtle rattle out from under the mattress. When his heart stopped beating fast, he examined his secret, incriminating possession, running his finger along the ridge between the twenty-four main scales on top of the shell, which was worn and colored deep brown, like petrified wood. He turned it over and examined the stiff underside. The rattle was very old, he was sure of that. He'd never seen one like this. Grandfather had some rattles with wooden handles. This one used the head and neck of the snapper himself as the handle. The leathery skin was easy to grasp. Two slender wood splints were inserted into the middle of the turtle's underside, and lashed to the neck with rawhide.

"I wonder how they made this," he thought. "How they got the snapper ready, and all. Grandfather says turtles are hard to kill. You think they're dead, but they're not. And they can take your finger off with one snap."

Leonard stood up. He gave the rattle a strong shake, then another. He did a couple of circle dance steps, shaking the rattle. It felt good. He crouched, ready to twirl.

A digital beep startled him so much that Leonard leaped into the air and almost tossed the rattle away. By the time he was back on the ground, he realized it was his cell phone. Heart pounding, he glanced at the screen, which announced Woody's summons.

Quickly, Leonard returned the turtle rattle back to its hiding place.

"I'd better be careful," he told himself. "Old snapper draws attention."

He stuffed his laptop into his backpack, which he slung over his shoulder. He rushed outside and ran to the path to the main house. Woody didn't like to wait.

As he sprinted along the sloping path that wound through woods and around rocky outcrops scraped clean by the glaciers, Leonard debated again in his mind whether he should tell what he knew about that terrible night, more than a month ago. How he was lying on his bed, awake, looking through the window at the clouds scooting across the moon, listening to the trees creak and moan in the arctic wind. How he saw dark shadows move against the snow. They were Levi Moon and his men passing near his window, heading to the path to the Lone house. How he dressed quickly, and followed them through the woods, to see what they were up to, on a night no human being should be outdoors. He would have texted Woody, but he knew he was away from home, because he had told the guys to be extra watchful while he was gone.

Leonard saw them go into a door at the rear of the mansion, and wondered why an alarm didn't ring. Maybe the power was down, from the storm. He crept to the front door, where he noticed the pile of snowshoes and skis just outside of it. Holding his breath, he carefully tried the carved wooden door; it was unlocked. He slowly opened it, and peered inside. No one was in the dimly lit foyer. A pile of wet jackets lay just inside the door. He tiptoed inside.

Then loud voices rang out. Leonard looked around quickly and saw a door; he jumped inside a closet, squeezing between thick coats. He left the door open a crack, hardly breathing.

He heard the fatal gunshots. They echoed through the foyer. Moments later, Leonard got the scare of his life as he saw three grotesque faces float down the staircase in the dim light. False Faces. He pushed himself farther back into the closet. As they came across the foyer, he could see that the Faces were masks carried by three men. One of them, the tallest and youngest, hesitated as the others grabbed their jackets by the door and started to put them on, just a few feet away from Leonard. He could smell sweet grass and tobacco.

"We should stay," the man said. His voice shook; Leonard could see tears on his cheeks, drops that glinted in the dim light, like crystals. The other men hesitated.

"There's nothing we can do for him now," the eldest man said, his voice shaking.

The sound of another gunshot rang through the foyer. The bullet shattered one of the sidelights next to the door, near their heads. The three men grabbed their jackets and leaped outside. A biting wind carried a burst of snow into the house. They slammed the door shut behind them.

"Let the fools go." Leonard recognized Levi Moon's voice, coming from the second floor landing. He stopped breathing, and waited.

Then, women's screams pierced the entire house. They were awful, worse than anything he had ever heard, or imagined. They weren't wails of grief but shrieks trying to chase away reality.

That was enough. Leonard made a run for it. He was out the front door just before all the house's lights went on. He didn't look back, but started to run through the snow on the path broken by the night's visitors. He was about to turn to run to the back of the house when the turtle rattle tripped him.

Leonard got a face-wash of snow when he fell to the ground. When he was able to sit up, the rattle was sitting between his legs. Not even sure what it was, he stuffed it inside his jacket, then hurried as fast as he could into the woods. He wasn't worried about leaving tracks. Snow was falling and would eat them before long.

Snow-heavy clouds hid the moon before Leonard was halfway back to the doublewide. He fought through lashing wind and blinding snow, worried that he'd take a wrong turn and get lost in the woods. He'd freeze to death by morning. Finally, through tree trunks, he saw the dim solar spotlight above the door. He was sure he'd wake up somebody by letting in the frigid wind, but Jemmy and the other guys didn't stir, even when he shook the snow off his jacket and the rattle fell on the floor with a clunk. They'd had a long day shoveling snow.

Leonard crept into his bed, shivering. He lay under his blankets, holding the turtle rattle next to his chest to warm it. He knew something terrible had happened. He saw it in the faces of the healers. He knew that's what they were. Somehow, they got in a deadly fight with Levi Moon and his men. He hoped that any magic that was in the turtle rattle would protect him, keep anyone from knowing he was in the house that night.

The next day was terrible. State troopers questioned everyone, even him and the guys, about where they were and what they saw the previous night. Fear, and Clint's warnings, made the lies come easily out of Leonard's mouth. He'd been asleep all night. He hadn't seen or heard anything because of the storm. He was sure the cops would figure out it was Levi Moon without his help. But then the story that came out made him question reality. The police report, which was quoted in all the news stories, said unknown intruders got into the house and killed Jerome. It said John Lone's family was wakened by two gunshots and found Jerome bleeding to death in John's room. It said Jerome must have heard the intruders and went to protect John. It said it appeared the same gun that killed John Lone also shattered a front window. Nothing was said about anyone else being in the house. There was no mention of Levi Moon.

When Leonard reached his office, out of breath, Woody was staring at the photo of himself and the Lone brothers on the Appalachian Trail. He didn't turn around to greet Leonard.

"See if you can fix it," he said, pointing to the computer.

It hurt Leonard to look at Woody. He'd lost a lot of weight. Raw grief lay over him, and the entire household, like a dark storm.

Leonard quickly got the computer operational. It hadn't really crashed. Woody had just given it some bad commands.

"Is there anything else I can do for you now?" Leonard asked, when he finished.

"No." Woody turned. "Well, maybe yes. Can you get old newspaper articles off the web?"

"Yeah."

"Find me anything you can on Jerome's ..." he swallowed, "on that night. And the investigation. Print it out for me."

"Sure, Woody."

"I wonder how much he knows, what he suspects," Leonard thought. He opened a search engine and scanned down the list of newspaper stories it brought up:

Intruders kill university professor
Police speculate on motives in Lone murder
Questions remain in gun battle at Indian estate
Sheriff asks FBI to investigate Six Nations conspiracy
Local group demands taxes on Indian businesses
Oped: Open business records to find motives in Lone killing
Lones involved in smuggling ring, informer says

Collecting the pages as they came out of the printer, Leonard worked up his courage. He asked, "Woody, why do they write this stuff?"

"Everything revolves around money to them. They can't understand anything else."

"What do you think happened?" Leonard's voice was just above a whisper.

Woody glared at him. "Why are you so interested?"

"I just, I just ..." Leonard stammered. "I liked Mr. Lone."

A tear oozed out of Woody's left eye. "Everyone's got a story." His voice was even more gruff than usual. "Don't believe any of them. I don't." He turned and walked quickly out.

Leonard's breath escaped his body in relief. For a brief moment, he thought Woody was going to keep questioning him. He finished printing the articles. The last one, in *The New York Times*, had a picture of Jerome under the headline, "In upstate Indian country, murder leaves community questioning family ties." Jerome's handsome face was smiling in the image.

Disgusted, Leonard shredded that one. Woody didn't need to see it. Whatever happened, he knew Jerome wouldn't turn against his brother. He decided he would wait, and watch. He would know the right time to talk to Woody. He was Jerome's friend. Leonard knew he was waiting, and watching, too.

CHAPTER THIRTY-SEVEN

Ben barked when the door chime rang. Anne, trying to concentrate on editing the draft report to the dean from the transformation committee, was annoyed. She wasn't expecting anyone. Ben kept barking. She sighed, and went downstairs. Through the lace curtain on the front door, she saw Quin standing outside. Ben leaped against the door, barking happily. With mixed emotions, she opened it.

Spring air, mixed wth a damp chill, wafted into the foyer. She sat on the stairs and waited while Ben greeted his friend with leaps and a slobbering tongue. After a few minutes, Quin got the dog settled down. Kneeling on the floor stroking Ben's side, he looked up at Anne and said, "Hey. Can I come in for a while?"

She tried to collect enough energy to feel glad to see him. They had barely been in touch over the last few weeks. After her initial relief that they were friends again, she kept herself distant. He was still working at the Turtle, and she didn't want to think about it. But here he was. After a moment, she said, "It would break Ben's heart if you didn't. Come on up." As she climbed the stairs, she pretended not to notice Mari's door open a crack, then close. "So, what brings you over?" she asked, as they walked into her parlor.

"Two things," he said. "First, I have something to show you." He reached into the pocket of his flannel shirt. "Look."

Anne took the folded piece of paper and opened it. Her jaw dropped when she saw it was a large check made out to him.

"Excellent, Quin." She handed the check back to him. "You were right about them making this job worth your time."

"Yeah. My mom cried when I told her how much I'd be sending home." He put the check back in his pocket. "But that's not the best part."

"No?"

"No." He looked uncertain for a moment, but then decided to speak. "I can't give you any details, in fact I shouldn't say anything at all, but I didn't get this money by helping set up the gambling operation. I got it for fucking things up."

"What?"

"Like I said, I can't give you any details. I can just say that the Turtle is safe for now. And I helped save it. I got a letter with the check that said all plans for the Turtle are on hold again. Some lawyer wrote it. But something terrible happened to Jerome Lone, the man I ended up working for. He was killed a month ago."

"I read about that in the papers," Anne said. She hesitated. "Do you think it could have anything to do with the Turtle?"

"Man, I hope not," Quin said. "I feel really bad about it. He was a good guy."

Anne realized that Jerome Lone was the man who had gotten Quin for her that fateful night. She felt sad, and uneasy. "How about some wine?" she asked, heading for the kitchen, where she collected wine and two glasses. They went into the parlor. After a few moments of silence, she asked, "What is your other news?"

Quin had been staring at Ben, and now he looked a bit confused. "I was just feeling bad thinking about Jerome. My other news is great, but it's hard to feel happy just now."

"You can't change what happened," Anne said, feeling the irony of her comment. "Tell me your good news. I can use some."

"It's about going to Mars," he told her.

"Is this a joke? What are you talking about?"

"Do you know who Lee Sanga is?"

"No."

"He's one of the tech billionaires. Get this. He's about to announce that he's put together a consortium to begin a new project to take a manned mission to Mars in five years. He's calling it the Malacandra Project. It hasn't been announced yet. But, man, it's unbelievable!"

"How can you know this?"

"It's too big to keep secret. It's all over the 'net. And the best part is this: in a few weeks the project managers will start accepting resumes and proposals. They're going to put together a whole scientific team dedicated only to Malacandra, starting from scratch like they did with the Manhattan Project. They're looking for talent at the universities. And my project team is putting a proposal together."

"Where will this project be based? And where would they launch the rocket from?" Anne asked.

"They don't know yet. That's the beauty of it. It could be anywhere in the world. They have to invent the whole project as they go along. With a short timeline, so they can catch the next optimum launch window. No fucking reinvention. The real thing."

Anne's mind reeled. "What's the name of this project again?"

"Malacandra."

"What does that mean?"

"It's C.S. Lewis." Quin grinned. "*Out of the Silent Planet,* the first volume of his space trilogy. I read it when I was eight. It's his name for Mars."

"Science fiction. That's perfect. All you guys are just acting out your childhood fantasies."

Quin smiled. "What's wrong with that?"

Anne scowled. "Do we have any right to go to another planet while we're still terrorizing each other here on Earth?"

"Man, we'd better start going to other planets. This one's almost all used up. We need a backup."

"I'm not joking, Quin."

"Neither am I. There are no more frontiers on Earth. It's overpopulated, polluted, and melting. We're killing each other off at a good rate, killer microbes keep mutating stronger, and the ozone is disappearing. We've gotta go off-planet, keep spreading our genes, or our species will disappear. It's biological destiny."

"So, you're saying that we should send humans to other planets so we can survive after we kill off our planet. What happens if there are life forms there?"

"Assuming they're not as technologically advanced as we are, we'll destroy them with our germs, or conquer them."

"Just like the Europeans did with the Native Americans?"

"Yeah."

"And you're saying that's okay?"

"No, I'm not saying it's okay. I'm just saying it's inevitable. We're a voracious species. We multiply, eat everything in our path, and move on."

"Humans are not just biological organisms, Quin. We have free will. We can decide not to be murderous conquerors."

"To a point," he said. He was serious.

Anne started to respond, but he interrupted her. "Look, if an aggressive, technologically advanced species landed on Earth, we'd be dead meat. Didn't you ever read *War of the Worlds*? It's where you are on the food chain, Anne. That's all it's about."

"Well, I think there's more to it than that, Quin. A lot more." Anne realized she wasn't angry at him, but at the whole world. But the anger felt good. It took her out of the despair she had been feeling for the past weeks. Her senses revived. She was hungry, and anxious to get out of the house. "Let's go eat," she said.

He grinned. "Liftoff."

Anne took him to her favorite pizza place on Pine Avenue. Quin took a deep breath of the aromas coming from the kitchen. A waitress led them to a booth and threw a couple of menus sheathed in plastic on the table.

"I'll be back for your order," she said, and disappeared.

"What's good?" Quin asked, picking up the menu.

"Everything." Anne took his menu. "Don't bother reading it. I'll order." When the waitress returned with a basket of Italian bread and a small bowl of butter patties, Anne ordered a pitcher of beer, two bowls of beans-and-greens, and a large pizza with sausage and mushrooms. When the beer came, she quickly poured two glasses.

"You know, Anne," Quin said, wiping foam from his mustache, "going to Mars most likely means we're going home. We're probably Martians, anyway."

"You mean because Martian meteorites landed on Earth billions of years ago?"

"Right. They seeded the primordial soup."

Anne shook her head. "Suppose Mars did have a civilization once. And then they destroyed their environment, and had wars, like we're doing, and now everything they were is dust. Just red dust swirling around an empty planet."

He nodded. "That's a possibility. We won't know until we get there, and see what's underground."

She stared at him. "You really want to get in on this project, don't you?"

"Hell yeah! I've been dreaming about Mars since I was a kid, when I first read Lewis' trilogy, and saw that little red dot through a telescope. Now, with Malacandra, it's the only thing I can think about, the only thing I want to do. I *have* to get in on it."

He began to tell her what his department's project might look like, rattling off technical details that Anne didn't even attempt to follow. As she listened, she grew jealous, then depressed. He had an exciting career path to follow. Her nursing school's transformational committee was at a dead end. The report she had been editing said nothing new.

Later, back home, Anne let Quin take Ben for his walk, even though she could have used it, after that meal. She started to brew a pot of coffee, dizzy with the contradiction of Quin's good nature versus his casual acceptance of the destruction of alien life forms and the probable demise of life on Earth. Going to Mars. It was the miracle the world needed, a distraction to keep us from focusing on the dying planet beneath us, an escape route to leave all our problems behind. Then we won't ever have to solve them. She was already tired of the discussion. She turned the coffee maker off, and tried to remember where she had put her martini glasses.

Early the next morning, Anne's cell phone rang. She reached across Quin's bulk to get it.

"Anne, it's Emily. Have you seen the morning paper?"

She tried to sound as though she'd been awake. "Not yet."

"There's great news. For once, wonderful news."

She sat up. "What is it?"

"There's an announcement that the Pickering Corporation has been dissolved. All its plans for a cyber casino in the Turtle are off."

"That's fabulous news, Emily," she said, pretending she hadn't heard anything about it.

"I've got to go, I have more calls to make. Bye."

Anne put her arms around Quin's naked chest. "So you really are one of the good guys," she said. She felt happy as Quinn kissed her. The Turtle really was saved, for now. And maybe humans would land on Mars before another casino opened in Niagara Falls.

CHAPTER THIRTY-EIGHT

"What's that you're looking at?"

Leonard jumped. Woody had snuck up on him again, while he was working at the office computer. He was supposed to be searching for any more news articles about the Lone family, but he had gotten distracted reading about a protest rally being planned for Niagara Falls. The federal government was establishing a national commission to renegotiate tribal and international treaties. Opponents of the commission said it was an attempt to negate treaties that protected land and water; its blatant purpose was to open up native lands to the extraction industries like mining and fracking. They were also examining who controls water – aquifers, lakes, and coastal waters. Native groups and environmental activists were joining together to fight this corporate assault on the planet's resources.

Leonard nervously turned to Woody. "It's nothing. I mean, well, it's this article about a rally in Niagara Falls in a couple of weeks. The guys and I were thinking we might go. If it's okay with you, that is, if we take the time."

"What kind of rally?"

"Take a look." He stood and offered his chair. Woody ignored the chair and squatted down until his head was almost low enough to be in front of the computer screen. He read, amid colorful graphics:

Save Our Planet
A Demand for Respect for Native Sovereignty
Stop Corporate Plundering of Earth's Resources
Clean Air and Water Is a Human Right

Native American and environmental leaders nationwide are organizing a series of rallies across the country to oppose Congress in its latest attempts to break treaty agreements and open up tribal lands to mining, timber and oil interests. A new National Commission on Treaties and States Rights headed by former Senator Gordon Spade is planning a systematic attack not only on native sovereignty, but on Mother Earth herself. The commission proposes to renegotiate all native and international treaties, including treaties that cover international waters. The Great Lakes and all rivers are in jeopardy. The people must act!

**The first rally will be held in Prospect Park in
Niagara Falls, New York
First Sunday in May**

Links:
Sign petition to Congress
Native sovereignty: George Washington's pledge
Broken treaties
Treaties America kept

Woody's knees cracked as he got up. "We'll see what's going on then. If I don't need you, I don't care if you guys go." He looked as though he didn't care much about anything, anymore.

Leonard hesitated, then decided the time had come to speak. How could he legitimately go to a rally for justice if he was afraid to stand up for the truth here, where he lived? If he didn't try to get justice for Jerome, whose murder was still officially an unsolved case? Moon and his men were still camped in the field. He stood in front of the office door. "Do you think we could talk sometime, Woody?"

"Don't tell me you want to leave. That would really screw me up right now."

"No, it's not that."

"You want a raise?"

"No." Leonard faced down his boss's annoyed look. "But I have to talk to you. It's important." He glanced at the open window. "But I can't talk to you here." Leonard knew that if Levi Moon even thought he knew anything about that night, they'd never find his body.

For a moment Woody looked as though he would just walk away. But he didn't. He stared at Leonard, then said, "I've gotta do some stuff in town this afternoon. You can ride with me. Be ready to go in an hour." He left the office.

Leonard breathed a sigh of relief. It would be good to get this over with. He killed time by going to the rally website's links, signing the petition to Congress, and reading about the broken treaties. On the link to <u>Treaties America Kept</u>, there was one word on the page: NONE.

Later, he waited until Woody started the engine to his pickup, which was parked just outside. Then he ran out the door and jumped in the truck as fast as he could, and sat slouched in the passenger's seat, his backpack wedged between his legs, so he couldn't be seen.

Woody said nothing about Leonard's curious moves. He drove quickly down the narrow, winding road through the woods, spewing gravel at every curve. The truck bounced Leonard all over the seat, even with his seat belt on. When they finally reached the smooth surface of the county road, Leonard began. "Woody?"

"Yeah?"

His nerve failed. "You know, I think you should upgrade your hardware. And your network connection. It's really slow."

Woody threw him a perplexed glance. "Is that what this is about? Computers? You want more toys?"

"No. Not exactly. Even though you do need better hardware. And some more stuff, like a scanner, a color printer..." Leonard couldn't stop himself from nervous babbling.

The big man growled, reminding Leonard of some of the stray

dogs he'd run with. "Get to the point, kid."

He looked at the big man's profile. "I know what happened that night. Some of it, anyway." He held his breath.

Woody reached over and grabbed his arm. "Don't you fuck with me, Leonard."

"I'm not." Leonard gasped with pain as Woody tightened his grip. "I swear it."

Woody let go of his arm, and accelerated the pickup so fast he went over the center line several times. Oncoming cars honked.

"Woody...," Leonard began, but his boss held his massive hand in front of Leonard's face. "Don't talk. Don't say anything."

Leonard leaned back in the seat, feeling oddly relieved. Even if Woody fired him, at least he'd be rid of the terrible secret he'd been holding. It was a heavy burden. He'd gotten nowhere investigating on his own. He'd kept his eyes open, but had seen nothing that shed light on Jerome's murder. Between spying on the trailer, and keeping up with his work, and hanging out so the other guys wouldn't get suspicious, he was exhausted. Now, he closed his eyes and dozed as the truck raced down the road.

When Woody shook him awake, they were in a parking lot at one of the New York State Thruway rest stops. They went inside. This one had an Italian fast-food counter. Eating was Jim's way of getting ready for something. They ordered lasagna and cokes. Woody paid and led the way to a booth in the corner. In mid afternoon, the eating area was fairly deserted. They ate quickly, without speaking. When he finished, Woody rose abruptly, and headed for the men's room. When he returned, with coffee, he rested his arms on the table and leaned forward. "Now talk. And it better be good."

Woody's face showed no reaction as Leonard described the terrible biting cold, how he followed Levi Moon's men, and hid in the closet, the sound of shouts, and gunshots, the three healers, and their rushed departure from the house, and then Levi Moon and his men revealing themselves to him. It wasn't until Leonard put his backpack on the table, and lifted the flap to reveal Old Turtle, that Woody looked like he believed the story. His face collapsed with grief. He pulled the backpack onto his lap, keeping Old Turtle hidden. Leonard saw his massive shoulders shake. He put his head down as Woody spoke in a low voice. "Jerome, why didn't you let me help you? Why did you send me away? You should have trusted me, Jerome. You should have trusted me."

Leonard said nothing. Woody's grief was big, like he was. But it was good for him to release it, so that his mind wouldn't collapse from trying to hold it in. He slipped out of the booth to the men's room. He was gone for a while. On his way back to the table, he bought more drinks and pizza slices.

By then, Woody was back in control. He ate a slice of pizza in a few bites. Then he leaned back and examined Leonard. "Why did you wait to tell me all this?"

"I've been wanting to tell you since it happened, but, well, no time seemed right. I really thought the cops would solve it. I mean, who else could have done it?"

"That's always been the big question. Jerome turned off the security system himself – that was the last thing on the surveillance tape. We couldn't figure out why. He wouldn't have turned it off for Moon. So then – for who?"

"Sometimes I thought I dreamed the whole thing," Leonard said. "But then I'd feel so bad I knew it all was true." He took a swig of vitamin water. "I've been trying to get more information. I've been watching Levi Moon, and those guys. They've been mostly staying put."

"Have you listened in on what they're talking about to each other?"

Leonard bowed his head, feeling ashamed. "I'm afraid to. The ground's still too wet, and I'd leave tracks. If they caught me, they'd kill me for sure."

Woody nodded. "They would, so be careful. Be very careful." His face still sagged. "Man, I wish Jerome hadn't tried to do it alone. It's obvious what his plan was. He tried to bring in some real healers to take a look at John, and figure out how to cure him, how to get Moon away from him. But he had no idea what he was up against."

"What do you mean?"

Woody stared at him hard. "We're in this together now, right? Partners. This goes no farther."

"Yes. I swear. I want to help."

"Okay, then." Woody leaned closer. "Jerome sent me to New York to meet with this private investigator he hired a while back to check on Moon. The guy gave me his final report. They found out a lot." He glanced over his shoulder; no one else was in the eating area, but he still lowered his voice. "They think Moon was born on or near the Matachewan Indian reserve in Ontario, up near Quebec, around nineteen-forty. His birth name was Claude Anguiné. His mother was Quebecois. His father had relatives on the reserve. His mother abandoned Claude when he was still a baby, and he was raised in a missionary school near Three Rivers in Quebec. That school was closed about twenty years ago, after a big scandal that the priests were physically and sexually abusing the students. Anyway, when Claude left school he found a career in robbery, assault, and battery, and served six years in prison. He disappeared for a long time after he was released, but in the sixties they picked up his trail again. He started showing up on various reservations, always just passing through. The investigators are certain he was in the smuggling business, transporting contraband across the U-S-Canada border at various points. He got turned back at the Niagara Falls bridges a few times, for having forged documents. He was arrested once at the Whirlpool Bridge on the American side for trying to get drugs across. In the seventies, he got involved with the Warrior Society for a while. Then he dropped completely out of sight. Some people say he went underground, in the Caribbean and South America, to learn about medicinal herbs and black magic."

Leonard sucked in his breath. His eyes were wide.

Woody glared at him. "You don't believe in that crap, do you?"

"I ... I don't know. I mean, you hear a lot of stuff about it, and I saw a program on the Discovery Channel about voodoo and zombies ..." He felt defensive when Woody snorted. "You said yourself Jerome didn't know what he was getting into. What did you mean, then?"

"I was talking about Moon's criminal record, and his potential for violence. Sure, I think somehow he's using some weird drugs on John, and maybe Mrs. Lone, too, but that's pharmaceutical, not magic."

Leonard decided not to push the point. He wasn't sure what powers he believed in, but he wasn't going to rule anything out.

"Just listen," Woody said. "About ten years ago, our friend Claude started showing up again, only now he's Levi Moon and he's pitching himself as some sort of healer. He's been successful at hustling people, performing fake cures. He's also been arrested for fraud and embezzlement, but the charges never stick. People usually drop them. The police think they're scared off, but they can't prove it."

Leonard was tense with excitement. "Why did Jerome ever let him go near his brother?"

"Jerome never did. It was Mrs. Lone. We never figured out how those two got together. Maybe he contacted her, after he found out about John, maybe through newspaper articles, and figured to give it a shot. Then he discovered a gold mine. Better than gold. Moon even tried to set up a cyber casino operation in the Turtle in Niagara Falls, using phony papers with John's signature, and his mother's, too."

Leonard gasped. "My friend works there!"

Woody's eyes narrowed. "Doing what? How does he know Moon? And how do you know him?"

Leonard's head spun as he contemplated the connections. "I ... I don't think he knows Moon. His name's Quin, he's a computer guy, he works at BU. He's setting up the computer network. He was going out with my, my friend's aunt, and she dumped him when she found out, because she's anti-casino, she has a house by the upper rapids, but they got back together again, I think." That was Leonard's impression when he last saw them, at the Buffalo airport, but he didn't stick around long enough to ask any questions, or answer any.

"What else do you know about it?"

"Nothing. No one ever heard about Levi Moon. Everyone thinks John Lone is setting up the cyber casino."

"Yeah. Only he's still in a coma. But Jerome's lawyers put a stop to that sleazy operation in the Falls."

"Do you see him? John Lone, I mean."

"No." Leonard could tell Woody didn't like admitting that. "Mrs. Lone keeps everyone away, except the family and Moon."

"Maybe we could get those healers to come back."

Woody shook his head. "They won't get in a second time. But it would be good to talk to them. Find out what they know, what they think we could do to help John."

"Maybe my great-grandfather would know how to contact them."

"Who's that?"

"Wallace Mountview. He knows people on the Haudenosaunee Council. He could find out who the healers were."

Woody looked impressed. "The word's gotta be out on this to the Council."

Leonard leaned across the table. "Everything you said about Moon makes this even scarier. And it's really creepy to know he's connected with what's going on at the Falls. Things have been really weird there lately."

"Things are always weird there." Woody wiped his mouth with his napkin. "First thing we need to do is find those healers. We'll do it this week. Tell people we're picking up new hardware in Buffalo, like you said we need. We'll take a little jog north to see your great-grandfather."

"Okay."

"In the meantime, keep your eyes open and let me know if you see or hear anything, no matter how trivial it seems. Don't try to get too close to that RV, though. You're right to be afraid."

"Okay."

"Do you think we can bug it?"

Leonard laughed. Woody was cool, when he wasn't scary. "Yeah, we can try. Let's look for some stuff when we go to Niagara Falls."

CHAPTER THIRTY-NINE

Anne was relieved to see Bill's gray SUV in the small parking area outside the Giacometi Construction Company headquarters, a series of long trailers squatting among company trucks, piles of lumber and pipe, and shipping containers. It was just outside the city limits, on a lot bordering the New York State Thruway, just north of the OHA-RAS landfill. Everything, including Bill's car, had a grimy sheen to it. She went inside the first trailer. The walls were covered with company calendars and renderings of office buildings and strip malls.

"Can I help you?" The receptionist looked harried, and it was only eight in the morning.

"Is Bill Techa here?"

The woman looked Anne up and down. "Is he expecting you?"

"Not really. I'm his sister. I just need to pop in and see him for a minute."

The woman cocked her head to the right. "His office is at the end of the hall."

The hall was a path between two rows of cubicles, culminating in one large office that spanned the end of the trailer. Anne heard Bill's voice before she was halfway down the hall. "No, we need that shipment today. You're already a week late. If it's not here by noon, the order's cancelled. Yeah, well, screw you, too. Goodbye." She heard the receiver get slammed down, and hurried into the office before he could dial another call.

"Hi, Bill." She sat on a metal chair across from his messy desk.

"What the hell are you doing here?"

"I need to talk to you. Do you have five minutes?"

"Does it look like I have five minutes?"

"It's about Phoebe." The look on his face scared her. "It's not bad news, Bill, don't worry."

"I'm not worried. I don't give a shit anymore."

Anne knew better than to argue. "Since you won't answer my phone calls, I just want to tell you that she's okay. She's staying at my house now, not in Buffalo. We had a good conversation about it. She'll be more comfortable with me, and I feel better with her close by. She's better, I think, but she's still ... exhausted. We made a deal. She'll finish the school year – I'll get her back and forth to school in Buffalo every day. So she'll stay with me until we figure out the next step."

"You mean until that Indian kid shows up again."

"Bill, I really think that's the least of our worries."

"Yeah, well, I don't care what you think."

Anne accepted that Bill was still furious with her. She knew he'd never forgive her for not telling him Phoebe was in Las Vegas. What he didn't understand was how important Phoebe was to her, too, how important he and his whole family were. They were the only family she had. Not wanting to make things worse, she stood up. She had prepped herself to be absolutely professional during this meeting.

"Well, okay, I won't take up any more of your time. I just wanted you to know where Phoebe is, and that she's safe. Mari's keeping an eye on her while I'm gone. We won't let her be alone. I have to get back home now. I want to be there when she wakes up."

"Wait. I'll walk you out." Bill stood. Grabbing his jacket, which was hanging on a hook next to the door, he felt the pocket and pulled out a pack of cigarettes. As he and Anne walked past the receptionist, he said, "I'm going out for a smoke." Anne felt the woman's eyes boring into her.

Outside, he motioned Anne to an area behind the trailer, where a picnic table, benches, and tall cans of sand had been set up for breaks. They sat on the table, their feet on the bench, huddled against a chilly wind. Anne watched a truck maneuver its way through the cluttered complex, toward a metal warehouse at the back of the site.

Bill inhaled deeply, then blew out a cloud of smoke. "So you really think it's okay for her to be at your house?"

"I hope so. I had a good talk with her, and her counselor. Sister Bea says she doesn't seem to be suicidal. She's improved over the past few weeks."

"I wouldn't know. She won't talk to her mother or me."

"I'll watch her as closely as I can, and Mari will, too. I won't leave the house unless Mari's there."

"Well, there's nothing I can do for her." Bill threw the smoked filter down on the ground. He pulled out another cigarette and lit it.

Anne pressed her hands against her throbbing forehead. She knew she shouldn't give Bill any assurances; she wasn't as optimistic as she tried to be. He couldn't pretend that he had forgiven Phoebe, or her. But she'd done the right thing in telling him where his daughter was, and now she could leave. She stood. "You'll tell Ellen where she is? That I'm doing my best for her, keeping her under close supervision?"

He snorted. "No way."

"Bill, she should know where her daughter is."

"Why?" His face was red, and he breathed hard. "So she can worry every minute that the kid's gonna take off again? Or jump over the falls? So she can go back on tranquilizers? Forget it, I'm through letting that kid run our lives."

Anne stared at him, not daring to speak. He stood up. "Guys like me, we work hard, we don't complain, we try to raise our families, and what do we get for it? We get shit, Anne. That's what we get. Shit from our bosses. Shit from our wives. Shit from our kids. Just shit."

Anne wanted to comfort her brother. She wanted to acknowledge how hard he worked. She wanted to tell him that Phoebe would be okay, and that his daughter loved him. She started to speak, but Bill held up his hand. "Don't say anything, Anne. Don't even try. And don't come back here again." He turned and walked quickly back into the dingy trailer.

She stood motionless for some minutes after Bill left. She was glad she couldn't see OHARAS from there. It was better not to see it, while you were within range of the tiny toxic grit that blew off the poisonous heap. Tiny toxic grit that permeated people's hearts, and minds, and everything they cared about.

That evening, her cell phone rang as Anne was clearing dinner dishes. Phoebe hadn't touched her food. She was lying on the floor in the parlor, watching TV. Ben was stretched across her legs. Anne was debating whether to save the pasta primavera, or just toss it, as she picked up the phone.

"Hey, Anne."

"Quin?" She hadn't expected to hear from him; he had told her he'd be busy all week working on his ideas for the Malacandra Project.

"Yeah. Hey, listen, I've got a really big favor to ask you."

"What kind of favor?"

"Like I said, a big one."

"Well." She hesitated. "You know I have Phoebe staying here now."

"Yeah. Well, listen, late last night my mom called. She was pretty upset."

"Oh, Quin, has your dad gotten worse? Or is it your brother?"

"No, actually, my dad's been doing pretty well, with the new drugs and all. The thing is, he got it into his head that he's coming to Niagara Falls to see this big environmental rally in a couple of weeks. He got the plane tickets without even asking my mother. She can't talk him out of it. All of a sudden he's really into saving the planet."

Anne had seen posters for the rally on campus. "Is he strong enough for the trip?"

"My mom doesn't think so."

"Why does he want to come here for that?"

"You got me. All I know is, my mom says they came to Niagara Falls on their honeymoon, and she thinks he wants to see it one last time, and this is a good excuse because he always said the Indians were the only ones treated worse than the Irish."

"Oh." Anne hesitated. "What do you need from me?"

"Can they stay at your place? Just for the weekend?"

Her jaw dropped. "Oh, I don't know, Quin, I, I mean, Phoebe is here, and ...."

"Listen, I can't get them a hotel room anywhere, everything's booked. And they can't stay at Pete's place, it's a fucking wreck. And my mom would be really relieved if Dad was staying with a nurse, and all."

"What did you tell them about me?"

"I just said you're a nurse I know from BU."

Anne felt a twinge of disappointment. She considered telling him it was impossible. But how could she, really? She couldn't; she was even planning to go to the rally herself. "Okay," she sighed. "They can stay here. I'll move into the guestroom. It'll let me keep an even closer eye on Phoebe."

"What do you mean?"

"She's moved into the tower room. I can't talk about it now. I'll tell you later."

"Okay. Hey, listen, Anne ...," he hesitated.

"What?" She was ready to hang up.

"Thanks. I mean, a lot. You're great."

She managed a smile. "It's okay. Bye." As she ended the call, she tried to forget his words, "a nurse I know."

CHAPTER FORTY

Loud voices and heavy footsteps woke Phoebe from her deep sleep. Lying on her back on an inflatable mattress on the floor of Anne's tower room, she let her mind drift up from sweet oblivion to sunlit reality. She opened her eyes and dreamily watched the lace curtains flutter in the breeze creeping through the open windows. Scattered sunbeams flowed across her and the wooden carving of the Warrior. She was relieved Quin's parents were finally there. That meant Anne wouldn't be checking on her every five minutes, listening at the bottom of the stairs to see if she was awake. Why was everyone still so worried about her? All she wanted to do was rest. Not even think, just rest. The sooner they understood that, the better. She turned her mind to the frequency of the Niagara channel. That's what she called it when she shut out every sound except the rush of the river. When she concentrated very hard, she could feel its vibrations surge through her whole body. She wasn't afraid of the falls anymore. Now she listened to it. Sometimes, she was sure it was speaking directly to her.

The odor of coffee and hot roast beef wafted into the tower. She stood up and stretched. She felt pretty good today, for some reason. She pulled on a pair of jeans under her big tee shirt. She tiptoed down the stairs and scurried along the hall to the bathroom.

"I think I've spotted the elusive Phoebe."

She froze when she heard the loud male voice. She locked the bathroom door, and got into the shower. She stood under hot water for a long time. Afterward, she dried her hair; it was almost back to shoulder length. After getting dressed, she debated what to do. She didn't want to be spotted again.

Anne knocked at the door. "Phoebe? Do you want to join us for lunch, Hon? Quin and Mari are here, and Quin's parents."

She could smell the meat even stronger now, and that drew her out. Quin grinned when she entered the dining room. "Hey, squirt, what's up?" Ben was sitting between him and his father. The dog had abandoned her for treats.

"Nothing. Hi, Mari."

Mari rose from her chair and hugged her, as Anne announced, "This is Mr. and Mrs. McCarthy, Quin's parents."

"We're Tommy and Kat, Phoebe," said Quin's father, who rose slowly from his chair. "Happy to meet you."

"Nice to meet you, too." Phoebe held her breath as the man grasped her hand in a clawlike grip. She was surprised that such a small man had such a loud voice. But as she looked at him, she realized that he had shrunk, somehow. Folds of skin hung from the bottom of his cheeks and arms. He looked like an old, shriveled Quin; he was so pale, it seemed as though he was fading out of a picture. She was repulsed by him, but didn't show it, because he was Quin's dad, and she liked Quin. If he were a stranger, she'd run.

Anne bustled around the table, putting out more hot beef and gravy, and pasta salad, and rolls, and sticks of fresh vegetables. Mari went into the kitchen and came out with a plate of small cakes. Quin ate nonstop.

"More coffee, anyone?" Anne asked.

"This is a wonderful lunch, Anne," Kat said, holding up her cup. "You're so kind to let us strangers stay in your lovely home." She glanced at her husband.

Phoebe recognized the look. Her mother had it, too. It meant he was driving her nuts.

"Oh, think nothing of it," Anne said, managing to sound sincere. "I like company."

"Is this your first trip to Niagara Falls, Kat?" Mari asked.

"No." Kat reached for a carrot stick. She was a thin woman with graying hair and a deep, tobacco voice. "We came here more than forty years ago, while we were on our honeymoon trip to Chicago. We stayed a couple of nights in Canada, in a one-story motel with flower boxes on all the windows. We enjoyed it so much."

"That we did," her husband agreed. "It's a wonderful thing, a great waterfall like Niagara. I've never gotten the vision of it out of my mind, not in forty years. Or the sound of it, either."

"You must love living so close to it in this beautiful house, Anne," Kat remarked.

"I do."

"And you must love visiting your aunt, Phoebe."

The girl froze as all eyes turned toward her. Why was this woman babbling like that? Luckily, Phoebe's mouth was full of gravy-soaked rye bread, so she escaped having to answer with anything but a nod.

Tommy swallowed a mouthful of coffee and leaned back. "I'm glad the Indians are standing up for themselves. It's about time. You can't wait for the enemy to give you justice. That day will never come, as the Irish know only too well. You must demand justice. When the oppressors come and take your land, they won't give it back without a fight."

His wife glanced nervously around the table. "Tommy, you know they can't give back all the Indian land."

Tommy's fist pounded the table, making the dishes, and Phoebe, jump. "Compensation! There must be compensation." He started to cough. Everyone sat very still. Anne rose and gently moved him to a better sitting position. She handed him a glass of water. He took a swallow, then glared around the table. "I'm not gone yet, so stop staring."

"I'm not staring," Phoebe told him. "My dad does the same thing. Yells until he coughs. It's because he smokes too much."

"The world takes its toll on a man, Phoebe," Tommy replied, in a sad voice. "On his body, and on his soul."

"Come on, Dad." Quin stood up, shoving a piece of cake in his mouth. "I'll take you for a ride around the falls. Wanna come, Ma?"

"No, I'll stay here and help Anne clear up."

"Oh, there's no need for that, Kat," Anne said. "Mari will help me. You go enjoy yourself."

"Well ...," Kat glanced at Tommy. "If you don't mind, I'd like to unpack, and perhaps lie down for a while."

Phoebe could see how desperately Quin's mother wanted to get away from her husband, and suddenly Phoebe wanted to get away from her. She looked like she was going to crack. She liked Quin's dad, though. He had real feelings. "Can I go with you, Quin?" she asked.

"Sure, come on."

"Here, take my car, it's more comfortable than your old Jeep." Anne handed him her electronic key. She looked at Phoebe and mouthed the word "thanks." That made Phoebe feel good; for once, she wasn't the problem.

As they walked down the front steps, Phoebe saw cars parked along both sides of Cataract Lane. "What are all these cars doing here?"

"They're for the big rally tomorrow, Phoebe," Tommy told her. He was holding the railing as he walked down the steps, one by one. "I tell you, the time has come. This country has got to settle things fairly. And do a lot of other things that people are demanding, like taking care of the planet. Then this new century can really begin."

"Oh, right, the rally's tomorrow." She had forgotten. She started to get excited. She knew Leonard would have to be there. He wouldn't miss it. She'd find him and join up with him. She'd go to the secret place where he lived — it had to be in the woods, and there had to be animals, and big trees, and sacred places. The rest of the world was too full of mean people. Phoebe couldn't stand it anymore.

She stretched across the back seat as Quin drove to Buffalo Avenue and joined a long line of cars crawling toward Goat Island. They crossed the traffic bridge and cruised slowly. Near the Three Sisters Islands, traffic came to a halt as a large crowd of tourists surged across the road.

"Who in the hell is that?"

Quin and Phoebe looked where Tommy was pointing, toward the stone bridge to Asenath. A bearded man in filthy clothes and sandals was standing on a bench, shouting.

"That's the Hermit," Phoebe told him. "He's reincarnated."

"He's what?"

Quin laughed. "He's crazy, Dad. But uniquely delusional. He thinks he's the reincarnation of a guy who lived on Goat Island in the early nineteenth century. Let's see what he's saying." He opened the car windows. Above the noise of the crowd, they heard the Hermit yell: "... but not to me returns Day, or the sweet approach of ev'n or morn, or sight of vernal bloom, or summer's rose, or flocks, or herds, or human face divine, but cloud instead, and ever-during dark surrounds me ..."

"That's weird. Close the window, Quin." Phoebe didn't want to hear any more. "Come on, the traffic's moving again."

Quin drove forward. Cars slowed again as they passed by Terrapin Point. Tommy craned his neck to see the water. "Want to get off here, Dad?"

"No, I'd rather see it from the other side."

"Maybe you should go back to Anne's and rest for a while."

"I'll rest when I'm dead, and not before."

Phoebe saw the back of Quin's neck get red. She tapped him on the shoulder and said, "It's better from the other side."

It took more than an hour to get over the Rainbow Bridge, but Phoebe didn't mind. Quin and his father didn't say much, but none of them were bored. There was too much to see.

Once over the bridge, Quin scanned the crowds on River Road, which was lined with colorful baskets of flowers. "I'll never find a parking spot. How 'bout I drop you guys off by the Horseshoe Falls, and come back in about fifteen minutes and pick you up? That should be long enough to see the view."

"Good plan, son."

Quin made an illegal U-turn to drop off his passengers near the overview for the Horseshoe Falls. Phoebe jumped out and waited for Tommy, while cars honked impatiently.

"We're going to get wet," she yelled over the roar of the falls, as they made their way through the crowd to the railing. A strong breeze was blowing the Horseshoe's mist toward them. A huge blue-and-white Cataract Cloud balloon ride was hovering overhead, just above the great basin of the falls, swaying gently on its tether.

"It's the taste of nature, Phoebe." Tommy breathed hard. "Nature is life."

Phoebe pushed through people to make the path easier for Tommy, and squeezed them into a space at the stone wall at the edge of the gorge. Tommy grinned at her. "You're a good tour guide, Phoebe."

She shrugged. "I know how to deal with tourists."

They watched the river form a green-tinged crown as the water rushed over the brink. When Phoebe focused her eyes on one point, the water seemed to fall in slow motion, hanging like ribbons of crystals. White clouds swirled up from the foot of the cataract. Down below, the tour boats, bursting with passengers, sailed the forceful currents.

"Look at the balloon, Mommy!" a little girl shouted.

Phoebe looked up. The Cataract Cloud balloon was pulling on its tether, its large open gondola swaying in the gusts of wind. She could see people in the gondola waving to the crowd. Holding onto the curved iron railing, she leaned forward to see better. "That looks fun."

"I'd like a little more under me than that flimsy basket," Tommy replied. He looked away from the balloon and stared at the falls. "It almost makes me believe in God again."

Phoebe wasn't sure if Tommy was talking to her. His face was covered with droplets of mist, or maybe tears.

"I don't believe in God," she told him. "What's the point? God can't help you with anything. There's the story about the Maid of the Mist. About a god who lives behind the falls, who fights a demon and saves a girl who sacrifices herself by going over it. That story makes sense to me. You should pay attention to gods that live on Earth. Why bother with some God who only lives in Heaven, and just looks down on us, like we're some kind of experiment or something?"

"Phoebe, you present an interesting theological argument," Tommy replied, looking a bit confused. "I'll have to think about that."

"We'd better start back and look for Quin," she said.

As they turned, a woman screamed. Then everyone around them started yelling. Whirling around, Phoebe saw the lovely balloon dancing crazily in the sky, its gondola swaying back and forth like the pendulum on a clock.

"The tether snapped!" a man shouted. "It pierced the balloon!"

"Lord help us!" Tommy cried.

The giant balloon sped toward them as air spewed out of the other side, until it was caught in the heavy mist surging from the Horseshoe's cauldron. Then it started to spin like a top. One man, then another, jumped feet first from the basket into the swirling green water below, and disappeared. Other passengers were half-hanging off the sides, or reaching out as though they could grab onto the horrified onlookers along the top of the gorge. Phoebe thought she could hear the passengers' screams above those of the people around her, and wished she was watching this happen on TV, instead of for real.

Slowly, the balloon deflated, and sunk toward the surging waters below. The gondola disappeared into the swirling waters. The balloon's skin hung in the heavy air for long moments, then twirled like a dancer's shawl, and fell into the water, where it lay in a bright nylon puddle, swirling in the currents. None of the passengers could be seen. The tour boats in the water turned toward the disaster.

Tommy grabbed Phoebe's arm. "Are you all right, Phoebe?"

"I'm fine." She pulled her arm out of his hard grip. "This isn't the first time I've seen an accident at the falls." She remembered watching the boat *Marilyn* struggle in the rapids below the falls. Then, like now, it seemed unreal. The only way to deal with it was to treat it like it was a story, and not real people. Otherwise, you couldn't stand it. To see how death came – like a thunderbolt out of the sky.

Tommy stared into the rocky basin. "I've never seen anything like this. Maybe there *are* demons around here."

"Lots of people think so. You should talk to Mari."

"Dad! Phoebe!"

They turned and saw Quin pushing his way through the crowd. A wall of people was rushing toward the railing. Quin took his father's arm. "Phoebe, let's get him out of here." They fought their way back to the street; Quin had left Anne's car parked illegally, with its emergency lights flashing. Sirens were wailing all along the congested street.

It took a long time to get back across the bridge. When they finally pulled up at Anne's house, she was sitting on the front steps with Mari, Kat, and Ben, waiting for them. She rushed to the car and opened the door for Tommy. "How are you? Did you see the accident?" She looked in back. "Phoebe, what about you? How do you feel?"

"We saw it, but we're fine," she reported.

Anne and Kat took Tommy's arms and helped him out of the car. "They said on the radio that it could be ecoterrorists," Kat said. "Do you think so, Tommy?"

"No." He winked at Phoebe. "But it could have been demons."

"My God, he's delirious," his wife said. "Quin, how could you keep your father out so long?" She glared at him. "Anne, please help me get him into the house."

Phoebe and Quin watched the three women fuss over Tommy as they slowly went up the front stairs. He seemed to enjoy the attention, as he dramatically described the scene of horror and death on the river.

Quinn looked upset.

"Don't worry," Phoebe told him. "He's not delirious. He's just thinking."

CHAPTER FORTY-ONE

Leonard made sure he woke up before the other guys did, because he wanted to check again that Old Turtle was packed carefully enough in his backpack. Not just enough to keep him safe, but enough to keep him quiet. Old Turtle was making a lot of noise lately; Leonard thought it was because he wanted to go to Niagara Falls, too. They had a long day ahead of them – it was the day of the rally at Niagara Falls. Leonard had no idea what would happen. And no plan, either, other than to look for his great-grandfather and find out if he had made contact with the healers, and if he could tell him what to do next.

The previous night, he and the guys had watched local news reports to see advance coverage of the rally. Homeland Security was warning it could create a state of emergency in downtown Niagara Falls. Most news programs opened with coverage about the search for bodies of the victims of the balloon accident the day before. Eight people had gone into the river, and none had been recovered.

"Man, that's a bad way to go," Jemmy said.

Leonard watched closely as the names of the missing and their hometowns were scrolled onscreen. They were all tourists from other countries and states. But then, who else would go on that thing? He felt edgy, as he tried to figure out what this disaster could portend.

Later, one local news report had interviews with Native Americans among the rally organizers. After interviewing an Oneida clan mother, the reporter put the microphone close to the face of a tired-looking man. "Sir, can you tell us who you are and why you are marching?"

His dark eyes looked straight into the camera. "My name is Ely Walker and I'm a member of the Cayuga Nation, the people for whom the longest of the Finger Lakes is named. We want to come home, to the land of our fathers; we have fought in your courts for two hundred years, and we have never found justice. Today we are marching to say enough! Senator Spade and the Congress say they want to negotiate treaties for the twenty-first century. First, let the United States honor the treaties of the eighteenth century."

The news anchor then ran a taped interview with Auburn Burdett, president of the Central New York chapter of White Citizens for Equality. His thin face was cracked like dry leather. "These people want land my family has farmed for three generations. They won't have to pay taxes on it. And now they want to control the oil and water? What gives them the right?"

There were other interviews. A sixtyish man, his head haloed with frizzy gray hair, said, "This is our last stand to save the planet. If Congress guts the treaties and lets corporate greed run rampant, our children won't have anything left on this planet."

The news coverage got the guys totally psyched for the rally. Leonard tried to quell the anxiety he felt because he hadn't heard from Grandfather yet. Wallace and Rose had been overjoyed to see him when he and Woody had gone to their house the week before. Woody ate three bowls of Rose's five-bean soup while Leonard told their story. Grandfather didn't say much, except to warn Leonard again and again to stay far away from Levi Moon. He said he would get word to him, one way or another, if he learned anything. Sometimes Leonard wondered if Grandfather had believed the story. Sometimes, he almost didn't believe it himself. Sometimes, he almost convinced himself it had all been a terrible dream. But there was Old Turtle, carefully muffled in his backpack. He was no dream. He was real.

Before eight o'clock in the morning, the guys were ready to hit the road. Leonard was wearing a "Free Leonard Peltier" tee shirt.

"Come on, hurry up," Jemmy urged. "There's gonna be lots of traffic, especially at the bridges." They were about to climb into Jemmy's SUV when Leonard's cell phone buzzed. Jemmy groaned. "Oh, man, it better not be the Woodman."

Leonard answered the call. "Woody?"

Woody's voice came through thick static. He was shouting. "I need all you guys at the main house now! Come to the front door. Hurry!" He ended the call.

If he didn't know better, Leonard would think Woody sounded scared. The guys roared off. The road was longer than the trail through the woods, but Jemmy sped all the way. As they neared the house, they saw Levi Moon's huge black SUV parked in front of the main door. Archie was at the wheel. Mal and Samuel were standing next to it. Woody was just outside the door of the house, looking in. Jemmy squealed to a halt near it, and the guys ran to their boss.

"What's happening?" Leonard asked.

"I don't know, but we have to stop it somehow. Look." Woody stepped away from the door. Leonard peered inside. Mrs. Lone was standing at the bottom of the stairway, with her daughter Loraine and Andrew. Leonard felt his knees go wobbly when he saw what was coming down the stairs.

Levi Moon was stepping backward, motioning to a thin man, dressed in black, to follow him. The man stared straight ahead, putting one foot ahead of the other with tentative steps. His right hand gripped the handrail, the left was on Reg's shoulder. Leonard recognized his handsome face, framed by long black hair flecked with silver. It was John Lone. He felt as though he couldn't breathe. He glanced at the waiting family. Andrew looked grim. John's sister was crying. His mother had a proud smile on her face.

When Levi Moon and John were both on the solid floor, Andrew grabbed Moon and whirled him around. Leonard followed Woody as he rushed into the house.

"You're not taking him anywhere!" Andrew shouted. Loraine tried to reach John, but her mother held her back. Samuel and Mal ran into the house. Two lines were formed, with John Lone between them. The sides glared at each other.

Levi Moon stepped forward and stood next to John. "We are going now," he said in a calm voice. "Anyone who really cares about Mr. Lone will not interfere, lest he disturb the careful balance we have attained."

"Just where do you think you're taking him?" Woody growled.

"It's none of your affair," Moon replied. "We have a duty to perform. Then his recovery will be complete." He took John's arm, and led him slowly toward the door.

Woody and Andrew moved warily toward them. Leonard tried to grab Mal, who pushed him roughly to the ground.

"They have guns!" Leonard shouted. With an evil grin on his face, Mal moved his hand under his jacket. They could see the bulge, and everyone froze. Leonard had no doubt Mal would use his weapon, and that all of Moon's men were armed.

Moon and his men helped John into the black SUV, while the others looked on helplessly. As soon as the doors closed, Woody turned toward Andrew. "Do you have any idea where they're going?" Andrew shook his head.

Loraine turned on her mother. "Where are they going, Mother? Tell me. Quick!"

Mrs. Lone's eyes were wild, darting here and there. "They are going to a healing ceremony. I wanted to go, too, but he wouldn't allow it. Not for women, he said."

"How could you let him do this?" Loraine sounded hysterical. She grabbed her mother's arms and shook her. "Where are they going, Mother? Where?"

Mrs. Lone seemed not to mind the shaking; she seemed not to be aware of it. She said calmly, "To Niagara Falls. To the Turtle. That's the only place it can be done, the Healer says."

Woody let out a roar. "Come on," he shouted. He ran outside, and jumped into his red SUV, which was parked along the drive. Leonard and Andrew got in with him. The other guys got into their vehicle, and followed. They soon caught up to Moon. Leonard pulled out his cell phone. His hands were shaking. "Please be home, please be home," he whispered as the phone rang at his great-grandfather's house.

Rose answered.

"Is Grandfather there?"

"Leonard, how fine to hear from you. He's left for the rally already. He said he had to meet some people."

"Will you see him? Before the rally, I mean."

"I might. Is something wrong?"

"I just need to get him a message. I have to see him."

"Alright, I'll tell him that."

"And, tell him ...," Leonard hesitated. "Tell him everyone is coming. *Everyone.* Tell him to be ready." He signed off before she could ask any questions.

The three vehicles soon reached the 219 and sped north toward Buffalo.

"What do you think this is about, Woody?" Andrew asked.

The big man's lips barely moved. "Advertising," he said.

Andrew gasped. "Huh?"

Leonard leaned forward from the back seat. "What do you mean?"

"He wants John to be seen at the Turtle when he knows a big crowd will be there, lots of folks from the Nations, and reporters, too. That confirms John's his partner. And it also advertises Moon's supposed healing powers. Imagine the business he'll drum up."

Leonard considered that. It made sense, but it was too easy. "It's more than that. I don't know how I know, but I feel it. I think it's about his power, not just marketing. I think he *has* to take John to the falls."

"Get a grip, kid," Woody growled. "You've been watching too much TV."

"Maybe." He leaned back in his seat. Maybe. But Niagara Falls was the most powerful place there was. And maybe Levi Moon knew black magic, and maybe he didn't. But it was a dangerous conjunction of powers, as Mari would say. Anything could happen.

It was a long drive as they followed Moon onto the Youngmann Highway near Buffalo. The Grand Island bridges were backed up so he drove to Niagara Falls along River Road. Mal got ahead of them when he ran a red light on Buffalo Avenue. By the time Woody pulled into the Turtle's parking lot next to Moon's car, they were already inside. All the doors were locked.

Woody and the guys settled in to wait, while Leonard searched for Wallace. The rally had drawn hundreds, maybe thousands of people. A stage was set up near Chief Clinton Rickard's statue. There was a lot of law enforcement keeping a close eye on the crowd. Some officers had big German shepherds. The air was tense, not at all festive. People meant business; many believed they were making a last stand for the Earth.

Woody was in an extremely bad mood when Leonard returned. "Did you find him?"

"No. He might not be here yet."

"Well, a lot of good he turned out to be." Woody turned and walked to a shaded area next to the Turtle's big white head. He lit a cigarette.

Leonard felt ashamed. He had been sure Wallace would meet them. Then a thought hit him. Maybe he was at Anne's. Maybe he figured Leonard would go there. Leonard looked up the street toward Cataract Lane. He had to take the chance, even though he knew it could be difficult. He knew Anne would want a lot of explaining from him.

"I'll be right back, Woody."

"Don't you dare disappear."

"I won't." He ran as fast as he could to Anne's house. He pushed on the bell several times. There was no answer. Turning, he took the front steps in one leap. He ran toward the falls along the path by the river, noticing a fresh Ben-dump near the Knobby Tree. Anne must be slipping, or else maybe it was Phoebe who was walking the dog. She never picked it up. He was as cranky as Woody when he got back to the Turtle. They didn't look at each other.

Soon Leonard saw a crowd of marchers with signs heading toward Prospect Point, following a tall puppet of a snake representing corporate executives. The signs read, "Honor the Treaties," "Save the Lakes," "Water is a human right," and other slogans. One man had a smaller puppet representing corporate greed – a skeleton stuffing children and trees into its mouth.

"I'm going to see what's going on," Leonard told Woody. He hurried across the street, followed by Jemmy and Darman, ignoring Woody's shouts to come back.

"What's happening?" Leonard asked a man wearing a ribbon shirt and a *gustoweh*, who was trying to direct the marchers.

The man shook his head sadly. "Some rightwing bystanders attacked the anti-globalization militants. It's not our people fighting, but the police have stopped the rally. They cut the power to the sound system. Ely Walker won't leave without speaking, so we moved."

A makeshift stand was quickly set up on the plaza near the brink of the American Falls. A tall man whose *gustoweh* held a single upright eagle feather stepped on it and faced the crowd, speaking through a bullhorn. His amplified voice could barely be heard over the roar of the cataract behind him. Leonard moved closer. Walker said, "Three hundred years ago, Europeans sailed west along the Lake Ontario shoreline, and landed in places they had never seen before. They were met by our forefathers. You could say our forefathers discovered them, standing on the shore trying to figure out where they were."

Leonard and most of the crowd laughed. But there were some boos.

"This is our homeland," Walker continued. "Turtle Island, the homeland of all the native peoples. As the years passed, from the first encounters, our homes were taken from us. This is a long story, full of pain. It is a story of lies and trickery, and of breathtaking dishonor. Colonials claimed they bought land from us – a people who know that no man owns Mother Earth. Every treaty signed by the United States, and the State of New York, and other states, was broken. This web of lies and betrayal is still breeding bitterness and enmity throughout the United States."

"Go back to the reservation!" The shout came from a man wearing military khaki standing above them on the lawn, waving an American flag. A rifle hung across his back. "This is America. The white man won!" He retreated as several demonstrators started to walk toward him. Holding the flagpole under his arm like a lance, he ran up the slope and disappeared into the crowded street, the flag trailing on the ground.

Walker's somber expression didn't change. "'Great nations, like great men, should keep their word.' Those are not my words, but the words of the late Supreme Court Justice Hugo Black. The United States must honor the treaties that they signed, treaties that guarantee sovereignty to the Indian nations forever. It is a matter of honor, and simple decency. We do not need the National Commission on Treaties and States Rights, headed by an enemy of Indian sovereignty, the former Senator Gordon Spade. If men like Gordon Spade have their way, the dishonesty, the hypocrisy, the injustice will continue through another century. No nation that has lost its honor can be a great nation. It cannot survive."

Leonard joined the crowd in raising a fist and letting loose a torrent of yells for "Justice! Justice! Justice!" Then, glancing back at the Turtle, he saw movement across the street. Levi Moon's big SUV was pulling out of the parking lot, left onto Buffalo Avenue, with Woody and Terrence driving their vehicles right behind him.

"Come on!" he shouted to Jemmy and Darman, and ran. At the corner of First Street, Moon made a right turn, heading onto the bridge to Goat Island.

As he ran across the bridge after them, Leonard felt as though the raging rapids beneath him were surging through his bloodstream, as though he were in a nightmare, running toward an inevitable terror he couldn't foresee. Levi Moon was taking John Lone to the Horseshoe Falls. It was a very, very dangerous conjunction of powers. Now, Leonard could only hope to do his best, to be brave and loyal.

CHAPTER FORTY-TWO

After playing cards with Quin and Phoebe until almost midnight, Tommy slept late on Sunday morning, but he assured Anne and Kat that he felt strong enough to go to noon Mass at St. Mary of the Cataract church. Anne was especially anxious for them all to attend, since Father Joe was offering the Mass, and he had told her there would be some surprises.

It was herding cats to get everyone ready and out the door in time to get there early enough to get seats. Anne drove Tommy and Kat, while Quin, Phoebe, and Mari walked to the church from Cataract Lane.

Anne gave the Quins a short driving tour, down Buffalo Avenue past the covered terrace of the Red Coach Inn, to Rainbow Boulevard and then Niagara Street, before turning on Fourth Street to the church. They had to drive under the massive arch of the Seneca casino to get to the church parking lot. Tommy looked longingly at its entrance.

"You've really managed a miracle, Anne," Kat said, as they were exiting the car. "This is the first time Tommy's been to church in years."

"Now, now, Kat," Tommy said. "It's the least I can do to honor our Irish ancestors who started building this church during the War of 1812. I read a pamphlet about it last night. Just look at that stonework! And the steeple – it's as high as the American Falls."

Kat asked Anne to take a picture of them in front of the intricate masonry of the church wall made of dense gray slate. Every stone had been carved by hand and placed with reverence by Niagara's early white settlers, mostly French and Irish Catholics. The historic church fought to survive the desolation of urban renewal during the nineteen-seventies. Now the church, and its rectory next door, stood amid large empty lots where the houses of a prosperous middle class once stood. Formerly the dominant structure in its neighborhood, St. Mary's was now dwarfed by the towering casino hotel next door. At night, it was almost invisible in the aura of the glittering neon waterfall that flowed down the facade of the hotel's twenty-six stories.

Inside the church, they took seats near a marbled column. Anne felt the serenity of a site made sacred by centuries of prayers, songs, and tears. The arched ceiling was decorated with gold crosses; the lovely stained glass window over the altar pictured the Virgin Mary's coronation by the Holy Trinity. Gold fleurs-de-lis on a deep blue background bordered the carved wood altar. The columns, which ran along the length of the church, supported arches on which round mosaics depicted American saints and blesseds. Anne's favorite mosaic was of Saint Kateri Tekakwitha, the first Native American saint, the Lily of the Mohawks. She pointed it out to the Quins.

"I've been in much fancier churches, but I think this is the loveliest one I've ever seen," Kat told Anne, who was pleased that Kat finally seemed to relax a bit as they sat waiting for the ceremony to begin. Kat took a rosary with white beads and a silver crucifix out of her purse, and knelt to pray, fingering the beads. Tommy leaned back in the pew and closed his eyes.

The church filled up early and quickly; people stood along the walls, as many as could squeeze in. Joe's surprises were an Indian ceremonial drum that welcomed the worshippers and beat softly during the hymns. Instead of the usual musky incense, the nourishing smell of native plants – sweetgrass and sage – wafted through the pews. Joe ended his sermon by quoting St. Francis' "Canticle of Creatures": "Praised be You, my Lord, through our Sister Mother Earth, who sustains and governs us, and who produces various fruit with colored flowers and

herbs." During the Prayers of the Faithful, he made this plea to God:
"Please let the voices of the people gathered in this city today be heard
by the nation's leaders. Grant them the humility and wisdom needed
to guide our country in peaceful ways for the benefit of *all* the peoples
and living beings on our Mother Earth."

"Lord, hear our prayer," the congregation responded.

After Mass, Anne took Quin and his parents back to Cataract
Lane, then gently refused their invitation to join them for lunch. Quin
was taking them to Buffalo for chicken wings at the Anchor Bar; after
all the official warnings, he was trying to keep his father away from the
rally. "I need to keep an eye on Phoebe," she told them. "She's planning
to go to the rally and I want to stay close to her."

Kat nodded knowingly.

"We'll see you there after we get back," Tommy said.

When Phoebe returned with Mari, she was anxious to leave for
the rally. After eating quick sandwiches, they left with Ben and took
the upper rapids path toward Prospect Park.

"I'm really glad you came to Mass today, Phoebe," Anne told her.
"Did you see Father Joe smile at you?"

"Yeah," she replied.

"And thanks for helping convince Tommy to go, too, by giving
him that pamphlet about the church. I'm so glad he went. He seemed
to enjoy it."

"He's still all shook up from the balloon accident yesterday,"
Phoebe said.

Anne looked at her closely. "Are you still upset about it?"

"He's dying, isn't he?"

Anne hesitated for just a heartbeat. Phoebe was staring at her,
daring her to answer. She spoke slowly, careful with her words, because
she knew death could fool you, just like life. "From what I can see, the
cancer treatments have taken a toll on him. He needs rest, and lots of
good health care," she told Phoebe. "But you can't always predict what
will happen."

Phoebe didn't respond. She watched Ben as he crouched near the

Knobby Tree.

Anne found some optimism in this exchange. It was a good sign that Phoebe was empathizing with others.

When they reached the American Rapids Bridge, Phoebe stopped. "Let's go on Goat Island. I want to check out something."

Anne readily agreed. She was in no real hurry to join the massive crowd gathering in Prospect Park near Chief Rickard's statue. The news had been full of warnings about the possibility of violence at the rally. But she still wanted to make a gesture of support. She knew there were at least a couple of busloads of BU students there.

They walked at a leisurely pace under the blazing sun to Terrapin Point, where a fine mist cooled them a bit. The area was unusually deserted for a Sunday afternoon; most people were at the rally, or had stayed away from downtown because of it. Only a few tourists were around, taking advantage of the opportunity to get images at the Horseshoe Falls without a lot of strangers in them. Ben plopped down at Anne's feet, panting. Phoebe leaned against the railing and stared at the rushing torrent. Anne stood close to her. A low cloud of mist swirled in the rocky cauldron below. A perfect rainbow arched across the gorge.

Anne asked, "What are you thinking about, Phoebe?"

"I'm wondering what it would be like to live behind the Horseshoe Falls."

Anne felt a twinge of fear. "What do you mean?"

Phoebe looked at her, and laughed. "Anne, don't worry already. I'm thinking about writing a movie. When I saw that balloon go down yesterday, it sort of reminded me about the Wizard of Oz. And I've been wondering, what if the people in the gondola weren't killed, but went into a magic place behind the Horseshoe Falls, and had adventures?"

"Why, that sounds like a plot with a lot of possibilities, Phoebe." Anne was thrilled that Phoebe was thinking creatively. She let her take her time staring at the tumbling waters. Finally, Phoebe was ready to move on, and they walked up the concrete path toward the tourist center. As they drew close to the top of the long slope, Anne noticed a small group of men clustered around a bench. "Look, Phoebe, there's Leonard's great-grandfather. Let's go say hello."

They walked up to the bench where Wallace was sitting with another elderly Indian man. "Hello, Chief Mountview." Anne held her hand out to him. When he looked up at her with a surprised stare, she knew she had caught him off guard. She didn't want to embarrass him. "It's Anne Techa, from the preservation group."

"Oh, yes." He rose slowly. "Doctor Techa. Of course. Hello."

Two men who were standing nearby, one of them very tall, moved away from the bench. The sitting man didn't look at her at all. Wallace smiled pleasantly, but did not introduce her to his companions. He didn't look unfriendly, only distracted. She could see she was intruding. "Well, I just wanted to say hello. And to introduce my niece, Phoebe, to you."

"You're Leonard's friend," Wallace said to her, taking her hand for a moment.

"Yes," she replied. "Do you think he'll be here?"

"You should try to find him at the rally," Wallace said. "Not here."

"That's where we're going now," Anne said. "We've got to get moving."

She said a quick goodbye and they left.

Phoebe seemed to be lost in thought as they walked. Halfway over the pedestrian bridge to the mainland, she stopped suddenly and cried, "Look!" She pointed toward Buffalo Avenue. Several young men were running along it, against the current of people heading toward Prospect Point; one of them was far ahead of the others.

"That's Leonard! They're going to cross the other bridge!" She turned and ran back on the island.

"Phoebe, stop!" Anne ran after her, but Ben slowed her down. Phoebe followed the shortest path back to Terrapin Point, across lawn and around the woods. As they got near the tourist center, they saw a huge black SUV race past them at a dangerous speed.

When they reached the front of the tourist center, they saw Leonard talking to Wallace. Someone had left a red SUV parked illegally on the road near them. The black SUV had been driven down the narrow lane for the tourist trains, past the point where cars were allowed, and stopped in the middle of the wide lawn. Two men helped another man get out of the vehicle; he seemed to be ill. They walked slowly toward the railing at the brink of the falls. Two other men, one of them very large, were on the lawn nearby. The three men who had been with Wallace were at the top of the path, slowly moving toward the group. Leonard and other young men stood off to one side. To Anne, the whole scene looked formalized, like pieces on a chessboard. She felt the tension between the players, and began to get nervous.

Phoebe squealed. "There's Leonard!"

"Don't bother him now," Anne warned. But Phoebe ran to get closer to Leonard.

Anne couldn't know it, but Wallace and the three healers who had been in the Lone residence on the tragic night Jerome Lone was killed were on Goat Island to confront Levi Moon. The eldest healer had had a vision of John Lone and the Horseshoe Falls, and they were waiting for him to be brought there. Wallace hadn't told Leonard about the plan, because he hoped Leonard would not be on Goat Island when the confrontation occurred. The vision had been dark and chaotic, and he was full of dread.

The tall healer, Jake, spoke with Wallace and Leonard. Then they hurried down the path to overtake Reg and Mal, who were supporting John Lone as they took him toward the brink. They were almost at the center of the wide, sloping terrace. Andrew, Jemmy, Terrence and Darman stayed close to them, wondering what to do.

Phoebe was upset that Leonard ignored her. "What's going on?"

"I don't know," Anne told her. "It looks like they're involved in something important. We should go." Anne wondered how she would get Phoebe out of there.

A parks employee on a scooter pulled up next to the red SUV. He got on his radio and called for a tow truck. That made up Anne's mind;

it was the excuse she needed. She walked up to the closest man, not intimidated by his size.

"Excuse me," Anne said. "Excuse me." He ignored her until she said, "They're going to tow that red SUV up there."

"Oh, shit!" Woody cried, and ran back to the road.

Phoebe and Ben slowly approached Leonard, who was standing near Wallace. Anne stared at the participants in this strange gathering. All had grim expressions, except for the one who was being treated as an invalid. His handsome face was drawn, as if he were in pain; his eyes darted wildly about, not focusing on anything; his arms and legs were rigid. Anne thought the man could be drugged, and not there of his own will. She turned away and keyed 911 into her cell phone. The call didn't go through.

Wallace was speaking to a small man dressed in an expensive black leather jacket, despite the heat. He was carefully groomed; his face was so smooth and unblemished that Anne wondered if he was wearing makeup, if he were someone who appeared on TV.

"Yes, we met before, a long time ago," Wallace was saying. "Back in 1958. In the old jail by the falls."

"I was never there," the man replied. "You can check the records."

"Oh, not as Levi Moon, I know that," Wallace replied. "The man I remember was known as Claude Anguiné."

Moon's eyes narrowed into thin slits. He spoke gruffly. "Get away from me, you old fool." He glared at the men behind Wallace.

Jake stepped forward. "We're ending this now. We're taking him back."

"You're fools, all of you," Levi Moon said to the men encircling him. "I am so far beyond anything you can reach. I'd laugh, if you weren't so pathetic." He glared malevolently at Wallace. Wallace met his eyes. The two men stood, staring, until suddenly Moon seemed to puff himself up. He clenched his fist, and raised it, closed his eyes, and muttered. "Here, old man!" he shouted, and cast his pitch, seeming to throw something at Wallace.

At that moment, John Lone cried out, and lurched away from

his handlers. He ran, his limbs barely under control, down the slope, toward the raging river. At first, everyone stood stunned. Then all the men shouted, each in his own terror, or wonder, and ran after him.

All except Wallace. He was kneeling on the ground, clutching at his throat. Anne dropped next to him. He seemed to be choking on something. She got him lying down on his side, and checked his throat for obstructions. She couldn't see any.

"Phoebe!" she yelled. "Run to the tourist center. Have them call an ambulance right away!" The girl took off, with Ben loping beside her.

Leonard threw himself down next to his grandfather. "He's choking! Do something!"

"Stay calm. We're getting an ambulance."

"That won't help!" Leonard cried. "This is black magic!"

"Leonard, there's no such thing!" Anne tried to reposition Wallace so that she could do CPR. The old man fought her. He grabbed Leonard's arm and pulled the youth toward him. He tried to speak, but the effort cost him. He coughed until his face changed color.

"Leonard, move away," Anne ordered.

His face showing anguish, Leonard backed away, but Wallace held his arm. He tried to speak again. Leonard stretched out on the ground, his face close to his grandfather's. Wallace's skin was starting to go gray.

Phoebe returned, breathless. "They called the ambulance." She knelt next to Leonard.

Anne saw that Wallace's bolo tie was twisted around his neck. She couldn't loosen it. She remembered her knife, the gift from Mari, hanging on its silver chain on her belt loop. She might have to do a crude tracheotomy. Holding Wallace's head, she said, "Phoebe, unfasten that knife on my jeans, and open it."

"What are you going to do?" Phoebe fumbled with the small chain, but got the knife off quickly, and handed it to Anne.

As she opened the knife, its silver blade caught the sun and reflected it with a bright light that made Anne blink. She cut his tie. She got him in a face-down position and hit him hard on his upper back. He sucked in a deep breath, and started to cough again. Anne lifted him to a half-sitting position and did a Heimlich maneuver, once, twice, three times. Wallace heaved, lurched forward, and spat on the ground. A globule of black phlegm spewed out.

He could breath after that, but his pulse was dangerously fast. Anne put him in a comfortable position on the ground. Leonard stayed close to him, so he could hear Wallace's words, given between pants of breath.

It took almost an hour for the ambulance to reach them. By that time, Wallace was no longer speaking, and was almost unconscious. Leonard was still lying on the ground, with his face close to his elder's.

Anne was livid. "What took you guys so long?"

"Are you kidding?" the EMT replied, as he pulled the stretcher out of the back of the ambulance. "There's a riot going on. The police are blocking off downtown. They set off tear gas to break up the crowd. And the mob's heading this way."

They quickly got Wallace ready for transport. Anne looked around. "Where's Leonard?" she asked Phoebe.

"He said he had to go."

"Go? Go where?"

"To help those other men. His grandfather told him to."

"Those other men? What about his own relative?"

"We're ready," the EMT announced. "Is someone coming?"

"Leonard should go with him." Anne was distressed. Someone had to go and tell the ER staff what happened, who Wallace was. There couldn't be any delays. Someone would have to advocate for him, especially since there was a riot going on, and there could be many other people brought in. He might not be seen for hours.

"You go, Anne," Phoebe said, seeing her indecision. "I'll take care of Ben."

"We're leaving," the EMT called.

Anne was torn, but she knew what she had to do. Her first duty was to her patient. She had to trust Phoebe.

"I'm coming," she called. "Phoebe, promise me you'll go straight home with Ben."

"Don't worry."

"I mean it, Phoebe!" She ran to get in the ambulance.

Her godchild rushed up and kissed her on the cheek. "I love you. Bye." Phoebe backed away as the medic slammed the door shut and the ambulance took off.

The ambulance sped along the winding road, its sirens blaring. Anne's head throbbed. As soon as she made sure Wallace was being treated, she'd try to get hold of his wife or Emily. Then she'd call her own house. She tried to believe Phoebe would be there safe and sound. She tried to suppress her suspicion that Phoebe had no intention of obeying her.

As they reached the bridge, she saw a haze of white mist creeping up Buffalo Avenue. Her eyes started to sting. The EMT checked Wallace's oxygen mask. Anne prayed the riot wouldn't reach her house, or the gas or the mobs of people who were running down Buffalo Avenue to escape it. Many of the protesters ran across the bridges to Goat Island, carrying their signs. The driver could only inch the ambulance forward through the crowd, even with his lights and siren on. She hoped Quin and his parents were still in Buffalo.

By the time the ambulance cleared Buffalo Avenue and was speeding toward the hospital, police helicopters were rushing toward the falls. Anne despaired that Phoebe wouldn't be able to get off the island, even if she tried. She'd be trapped between that raging mob and the brink of the most powerful cataract in the world.

CHAPTER FORTY-THREE

Crying and shivering, Phoebe tried to make her way through the crowd to get close to the bonfire in the middle of the slope at Terrapin Point. There was confused activity all around her, even though it was the middle of the night. Hours ago, she'd gotten caught up in the streams of running people who swarmed to Goat Island after the police shut down the rally. Ben's leash was pulled out of her hand, and he disappeared. The demonstrators had established an Occupy camp, and the police had since barricaded the bridges. People were saying terrorists were in the crowd, and that they had bombs and weapons. Phoebe was sorry she didn't get off the island before it was shut off, but she couldn't leave without Ben. She'd been calling him for hours; she last saw him running toward the Three Sisters Islands. She could never face Anne if anything happened to him. All she wanted to do now, though, was to get dry. Her clothes were damp from the mists blown over the island by the constant police and news helicopter flyovers.

After trying for some time to get to the bonfire, she gave up. There were just too many people around it, hundreds of people jammed together in an odorous mass. Some were in organized groups under banners. Others were in loosely-knit coalitions that had no unifying logo. She was scared of small cadres of militants who huddled in small groups. They wore masks or bandanas over their faces as they used flashlights to look at maps of the island. Maybe they *were* terrorists. The huge bonfire, its flames fed by picnic tables and benches, and anything else that burned, looked like a pagan ritual. The roar of the Horseshoe Falls was an echo in the roar of the mob huddled at its brink.

Phoebe was extremely cranky. She wondered why they couldn't have built the bonfire farther back, where the wet wind blowing off the falls wouldn't be in her face. Wolf was in that crowd, somewhere, avoiding her. When she had approached him earlier, he just kept saying, "Phoebe, go home," in a really cold way. He even pushed Ben away.

She knew it had to be past midnight, but her phone was dead and it was hard to tell just how late it was because the whole plaza was lit up by spotlights from the Canadian side, which were focused on the demonstration instead of the water. A thick mass of gray clouds overhead reflected the light back, making the air seem thick, and putting everything a bit out of focus. The spotlights, filled with droplets of mist, cast stark shadows. Other lights beamed down from the sky, like UFO's, as helicopters scanned the crowd. Every once in a while someone would yell that they saw a drone, and people would rush around in terror. Police vans circled the island, warning people through loudspeakers that the demonstration was illegal, and that everyone participating in it would be arrested. People yelled back, "This is our island!" They booed and jeered when the police announced that the island was in a state of emergency.

Phoebe turned away from the bonfire and walked up the path, toward the tourist center. The farther away she got from the bonfire, the more the people, and their mood, changed. It was less intense near the top of the slope; people were sitting and lying on the lawn in small groups. There were the usual demo types – skinny buzz-heads, girls with wild hair, bearded old hippies, hyper women with lots of slogan buttons on their jackets, and just plain old weirdoes, as her father would call them. There was a circle of Goddess-worshippers holding hands and singing. Phoebe looked for Mari, but she wasn't among them.

She saw a flurry of activity near the tourist center. People were scooting away from a side emergency door, like ducks chasing bread tossed on water. When she got closer, she realized that some people had broken into the center and were tossing food – wrapped sandwiches, bags of chips and candy, cans of pop – onto the lawn. She scurried like a duck herself and came away with some sandwiches, several bags, and a can of grape soda. She sat on the ground and tore open a bag of red licorice.

But she was still damp, and really cold now. Every once in a while a sharp gust of wind or helicopter blades blew icy mist over her. She wrapped her arms around her legs and swayed back and forth, trying to warm up. She was lonely in the middle of all those people. She wondered where Belle was now, and if she and Val were still partying, and if her friends ever thought of her, their lucky charm, who they had so cruelly rejected. Now even Leonard turned her away, and Ben abandoned her.

Suddenly, a man seemed to appear out of nowhere, right in front of her. A loud voice announced: "Light thickens; and the crow makes wing to the rooky wood; good things of day begin to droop and drowse; while night's black agents to their prey do rouse."

Startled, Phoebe jumped to her feet. When she saw who the speaker was, she was more annoyed than afraid. "Leave me alone, Hermit. You scared me."

"If I do wrong, forgive me or I die; And thou wilt then be wretcheder than I." The Hermit tossed something on the bench, then rushed away, toward the woods.

Phoebe picked up the white objects, which turned out to be a tank top with a rainbow across the front and a hooded sweatshirt with a picture of Niagara Falls on it. He must have stolen them from the tourist center; the price tags were still attached. They were dry! Gratefully, Phoebe ripped off the tags and yelled, "I forgive you, Hermit!" in the direction in which he had fled. She crouched behind the bench and changed into the dry clothes.

Energized by sugar and warmth, she decided to try one last time to find Ben and then she would get off the island. She didn't care if they arrested her, or even tortured her for information. They'd soon find out she didn't know anything.

She walked around to the back of the tourist center. Something damp and big rubbed against her legs. She turned around to see a scroungy dog. "Oh, Ben!" She hugged him as if he were her last friend on earth, damp and smelly as he was. Then she noticed another fire, a small one just a few yards in back of the tourist center, sheltered from the mists and winds blowing out of the Horseshoe's cauldron. A circle had been cleared under the tall trunks of a stand of maples. Two groups of men were sitting on opposite sides of the fire. Ben whined and walked toward it, then turned to see if Phoebe was following. She tried to grab his leash, which was dangling from his collar, but he kept drawing her closer to the fire. Then she saw Leonard sitting there.

Quietly, she sat down right behind him. Ben inserted himself between them, his shaggy body pressed against them both. Leonard ignored them, and kept staring straight ahead, until Phoebe leaned forward and tossed two sandwiches and a bag of candy in his lap. Then he smiled, a little bit. He handed one sandwich to a huge man sitting next to him, who glanced back at Phoebe and acknowledged her with a slight nod. They ate ravenously.

Leonard leaned back, and whispered, "Thanks, Phoebe. Now go home."

"I will. I just want to rest for a while," she whispered.

Leonard leaned back and put his arm around Ben.

Phoebe leaned against the dog's flank and relaxed. The roaring falls and the noise of the crowd were dimmer here, not overpowering her. She recognized the men who were with Leonard's great-grandfather earlier, sitting nearby. Almost directly across the bonfire from where she was sat was the man she thought was too weak to walk, until he yelled and started running for the falls. He was sitting with his back straight, legs crossed, his eyes closed. The fire cast a reddish glare that was caught in the contours of his face. Long black hair with strands of silver framed his face. Phoebe stared. He was the most beautiful man she had ever seen, like a hero from a movie, the kind of movie where there was the good kind of hero, like from days of old. He was more beautiful than any of the dancers and actors in Las Vegas, and he didn't even wear makeup. He was naturally beautiful, like a mountain.

She tapped Leonard on the shoulder. He leaned back. "What?" he whispered, tensely.

She pointed at the handsome man. "Who is he?"

"His name is John," he said softly.

Phoebe glanced warily at the mean-looking men sitting around John. Then she almost jumped. The small man she had seen earlier, who had looked so fashionable, was sitting, hunched over, in front of the others, closest to the fire. His silver hair was loose and hung from his head in limp strands. Maybe he was sick, Phoebe thought, because in the firelight his face looked pale green. He held his head down, but his hooded eyes were staring past the fire, as though they could look right through her. She hated the sight of him. It forced her to remember the time she tried not to think about, the time when she couldn't move, and there was a mean, hungry face bearing down on her.

Pulling her hood over her head, Phoebe moved closer to Leonard, shifting her position so that his shoulder hid her from the evil man's view. Ben, fast asleep, was a warming hulk snuggled between them. She rested her head on the dog's back.

Staring at the man named John, Phoebe imagined that he was the king of the secret land behind the Horseshoe Falls. She was the maiden he loved, a maiden who fell from the sky, and landed in his enchanted country. She hummed her favorite love song, and imagined herself dancing with her lover, behind the tumbling crystal waters of the Horseshoe Falls.

CHAPTER FORTY-FOUR

"Look, I'm getting totally desperate here. My niece is caught in that crowd on the island, and my dog, too." Anne pulled off her sunglasses. She blinked hard as hot, salty droplets trickled down her cheeks. "I have to go look for them. She's on medication, she may be in crisis."

She might as well have saved the effort, and her dignity. Dan Gallo couldn't help her. The local police were part of the law enforcement blocking off Goat Island, but they answered to military commanders in a state of emergency.

"You know I would if I could, Anne," he said, glancing around nervously. "But we're not in charge here. It's getting ugly. They're talking about clearing out this area, too." He pointed to the conglomeration of demonstrators, reporters, videographers, and onlookers massed behind police barricades along Buffalo Avenue. A similar crowd was gathered at the entrance to the American Rapids Bridge, where Anne had just made another futile attempt to get on the island. Phoebe and Ben had been there all night. It was mid afternoon, now, of Day 2 of the Takeover at Niagara, as the news networks were calling it.

"Please, can't you send me with an escort, or something? You can arrest me when I come back, if you want to. But I have to find my niece. And my dog. They're not demonstrators, they're innocent bystanders."

He shook his head sadly. "We have orders. No one goes on the island except police and military personnel."

Anne had an idea. "What about medical personnel?" she asked.

"If we get a call for them from units on the island, they'll let them in."

Putting her sunglasses back on, Anne dodged through the crowd as she ran home along the river path. Her mind lurched between anger at Phoebe for disobeying her order to go straight home, and worry that something terrible had happened that had prevented her from doing so. Anne hadn't even tried to sleep last night. Quin had stayed over, sleeping on the couch, and gone with her several times through the night to try to get on the island. But they couldn't. Goat Island was as completely blockaded as a fort.

Anne had been glad of Quin's company, and even for that of his parents, who had missed the riot because of their quest for chicken wings. Tommy had managed to make her laugh a few times. He saved her from disaster, too, by answering the phone. Bill had called several times to check up on Phoebe. Tommy lied smoothly, and skillfully, even inviting Bill over to play poker.

"Phoebe will be home when she gets bored and hungry enough, Anne," Tommy assured her. "All of my kids have been in demonstrations of one sort or another, and survived them."

As she unlocked her front door, Anne hoped he was right. She heard Kat's voice as soon as she entered.

"Anne?"

"Yes, it's me." She ran up the stairs.

"I have an important message for you, from Emily."

"What is it?"

"She said to tell you that Chief Mountview is being released from the hospital this afternoon. They did some tests and didn't find anything serious enough to keep him. She'll call you again later."

"That's good news, I think," Anne replied. "As long as they really checked him out."

Kat's expression was sympathetic. Feeling helpless, Anne went into the kitchen and pulled a bottle of cold water out of the refrigerator. She held it against her throbbing forehead.

Kat joined her, looking more stressed than ever, as though she were about to burst into tears. "I have more to tell you."

"What is it?"

"I'm really sorry about this, Anne. You know we were supposed to leave this afternoon. But my husband has decided that we're going to stay another day. Without even asking if you minded. Tommy really is worried about Phoebe, despite what he says."

Anne was beyond caring about such a minor complication. "Kat, it's all right. Your staying longer is the least of my worries right now."

"But it's such an inconvenience."

"Not really. I'm too worried about Phoebe and Ben to notice most of what's going on around me."

The muscles in Kat's face and neck tightened. Anne watched her with sympathy. Kat always wore an expression of worry as tangible as a wooden mask. Anne had seen that look on many caregivers. The wives were the saddest, stoically enduring a sort of forced march. It was awful when they didn't even like their husbands anymore. Anne could pick these women out of a crowd, anywhere, members of a Greek chorus of despair.

"Well, it's an inconvenience to *me*," Kat said, her lips tight. "He didn't even ask me if I wanted to stay. He and Quin just ran off with your brother."

"My brother?"

"That's another thing I have to tell you. Your brother Bill came here, a couple of hours ago. Checking to see where his daughter really is." Kat's right eyebrow arched accusingly. "After you tolerated his sins last night, Tommy told another bald-faced lie, about Phoebe and you just being out for a walk. Then he told Bill about something he heard on television this morning, how the casinos in Canada have special betting boards where people can wager on when they think the police will clear the mob off Goat Island, and how many arrests there will be, and things like that. So the three of them took off for the Indian casino, which they hope is doing the same thing. Tommy will be exhausted when he comes back."

Anne rubbed her temples. "Oh, God. I only hope that this whole thing ends before then."

Kat walked over to the counter. "I've got half a mind to get on the plane without him. I just made more coffee, Anne. Do you want some?"

"No, thanks. If I have any more caffeine it'll make me sick to my stomach. I haven't eaten since around midnight." She reached into the cupboard for a bottle of ibuprofen. She took two tablets and washed them down with water. She cut a slice of rye bread off a loaf sitting on her counter, and forced herself to eat it.

Holding a mug, Kat said, "Come into the parlor, Anne. They're showing the demonstration live on TV now."

"Just a minute." Anne cut herself another slice of bread, and poured coffee into a mug. It smelled good. As long as she ate, she figured, she could handle more caffeine. She joined Kat.

The image on TV seemed to go in and out of focus, until Anne realized that clouds of mist spewing from the basin of the Horseshoe Falls blurred the scene. In the lower-right-hand corner of the screen, green-tinged water fell in an unstoppable torrent. Terrapin Point took up the rest of the screen. Anne stood a few inches away and peered at tiny figures moving to and fro. A dark blotch was in the center of the field of vision. After peering closely for some seconds, Anne realized it was a solid mass of people. Flames blazed in its center. The images seemed unreal, sometimes hazy, sometimes clear, and always on the edge of sight.

"They have a live camera up on one of the Canadian towers," Kat told her. "They've been showing this nonstop for quite a while. You can get a better look at the demonstration on the regular news shows, when they send a helicopter right over it."

"Has anyone said what this takeover is about, exactly?"

"Not that I've heard. I think they're just mad at everything. Eco-terrorists."

Anne continued to examine the screen close-up. "I'm trying to see where the police and medical units are stationed."

"The news said they've been ordered off the island, near the bridges, to avoid confrontations," Kat told her. "For now, anyway."

Anne's bird's-eye view was making her dizzy. "I wish to God they weren't so close to the brink."

The doorbell rang. She set down her mug and rushed downstairs to the front door. Opening it, she saw a thin, dark-haired woman in a bright blue jacket and black pants. Anne smelled the odor of a heavy smoker. "Yes? Can I help you?"

"I hope so," the woman replied, holding out her hand. "I'm Jane Kirby, a producer with SNI, Satellite News International. I've got a crew with a satellite van arriving from Toronto in less than an hour, and I've got to find us a place to stay. I heard you might be interested in renting your house, for the duration of this news event at the Falls."

"Who told you that?"

"We'll give you a good daily rate, US dollars."

"Who told you I might rent my house?"

"The man at the tourism office downtown."

Anne felt as though her head would explode. "Was it Nick Valli?"

"Yes. Look, I don't have a lot of time ..."

"I'm not interested in renting my house," Anne was almost shouting. "And I would *never* let a smoker inside!" She slammed the door shut and ran back upstairs, her mind racing. After splashing cold water on her face, she quickly brushed her hair and shoved it under a cap. She put sunblock and powder on her sunburned nose, and applied lipstick. She hurried into the parlor.

"Kat, I've got to run out for a bit. If anyone calls, please give them my cell phone number." She took a piece of paper from her desk and wrote the number down. "It's right here."

"Okay, Anne." Kat's voice was tired. She was lying on the sofa, her right hand resting on her forehead.

Anne ran most of the way to Niagara Tower.

"Where is he?" she demanded in a loud voice as she strode into Nick Valli's office. There was a young, pretty secretary, not the one who was there the last time she had stormed in.

"Excuse me, ma'am?" the young woman asked.

She rushed past her to Valli's office door, and tried the knob. It was locked.

"Mr. Valli is at lunch, ma'am." The secretary was standing, with her hand on the phone. She looked nervous.

"You give him a message from me," Anne told her. "You tell him that if he ever sends anyone else to my house, I'll sue him for harassment."

"Who are you? Will he know what this is about?"

"He'll know." Anne glared toward the locked door, thinking that the odds were eighty-twenty that the little worm was in there, hiding from her. "You just tell him to watch himself."

Back on the sidewalk, after running down five flights of stairs, Anne leaned against the outside wall of the red sandstone building, appreciating its sturdy bulk, and took a deep breath. People hurried past, excited, toward the falls. Two military helicopters rushed overhead, racing toward Goat Island.

She felt like crying. Was she going insane?

This was just a media event to most people, but to her it was a nightmare. Phoebe wasn't stable. Anne forced herself to admit that fact. And she was in the middle of a tense situation that could turn violent at any moment, at the edge of the most powerful waterfall in the world. Anything could happen. The only ray of hope was that Leonard and Ben were with her. Leonard would watch out for her. She forced herself to quell a nasty glimmer of doubt, that Leonard might not be keeping an eye on Phoebe. That whatever was going on among all those men was more important than her niece. But that wouldn't happen, she told herself. Not when Leonard was the great-grandson of a man like Wallace Mountview. She had to have faith.

CHAPTER FORTY-FIVE

Hugging his backpack close to his chest, Leonard waited for Jake to emerge from the men's restroom in the tourist center. He hoped none of the people nearby could hear the rattling coming from inside his bag – they might think it was a bomb. Old Turtle was trying to say something – he'd been rattling away for hours now – and Leonard knew he had to get him in the right hands. He also knew he'd get snapped if he tried to reach inside his backpack. He strolled back and forth, trying to look like just another person whiling away time on an island in the middle of a homeland security emergency. He kicked an empty pop can that was lying near his foot. It bounced off a lamp pole and landed near the side of the building. The tourist center was totally trashed. Garbage was strewn all over. The restrooms were putrid. The gift shop was vandalized and looted. The police had not bothered to defend it; the image of the ransacked building would help make the case later for the use of force to clear the island. It didn't matter that the Indians weren't the ones who did the damage. Leonard knew they'd get the blame for organizing the rally in the first place.

"Where is he already? And be quiet, Turtle!" Leonard hissed into his backpack. He looked around. No one was paying any attention to him; guys were mostly hurrying into the restroom, then hurrying even faster out of it.

Leonard didn't want to leave Phoebe for too long. She was acting funny, but at least she was staying in sight around the bonfire, dozing off and on, not being a pest. A little while ago, when Jake got up and walked away from the fire, she had said she was going to the women's restroom, but he followed her to be sure. She ran into someone there – that girl with weird hair who was at Anne's meeting. She and Phoebe started talking, and the girl kept petting Ben. Leonard remembered her name then, Chani. She was the type who stuck to a person, so Leonard felt safe in leaving Phoebe with her for a while. Now if only Jake would come out.

Finally, he did. Leonard stepped in front of him. The tall man's eyes, set deep in his lined face, coolly examined Leonard. It was the first time they had been alone together.

"Can you hear this?" Leonard held up his backpack. Jake's eyes narrowed, but he said nothing.

Leonard looked around. "I need to talk to you. Just for a minute. In private." He walked a few steps toward the woods, then turned to see if Jake was following him. He wasn't. "This is really important," he urged.

"I have to get back to our group." He started to walk away.

Leonard ran and stood in front of him. "Listen. Wallace Mountview is my great-grandfather." He felt a swelling of pride as he said that. "I know who you are. And what you are. I was there that night. I saw you, and the two others. And now I need to give you something that's important. You have to come with me."

Jake's eyes narrowed again. "So you are the witness Wallace told us about."

"He said I should stay here and help you. But I don't know what to do."

"Neither do we." Jake gave a short laugh. "Yet."

"Will you come with me now?"

Jake nodded. They walked away from the tourist center, under the canopy of the tall trees that filled the middle of the island. The rock-hard soil did not allow for underbrush. They aimed their steps carefully to avoid tripping over long, bare tree roots clutching the earth. They finally sat, facing each other, near the wide trunk of a maple that towered above them. Spotlights reflecting off the clouds gave them a dim light to see by.

"He's been driving me crazy." Leonard carefully opened his backpack, making sure to grasp the outside of the leather sack well away from Old Turtle's head. He handed the sack to his companion. "Be careful," he said.

Jake took the sack gingerly and peered inside. He exclaimed a long word in Seneca that Leonard did not understand. "This belongs to me. I thought it was in evil hands." He looked closely at Leonard. "How did you get it?"

"He got me," Leonard replied. "I was running away from the house, right after you left, and he tripped me in the snow. I just grabbed him and kept running. I kept him hidden, and safe, until I could return him." He leaned forward. "He's very old, isn't he?"

Jake nodded. "Many generations old."

Leonard smiled. He felt proud that Old Turtle had chosen him as his keeper for a while. "I think he's got something to say," he told Jake. "He's been rattling for days."

Jake focused his dark eyes on Leonard, who looked down, not wanting to appear familiar, or arrogant. He spotted a small nub sticking out of the ground. He jostled it loose, and pulled out a small rock, pitted with holes, heavy for its size, about as big as a child's fist. Its travels by water had rounded its edges. Some of its surface was as dense and smooth as dark glass. Leonard pushed the stone into his pocket. "What's going to happen?" he asked Jake.

"I don't know. We're trying to get John Lone away from Moon. But we have to do it carefully. Even Moon had a hard time calming him down, when he tried to get away yesterday. Lucky we caught him before he got to the railing."

"Why don't they just leave the island? They could keep us back. I know they have guns."

"That's why, I think," Jake replied. "They have to go through the military checkpoints. They didn't count on getting caught up in this riot. Even if they dumped their guns on the island, I'll bet some of their names, at least, would turn up in the police database. And there's something else afoot. Woody told me that when he took his car to the parking lot, he saw Mal pulled over on a service road, meeting someone in a van, and they were putting boxes into the back of Moon's SUV. But I don't care about that. I just want to get John away from him. The only good thing is, I think Moon is as unsure of what to do as we are. He didn't expect to get trapped here."

"What do we do if they start rounding people up?"

"I don't know," Jake said. "Just be ready for anything."

As they walked back to the others, Leonard heard giggling nearby. Ben ran up to him. He saw Phoebe and Chani peering at him from behind wide trees. He tried to ignore them. Then he spotted the Hermit with them.

"I've got to check something out, Jake. I'll be right back."

The tall Healer nodded, and kept walking.

Leonard turned. "What are you guys doing? Come on, Phoebe. Let's go back to the fire."

She danced out from behind the tree, wearing the white tank top with a rainbow across the front; her hoody was gone. Phoebe sang, skipping among the trees, "We're dancing and dancing, as happy as can be. Look what the Hermit has given to me."

Leonard didn't have time for this. "Chani, make her stop."

Chani came out from behind another tree, wearing Phoebe's hoody. "She'll stop if you come with us. We want to show you something."

"I can't. I have to get back to the other guys."

"This is important, Wolf," Chani said. When Leonard looked surprised, she explained, "Phoebe said that's your Indian name. It's cool. I'm going to call you that, too. Now come on. You'll really want to see this."

Leonard almost groaned. Calling himself Wolf to Phoebe seemed cool before, but it wasn't his real Indian name, and now it was just embarrassing. He went with the girls and the Hermit just to be sure they wouldn't call him that in front of Woody. They led him farther into the woods, to a sort of drainage ditch. The Hermit jumped inside it, moved a big rock, and came out with a green plastic recycling bin.

"You should see the stuff he's got hidden away all over the woods," Chani said. "Food and everything. But show him what you got last night, Hermit."

The Hermit pried the cover off the green bin, and lifted out a large bundle wrapped in white cloth. Unwrapping it a bit, he took out a small item that gleamed in the dim light, and held it up in his long fingers. It was a small human figure.

Leonard gasped. "That looks like gold."

"It is gold," Chani assured him, as he stared at the square figurine. "It's Egyptian. And there's more."

"Where did you get this, Hermit?" Leonard asked.

Chani answered for him. "He got it out of the trunk of that weird guy's SUV."

Leonard's eyes went wide. "It must be stolen."

"No kidding," said Chani. "Show him what else you have, Hermit. The big thing."

Reluctantly, the Hermit slowly unwrapped part of his bundle. Then he stopped and looked at Chani.

"He won't do it," Chani said, "but I will. Look!" Quickly, she unrolled the object and held it up. It caught a gleam of light, and it seemed to Leonard that it blazed. It was a gold mask, attached to an object that had long strands of grimy gauze hanging from it. It stank.

Leonard stepped back. "What ... what is it?"

"It's an Egyptian mask, on a mummy head," Chani told him. "It's stolen from the Niagara Museum. There's a reward for it."

"How did Levi Moon get it?"

"I'm not sure. But at least your spooky friend doesn't have it now."

Leonard took another step back. "Cover it up!"

Smugly, Chani re-wrapped the ancient remains, and put them back in the Hermit's box. He covered it, and hid it again.

Leonard looked around. "Where's Phoebe?"

"Dancing around the trees again, probably," Chani replied. "Do you guys have pot, or something? She's been acting like she's high, all of a sudden."

"No," Leonard said. "I want her and Ben to get off the island. And you should go, too."

"Me? No way. I'm having too much fun. Look." She led him to a spot a few yards away, where a neat square of soil, about a yard wide and an inch deep, had been carefully scraped out. A small toy plastic shovel and sand sifter were inside.

"What's that?" he asked.

"My first Goat Island dig," she said, proudly. "I got the beach toys out of the tourist shop. I'm hoping to find something important before they chase us off the island."

"Dig, dig, dig, Chani, dig, dig, dig ..." Phoebe stepped past them chanting, stepping as if she were doing aerobics. Ben stood next to Leonard and watched her.

Leonard didn't know what to do. He considered going to the checkpoint, and asking the soldiers to drag both girls off the island. He looked down at Ben, who was filthy and wet. Anne would be so pissed if she saw him like this, he thought. He felt a tap on his shoulder. It was the Hermit, who handed him a plastic bag full of sandwiches and cans of pop. That made up his mind, at least for now. He had to take these back to the guys at the fire. He'd deal with Phoebe later. "Thanks a lot, Hermit," he said.

Chani knelt down and started scraping the ground with her toy shovel, her nose just an inch from the surface. Leonard wondered how she could possibly see anything in the dim light.

When he got back to the fire, Leonard's companions gratefully took the sandwiches, and ate them under the surly gaze of Mal, Reg, Archie, and Samuel. Levi Moon still seemed to be looking beyond them. John Lone sat with his eyes closed against the world.

After a while, to Leonard's great relief, Phoebe came back and settled down; she sat off to one side, where she stared at John for a long time, then finally fell asleep. Leonard felt she was safe, as long as he kept his eye on her. He gave Ben half his sandwich, and the grateful dog licked his face. Leonard tried to stay awake and alert, but the crackling of the fire and Ben's warm, soft body finally lulled him to a restless doze.

CHAPTER FORTY-SIX

Phoebe laughed as she ran among the old trees, chasing fireflies. She was as lightheaded as though she had been drinking champagne, but it was better than champagne. She was giddy with happiness. She had finally found her place, her sacred place, where she was safe. She was in the middle of the woods on Goat Island. It felt like the center of the world to her.

In the woods, Phoebe felt as though she had left everything behind – all the noise of the falls, and the angry people, and the helicopters. Best of all, she'd left behind the lights from the illumination beams that were supposed to be on the falls, not her, and she'd lost all the people watching her, like Leonard, and Ben, and Chani, who wouldn't stop talking, and the Hermit, who wouldn't let her just be alone, and the evil man in black, with his gleaming eyes, like a snake's.

The only person she wanted to look at her was John, but he was lost in his own world, just like her. That's why she crept away from them all, so she could find her own special place, where she could rest, like John, until the time came when he would finally see her, and they would be together, in their rainbow world behind a sparkling curtain of water that fell in a cascade of crystal and pearls.

Phoebe stopped chasing the fireflies. She realized, suddenly, that they weren't running away from her. They were dancing with her. She should dance, too. She tried to forget about gravity. She was a firefly now, able to glow from within whenever she wanted love.

Twirling slowly as she danced among the trees with her new, bright friends, stepping lightly so the roots wouldn't trip her, Phoebe saw a thin dark figure coming through the trees, toward her. He was singing something. She heard him sing, "Come, come, come away ..."

It was that old Hermit trying to spoil her fun. She turned and ran away from him. She darted from tree to tree, and he followed her, repeating his boring song. She led him in a hide-and-seek game from one end of the woods to another, until he finally got tired, and went away.

Phoebe left the woods and ran across the old stone bridge to First Sister. No one else was there, because it was her little island now. She climbed over the railing, found a calm pool between two Sisters, and knelt beside it. Its gentle flow made her forget the angry river just beyond.

Her eyes felt so heavy. Phoebe laid herself down on her stomach, and rested her head on her right arm, stretching her body along the stream, which sang the river's song. She put her left hand in the water, and let it caress her.

Sighing, she closed her eyes. She imagined she was floating in a warm pool, Phoebe's pool, waiting for her lover to take her to their magic place, under the rainbow.

CHAPTER FORTY-SEVEN

At the barricade to the pedestrian bridge on the following day, Anne was completely frustrated. Joe pulled gently on her arm, trying to pull her away. "Keep calm, Anne," he said, softly. "We'll try again later."

"Later may be too late, Joe! And we've tried four times, since yesterday – every time they've changed shifts. And we don't know when the National Guard will move in." She pulled her arm away and turned on him. "You saw it – Showdown at Niagara! That's what the media are calling it now. They say they've confirmed that terrorists are on the island with guns and bombs! They're getting ready to attack it. And Phoebe is somewhere in that mob. And Ben." She sobbed, her throat constricted by an overwhelming feeling of helpless anger. "Oh, God, Joe." She looked at the crowd around them. Most people looked excited, not anxious. Many of them were even wearing blue or red "Showdown at Niagara" tee shirts. "How could I let this happen?"

"None of this is your fault, Anne," Joe said. "Let's go back to your house. We'll try again."

Anne turned away from him and walked slowly through the crowd, looking for a place to sit down on the grass. She couldn't figure out what they were doing wrong. Joe was wearing his Roman collar, she a white clinical jacket and medical badges. She told the guards that Joe had received a call to assist someone he was counseling who was trapped on Goat Island. They had to get to that person. And it just wasn't working.

Finding a clear spot, Anne slumped down on the park lawn. She covered her face with her hands.

Joe sat beside her. "It's a good plan, Anne. We just need to find the right person to pitch it to. Someone with a bit of heart left."

"I don't think anyone has any heart left, Joe." She was trying not to cry from frustration and despair. She could handle anything, even a patient's impending death, as long as she could do something, even if it was only to counsel the family. Passively waiting was the only thing she couldn't endure.

"Come on," Joe urged. "Let's go get some coffee, and we'll try again later."

She looked up at him. "I can't go to my house. I'm avoiding Bill. He doesn't know yet that Phoebe's on the island."

Joe didn't say anything. The afternoon sun was getting low in the sky. Then Anne saw him. "Quin!" she called. She stood up, waving her arm. "Up here."

Quin dodged through people to get to them. "Hey, Anne. I was looking for you. Hey, Joe." He looked as calm as if it were an ordinary day.

"Did your parents' plane get off okay?" she asked. "I hope they didn't mind that I didn't go with you to the airport."

"Nah. Dad was still counting his casino loot. He was practically singing."

"How much did he win?" Joe asked.

"More than ten grand, mostly on slots, but a few hundred on the Niagara Showdown board. Most people bet it would've ended by now. Dad knows a lot about demonstrations, though." Quin grinned. "He's thinking about a trip to Vegas. Bill lucked out, too. He made almost fifteen hundred at blackjack."

"Did you play?" Anne asked him.

Quin snorted. "Naah. I went to the game room. They have some cool ones."

Anne said, "I'd invite you both to my house for some food, but I'm afraid I'll run into Bill, so I'm hanging out here."

"Don't worry about him," Quin told her. "He's cool."

"How can I not worry? If I see him, I have to tell him that Phoebe's on the island."

"He knows. Dad told him."

"He did?" Anne was dismayed.

"Yeah."

"What did he say?"

"Nothing. He just kept yanking the slot machine."

"Well, this is it." Anne felt as though she had been beaten up. "Bill will hate me forever. Especially if anything happens ...." Her voice faded away.

Joe and Quin exchanged a glance. "We'll try again, Anne," the priest said.

"Try what?" Quin asked.

Joe explained the plan.

Quin nodded his approval. "The best time to try," he advised, "is around three, four a.m. That's when people are most sleep-deprived, and off their mark. It's when big accidents happen, like Bhopal and Three Mile Island and the Exxon Valdez. Besides, I think that's when the feds are going to make their move. Tonight, before sunrise."

"What makes you think that?" Anne asked.

"They'll want to do it at night, in the dark. They already announced that at noon, tomorrow, they'll start arresting people on the island, but they won't want to have that confrontation in broad daylight with all the cameras on them. I say they'll move just before sunrise, go in and start arresting as many people as they can, and hope a lot of the crowd disperses peacefully."

"What if people fight back?" Anne asked. "The police say the demonstrators are armed."

Quin rolled his eyes. "They always say that."

Anne looked at Joe with new hope.

"I say we try again tonight," Joe said. "We have nothing to lose."

Anne felt better. They had a plan. "Okay." She managed a thin smile. "Let's go to my place. I still have lots of food left."

"I'll come by later, Anne," Joe said. "About, say, three this morning?"

"What are you going to do between now and then?" Anne suspected that he didn't want to intrude on her and Quin.

"I need to sit in my church and pray, Anne. I haven't felt much like praying over the past few days, but I do now."

Anne gave him a quick hug. "See you later then, Joe. I'll pray, too."

She was falling, plummeting through white mist, swirling in a faint, purplish light. Anne frantically tried to grasp something, anything, to break the fall, but there was nothing substantial to hold onto. She felt only the harsh wind, rushing up past her. She jerked her body up, as though she could reverse the fall. The clouds fell away, and she realized where she was – in her parlor, on the loveseat, clutching the corner of her mother's crocheted afghan. In the dim light from the television screen, she saw Quin stretched out on his back on the sofa, emitting a low snore.

Unwrapping herself from the afghan, Anne glanced at the mantel clock. It was just after two in the morning. The television was still airing the live scene at Terrapin Point. She had the illusion she was looking at life forms deep under water; she could make out only dark splotches and indistinct movements, caught in the glare of artificial illumination.

She walked quietly out of the parlor, feeling lonely about not having to be careful that she didn't trip over Ben. In her bedroom, Kat had stripped the bed and left used sheets and towels in a neat pile. Anne opened the door to her porch and walked outside. The hot night air was muggy. Heat lightning flashed in waves across the sky. The two cities of Niagara Falls – Canada and USA – gleamed with light. The high-beam illumination lamps fixed on Terrapin Point gave that area the brightest glow. Portable spotlights glared over the National Guard outposts along Buffalo Avenue. Helicopters roared over Goat Island. The city was under siege.

Standing in the quasi-darkness, Anne was convinced more than ever that Quin was right. The world was nothing but chaos. She'd been as delusional as Mari and her Wiccan friends to think that she could do anything to control it. "Oh, God," she prayed aloud, her eyes fixed on the bulbous cloud of purplish mist hovering in the lights over the Horseshoe Falls, "please watch over Phoebe, please God, watch over her and keep her safe. Let her come home, safe. Let Leonard be safe. And, please, please, let Ben come home safe, too."

Anne felt as though her chest was being squeezed by a giant hand. The last time she had really prayed, she realized, was when she was ten, sitting on the cement step of her family's front porch on a hot summer night, waiting to find out what had happened in the Hooker explosion, waiting for her father to come home. Her attending Mass was just ritual, was just because of Joe. It gave her some peace to keep the tradition of her family going. Now she remembered the sharp odor of chlorine in the air that night, and her despair when she realized her prayers were nothing but words sent into a vacuum. An odor of tear gas came on a breeze; she felt nauseous, and went back into the house. She realized now that she had never believed in God again, after that night.

After minimal grooming and a change of shirt, she went into the kitchen. She put on coffee, and started to make French toast, battering the eggs-and-milk mixture with a whisk. Quin appeared at the kitchen door soon after she began to fry a pan of leftover baked ham. She gave him a mug of fresh coffee. Joe arrived shortly afterward. They ate quickly, in silence.

Soon the three of them were walking along the river path to Goat

Island. The illumination along the upper rapids was at full strength. Anne carried her medical jacket on her arm; it was too muggy to put it on before she needed it.

"Man, I miss Ben," Quin said, as they walked past the Knobby Tree. Anne couldn't reply. Then she noticed something. She stopped walking.

"What's up?" Quin asked. He and Joe turned back.

"Look how smooth the rapids are." She pointed at the waves flowing limpidly past them. "The water's really low. They must be diverting as much as they can into the power intakes."

"Gives them some maneuvering room along the river," Quin commented.

"Not much," Anne replied. "Come on, let's hurry."

They stopped just before they reached the police barricade at the American Rapids Bridge.

"There's definitely something going on," Quin said. "They've got reinforcements."

Military vehicles were lined up all along Buffalo Avenue. Several boxy MASH Urgent Care ambulances were parked near the bridge; their drivers stood a short distance away, smoking. Anne felt her knees get weak when she spotted the black-clad SWAT teams, assault weapons ready, squatting behind their vehicles. She clutched Joe's arm. "I hope you prayed really hard, Joe."

"Mother of God, have mercy on them." Joe made the Sign of the Cross as he looked at the armaments.

"Man," Quin muttered. "They're serious."

Suddenly, they were in darkness. The falls illumination lamps were turned off. So were all the lights on Goat Island, and on mainland streets, and in nearby buildings. It was as dark as it had gotten at Niagara Falls in a century, as dark as it could get, given the ambient light that hung over the Canadian side, and the colored glow from the towering Seneca casino. It was dark enough to unnerve everybody, to make the world alien.

The SWAT teams rustled by like swarms of bats, men crouching as they ran over the bridge. The military vehicles, their headlamps off, followed them. The green glow of their night-vision screens gleamed. The ambulance drivers stayed where they were, waiting to be called.

Quin, walking low, went to the driver's side of one of the ambulances. He waved Anne and Joe forward. "Get in, from this side," he hissed. "It's now or never."

Anne pulled on her white jacket as Joe jumped across the front seat. She followed. Quin turned the motor on, and drove over the bridge, headlights off.

"How did you get it started?" Anne asked.

"I'm brilliant." Quin paused. "The keys were in the ignition."

Anne grinned and squeezed his arm.

The military caravan veered to the left after crossing the bridge. Quin turned right.

"Get as close to Terrapin Point as you can," Anne directed.

"Man, it's dark," Quin remarked, as he drove slowly along the road, closed in by thick foliage. Heat lightning flashed. A purple haze shone wherever there was any light. Anne noticed she was breathing hard, as if oxygen had been sucked out of the atmosphere.

Quin pulled the ambulance to the side of the road as soon as he spotted vehicles parked ahead, near the power plant arch. They left the ambulance and walked along the parking lot. He stopped suddenly and held them back. "There's soldiers in the road ahead," he whispered. He led Anne and Joe through the trees, heading toward Terrapin Point.

Suddenly, the whole world lit up. A giant bolt of lightning streaked across the sky. In that nano-instant, Anne saw that there were other figures all around them, creeping forward. The explosive crack of thunder echoed so long in the rocky gorge that she was afraid it had started a rockslide. Her hair was standing on end. She turned to look back, inadvertently brushing against Quin. They both recoiled in surprise at the spark that sizzled between them.

As the last echo of thunder boomed down the gorge, a different sound grew, louder and louder. It took a moment for Anne to realize the sound was human, and when she did, a bolt of fear cut through her body.

The sound was the angry wailing of many voices, the keening of human beings who know they are trapped between the cold forces of social order and a point of no return.

Anne started to run to Terrapin Point. Joe and Quin were right behind her. Sinister sounds surrounded them – the metallic rustle of weapons, the stomp of heavy boots, the hiss of radios. She had no idea what she was going to do. She only knew that Phoebe was trapped, caught between armed men and the rocky chasm at the foot of the Horseshoe Falls.

CHAPTER FORTY-EIGHT

They were taking the water.

Leonard leaned over the railing at Terrapin Point to be sure. The shadows cast by the glare of lights from the Canadian side made it hard to make out details, this deep into the night, but he had no doubt. The water rushing over the Horseshoe Falls was lower than he had ever seen it, down by several feet from the usual nightly diversion level. There was a new stretch of smooth riverbed between the ledge along the shore and the torrent of water rushing over the brink. If he climbed over the railing and down to the riverbed, he'd be able to walk out a couple of yards that just hours ago had been covered by the surging flow. Two hundred feet below him, at the bottom of the gorge, water trickled over newly exposed boulders at the river's edge.

It meant they were coming soon. He felt someone grab his arm from behind. He jumped.

"Wolf, you've got to come. We need help."

He turned to see Chani, looking haggard in the glare of the spotlights. "What's going on?"

"Phoebe's in the river!"

He felt his heart go cold and heavy. "What do you mean, she's in the river?"

"I saw her go across the bridge to the Three Sisters Islands and followed her. She's laying by this little pool between the islands, and won't leave."

"Why did you leave her there alone?" He felt like shouting.

"She's not alone, the Hermit's there, and Ben. I came to get you. Maybe you can get her out, she's half in the water."

Leonard took off, running along the path. His heart was pounding, but not from running. This was the time of reckoning. Events were about to unfold, and fates would be sealed. Now, he thought, the water diversion was a good thing. The power of the river was weakened.

On Asenath, Leonard stood still. Phoebe's laughter rang out over the sound of water dribbling around the islets. He followed the laugh over the bridge to Angeline, and across that small bit of land to its outer edge, where a channel separated it from Celinda Eliza. Phoebe was standing in a foot or so of water, bent over with laughter. She seemed to glow, as ambient light reflected off her white jeans, white tank top, and light hair. The rainbow on her chest stood out against the gleam. The Hermit was standing in the water, too, downstream from Phoebe, his skinny bare legs barely keeping him upright in the flow. Ben rushed back and forth along the shore, whimpering. Leonard knew that if the water flow was at its normal level Phoebe already would have been swept into the rapids surging over the Horseshoe Falls.

Leonard tried to keep his voice calm. "Phoebe, what are you doing?"

She laughed, and held out her hands. "Wolf! Come in. The water's so warm."

He kicked off his boots and stepped into the stream. The water was freezing cold. He walked carefully, so he wouldn't slip. When he got close to her, Phoebe jumped and wrapped herself around him, like a lover. That breaking of their unspoken boundary stunned him, even though he was relieved. Slowly, balancing on the slippery rocks, he turned around, and, with the Hermit's help, got her back onto dry land. He disengaged himself from her, counting on the Hermit to keep her from running off. She laughed, and stroked his legs with her bare feet, while he put his boots back on. He was angry. "What's going on, Phoebe?" His voice was harsh.

"Nothing. I was just waiting."

"Waiting for what?"

She giggled harder. "For someone to come. Someone like a prince, you know?"

Chani ran up, breathless. Leonard turned on her. "Did you give her drugs?"

"What? No way. Don't be an asshole." She looked hurt.

The Hermit took Phoebe's hand. "All was so still, so soft, in earth and air," he said, coaxing her to walk with him. "You scarce would start to meet a spirit there; Secure that nought of evil could delight to walk in such a scene, on such a night!"

"What are you talking about, Hermit?" she asked, but followed him as he led her over the bridge, back to the main island. Ben followed them.

Leonard glared at Chani. She shook her head. "I don't know what happened, man. She started dancing and running. It's like she freaked out, or something."

"We've got to get her out of here." He and Chani walked after the others. Leonard stepped forward.

"Hermit," he said firmly, as he grabbed Phoebe's other wrist, "we're going to take her to the men by the bridge. They'll take her home, where she'll be safe. Ben, too."

The Hermit nodded. They started to cut across the wide lawn.

Then, all the lights went out. They froze. Phoebe jerked her hands out of the grips of her guardians, and started to run back toward Terrapin Point. Leonard saw her white form head for the woods, and ran after her. The others followed. Still wet, Phoebe was able to wriggle away when he tried to grab her. She slid around trees, heading for the gleam of light from their campfire. The air was full of din, as hundreds of people all over the island started yelling and screaming over the roar of the waterfalls.

"Go to the bonfire!"

"Stay together!"

"They're coming!"

Phoebe ran to their fire, Leonard right behind her. They both stopped, shocked, when they saw that John and the others were gone.

"Where did he go?" she asked no one in particular, as Chani and Ben came up.

"Stay right here," Leonard ordered. "Chani, hold on to her." He ran the short distance to the parking lot. The red and black SUV's were still there. Leonard leaned against Woody's vehicle and tried to think. "Where would they have gone?" He didn't have an answer and rushed back to the fire. Phoebe, Chani, and Ben had disappeared.

"Phoebe!" he screamed. "Ben! Woody!"

The dog was the only one who responded. He ran to Leonard, panting. "Good, boy, Ben!" Leonard roughly caressed Ben's big head. "Find Phoebe!"

Ben took off toward the mob crowding the center of the plaza. People were pressed against each other around the bonfire, like one big organism, holding hands, whispering instructions: "Peaceful resistance." "We'll make them arrest us all." "Go limp so they have to drag us out." "Make it last as long as you can, until daylight, so the news cameras catch it."

"I've got weapons," a man yelled. "We'll make a stand on Luna Island." A large group of people tore off from the crowd, running into the darkness toward the Tesla statue.

Glancing back up the slope, Leonard saw the bulky, metallic hulks of military vehicles, gleaming from casino lights across the border, as they lined up along the road. He pushed his way along the edge of the crowd, following Ben, until they could see the Horseshoe Falls. There weren't many people in this no-man's-land between the demonstrators and the edge of the gorge. Outlined against the white curtain of flowing water he could see dark forms, and thought he recognized Jake's tall figure. He looked desperately for Phoebe's slim white figure.

A lightning bolt flashed. The thunder blast was right overhead; it rumbled down the gorge, toward the Whirlpool. As it died down, the demonstrators began a high-pitched wailing, led by experienced veterans of anti-globalization street wars. Ben whimpered and rubbed against Leonard's legs. Leonard held his palms against the dog's ears, sympathizing with him. This was the kind of sound made to drive men crazy, or to send them off to war.

Daylight came suddenly, as the giant illumination lamps went back on, relighting the scene. Rubbing his dazzled eyes, Leonard got a glimpse of Phoebe at the railing a few yards away. He rushed over to her, and followed her gaze looking out at the brink of the Horseshoe Falls. He couldn't believe what he saw in the shining lights.

John Lone was standing on the smooth riverbed, a few yards upriver from the brink, just inches from the torrent rushing past him. Jake and the other Healers were standing on different levels of the rocky ledge. Jake was calling to John in the Seneca language. He did not respond, but stared in the direction of the river's flow, downstream, toward the Whirlpool.

"Damn, damn, damn!" That was Woody. Leonard turned and saw him go over the railing in one step. He followed and asked, "Woody, what happened?"

The big man didn't turn to look at him, but stared at John as he answered. "When the lights went out, Moon tried to get John away from us. Jake followed them, talking in Seneca, and shaking a rattle. Moon took hold of John's arm, but John gave a roar and took off running, like before. We all tore after him, but we lost him when the lights went out. Now this." He gave a helpless gesture toward John. "I'm going after him." He climbed down the ledge to the riverbed, and stepped carefully, as quickly as he dared on the slippery rocks, going toward John.

As Leonard considered what to do, he felt something slide against his leg. Looking down, he saw Phoebe climbing between the lower bars of the railing. He grabbed at her and managed to catch her by the waistband of her jeans. "Phoebe, come back here!"

The Hermit appeared out of nowhere, and tried to grab hold of Phoebe, too.

"Let me go, Wolf. I have to be with him." She tried to pull away.

"What are you talking about?" Leonard yelled.

"Don't you understand?" Phoebe stopped struggling for a moment. She looked right into Leonard's eyes. "I'm the Maid of the Mist."

"What?!" Leonard almost let go of her in his shock. The Hermit stood back, a look of awe on his face.

"What do you mean, you're the Maid of the Mist?" he shouted. "There is no Maid of the Mist, Phoebe. It's a stupid story, made up by some white man. It's stupid, Phoebe, and it's fake. There's no Indian sacrifice. Listen to me! I'm telling you there's no stupid sacrifice, and no Maid of the Mist!"

She gave him a sweet smile. He was yelling into her face, and didn't notice her smoothly unfasten her jeans. She grabbed the top rail, as though she were going to climb back over, but only kicked off her jeans, and left them hanging in Leonard's hand. Then, wearing nothing but the rainbow tank top and her white panties, she scrambled down the rocks to the riverbed, which was flecked with shallow black pools of water. Woody and the Healers were too shocked to move as she calmly walked past them, barefoot, to stand next to John Lone, and shine in the glare of the illumination lamps.

The blood roaring through Leonard's head deafened him. He couldn't even hear the roar of the falls. He felt as though time had stood still, like the moment when the atom bomb went off and froze people's shadows on walls. Standing in the harsh light that cast a thin, elongated shadow from her form onto the rock, Phoebe looked as slender and fragile as one of Rose's poppies. Even John's figure was diminished as he stood in that light, near the raging torrent that, if unleashed, would sweep them both to their doom in an instant.

Leonard saw more figures climb over the railing – Levi Moon and his men. Mal and Reg started after Woody. The eldest of the healers stepped in front of them. Leonard saw Mal raise his arm to strike Woody and tackled Mal from behind. They both grunted as they crashed on the stone, only a few feet from the rushing water. Leonard lay half under Mal, stunned.

Mal managed to raise himself up. He sat astride Leonard's chest and brought his weight down, pushing the air out of Leonard's body. Looking down at him with an evil grin, Mal lifted his fist. Trying to breathe, Leonard braced himself, but the blow never came. Jemmy pulled Mal back, and Leonard slid out from under him. Mal twisted out of Jemmy's grasp and turned on them both. The two youths repulsed the tough man with a push that sent him sliding backward. He scrambled to catch his balance, but his feet gave out on the slippery stone. Momentum carried him into the rushing water. The youths watched in shock as the river swiftly took Mal, lying on his back, into the abyss.

"Oh, man, Leonard."

Staring at Jemmy, Leonard saw his own horror reflected in his friend's eyes. Did they just kill a man? Was it self-defense? Would Mal have tossed them into Niagara, to be carried to their deaths over the terrible brink? Leonard fell to his knees, overcome by the power he had just wielded, overcome by the power raging past him. Jemmy stood behind him, barely breathing.

They heard shouts. Looking toward the brink, Leonard saw John Lone and Phoebe standing side-by-side, framed by the spotlights. Woody, crouching, was coming up behind them. Levi Moon was right behind him, holding a stout piece of driftwood, about to slash the big man's legs right out from under him.

Leonard scrambled to his feet. He and Jemmy stepped as quickly as they dared on the slippery rock to help Woody. They were too far away. But the Hermit was closer, standing on a ledge near the brink. As Levi Moon was about to strike Woody down, a flashing object came hurling through the air and hit him hard on his shoulder. He dropped the stick and, holding his arm, saw the mummy's head with its golden mask fall with a loud clank on the naked stone. Leonard heard its voice echo deep, deep into the bedrock as it bounced toward the brink. Moon shrieked, and went down on all fours to try to catch it. He watched helplessly as the precious, ancient artifact slid smoothly over the rocky ledge, into the chasm below. He raised his head and screamed like a wounded beast.

At that moment, Woody reached out his long arm and grabbed Phoebe from behind. He flung her backward, away from the brink. She lost her footing and started to fall. Leonard by then was in position to catch her. He brought her down, mostly on top of himself. She tried to get away, but he held on; she struggled against him until she hit her head on the rock bed, and was stunned. He tried to stand, but the rock was too slippery. Strands of algae slithered through his fingers as he tried to find something to hold onto. He and Phoebe slid slowly down the sloping riverbed, inexorably, toward the brink.

"Maybe you'll be the Maid of the Mist after all, Phoebe," Leonard muttered. He felt as though a magnet were pulling them.

Phoebe's eyelids fluttered and opened. She started to cry. "This hurts, Wolf. I'm cold. I feel all slimy. It smells here." She sounded like the old, normal Phoebe. "Wolf, I'm scared. I don't want to go over the falls!"

"Then hold still." Twisting toward shore, Leonard desperately reached for anything to grab onto. His efforts only made them slide more quickly to the brink. Then he felt something pulling hard on his shirt. It was Ben. The dog dug his paws into cracks in the rock and stopped his friends' downward slide.

"Hang on, Phoebe," Leonard grunted, as he rolled over her and managed to wrap his arm around a jutting rock. A moment later, he felt strong arms pulling them off the riverbed. It was Jemmy and Terrance. They lifted Phoebe and passed her on to other arms waiting to get her back to solid ground. As he pushed Ben up the ledge, Leonard heard a familiar voice yelling, "Phoebe, Phoebe! Over here!" It was Anne. He wasn't surprised.

Phoebe turned to Leonard and held out her hand. "Wolf, come with me."

"I can't. You go." He turned his back on her. She was safe now. She wouldn't escape Anne's clutches again.

He tried to make out what was happening on the riverbed. Woody had gotten hold of John and, with Jake's help, had pulled him away from the brink, back upriver, and toward the shore. Levi Moon, Reg, Archie, and Samuel were standing nearby, watching. The Hermit was lurking behind them.

Suddenly, Levi Moon shrieked and flung himself on John, pulling him out of Woody's grasp. The other three men attacked Woody and Jake and tried to bring them down. Woody struggled to push them off; he tried to grab John, but couldn't reach him. The Hermit grabbed onto Levi Moon. The force of the men's struggles knocked all of them down, and they slid along the riverbed toward the brink.

Leonard followed their course, staying on the ledge. Jemmy shouted to him from above. Leonard grabbed Jemmy's outstretched hand to anchor himself, and grabbed Jake, who was closest to him. Jake grabbed Woody; centrifugal force swung the two men hard against the rocky ledge. The swarming, struggling mass of Levi Moon, who still held John, and the Hermit, Reg, Archie, and Samuel kept sliding toward the brink as though the river itself were carrying them. As they plunged over the edge, Levi Moon's shriek fell with them until it was swallowed up in the swirling cauldron at the base of the mighty Horseshoe.

Jemmy and Leonard pulled Jake and Woody off the riverbed. Woody sat on the ledge, in shock. Leonard sat beside him, saying nothing. Dawn began to brighten the sky.

For a long time, Leonard was numb. He couldn't even think, didn't want to think. But as the sun burned away the dawn's haze, his senses started coming back to him. "Why did he do it, Woody? Why did Moon attack you when you were trying to save John?"

Woody could only stare straight ahead. His face looked shattered with grief. "He was crazy." After some moments, he added, "John was breaking away from his power. After that, he wanted him dead." He rubbed his eyes, stood up and started climbing along the ledge.

"Where are you going?" Leonard asked.

"I just want to take a look over the edge. So I'll never forget."

Leonard followed him. When he got to the sharp edge of the rocky brink, Woody took a strong hold on the shrubby growth pouring out of cracks in the rock. Leonard came up behind him and held on, too. Suddenly, the big man dropped to his knees. Leonard grabbed at him, afraid he was falling over. But Woody pointed down. "Look!"

369

Peering over the edge, Leonard gasped. About five feet down, a narrow ledge of rock jutted out. John was lying there, in a shallow pool. His face was above the water. His eyes were closed. He could still be alive.

"Go get the guys," Woody ordered.

Leonard scrambled up to the railing. Jemmy and the others were standing nearby. He called them over, and they quickly climbed down to Woody.

They devised their plan hastily. Holding Leonard's arm, Woody dropped him down to the ledge, where he knelt beside John. Cautiously, Leonard touched his neck. He felt blood gushing.

"He's alive!" he called up.

Woody dropped Jemmy down. The two youths lifted John under his shoulders, up to Woody and Jake. Then the two men brought the youths back up. Quickly, stealthily, they carried John to the edge of the plaza, and carefully placed his unconscious body on the ground. The healers crouched near his head, speaking the old language in low voices. As Leonard sunk to the ground near them, he could hear Old Turtle rattling. Woody sat down heavily near Leonard, as Jemmy, Darman and Terrence collapsed around them.

For the first time, Leonard noticed the chaos happening on the island. Police and National Guardsmen were busy trying to herd the crowd into controlled groups. Helicopters were buzzing overhead. Wafts of tear gas came from the direction of Luna Island, where an armed standoff was being waged. Leonard saw Phoebe standing near one of the sets of stairs, with a crowd of cameras focused on her shivering, almost undressed, form. Anne had her arm around Phoebe's shoulders. Ben was jumping and barking. Anne was trying to get away with Phoebe, but was pinned by the media mob.

A young Guardsman walked up to Leonard's group, huddled around John's unconscious form. He was dressed in black combat gear, with body armor and a helmet. He pointed his assault weapon at them. Woody thought he looked nervous, and that made him scared.

"We haven't forgotten you guys," the Guardsman said. "We'll

be taking you into custody as soon as we get this scene under control. Don't even think about getting off the island – we've got the bridges barricaded. We've heard about your plan to blow up the Horseshoe Falls. You guys will never see daylight again."

Leonard couldn't stop himself from blurting out, "Why would we want to blow up the falls?"

The Guardsman's eyes narrowed into slits, and he pointed his gun directly at Leonard. "You tell me. You're the one working for ISIS. Or is it your old beef, your grudge against America?" He glared for another moment, then turned abruptly and walked a few steps away, his weapon still pointing at them. He looked up the slope, where Anne was waving her arms and yelling for help.

"Oh, man, Leonard," Jemmy said. "He almost shot you."

"Just keep your mouths shut, all of you," Woody ordered. "Let me think."

"We're doomed," Darman said. His voice was thick.

Leonard watched the situation around Anne and Phoebe. They looked alone, besieged. He wondered if the police were letting the media have the two women as a distraction while they did their work on the demonstrators. He could see people being dragged up the slope and thrown into police vans. Leonard knew Anne couldn't be enjoying the scene, but she could handle it. He suspected Phoebe was in her element. The Maid of the Mist. Phoebe had made her real. The white man's fantasy. And Phoebe's, too.

Leonard's mind suddenly cleared and he knew real fear. He pulled his knees close to his body and dropped his head down on them. He'd been too busy, too high on adrenaline to feel afraid when he was running around on the slippery bed of the Horseshoe Falls. But now – now the next step would begin his processing in the American so-called justice system. They'd all be called Indian terrorists, with no chance of getting a fair hearing, let alone justice. They'd committed the crime of being Indian. Look what America had been doing to his namesake, Leonard Peltier, for more than thirty years. Here was another Leonard to throw into the hellish soul-eating American prison machine. He'd never feel the fresh air, never see the sky, or the Milky Way. All the cold cruelty of the white man would be unleashed on him and his friends.

Leonard decided he wouldn't let them take him, or endure what Peltier had endured in his decades of unjust confinement. He wouldn't be shackled, beat up, put in solitary confinement. He'd rather die than have Grandfather go through the ordeal of a trial by media; they'd probably arrest him, too, call him a terrorist mastermind for all his work for Native justice.

Cautiously, Leonard looked about and assessed the scene around him. He was so close to the railing, just yards away from the brink. He could make it in a few leaps. There was only the one armed Guardsman near their group. He'd wait for his moment; three or four leaps would get him over the railing. So what if they shot him down before he made it into the rapids? It would still be a quick death. He'd be a YouTube sensation, and live online forever. He looked up at the full height of the tower of white mist rising from the Horseshoe's basin. He'd rather die quickly going over the falls than tortured and broken in a cement cell. His spirit would be free.

Then he noticed a bulky MASH ambulance driving slowly over the lawn, toward them. It parked close to Leonard's group and the armed guard. Leonard rubbed his eyes to be sure of what he was seeing. Father Joe jumped out of the passenger side and ran to the Guardsman; he was carrying a blanket. The priest handed the blanket to the guard, and pointed up the slope, at Phoebe and Anne. The Guardsman nodded and took the blanket from Joe. He lowered his gun and went to drape it around Phoebe's shoulders.

The moment the Guardsman turned away from them, Quin leaped out of the driver's seat and quickly opened the back door of the ambulance.

Leonard couldn't believe it. They were going to beam out of there.

PART FOUR

"Every living being is an engine geared to the wheelwork of the universe."

Nikola Tesla, 1915

CHAPTER FORTY-NINE

"Ani, Phoebe, this is me again, Nick. Listen, you really need to talk to me. Give me a call right away. I have an offer for you – a very serious offer – from Universe Las Vegas. They want to sign you on as an attraction in their new pavilion, where you will get top billing as The Maid of the Mist. All you have to do is jump from a platform into a pool. Not too high, nothing like the real thing, but lots of special effects to make it dramatic. Did I tell you how awesome you looked on the news? That was a brilliant stroke of marketing you thought up, babe. I've got your pictures up on our web site, the home page, doll. Let me pick you up in a couple of hours, I'll take you to dinner in Buffalo, there's a hot new place on the waterfront. Don't talk to anybody, and don't sign anything. You're not going back to Vegas without me along to fend off the sharks, represent you, you know ..."

BEEP.

Phoebe was glad her voicemail cut Nick off. She deleted his message. He was so old and creepy. She couldn't imagine how she ever thought he was cool. Well, she was still inexperienced then. Not any more. She never had to be afraid of him again, or of what he might say about her. It would just be more buzz for the media, the noise that follows its stars.

"Phoebe, are you almost ready? The limo's outside waiting."

"I'll be there in a few minutes, Daddy."

"Okay, Hon. I'll tell them to sit on it."

Phoebe smiled at herself in the mirror as she continued to re-fine her makeup. She tried not to let the emotions of the days since the Showdown at Niagara alter her wide-eyed facial expression, and smudge her colors. The best result of all the things that had happened – besides the fact that she was now world famous – was that she and her Dad were best friends again. He actually cried when he saw her at the hospital after Anne got her off Goat Island. Her father! It was some-thing she never expected, for him to cry, instead of just grunt, get a drink, and smoke. Anne cried, too, right there in the emergency room, in front of all the other nurses. Phoebe didn't cry herself. She just wait-ed to see what would happen when they all got calm again. Her dad even forgave Anne for letting Phoebe get loose at the demonstration, and now they were one big happy family again, as much as they could be.

It was so cool to have a limo sitting out in front of their house, waiting to take her and her family to a photo shoot at Terrapin Point. A British magazine that did photo spreads about exciting personalities had arranged it. Her parents and twin brothers were coming along, too, because the editor wanted a shot of the whole family. They were all nervous, but Phoebe wasn't.

She wished Leonard were around, but he'd disappeared again. Homeland Security was looking for the missing Indians that were at the rally, but they couldn't find them. Everything was so confused, the authorities didn't even know how many men they were looking for, or what exactly had happened on the riverbed when the lights were out. Phoebe had given the press her Ani Shanando name, and told them that a Mysterious Warrior had saved her life. She had her story down pat: she was on Goat Island walking her aunt's dog when she innocent-ly got caught up in the occupation. She came under the spell of the riv-er and somehow found herself standing on the brink of the Horseshoe Falls; a Warrior came and saved her. She said nothing about John Lone or Levi Moon or the other Indians, the Hermit, or Chani. She was sup-posed to give a statement to the FBI, but her dad's lawyer kept getting it delayed. He told her not to say anything under oath. Even Anne said that was good advice. They didn't have to worry, though, because she wasn't going to talk until she got the best offer for her story about being The Maid of the Mist. She already had lots of serious offers, and calls from agents, in just a week. So far, a German newspaper was in the lead with the biggest advance.

She finally understood what Belle-Aurora meant when she told Phoebe she had to *become* the Maid of the Mist, the way Belle had become the Riverboat Queen. She lost the Universe Las Vegas contest, she realized now, not because it was all fixed, but because the judges could tell she didn't believe she was the selfless Indian maiden. But that changed at the brink of the Horseshoe Falls.

Leonard would have looked great in the photo spread as the Warrior, but she understood why he had to disappear. He must be so sad about the handsome man called John going over the falls. She saw it happen. Phoebe sighed, and blinked her eyes hard so they wouldn't tear, and she'd have to do her makeup all over again. She'd loved John, too. He was the most awesome man she had ever seen. If he had taken her hand, at that moment when they were standing in the spotlight at the brink, she would have jumped over the falls with him. For love. That would have been legendary.

But, in the end, when it came down to it, Phoebe was glad Leonard had saved her. She did get carried away on Goat Island, what with the music of the river, and the fireflies, and John's beauty, and her fantasy about living behind the falls. She sighed, thinking about the Hermit, and how he was a hero, too. Poor Hermit. She forced herself to think of him now living in her magic cave, where he would want to be, because he loved the falls so much. Anyway, things must have been meant to turn out the way they did, because now wonderful opportunities were coming to her, and she didn't even have to die.

Pictures of her standing at the brink of the falls had gone viral. The original image was blurry from the lights, mists, and shadows, but people had created all kinds of versions of the image. Some even showed her naked, with huge boobs. Most of the photos didn't show John; his image, where untouched photos were shown, was dark and indistinct. But Phoebe was an instant icon: images displayed her slender form reflecting the spotlights shining on her, in her small tank top with the rainbow across her chest, and her white panties, standing on the rocky brink next to the surging torrent of the most powerful waterfall in the world. The whole world knew, now, that Ani Shanando was truly The Maid of the Mist.

Finally, Phoebe was satisfied with her face. She went into the living room, where the family was waiting. She was relieved her mother had finally done something with her hair; Anne had taken her to Buffalo to get it done, just for the shoot.

Josh and Jon, her six-foot twin brothers, stood on either side of Phoebe, protectively, as she encountered the production editor, who was obviously annoyed at her delay. Tylor Regan had the perfect close razor haircut for his angular face; he wore shades of gray and black, and had absolutely no body fat. He said, in a British accent, "Ani, we've got to run. The camera crew is set up and waiting for us at Terrapin Point. We need to catch the light, and the rainbow."

When he turned, Phoebe mimicked him behind his back, to make her brothers laugh.

She couldn't help but notice that her family members did not manage to look cool as they did their celeb stroll down their front sidewalk, past a small group of neighbors. The twins grinned like idiots, her mom's face was red, and her dad lit up a cigarette. She, of course, was used to cameras, so she was perfectly natural.

"Tell me, Ani, are you recovered from that dramatic moment at the brink of Niagara Falls?" Tylor asked her, as the limo rushed down Route 31. He had his phone video on her.

"Oh, I'll never recover from it fully, Tylor," she replied, making her eyes go wide, as she had practiced. "I mean, who could? I've been going over those moments in my mind, over and over again, and I realized that I'm the only woman in the world who has ever survived being the Maid of the Mist."

The editor looked confused. "But, I thought the Maid of the Mist was a beauty contest, and the backstory is a legend, not a real story."

"Oh, it's real," her dad interjected.

"It's real now," Phoebe clarified. "Yes, it is a legend, but it's also real, because I was there, at the brink of the Horseshoe Falls, and I was ready to sacrifice myself for love."

Even her mother nodded in agreement.

Josh leaned toward Tylor; the editor's eyes shifted to the young man's face, and scanned his wide shoulders. "Can you help me get an internship in New York?" Josh asked.

"Are you in college?" Tylor asked him, his sharp eyes scanning the young man's face.

"Yeah. I just finished my third year in marketing communications at Oswego State. I got a 3.8 last semester."

"Very good." Tylor handed Josh his card. "We'll talk."

"I go where he goes." Jon made his pronouncement with his long arms stretched across the back of the seat.

"I expected that." Tylor's thin lips creased into sort of a smile. He surveyed each of the twins from top to bottom. "I think after we finish our shoot with your sister, I'll put you two in front of the camera for a few exploratory shots."

"Cool." The twins flashed identical toothy smiles.

"This isn't like family pictures," Phoebe warned them. "You can't act stupid."

The twins made faces and mock-punched each other. Phoebe glanced at Tylor. He was leering at them. Her father was grinning proudly. Her mother looked confused, as usual. Leaning back in her seat, Phoebe closed her eyes, and forced herself to be calm. Pretty soon she'd be out of Niagara Falls, and never have to come back, except for occasional Maid shoots.

At Terrapin Point, the driver parked as close as he could to the production set-up near the railing. The viewing area was crowded with tourists. A bright blue sky shimmered overhead. The river's jade green waves surged. A perfect rainbow spanned the gorge. The production assistants tried to keep people from getting too close to their equipment, but it was a losing battle, since they were set up in the best viewing spot, and the tourists wanted their selfies.

When Phoebe emerged from the limo, with feathers in her hair, wearing white shorts and a tank top decorated with rainbow-colored beads, the crowd rushed to her.

"Look! It's the Maid of the Mist!"

"The Maid of the Mist!"

"The Maid of the Mist!"

She was thrilled to hear people refer to her in foreign accents. The production assistants moved the crowd back. The session went smoothly, and quickly.

"Hurry. It's nothing without the rainbow," Tylor kept telling the photographer as Phoebe posed under the colored arch.

When the rainbow dissipated about a half-hour after their arrival, Tylor announced, "That's it." He led the twins and the photographer off the crowded plaza for their trial shoot.

Phoebe walked toward the limo with a crowd following her for autographs. Her dad ordered everyone into a line, and then stood off to one side, talking to the driver, and smoking.

She smiled and was nice to everyone who asked for her autograph, even if they were rude or stupid. No one was going to call *her* a stuck-up bitch. She patiently signed postcards, tee shirts, tourist maps, and even one guy's muscled arm. She jumped when she felt something brush against her legs. Looking down, she was relieved.

"Hi, Ben!" As she knelt down to hug the dog, she saw people aim their phones at her. So she posed, with a big smile and her arms around Ben's neck. She noticed Anne letting out the leash, so her aunt could stay out of camera range.

When Phoebe resumed signing, Anne came forward and gave her a quick hug. "Just wanted to say hi, Hon. You look great."

"Ben looks a lot better, Anne. Like his old self."

Anne's smile faded a bit. Then Phoebe knew she was still upset about Ben staying on the island with her, and how scrawny and dirty he was when she got him back. Phoebe suspected that Anne had cried as much about Ben's condition as about hers, when it was all over. But her aunt didn't say anything to Phoebe about Ben, and she was very glad about that.

Just then, a female screech pierced through the crowd, causing everyone to freeze. "Ani! It's my little Ani!"

The crowd in front of Phoebe parted. At first she couldn't believe what she saw. It seemed like a vision. Belle-Aurora Boyette was standing just a few yards away. A flaming-red blouse and black skirt looked as though they were painted on her statuesque frame, which was balanced on high, thin heels. Her hair, now blonde, was curled around her face. She held out her arms. "Come to Belle, Ani Honey." Her deep voice easily carried over the roar of the falls. "Come to your girlfriend Belle."

Phoebe felt Anne's hand clutch her shoulder. Her dad stepped close behind her. "Who the hell is that?" he asked.

"It's, it's Belle-Aurora Boyette, the Riverboat Queen, Daddy." A flood of images surged through Phoebe's brain — of Belle, Belle, Belle, who overwhelmed almost all other memories of her days in Las Vegas. Belle, her good friend, who taught her everything she knew about show business. Belle, who came to her rescue just in time. Belle, who made her go home.

While Phoebe was sorting out her emotions, Belle rushed forward, flung her arms around Phoebe, and twirled her around, holding her close against her hard-muscled body. Dizzy, but aware of the cameras, Phoebe air-kissed Bell's cheeks when she was set back on the ground.

"We saw you on TV and just had to come by and see you again, Ani, Honey." Belle posed with glam smiles as she spoke.

"You changed your hair." Phoebe put her finger through a long blonde curl that hung just above Belle's left ear.

"It's my Marilyn look." Belle took a step back. Placing her right hand on her cinched waist, she turned, and did a hip-jiggling walk away from Phoebe, teetering on her high heels. Men cheered and made rude noises. Phones took images. She turned, and walked back. "Just like in the movie, remember?"

Phoebe had no idea. "Where's Val?" she asked.

"I am here." Val came up from behind her. He looked exactly the same as he had in Las Vegas, except maybe a little whiter along his hairline. Phoebe gave him a quick hug.

"So, who's this lovely lady, Phoebe?"

She turned to see her father staring up at Belle as though she were a holy statue. She made quick introductions, noticing that Anne had a suspicious look on her face. It was weird to see her family and her friends together; two totally separate pieces of her life from two different planets had merged, unexpectedly. She felt disoriented. Her Dad and Anne looked drab, suddenly, while Belle and Val seemed too jarring. What in the world was she going to do with all of them now? It was too much for her to handle, this mingling. She wished everyone would disappear, even Ben, who was sniffing around Val's boots.

"Excuse me for a minute." She walked quickly away from them, up the stairs toward the visitor center. She had to think. Why were Belle and Val here, really? Just because she was famous now? After they had sent her away, when she begged them not to? An ugly suspicion started to well up.

Then she heard another familiar voice. "Ani! Babe! I knew I would find you here." Nick Valli was walking toward her. She couldn't move.

"Your autograph, please?"

Phoebe turned, gratefully, to a young Asian man who was holding out a pen and Niagara tourist book for her to sign. As she reached for the pen, Nick stepped forward and rudely pushed him away.

"Later," he said, taking Phoebe's arm. "Come on, we have to talk."

"Get away from me, Nick." Phoebe pulled, but he held her arm tight.

A loud voice rang out. "Ani, Honey, is this worm still botherin' you?"

"I think he did not learn his lesson from before." Coming up quickly behind Nick, Val twisted him in an arm lock. Then he let go,

and socked Nick in the mouth as he twirled around. Nick fell to the
ground like a stone, and lay there. Belle shoved him off the walkway
with her high-heeled foot.

"That was great!"

Phoebe was shocked to see Anne go up to Val and hug him. "I've
been wanting to do that for a long time," she said. She bent over Nick
and felt for his pulse, letting Ben sniff the unconscious tourism official.
"He's still alive," she announced. And then she walked away.

Phoebe felt that was a bit much coming from her godmother,
who was always lecturing about self-control, though it did give her
relief, too, to see Nick lying there. He'd leave her alone now.

"Why don't we go to my house and have a toast?" Anne suggested. She seemed giddy. "A toast to Nick Valli finally getting what he
deserves."

"We must be at the Seneca casino in a few hours," Val said. "Belle
is performing."

"You are, Belle?" Phoebe asked.

"Yes, I'm doing Marilyn." Belle did a pose. "Some of her songs.
Will you come tonight, Honey? It'll make me feel less nervous, and
give me a boost in publicity, too."

"Well ...."

"Sure, she'll come, won't you, Phoebe? We'll *all* come!" Bill announced. He put his arm around Phoebe's shoulders.

Phoebe glared at her father. He didn't even try to resist Belle's
spell. He just surrendered, like all men did, to her awesome feminine
force.

"Okay. I guess so," she stammered.

Noticing the young man Nick had so rudely swept aside, Phoebe walked up to him, and signed his book. It was a history of Niagara
Falls. One of the pictures on the cover was of Marilyn Monroe posing
in front of the Horseshoe Falls. Now Phoebe got it. After she signed
his book, the young man walked up to Belle. Phoebe tried not to be
jealous, but she could see now how Belle was competition.

Tylor and the twins returned. Anne quickly organized their plans, and it was arranged that the limo would drop her family, Belle, and Val off at Cataract Lane. As they walked back to the limo, Phoebe heard her father mutter to Anne, "... like a brick shithouse." What did that mean, anyway, and why did all the guys from Niagara Falls talk like that?

In the limo, Phoebe listened in admiring amusement as Belle told Tylor the history of their friendship: "Ani should have won that contest. She was the real star of the competition, anyone could see it. But the fix was in. They gave the prize to one of the big casinos that they want to expand. Just for the extra publicity, as if they need it. But I told Ani then and there: you just keep working hard, Honey. You are going to be a star. You are somethin' special."

Tylor handed Belle his card as she exited the limo in front of Anne's house. "I'll be in touch," he told her.

By then, Phoebe had made up her mind about her near future. She would go back to Las Vegas and star in The Maid of the Mist attraction, on the condition that Nick Valli couldn't come near her. She'd prove she wasn't a loser. She'd work on her screenplay, too, about the secret world behind the Horseshoe Falls. That would be better than visiting the list of colleges Anne had made up for her. She couldn't imagine going to school, when the world was full of so many more exciting opportunities. She and Belle could help each other. The Maid of the Mist and The Riverboat Queen. They were in the same boat together. It worried her only a bit that she couldn't decide whether their vessel was a sturdy riverboat, or a small canoe headed for the brink.

CHAPTER FIFTY

John pounded the unresponsive earth until his hands were flayed by nettles and stones; his blood smeared his face as he wept. The salty taste of grief filled his mouth. He pressed his cheek against the thick layer of wild grass and weeds crushed under his body; he wished he could burrow into the ground. Every cell ached with the pain of his broken heart.

"Jerome. Oh, Jerome." He lifted his head and let his anguish surge out like the howls of a wounded animal. Then he collapsed, and let his tears flow again.

When all his tears were gone, John forced himself to sit up. He was in a wide field near the crest of a hill on his property. The slope of the hill faced west. Before him, the field flowed down into a wide, flat valley. Beyond the valley were wooded hills, which seemed to march endlessly into the west. This was one of Jerome's favorite places; he loved to come here and just sit and look at the beautiful landscape the Creator had taken special care to make for his people. Somewhere on this hill slope, under the dry, golden grass, his little brother Jerome was buried, with no monument or sign to mark where his body would mingle with Mother Earth.

John sat up and looked for his brother's spirit among the seed heads dancing in the breeze that flowed up the hill. He looked for it in the shadows under the white pines clustered along the edges of the field. He looked for it along the rocky outcrops at the top of the hill.

"Am I close, Jerome?" The words came hard, from a broken voice. "They said they buried you on this hill. Am I close?"

There was no answer.

"Am I close?" John shouted. He was angry now. The elders were always talking to spirits. His mother, especially – she babbled like a brook when she walked through woods and fields. Why had he never seen a spirit? Why couldn't he see Jerome, his own brother?

He buried his face in his hands, his body rocking back and forth. He was unable to get himself under control. "Damn them all!" John spit his words into his clenched fists as he tried, for the thousandth time, to find his memory, to figure out what had happened to him. Almost a year of his life was missing. They said he had been in a coma after he smashed his car. But it was no coma. A coma means your mind and body are paralyzed, in a suspended state. He wished his mind had been asleep and unaware, instead of fighting a battle against a darkness that tried to overwhelm him. He had no weapon, only the strength of his will, with which to fight back.

John wondered if his mind had been thrown back in time, to a pre-human consciousness, when the human brain was still forming, and everything outside one's self was a cacophony of terrifying, over-whelming sensations. He had felt lost in chaos, as though serpents were trying to entangle him and drag him down into an abyss. After long, long days, the darkness lifted, somewhat, into a gray haze, and he was on the verge of awareness. But some other will was there, directing him, not freeing him. He remembered the horror when he could see clearly the embodiment of that will, the face and lidded eyes filled with hate, envy, and greed.

He ran from it, toward the one sound he recognized in the dark-ness, the roar of Niagara Falls. He was ready to jump over the brink to escape that evil, but something stopped him – the fear that perhaps the face was his own, the culmination of what he had become in his desire for more money, more land, more totems of wealth. That hesitation almost doomed him, for it allowed the demon to catch up with him. Then John knew he was himself, not the demon, and fought again for his life, until he fell over a rocky cliff, and the serpents finally let go of him, and disappeared.

Then there was peaceful darkness, and healing. He awoke in a room full of smoke that smelled of tobacco, sweet grass, and life-giving herbs. The False Faces were there. Healers. They tried to give him food, but he was too weak to eat, at first. He slept, a long, restful sleep, and when he awoke again he was in a guest bedroom in his own house.

For days, they lied to him about Jerome. They said he was away, on a trip. He never believed them. He knew Jerome would never abandon him. After he had gotten stronger, he forced himself out of bed, practically crawled up the stairs, and found his bedroom suite locked. They finally told him the truth. Jerome was dead. He was killed while he was trying to protect John. That was the most bitter part, that Jerome died for him. It was wrong. He was the older brother, the protector. He was the one who always looked out for Jerome; he had to, because Jerome would never fight for himself, only for others. He was always lost in his own thoughts. He worried about people he loved. He worried about future generations, and Mother Earth, and the trees, but never about himself. He was the kindest person John had ever known.

Sobs wracked his body. Even Woody wouldn't tell him the details of how Jerome had died, and who killed him. Loraine gave the order that John had to get stronger. She was in charge of the household now; his mother had aged during the family's ordeal. She was an old woman now, a shadow of her former self. John didn't argue with his sister, for now. The details were irrelevant. Jerome was dead. And John knew he'd never get stronger, never heal, while he had this gaping hole in his heart.

Scrreeeeeeeeeeeeeeeeeech.

He squinted into the clear blue sky toward the sound of the bald eagle. He could see it circling high overhead. An answering call came from the south, and soon two eagles were soaring high over the valley, lazily, riding the air currents in wide circles. John fell on his back and closed his eyes. He remembered how happy Jerome was whenever he talked about bald eagles thriving again in their homeland, as they had in the old times. In spite of the hot sun, he felt cold permeate his body. He wished he could sink into the earth, into nothingness.

"John."

Startled, he sat up and looked around. Someone had said his name, from close by. Not Jerome. He knew he wasn't hearing ghosts. And Woody was still waiting for him beyond the grove of white pines. But he had heard his name, and no one was around. He rubbed his eyes.

John watched the red sun sink heavily toward the western horizon. A cool breeze ran up the long slope. He watched it bend the heads of the grasses as it came toward him. It washed over him, and ran over the hill. He glanced at the groves of white pines as they swayed in the wind. Those trees were old; their long, graceful branches were thick with soft needles, and heavy at the ends. The arms of the white pines kept swaying long after the wind had passed. They seemed to be beckoning him.

Come. Come.

He rose. Still unsteady on his feet, he had to stretch his arms and legs to get feeling back into them. He stomped the ground until he felt some warmth creep up his body. He looked out over the field again. It was full of whispers now.

When he reached a grove near the top of the hill, John saw, just beyond it on the higher hill slope, an outcrop of gray rock speckled with quartz reflecting the last rays of the sun. He walked over to it. Thick layers of sedimentary rock had collapsed over a layer of soft shale that was embedded with the imprints of small shells; it formed a rocky wall about four feet high. He climbed it, then walked along a treeless ridge scattered with large gray slabs and small, round white rocks, until he was at the highest point of land.

John looked across the golden field, where Jerome's body rested, to the far horizon. The sky was changing from blue to shades of pink and gray.

He had stood on this spot before, he remembered, just after he had bought this parcel of land, years ago. Jerome was with him. He had boasted to his younger brother that he owned this entire hill, and the next one, and parcels of land for miles. His old pride helped him feel his heart, for a moment, instead of his pain. Jerome had said nothing, but listened to his brother's words in silence.

Now, when he turned to the south and the east, where the land fell away into shadows, John felt immeasurably alone. He remembered his short vacation with Jerome the summer before. They had gone to the Adirondacks with Woody, but John had hiked for only a week, before he returned to his businesses, leaving his brother to go on alone. He felt tears well up again as he remembered Jerome urging him to forget the business and stay on the trail.

Then he knew. If his brother's spirit was anywhere still on Mother Earth, he'd be in some high place, a stark, beautiful place in the mountains. John would have to go to the peaks Jerome loved, the high mountains of the ancient homeland. That's where he would find his brother, and maybe himself, as well.

He felt life beating through him again as he started back down the hill. He would go where Jerome was leading him. His brother had never commented when John boasted about buying this land. Now John understood the emptiness of his arrogance. Jerome had known. No man could own the land. It was a gift from the Creator. If John had died in his accident, the land would still remain. A man could hold on to land for his lifetime, and honor the gift by cherishing and protecting it. Or he could dishonor his own memory by despoiling the land, earning the curses of future generations. Jerome knew that, too.

As he walked down the hill, back to the place where Woody was waiting for him, John's mind flashed back to one of his last clear memories, of standing in the hot sun in Buffalo reading the lament engraved under Red Jacket's statue. The great orator's fear that the Haudenosaunee would be forgotten had not come to pass. His people had survived.

John stopped to rest for a moment when he reached the cool shade of a grove of white pines halfway down the hill. The soft rustle of their long, delicate needles soothed him. He ached with loss for Jerome, but he resolved that his brother's life would have meaning. He would open the Turtle in Jerome's honor, as a place where art and memory could flourish.

But first he had to find his brother, and say goodbye.

CHAPTER FIFTY-ONE

Father Joe was waiting in the middle of the arched bridge to Asenath, the first Sister island, staring at the small cascade burbling over the gray rocks. He was holding a small black box. He looked up when Anne and Ben reached the bridge.

"Thanks for coming, Anne."

"I'm glad you asked me, Joe," Anne told him. "This will be beautiful. The island is so peaceful just after sunrise."

"I come here often before first Mass. It feels holy here, and puts me in the right frame of mind."

Anne looked at him closely. The priest looked exhausted. But their task had to be done early, before staff and tourists arrived to witness or disrupt the private ceremony. They were about to perform an illegal act. Emily and Don, the island walker, soon arrived. After they exchanged muted greetings, Joe said, "It's time."

Holding the black box in front of him like a chalice, Joe led the way across the bridge to Asenath. They each climbed over the railing along the left of the path, then walked down a short slope to the edge of the Hermit's Cascade. Overhung by tall trees, the spot was shady and cool. Joe placed the box on the hard ground next to the flowing water. The small group arranged itself in a circle around him. He took his priest's stole out of the pocket of his jacket, kissed it, and draped it over his neck. Moving his hands in blessing, he sang, "*In nomine Patri et Filii et Spiritus Sanctus.* In the name of the Father and the Son."

The small congregation made the Sign of the Cross.

Joe prayed quickly, in Latin. The traditional phrases seemed to suspend time, in this timeless place. Anne felt as though she could be in 1831, the time of the original Hermit, who died that year in the river he loved.

Joe switched to English. "We gather here to commend our brother, whom we knew as the Hermit, to God our Father and to commit his body to the elements. In the spirit of faith in the resurrection of Jesus Christ from the dead, let us offer our prayers." He nodded to Anne.

She unfolded a piece of paper and read the words of Jeremiah: "More tortuous than all else is the human heart, beyond remedy; who can understand it? I, the Lord, alone probe the mind and test the heart, to reward everyone according to his ways, according to the merit of his deeds."

"Let us pray in silence," Joe said.

Anne bowed her head and stared at the Hermit's Cascade, whose lacy curtain of water inexorably ate away at the living rock. The sound of the river calmed her as it flowed gently between Asenath and Angeline, sisters of land in the midst of a raging torrent. Ben slurped the water at the edge of the shore noisily, his front feet standing in the cold water. Anne tightened her grip on his leash.

Joe knelt. Scooping water from the rivulet into his hand, he sprinkled the box, then blessed it, intoning, "*In paradísum dedúcant te ángeli, in tuo advéntu suscípiant te mártyres, et perdúcant te in civitátem sanctam Jerúsalem. Chorus angelórum te suscípiat, et cum Lázaro quondam páupere aetérnam hábeas réquieum.* May the Angels lead you into paradise; may the martyrs greet you at your arrival and lead you into the holy city, Jerusalem. May the choir of Angels greet you and like Lazarus, who once was a poor man, may you have eternal rest."

The priest took the lid off the box. Slowly, carefully, he poured its contents, a mixture of black dust and crystalline fragments, into the water. He shook the last bits out of the box, and tossed it into the water. It was carried away quickly on the sparkling surface, on its last journey, through a cathedral of towering trees, toward the surging upper rapids, and the brink of the Horseshoe Falls. He prayed, "To you, O Lord, we commend the soul of your servant; in the sight of this world he is now dead; in your sight may he live for ever. Forgive whatever sins he committed through human weakness and in your goodness grant him everlasting peace. *In nomine Patri et Filii et Spiritus Sanctus.*"

"Amen," the small group said. Everyone made the Sign of the Cross.

The service over, Joe quickly removed his stole, kissed it, folded it, and placed it in his pocket.

"That was beautiful, Joe," Anne told him.

"It wasn't exactly regulation, with the Latin."

"It was exactly right."

The small group quickly dispersed. Anne walked with Joe. She could feel the early sun's hot rays as they hurried up the long slope to the American Rapids Bridge.

"Joe, slow down a bit," she urged; she had to wait for Ben, who was slower.

"Sorry." He stopped and waited for her to catch up.

"Can I buy you breakfast?"

He hesitated.

"Come on, Joe, you know it's tradition," she urged. "After you lay someone to rest, you have to eat. Share bread."

He inhaled deeply, and faced her. "Okay. You're right. We need sustenance. But a quick breakfast. I've got a busy day."

"So do I." That was a lie. Anne didn't have any plans. She didn't have to go to campus. Her usual summer course had been cancelled because of low enrollment. And just the week before, she'd learned the Veterans Administration did not select her grant for funding. That project was over. She hadn't heard from Quin in more than a week. Or from Phoebe and Bill in Las Vegas. For the first time in her life, it seemed that no one needed or wanted her, that there was no place she had to be.

At an outdoor cafe on Old Falls Street, Ben snored at Anne's feet as the waitress served coffee. Joe ordered pancakes with breakfast sausages. Anne asked for the veggie omelet. The waitress nodded and left the coffee urn on the table.

"Emily told me something strange when I called her yesterday to invite her to this service," Anne told Joe.

Pouring more coffee into his cup, Joe asked, "What did she say?"

"You know how the Hermit's body was recovered from the lower river eleven days after he went over the falls?"

Joe nodded.

"Well, Emily says that the body of the original Hermit was also recovered exactly eleven days after he was last seen, almost in the same spot. And they were never able to identify this man. She called the coroner, and he said they had no idea where he came from."

Joe's expression didn't change. "Are you starting to think maybe there's something to reincarnation, Anne?"

Though his tone was serious, Anne could tell by Joe's eyes that he was teasing. She decided to ask him about something that had been troubling her. "No, I'm not, Joe, but there is something else I'd like to ask you about. It's Sheryl Poloka."

Joe's face sagged, and Anne immediately regretted bringing up the subject.

"What about her?"

"Well, there was something odd about the way they found her, too, in the lower river, a day after that terrible night."

"What's odd about it? Isn't that where we always expected she'd turn up?"

"Yes, but ..." Anne decided to go on and settle the question. "But the police said she'd only been in the water a short time, not more than a few hours. And she must have gone in from Goat Island. But Sheryl was missing for months. And they haven't found anyone who said they saw her recently."

Joe shrugged. "They didn't recognize her, that's all. Sheryl would have kept in the background. Maybe she even hid herself. Who knows?"

"She was wearing a dress Mari gave her the day she disappeared, months ago. It was purple with a yellow iris on it."

Joe's expression told her to stop.

The waitress came with their order. Joe dug into his food. They ate quickly. Anne paid the bill, and they left. Anne and Ben walked with Joe across empty lots to the rectory building next to St. Mary of the Cataract church. As she was about to say goodbye, Joe said, "Come. I'll show you something. Maybe it will help give you some peace."

He unlocked a gate in a tall wrought-iron fence and led the way into a small, enclosed courtyard nestled between the church and the rectory. A lovely garden surrounded a monument to the Virgin Mary. Her white statue stood under a tall, ivy-covered arch made of hand-hewn stone. Soft water dribbled over stone bracketing the arch. Joe stood to one side of Mary's statue.

"She's here," he announced.

"Who?"

"Sheryl."

Anne felt the backs of her knees go clammy. "What are you talking about, Joe?"

He motioned for her to come and sit beside him on chairs on a small covered porch on the side of the rectory. "It's all right. I haven't lost my mind," he told her.

"Then what are you saying?" Anne tried not to reveal her fear.

Joe said, "After the medical examiner was finished with her, Sheryl's body was cremated. Her family wouldn't claim her, so he called me." He sighed. "I don't know, it just didn't seem right to put her in the charity plot at the cemetery, with strangers. I accepted her cremains. The other night, I lifted one of the flagstones in front of the statue." He pointed at it. "I dug a small hole, and poured her poor little pile of ashes in. Then I covered them. She'll be safe there, close to Our Lady."

Anne stared at Joe's face, searching for signs of dementia. All she saw was weariness and sadness, and his brown eyes, gazing calmly into hers.

"Oh, Joe." Anne shook her head slowly. "I, I don't know what to say."

"Just say a prayer for her once in a while, as you pass by." He stood. "And you can say one for me, as well."

Anne, her heart beating quickly, asked, "What do you mean?"

"I mean I'm leaving, too. Though not the way poor Sheryl did."

"You're leaving Niagara Falls? Or the priesthood?"

"Both. My resignation letter is on the Bishop's desk."

Anne fought the urge to beg him to stay just as he had been all these years, just where she needed him to be. She made an effort to use her dispassionate nurse voice. "Where will you go? What will you do?"

Joe opened his mouth to answer, then shut it. He looked uncertain.

Anne stared at him; she knew her dismay at Joe's leaving was pure selfishness. She tried to shame herself into a more noble frame of mind.

"Tell me, Joe, are you sure? And if you are, is there any way I can help you through the transition?"

"That's kind of you, Anne." He made an effort to lighten up his facial expression. "It's just that I'm not sure, yet, where I'll be going, or what I'll be doing." His words came slowly. "I know that first I'm going to take a long trip with some money I've saved – well, more of a sabbatical. I need time to get out of the priestly straightjacket."

"That's a good plan, Joe," Anne said. "Travel will give you fresh perspectives."

"Fresh perspectives." He snorted. "I'm sorry, Anne, I don't mean to insult you, but fresh perspectives are what have kept me trapped here for so long. Every time I was ready to turn in my resignation – and I have tried to do it for years – something would happen to make me think that things might change. Like when Pope Francis came out with his encyclical on climate change, *Laudato Si*, that talked about 'ecological conversions,' living our priestly vocations to be protectors of God's creation. I thought things might really start to change then. But they haven't. In spite of Francis' efforts, it's moving too slowly. The bishops still want to hold on to their old privileges. They don't want to rock the boat too much."

"What made you decide to quit now?" Anne asked. "Was it what happened during the showdown – the people going over the falls, and all the people hurt and arrested?" She paused, and spoke softly. "Was it Sheryl?"

"It was all of that and more, Anne." Joe sighed. "But I think the turning point was after the ambulance ride. I never told you how close we came to being caught at the bridge going off the island. There were soldiers in riot gear, and they made us stop to get searched. I thought it was all over. But just then, the gunfire started with those militants who ran onto Luna Island. They just waved us through then and started running there. Quin turned on the lights and sirens and hit the gas. None of us breathed till we crossed over Grand Island."

"They still haven't figured out how that ambulance ended up in Batavia, have they?" Anne managed to grin.

Joe was serious. "Some of the men we picked up were healers, members of an ancient society. They began to chant, to bring back a man near death, even before we figured out where we were going to go. They allowed me to stay with them. They took him to a longhouse in central New York, for healing rituals. I tell you, Anne, to actually witness some of the ancient ritual, to get a glimpse of how we are all connected in Nature, and how to give Thanksgiving, not to some paternal, strict godhead, but to a living spirit that encompasses all the atoms on this beautiful planet ..." His voice trailed off. "It was a holy vision. I saw joy." His eyes focused on the statue of Mary. "After that, I knew it was time. I went to Buffalo, and had a session with one of the bishop's counselors. They tried to convince me to stay, but it backfired on them. They showed me what Catholicism has become." He angrily punched his right hand into his left.

"Joe!"

"I'm all right. It's better to be angry than bitter."

"*Are* you bitter?"

"I'm trying not to be, but it's hard. It's terribly hard." He shook his head. "If I'm bitter, I'm bitter because of all the years I've wasted being deliberately blind."

Anne opened her mouth to speak but Joe's upraised hand stopped her.

"I have been blind, Anne, and I won't compound that defect by the sin of falseness to the truth. I surrendered myself to the authority of the church, and blinded myself to its corruption, and the suffering it's caused. Why, Anne? Why would I do that? Because the old men in Rome say they speak *Christus ipse locutus est*?"

"That means ...?"

"This is Christ himself speaking. They have the audacity to claim to speak for God!"

"Well, I never believed in the pope's infallibility. Does anyone? Did you, really, Joe? You always seemed to be able to keep a healthy separation from a lot of the old dogma."

"I made myself believe that the Roman Church was the closest man could come to God." Joe's eyes welled with tears. "That two thousand years of faithfulness to scripture and church authority had honed its leaders to spiritual purity. But it hasn't. It's tied them to the past, to decay. The dogma. Original sin, penance, the crucifixion, the denial of our physical nature, and condemnation of human longings. It doesn't speak to life, it speaks to death. It speaks to an exclusive, ethereal world, not the one we live in. And it led to unspeakable things, to all the sex scandals throughout the Church that have gone on for centuries. I've been ashamed to wear my collar in public, to have people look at me and wonder if I was one of them, one of the priests abusing peoples' bodies and souls. The charade has gone on for two bloody millennia. We can't carry it into this new century."

Anne felt helpless in the face of Joe's despair. "You should rest, Joe," she told him in a shaky voice, "take your trip, before you make a final decision. We've all been through so much."

"It's just that I'm wracked with indecision, about how best to begin the atonement."

"Atonement? Oh, God, Joe, you're the best person I've ever known. What do you have to atone for?" Anne stood and put her hands on Joe's shoulders. "Joe, listen to me. You cannot put this burden on yourself. You, alone, cannot make up for the failings of the entire Church."

"I can make a start." He stepped back, away from her. "And what better place to start than with the first people the Church encountered on this continent, the people it betrayed?"

Anne feared his passion, now that she saw how deep it was. "Joe, before you commit yourself to anything, you should take a long vacation, forget everything that's happened here in the past weeks. Niagara Falls drives everyone crazy sooner or later. Please don't make this huge leap while you're so devastated. You have to get away from here for a long while, travel, go someplace new, someplace far away."

He snorted. "I'm going to Rome. I'll stand in the middle of St. Peter's Square and I'll yell, 'Holy Father, come down! Why are you holed up in that castle, praying, while the world is being consumed? While the planet is dying and the people wail in despair? Explain to me, exactly, Holy Father, how you speak for Christ. Tell me! Tell me!'"

Joe glared at Anne, who was speechless. He said, "From the moment the first priest walked on this New World, the church was already corrupt beyond redemption. It had no right to come to a new continent, and help claim it for the Old World. There was no respect for the, the sanctity – yes, that's the word – the sanctity of the people they encountered, people who lived in God's primal world. What could they have told us, have taught us? I had a very small glimpse of it, Anne, and what we lost when Europe and the Church came to conquer this continent is immeasurable. They brought their bloody, endless wars here. They brought plague and slavery and Sin. And they did it all in the name of God, in the name of Christ, the Prince of Peace, in the name of His Holy Church!"

"Joe." Anne spoke as calmly as she could. "Joe, I never thought I'd be defending the actions of the Church, especially to you. There's no excuse for it. But you can't discount the many good things that it does, and the many good people who are part of it, people like you."

"It requires atonement." Joe's voice was firm. "Atonement, and renewal. Otherwise, it's just another decadent artifact of a dying civilization, and a dying planet."

Anne took a deep breath. Her hands were trembling. She was overwhelmed by Joe's despair. She had to get away from him, before she despaired, too.

"Joe, it's been a long morning." She couldn't think of anything else to say.

He stared at her, his face so familiar, but so distant now. Tears ran down her face. She said, "I'll leave you now, but remember, if you need anything – anything – I'll always be ready to help you."

He gave her a small smile. "I know. I'll keep in touch."

Anne rose, then turned away quickly and left the porch. She fumbled with the courtyard gate; she managed to open it and get Ben through it. As she passed in front of the church, she gave a quick glance back. Joe was standing at the side of the Virgin, near Sheryl Poloka's earthly remains, with his head bowed. He might have been praying.

CHAPTER FIFTY-TWO

When he got to the back door of Wallace's house, Leonard knew he'd made it in time for dinner. The homey aroma of baking chicken wafted through the screen door. He smiled.

He stood watching Rose through the screen as she moved efficiently in the small kitchen, taking plates down from the cupboard, setting the table. Grandfather would just be getting up from his afternoon nap.

Leonard scraped his shoes on the wooden step, trying not to startle Rose. Her face beamed with a wide smile when she saw him, then changed quickly to a worried expression.

"Oh, Leonard!" She hugged him hard as he came into the house. "Oh, I'm so glad to see you. But how did you get here? I didn't hear a car."

"My friend dropped me off a ways up the road and I ran here," he told her. "I didn't want to draw any attention."

Rose held on to his shoulders. "So many people are looking for you. The FBI. The media." She seemed to be amused. "You're a hero, you know. Even if they don't know your name."

"Yeah." He smirked. "The Mysterious Warrior. That's what Phoebe called me, and now everyone does."

"No one with any sense calls you that," a deep voice said.

Leonard turned to see his great-grandfather standing in the door to the parlor, with the widest smile he had ever seen on the old man's face. His heart beat fast, as he realized how much he loved him. And as he realized that Grandfather seemed to have gotten just a bit smaller since he had last seen him, lying on the grass on Goat Island, trying to help Leonard in the struggle against evil, even as he fought for his own life.

Rose made a clatter as she opened the oven door and took the baking pot out. She was noisy only when she got emotional. Both men turned to savor the smell of dinner. Soon they were sitting around the oak table, eating chicken baked with potatoes, carrots, and turnips.

Leonard ate slowly, savoring each bite. It had been a long time since he had eaten food this delicious. His chest hurt as he realized it would be a long time before he ate Rose's food, or anything nearly as good, again. He didn't talk much.

After he finished eating, Wallace had to be helped out of his chair. While he was in the bathroom, Leonard whispered to Rose, "How is he doing? Is he okay?"

"He's okay for his age," she whispered back. "He's taking medication for his heart now." She squeezed Leonard's arm. "Seeing you is the best thing for him. He's been so worried."

When Wallace emerged, Rose hustled the men into the parlor, where she brought his hot tea, and a glass of milk for Leonard. She set a plate of cookies between their chairs. Then she left them alone.

"No one cooks like her," Leonard said, as he bit into a still-warm chocolate chip cookie.

"You're right." Wallace held his mug of tea in both hands, as if he were warming them. He watched Leonard gobble the cookies.

When he finished his milk, Leonard leaned back in the soft armchair. It was his favorite chair anywhere. He liked to settle in it, and listen to his elder's stories, or just look at his face as he slept, or thought. He stared at the old man's face so that he could memorize every line in it, as though he were studying a cliff he intended to climb. Someday, maybe soon, his great-grandfather would go out of this world. Leonard knew that loss would be fundamental, as if the whole falls suddenly collapsed, and left a trickle of water where once a mighty roar had been.

"Seasons change." Wallace's words seemed a continuation of unspoken thoughts. "You will grow stronger for many more years, Leonard, and wiser, too, I hope. Then age will begin to take your strength away. But not ...," he placed his finger against his temple, "... not what is in here."

"Grandfather ..." Now that the time had come, Leonard searched for the right words. He swallowed.

"You're beginning a journey," Wallace confirmed.

"Yes." Leonard wondered why the thrill of it seemed dim, now. "In a few days. My friends who dropped me off, they're out getting camping gear. We're going to explore the high peaks, starting in the Adirondacks. We're going to go to wild places, and hike down the Appalachian Trail." Leonard let himself fall into Wallace's watchful eyes, as though they were a dark pool. "The man who's taking us is ..." Leonard knew Wallace would expect discretion, even here, "... is making a spiritual journey, to honor his brother, so he can say goodbye to him. The rest of us, well, we want adventure, me and my friends Jemmy and Darman and Terrence. And you remember the big man?"

Wallace smiled, and nodded. Leonard felt his excitement get strong again.

"I don't know how far we'll hike, or how long. But I'm going to go all the way into the Carolinas, even if I go by myself. I'll see it, Grandfather, I'll see the homeland of our people, before they came north." He was on the edge of his chair.

Wallace leaned back, and closed his eyes.

Leonard waited.

Finally, Wallace opened his eyes, and asked, "When you arrive in the land of our Fathers, what will you tell them?"

"I, I don't know." Leonard hadn't thought of that; his mind raced. What thoughts would be worthy? He stared at his hands, until his words came out, slowly.

"I guess I'll tell them that I'm glad to be there. I'll thank them for the journey they made. I'll tell them where we are now."

Wallace nodded his approval.

Leonard jumped to his feet. The longer he made this goodbye, the harder it would be.

"I've got to go now."

The old man grasped the arms of his chair. Leonard helped him to his feet. "I'll come to see you as soon as I get back to New York." His voice was thick. "I don't know when that will be."

They looked into each other's eyes for a long moment. Leonard realized he was making the journey for his great-grandfather, as well as for himself. That understanding, unspoken, was between them. Leonard embraced the old man, and quickly turned away; he rushed through the kitchen, and out the back door.

Rose was waiting for him by the garden. "Is your big, hungry friend with you?"

Leonard nodded, his voice too full of tears to be useful.

She handed him a parcel wrapped in brown paper. "Tell him these are from me."

Leonard smiled. He rubbed his nose on the back of his hand.

"Maybe I'll eat them myself," he teased her.

"You won't," she told him. "You're a good boy, Leonard." She put her arms around him and held him close. "I should say you're a good *man*, Leonard. That's what you are now. A good man." She kissed him on his cheek. "Use the gifts the Creator has given you. Carry in your mind the good things – love, and respect, and generosity." A tear ran down her cheek, as she hugged him once more. "And come back to us soon."

Leonard turned and ran, past the garden, over the low hedge that ran beside a narrow creek, across its dry, stony bed, and the scrubby field, and then along one of the narrow roads that wound through the small Tuscarora territory, taking him downhill from the escarpment. For a while, his heart was so heavy that it weighed down his feet.

Gradually, the lure of his journey lightened them, and he ran faster and faster to his waiting friends. He tried to imagine what he would see – lofty places looking out over mountainous vistas, and small places

beside brooks singing over rocky glens, and trees so old that his ancestors may have walked beside them, before the white man came.

He felt the grip of the falls at Niagara get weaker, its roar dimmer.
This wasn't his home, this flat, dingy place surrounded by gritty industries and a man-made hill of toxic waste. He thought briefly of Anne
and her friends, and their continuing efforts to make the city better.
Did they have any chance? He hoped so, but it occurred to him that
maybe their efforts were doomed. Maybe the falls doesn't want a city
there.

Phoebe was already gone. She'd texted him that she was heading
west to be the Maid of the Mist in Las Vegas. He'd hoped her experience at the brink would have taught her something, but it didn't look
like it, if she was going to be the Maid of the Mist in a desert city
where a real waterfall like Niagara Falls was impossible, and a fake one
was waste of a precious resource. Well, she was on her own now.

As the sun sank, a red glow started to rise from the western
horizon. Shadows deepened. A scruffy gray-and-white dog jumped out
of a ditch and ran alongside him. Leonard headed toward lights and
the noisy big-box parking lot where his friends would be waiting. They
were buying camping gear for their trip. His pace quickened. This was
just the first part of his long journey, the hardest part, the leave-taking.
In front of him, not so far away, were the everlasting high peaks, and
the ancient lands of his people. He was going home.

CHAPTER FIFTY-THREE

"Hey, Anne! Anne! Wait!"

Anne recognized the untidy figure running across the wide lawn toward her, emerging from the woods on Goat Island. She stopped to wait for her.

"Hi, Chani," she said, as the young woman, out of breath, bent down to stroke Ben, who wagged his tail in greeting.

"He looks a lot better," Chani said. "Like his old self again."

Anne still didn't like to talk about it. "He went through a lot."

"I'll say."

"So what are you doing here? Haven't you had enough of Goat Island by now?"

"Me? No, not nearly. Guess what? I might have a job here."

"On the island?"

"You won't believe it. With the state parks commission."

Anne laughed. "They hired *you*?"

"Yeah, unbelievable, huh?"

"It sure is. I was afraid you'd get arrested for digging that hole by the tourist center. What kind of job did they give you?"

"Well, you know how the center is still closed, after it got trashed during the showdown? Now a lot of people say it shouldn't be opened again, that the state should start returning the island to its original, natural state."

"I know. I've signed the petition, and our committee has written letters."

Chani giggled. "Your committee is too much, Anne. Anyway, I went to the parks commission and told them, as long as the building is closed, and the grounds all messed up, they should let me do an anthropological survey around it. I told them I'm looking for mastodon bones, that they'd be a big tourist draw. It's not an official survey, just an exploratory dig."

"Oh, Chani! Has your faculty adviser approved this?"

"It'll be okay, I promise. All I have to do is find one little artifact, one tiny piece of pottery, one bone. Then I stop digging, and get the story out on social media. The state would never be able to build anything on this island again. They'd have to start listening to you guys, and stop using it as a fucking parking lot."

"I have to hand it to you, Chani. You may actually get us somewhere."

"You'll never guess who gave me a recommendation. Sylvester Lindsay."

"Have you talked to him recently? How is he doing?"

"He's going crazy. I showed the police the stuff the Hermit found. It was my bargaining chip to not get arrested. They brought Sylvester in to try to help identify the items. There were things he had no idea where they came from – artifacts from the Caribbean and South America. And there was black magic stuff, too, some shrunken heads. Sylvester's really upset about the gold mask going over the falls. He's hoping the police don't leak out any information about it, or else people will be swarming all over the gorge to try to find it. He's hiring some professionals to poke around in the rocks under the falls to look for it. I might look for it myself."

"Have the mummies gone back to Egypt yet?" Anne asked.

"No way. Sylvester ran into more problems. He says he can't find a shipping company willing to transport them. People are talking about curses again."

"Too bad," Anne commented. "Well, I'm sure Sylvester will find a way to handle it in the end." Ben tugged on his leash. "I'd better get going, Ben wants his walk."

"Okay," Chani replied. "Hey, if you see your precious little Phoebe, tell her from me that she's a fucking jerk."

Anne stared. "What happened?"

"Nothing happened." Chani shrugged. "It's just that we were best friends on the island, and I only saved her fucking life by keeping her from jumping in the river, and now that she's famous, the fucking Maid of the Mist, which is a total joke, she won't even return my texts or phone calls."

"It's been incredibly hectic for her." Anne didn't know why she still felt compelled to cover for Phoebe. "I'm sure she isn't avoiding you. She's in Las Vegas now, with her father."

"Yeah, well, if you talk to her, just give her my message, okay?"

Anne was anxious to get away. "I'll come to your dig to see how you're doing. I'll let you know when our next meeting is." She tugged on Ben's leash.

"Okay. Bye, Anne. Bye, Ben. Good dog." She gave him a parting hug, and headed back to the woods.

Anne walked home quickly to get Ben out of the sun. It was just after eight in the morning, and the temperature was already more than ninety degrees. The weather guys were predicting one-hundred-plus degree days for the foreseeable future; authorities were urging people to conserve energy and water. Even this close to Niagara Falls, Anne mused, there wasn't enough water to keep the lifestyle of the twenty-first century going. The water in the Great Lakes was at its lowest level ever. Power production at Niagara had actually gone down recently, because the water just wasn't there. The upper rapids didn't dance anymore; they flowed limply around the big boulders in the riverbed.

As soon as they were home, Ben lapped all the water from his bowl. Anne's cell phone on the kitchen counter and her landline voicemail were buzzing with messages. She hit play. "Anne, did you read your email? This is Stephanie. Call me as soon as you get home." The second call was a hang-up, the third was from Stephanie again. Two more hang-ups. Then it was Quin telling her he'd be stopping by later.

Anne wondered how he suddenly found the time. The sixth message was from Emily, reminding Anne about a public hearing scheduled for that night. The parks commission was going to present its preliminary plan for restoring Goat Island facilities after the raucous Showdown at Niagara.

Anne went to her office and opened her email on her laptop. She saw a message from the president of the faculty union marked "URGENT ALERT!!!!!" She opened it, and read: "Dear Colleagues: I have obtained a copy of a confidential memo from the Chancellor that went out today to all university presidents and selected state officials. The memo details a substantial reorganization plan for the university system. Among the recommendations made by Central Administration is a call for such a radical restructuring of BU's College of Nursing, due to fundamental changes in the health-care delivery system, that the college as we know it will no longer exist. The plan would transfer the college's undergraduate academic programs to a new consortium of regional nurse training programs, and the research and graduate programs would be merged into the biomedical college. We must mobilize. We are arranging a meeting of the membership to be held later today. We need your voice. Join us." The memo ended with details of when and where the meeting would be.

Anne was surprised at how little emotion she felt. She re-read the email carefully. Yes, there it was, she had read it right the first time: "... radical restructuring ... the college as we know it will no longer exist ..."

After closing the email, she scanned her list of messages. She'd gotten more than a dozen from fellow faculty. There was already a hashtag called "Save Our Nurses." She didn't feel ready for battle, just then. She quit her email. She made herself a cup of herbal tea, forcing disruptive thoughts out of her head.

"I'm just going to have some tea, and stay calm," she said aloud, several times. She added a shot of vodka to her lemon-ginger brew.

While she was breathing in the alcoholic aroma from her cup, her home phone rang and went to voicemail. She listened as the Dean left a breathless message: "Anne, I'm sure you've heard the news. I need to talk to you as soon as possible. We're putting together a task force to reorganize – *not* restructure – our college and you are just the person we need to play a leadership role at this critical time. Please call me *immediately* and let's plan ..." The voicemail timed out. Anne turned off her phones.

Taking her mug out onto her porch, she settled in her rocker. Ben snuggled under her feet. The sun relentlessly heated the small space. All her plants looked wilted, even though she'd watered them earlier that morning. The maple trees looked even worse; their canopies were brittle brown. She leaned her head back, and closed her eyes. She didn't want to think, but the world wouldn't stay out of her mind.

Just like that. A simple statement in an email. A simple statement that marked the end of an era. Now she knew why the dean had formed the committee on transformative change. She must have known this plan was in the works. Restructure, reorganize – the terminology didn't matter. Repercussions of such drastic actions at a prestigious school like BU's would reverberate through the country. Buffalo was the beginning of the end of professional nursing as a distinct – and vital – partner within the health care system.

She laughed, but it was bitter. "Imagine," she said to Ben, "all these years we've been saying that nursing was an important, secure profession. That the human factor could never be taken out of patient care. Who could imagine it? Could you, Ben?" She pushed her rocker hard. Health care in America was a for-profit delivery system. And the bottom line demanded the diminishment of superfluous, expensive healing hands. All you needed now were technicians to monitor the machines.

Ben yelped when Anne's rocker went over his tail.

"Sorry, big boy." She scratched his ears until he went back to sleep, fighting the urge to go online and check her latest retirement plan statement. That's what every faculty member in the college would be doing now, she knew.

There was no breeze. The sky was silvery in the heat. Not a drop of mist hung over the basins of the two cataracts. She slowly rose from the rocker.

"Come on, Ben, it's too hot to be out here." She held the door as the groggy dog limped inside. He jumped on her bed. She sank down next to him, and immediately fell asleep.

The doorbell woke her up. Ben barked as he jumped off the bed and ran to the door. Disoriented, Anne checked her bedside clock. It was after four in the afternoon. She'd missed the whole day. It didn't matter. She pushed her hair out of her face as she walked down the foyer steps. She saw Quin's bulky form through the lace curtain, and opened the door.

"Hey, were you sleeping?" he asked, surprised.

"Yes. Come on up." She plodded back up the stairs, led him into the kitchen, and put on coffee while he played with Ben.

"I can't believe I slept for almost a whole day," she told him.

"What did you do, run around Goat Island before breakfast?"

"I feel as though I did. Twice."

He glanced at her quizzically. "I called and texted you," he said.

"I turned off my phones," she replied, leaning against the kitchen counter, gulping coffee.

He told her, "I saw Mari out front. She says she can't keep up with the demand for paintings of Phoebe as the Maid of the Mist. They sell out as soon as they go in the shops." He laughed, shaking his head. "She's mass-producing them now. She really misses Leonard."

"Phoebe gets a few cents for each image. She trademarked herself."

"How's she doing in Vegas?"

"I don't know. She hasn't called me." Her coffee tasted bitter. She dumped it in the sink. "How is your father feeling?"

"Pretty good, actually. He's been on a real high since his visit here. He's still ecstatic over the money he won at the casino. He says it means his luck has changed. He took Mike and his family to Disney World, and that seemed to cheer them all up. They were able to make some changes in Mike's house, to help him get around better, and they've got some extra physical therapy going for him."

"That's all great news," Anne said. She felt famished. "Let's go eat. Old Man River?"

"Blast off."

"I'll drive." She quickly changed into a summer print dress and pulled her hair into a ponytail with one of Phoebe's old scrunchies.

Anne drove swiftly along the Robert Moses Parkway toward North Tonawanda. The river was a limpid silver flow. Quin didn't say much, and that was fine with her.

While Quin waited for their order, Anne took Ben to look for a place along the river to lay her picnic blanket. There was little activity or noise. Even under the trees, it was sweltering. She swatted at bugs while she waited, and wished for a breeze.

"I got two beers for each of us," Quin announced as he knelt on the blanket, trying to keep the overflowing tray balanced.

"Good." Anne picked up a plastic cup dripping with sweat, and took long gulps.

They ate quickly. Because of the flies, she dumped their trash as soon as they finished. "Want dessert?" she asked, before she sat down again. She burped, tasting the beer.

Quin echoed her burp, louder. "Later."

She sat on the blanket, with her back against a tree, and stretched her legs in front of her. Ben lay at her feet. Quin was on his back with his hands under his head. She watched boats moving slowly up and down the smooth silver surface of the river.

"I got some news," Quin announced.

Finally, the point of his visit. "Good news, I hope," she said.

He sat up, smiling. "Yeah, it is. I've been offered a position with one of the Malacandra subcontractors. I'll just be a drone, a low-level techie, but I'm in."

She searched his face. "Where will you be, exactly?"

"Well, right now there are a bunch of labs doing stuff on contract, so the project is still scattered around the world. I can check in remotely for now. I actually won't be onboard till early next year. But there's some really cool news that's about to get out. Lee Sanga will be making the announcement later this week."

"What is it?"

He leaned toward her, his face shining like a blue-eyed sun, he was so flushed with excitement.

"Get this. The feds know Sanga's going to beat everyone to Mars. He's got backing from all the multinationals. Everyone wants a piece of this. There's no way the government can catch up – not any government. Hell, all the best space engineers and scientists in the world are working for Sanga now. The President's been throwing shit fits all over the place. He wants the USA to be a player on Mars. But there's no way Congress is going to give him funding for Mars missions – no one's lobbying them and paying them off for it. Private enterprise wants the Red Planet all for itself. So the President cut a deal: the feds are going to turn over Area 51 to the Malacandra Project."

"The place where all the UFO's are supposed to be?"

"Yeah! I mean, is that cool or what?"

"They're just giving that top-secret government facility over to private enterprise?"

"Not giving. There's some lease deal. To give the feds a piece of the action."

"What about all the government projects? Where are they going to go?"

"They're nothing, Anne. Nothing compared to Malacandra. It's the most important project on the planet right now. People have finally realized this planet is done. We have to become a multi-planet species, or we'll die out."

"Maybe our dying out would be a good thing," Anne said bitterly. "But I'm not even going to argue with you, Quin. You're right. This planet is done." She turned away.

"Damn right, I'm right." He stood up. "I'm going for ice cream. Want some?"

She nodded, feeling dizzy. When he returned, the ice cream was already dripping off the cones. Ben licked her hand as she ate.

"So, this means you'll actually be working at Area 51?" Anne didn't know whether to laugh or cry. "You'll get to see the alien space ships and bodies they're hiding there. What fun."

He laughed, not minding her sarcasm, and popped the last of his cone into his mouth. "You know," he said, lying down on his side, facing her. "Area 51 is real close to Vegas."

"So?"

"So, Phoebe's out there now. You ought to think about going, too. They'll be expanding everywhere. There'll be lots of jobs. They'll need nurses, for sure."

"Do you know, Quin, that there's nothing more obsolete than a nurse right now?" Anne couldn't keep the edge out of her voice.

"Not everywhere. Hell, they'll need nurses on Mars."

"You're wrong," she told him.

He looked at her quizzically.

"People are expendable," she told him. "They'll never send nurses to new colonies. It would jeopardize the profit margin. People are cheap, and easily replaceable."

"Wow! What have you been reading?"

"Just my email."

He didn't respond. She suspected he'd already heard the news. She slapped at a mosquito on her arm. "Time to go."

On the drive home, Quin described a robot he was designing, a small drone. "It'll be programmable for the terrain on specific sites on Mars. It'll be able to travel down into channels in crater walls, explore caves; that's where we'll find life, if there is any." He grinned. "I'm naming it Ben."

She managed a thin smile. "What an honor for him."

"Area 51 has the longest runway in the world. We're probably talking space plane instead of a rocket, first, I think. It'll take us to an orbiting station where the ships will be built. Then, Mars, here we come."

"So you'll get to see Earth from space," Anne said. "You know that's what you really want. To be out there. To look out at our beautiful blue planet from millions of miles away."

"You're thinking of the Apollo 17 picture of Earth," he told her. "I hate to tell you, Anne, but Earth doesn't look like that anymore. That shot was taken almost fifty years ago. The planet is much browner now, the atmosphere is thinner, especially at the poles, from climate change. There's tons of metal orbiting us, satellites and space junk. We're blasting out radio signals 24-7. You know what Earth is now, Anne? It's just a noisy little dirtball in space. We're like a bad trailer park."

She didn't respond. She didn't even disagree.

When they returned to Cataract Lane, they headed with Ben for the river path. The sun was low in the sky, a blazing red ball sinking slowly into a gray mist. They walked slowly, and wordlessly, to Goat Island.

Quin led the way to Tesla's statue. Leaning against it, he turned to Anne.

"Really, I was serious before. You should consider coming out west. I'm not saying sell your house or anything. Just rent it out, or something. But the future's out there. We're going to Mars."

"I'm not ready to make any decisions right now, Quin," she told him. She walked away.

Anne couldn't even look at the shattered remains of the tourist center at Terrapin Point. It was surrounded by big garbage containers and trucks.

In its chasm, the Horseshoe Falls churned mist that evaporated before it reached ground level. They leaned against the railing to watch a thin curtain of water fall over the brink. The Horseshoe's roar seemed muted in the heavy air.

Quin turned to her. "So tell me, what's going on? What's happening here that's so fucking important?"

Anne wondered that herself. What *was* going on in Niagara Falls? She thought of Chani and her search for artifacts, and the effort to turn Goat Island back into a natural paradise. There was the restructuring of the nursing school. Could she just give up, abandon the students and patients? Or should she contribute to the transformative shift by being a voice for compassionate patient care? She thought of Father Joe and wondered where his passion for the Earth and its first peoples would take him. Could efforts on this planet help pave the way for justice for any microbes that might be living on Mars, unaware of the coming invasion from Earth?

No one could deny our own planet was in danger. Maybe humans did need to escape. Just before the end came, Anne thought, the falls would dry up. Maybe it would be the last thing to die before everyone blasted off to new frontiers in space.

She considered Quin's suggestion. She'd never been out west. It might be interesting to see the famous Area 51, and watch the building of a new city dedicated to science, and the first rockets to send humans to another planet. After all, exploration was our human destiny. The most beautiful, and most frightful cascade in the world – that was what Father Hennepin wrote back to the Old World about Niagara Falls in the seventeenth century. Imagine discovering the wonders of Mars in the twenty-first century.

"Anne." Quin's voice was insistent, and louder. "I said, what's going on here that's so important?"

She took a long look at the jade-colored water tumbling in a smooth arc into the rocky chasm below.

"The falls, Quin. The falls. Do you think you'll find one like this on Mars?"

The End

Acknowledgments

The seed of this book was planted during my English class at Niagara Falls High School way back in the twentieth century, when my dedicated teacher, Miss Bertha Storey, commented on the lack of any "great novel" about Niagara Falls. No novel can capture the mysterious allure of the mighty cataracts, but this book is my contribution to a growing list of attempts.

First I must thank my husband, George Kobas, for his unwavering and loving support, and my daughter, Jeni Mitchell Henaut, for her ongoing support and wise advice.

I would like to give special thanks to Barbara Abrams, one of the founders of Cornell University's American Indian Program, for her insightful readings of my manuscript and valuable input.

The quote by Chief Clinton Rickard in Chapter 18 is included with the permission of the late Barbara Graymont, editor of *Fighting Tuscarora: The Autobiography of Chief Clinton Rickard* (Syracuse University Press, 1973), from which it is taken.

My extended family – Niagarans all – has been a rich resource. Walter Romanek has been not only a staunch supporter of my efforts in writing the novel, but an inspiration for life, as well. Marci Viscuglia Gibbs, an immensely talented graphic artist, provided me with support, dynamic images, and thoughtful editorial advice. The late Helen Romanek Dixon was a rich fount of local history and lore, which she generously shared, and Bruno LaSota shared his knowledge of the

Niagara gorge gained from a lifetime of exploring. Emily Romanek Yerrick and her late husband, Mike, gave me an inspiring tour of Las Vegas and its surrounding area. Christina Grace Lopez enthusiastically explored the falls area with me.

Because I have received so much support from family, friends, and colleagues, I cannot mention everyone who deserves thanks from me. The following people, however, must be cited for their support, especially in my early days of working on this novel: Jacquie Powers, Anita Harris, Leslie Logan, Dianna Marsh, and Mia Pancaldo.

Lastly, I would like to extend my appreciation to Steve Rokitka of Spinetree Media for injecting his brilliant creative energy into the final stages of getting this book into print.

About the Author

Born just about a mile from the brink of the American Falls, Linda Grace has studied the history and geology of the Niagara cataracts and city since she was a child roaming over the rocks on the Three Sisters Islands. While studying journalism at St. Bonaventure University, she worked as a reporter for the then-independent morning newspaper, *The Niagara Gazette*, covering stories from local beauty pageants to small airplanes crashing in the Niagara River. Following an award-winning career directing news and science communications at the University at Buffalo and Cornell University, she lives in Ithaca, New York.